Darkness

Visible

"Yet from those flames no light; but rather darkness visible"

— John Milton, Paradise Lost

JOHN GRASHAM

ISBN: 0989870715
ISBN-13: 978-0-9898707-1-9

DEDICATION

To all of those who take a chance on their dreams.

CONTENTS

ACKNOWLEDGMENTS

To my wife Judy who encouraged me to take a big risk
and take the time I needed to write the next book.
I can't thank you enough for your faith in me.

CHAPTER 1 – PROLOGUE: THE INFANT

"Why is life given to be thus wrested from us?"
— *John Milton, Paradise Lost*

5600 BC

The drenching rain continued to fall. For days it had come down, soaking the earth, the rivers and streams, while poisoning the land. The woman walked through the downpour with her mind spinning. *Why is the rain salty? How can it be salty?* The rain had long ago soaked her to the skin and she staggered along, exhausted and bleeding. Her bare feet trudged through the unending mud, but they kept moving, step after stumbling step. Her gut clenched and she felt herself cramping again. She knew she was losing more blood. She cursed at the wrongness of it all. The rain, the death, the running and the blood: all of it was so wrong.

From under her sodden robe came the mewling sounds of a famished infant. She laughed bitterly under her breath. *Might as well ask why my son died, or why my Lord was captured by his enemies.* The baby wept piteously again. *Or why my baby won't eat. Gods! Why won't she eat?*

Chalara walked on; always it seemed uphill, staying far enough from the bank of the river to avoid its wild, swollen waters but near enough to navigate by it. *I must make it to Varnach today. The babe will not survive unless I can reach shelter, warm it and get it to suckle.* Sobs threatened to choke out between her clenched teeth, but she bit them back. Instead of despairing, she let her anger grow. She screamed mentally. *Why won't she eat?*

For three days now, she had been walking, ever since the baby was born, ever since she'd mustered her strength after delivering the child all by herself. She realized suddenly that she herself was starving. *Fool. You haven't eaten since the night before the rains started.*

She'd been so happy as the chief wife of the king. She and the other

1

wives had spent a sensual night with the king, though she had been constrained since she was so far along in her pregnancy. The king did not visit the women's quarters often, but he had that night. Afterward, when they'd all fallen asleep, she had been awakened by the baby kicking from within her. Unable to get back to sleep, she went for a walk along the shore and then all of her world had started falling apart.

A loud thunderclap snapped her out of her reverie. She lifted her head from staring at the ground in front of her and in the fog of fat droplets, she saw a stone hut seem to emerge from the curtain of rain. *Shelter!* She felt a surge of energy and quickened her pace, heading for the hut.

At the entry, she paused at the leather curtain that served as a door and started to speak. At that moment, a gust of wind blew the flap inward and she changed her mind. *No need. No one is here.* She stepped inside and gasped. For the first time in days, she didn't feel the pounding of rain on her head. It felt wonderful, though her skin crawled as if missing the constant drumming sensation. She turned and secured the leather door curtain with its trailing cords and then turned back to survey her surroundings.

The one room hut was no more than twice her arm-span across and the ceiling was slightly higher than her head. The thick thatch of the roof had some leaks, but fewer than she would have imagined. Overall, she was relieved at the condition of the inside of the little hut. She lifted her sodden robe and pulled out her weakly wailing daughter where she had been nestled in a makeshift sling against Chalara's skin. There was a wooden stool in a corner. She sat on it and tried again to get the baby to nurse.

What followed was almost an hour of frustration. Chalara was a determined woman, but try as she might, the baby would not suck. Every trick, every technique she remembered from her first child had no effect. The infant would not take the nipple for more than a moment and would not drink. The baby cried, squealed and thrashed, and would not eat. Chalara was so angry after trying again and again that she felt almost feverish with rage. She wanted to shout at the child, "Eat or you will die!" But it was all useless. There is nothing less reasonable than a baby. *The babe will die and there is nothing I can do!*

She huddled over the child, warming it with her body. She rocked gently, hoping to calm the little one. *I remember rocking your brother. He grew almost as big as your father, the King.*

The baby's brother had been Melekan, son of Moloch. He'd grown to nearly twice his mother's height, a giant of a young man, but still not as tall as his sire. *But that didn't save him from the giant water monster.*

Melekan had fought and killed the massive crocodile that had ambushed them from the river's bank, but not before he and the monster had both become mired and sunk into the nearby tar pit. Her son had been swallowed by the inky blackness and died calling out to her, "Mother!" The other men that had come with them had either run away or died in the beast's jaws before her son had killed it, so when Melekan had perished, she had been left alone. Alone and in labor. She remembered very little of the rest of it: the blinding white pain, the contractions and the blood. Surely there hadn't been that much blood when she'd given birth to her son.

Somehow she had endured even while wracked with torment over her son's death. This second child was going to be born and cared nothing for her sorrow or anyone else's. The baby had finally come and Chalara dimly remembered cutting the cord with the tiny dagger that her Lord had given her as a present. She tied off the knot in the umbilicus and then the dagger had slipped from her bloody grasp and gone tumbling into the same tar that had swallowed Melekan. Somehow the loss of the dagger on top of everything else had been the tipping point for her. Chalara remembered shouting and shrieking in rage at the death of her son, the loss of her husband, her home and the agony of birth. By the time she'd come back from the brink of madness and returned to her right mind, she realized the baby was crying nearly as loudly as she herself.

She snapped back to the present as the baby twisted again, turned its head toward her and opened its eyes. Those dark windows seemed to look deep into her as if wanting to tell her something. Chalara felt a stab of pain in her gut. *I know, I know! You're hungry. Why won't you eat, then?*

Chalara looked around the little hut again, searching its contents. They were meager indeed and consisted of the stool on which she sat, a few pieces of broken pottery and the leather curtain that served as a door. *Looters have already been here.* Chalara's stomach growled. *I can't stay. There's no way to start a fire and if I go much longer without eating, I'll lose my milk. Then the babe will have nothing to eat, even if I can get it to suck.*

She moved decisively and got the baby secured again and they were out into the rain in just a few moments. She headed back toward the river and walked again, her face set in grim determination. *I am the wife of the king. I will not die here and neither will my child.*

In no more than twenty minutes, she saw another building and then several more. She must be on the outskirts of Varnach. That hut she'd stopped at must have been the beginning of the homesteads around the city. She decided she would not stop until she reached the center. There she would find a midwife and get help with the child. There she would find some of Lord Mulciber's people. They would give her help. Besides, she must tell them what had happened to Lord Mulciber. *They need to know what I saw.*

She came to the central square and saw immediately that Mulciber's palace had been completely destroyed. Not a single stone seemed to be intact. Some giant crushing force had reduced many of the huge blocks to gravel and the building itself was no more than a large pile of rubble. She looked at it in despair. *Where are all of his people?* She heard a low murmuring above the sound of the rain and to her left saw the temple to Mulciber and Moloch. It was partially intact and there was a glow through one doorway. *They have a fire going in there!*

Chalara hurried through the rain and into the doorway. Inside she saw a small crowd of perhaps forty people. They huddled by a fire but faced the front of the partially collapsed room where an altar still stood. An old priest stood there with two younger men. They held between them a bedraggled looking man whose wide eyes darted from side to side in terror.

The priest raised his hands and called in a sing-song but stuttering voice, "Lord Mulciber. Return to us … your people, we pray. The earth groans and the sky weeps … at your absence. Rise from your imprisonment and come back to us. End the ceaseless rain and bring … the sun to us again! We offer … you this sacrifice that you may drink life and come to us again."

He motioned to the younger men. Chalara had failed to recognize their filthy garments as acolyte robes until now, but finally she saw through the grime and noticed the hammer and fire insignia of Mulciber's priests. They dragged the victim to the altar. He tried to wrench free and pulled an arm loose. The bigger of the men hit the victim with a short club and the man's legs went limp. He slumped forward and the men draped him roughly over the altar then flipped him face up.

Chalara heard her baby cry feebly and felt it hiccupping weakly. She uncovered the child and moved closer to the fire to warm them both. *She's dying. It's been too long without eating. How can I bear all of this horror?* Hate surged in her: hate for this disaster; hate for the monsters that took her husband; hate for the flood; hate for the rain; hate for these bedraggled remnants of people; hate for the calamity that had stolen her life away. Her eye fell on one of the men huddled around the fire, warming his hands. *He looks familiar.* The man next to him also jogged something in her memory. *Who are these two?*

The priest had begun his sacrificial rite. He poured a small amount of oil over the man prone on the altar. The victim started to raise an arm again and the acolyte with the small club hit him forcefully on the side of the head. The victim went limp again. The priest continued pouring the oil and droned on. "…return again, cleanse the land of the … demons that came down from the sky, shut the fountains of Heaven that rain down the anger of the gods…"

One of the men around the fire looked up at her. At first, he glanced at her and then idly away, but abruptly, his gaze darted back to her and a look of horror came over his face. *He recognizes me. Who is he?* The man jabbed his elbow at the other man beside him and whispered to him. The man looked up in alarm at Chalara and his eyes opened wide in fear. *They both know me.*

The priest at the altar lifted a stone knife and promptly lost his grasp on it and dropped it. The knife clattered to the floor and the priest ducked down to retrieve it. He popped back up from behind the altar with a ridiculous expression of embarrassment and several of the people huddled around the fire laughed at him. Chalara narrowed her eyes at them and glared up at the priest. *He is a bumbling fool. He is making a mockery of this sacrifice.*

The priest tried to recover but stuttered to a halt. He stood there with a blank expression as if trying to remember something. *He's forgotten the words. Unbelievable. A priest and he can't remember the words of sacrifice.* More people laughed around the campfire, all but the two men that stared her way. One of them backed up and looked for the doorway. *He wants to get away.*

Then all at once, she remembered them, both of them. Chalara gritted her teeth so hard her jaw almost cracked. Fury rose in her in a wave that seemed to dwarf even the world-ending flood outside. *These are the two men who deserted us.* When the giant crocodile had attacked her group by the river, killed two of her son's men and taken her son with it into death, these two had been with them and had run away. *They ran away. They left my son to die. They left me to die. They left me to give birth alone. They left me to walk for three days with a starving child.*

The priest still stuttered, unable to proceed. Finally, he gave up and started the ritual over again with the pouring of the oil. The crowd around the fire broke into raucous laughter at his fumbling. *I have had enough of this!*

Chalara leapt to feet and shouted, "Enough! All of you be silent!" With one arm holding her dying baby, she stalked to the altar and the confused priest. He started to protest her actions, but she lifted her other arm and pointed at him.

"I am the chief wife of Lord Moloch, the brother god of your own Lord Mulciber!" She continued shouting and stalked up to the befuddled cleric. "I will not endure this mockery any longer. Give me that!" She grabbed the stone blade from him and raised it over the twitching victim whose eyes had opened again in confusion. She looked down at him and shouted the words of the ritual.

"Your life now serves one greater than yourself. I take from you all that you were and are. From now on, you are remembered no more." His eyes grew round with realization. Clutching the baby to her, she plunged the knife into the man's chest. He screamed in agony and died.

Instantly, the baby in her arm twisted as if hit by a bolt of lightning. It inhaled and seemed to shriek out a cry louder than any earthly infant had ever uttered. The hair of Chalara's neck rose and every square inch of her skin crawled. The baby seemed possessed with energy and thrashed. She looked down and saw the child rooting around as if seeking a breast to suckle. *She is hungry!*

Seized by an inspiration, she turned to the amazed crowd clustered around the fire below the altar and saw the two deserters a few steps closer to the doorway, but reluctant to step back out into the deluge. They stood transfixed by the sight of her over the corpse on the altar with the bloody, dripping dagger in one hand and the screaming baby in the other. *The crowd isn't laughing any longer.* Chalara motioned to the mob and shouted a command.

"Hold those two men by the door. They betrayed Lord Moloch's son and abandoned him to die alone. Bring them to me."

The two men seemed confused and unable to understand what was happening, but six men from around the fire leapt to their feet and surged after the two deserters. One seemed to recover his senses and darted for the door. He went through and splashed into the water and immediately slipped and fell down. The other man was grabbed by three men and pulled toward the altar. The three other men grabbed the one that had slipped and dragged him to Chalara. She motioned them forward. The struggling men fought fiercely but uselessly. She turned to the mumbling priest.

"What happened here? How was Lord Mulciber's palace destroyed? What happened to this temple?"

The man stuttered, "Demons flew on great wings ... from the sky. The ground shook and the palace collapsed. Giant winged creatures with the faces of men ... some with bodies like bulls ... some with those of lions ... they descended on the palace. They crushed giant stones in their claws. They dug through the rubble and pulled out Lord Mulciber. Others wrapped him in chains ... they flew away with him."

Chalara remembered the scene she had taken in at Moloch's harem. From her vantage down at the shore, she had seen giant flying monsters descend with a chained form and from the twisted shape she had known it was Lord Mulciber. The invaders had captured her Lord and one of them as large as Moloch had dangled Mulciber's chained form in her Lord's face as if taunting him.

"What happened to this temple, fool?"

"They returned, my Lady ... the demons. They flew back but many ... more the second time. They carried a giant chest with them. One of them ... waved at the sky and called down fire and lightning. The earth shook and ... and ... a hole opened ... in the earth. They set the chest in the hole and I saw ... I saw..." His voice seemed to stick.

"What did you see?" She insisted. He continued stuttering and could not proceed. She slapped the priest. He staggered back and started to protest. She slapped him harder and blood streamed from his split lip. She screamed into his terrified face. "What did you see?"

Words gushed from him, "They put Lord Mulciber in the giant chest. They closed him in. The one who called down fire raised his arms and a

6

wave like water flowed through the earth. The earth closed over the giant chest where they put Lord Mulciber. The temple shuddered and much of it collapsed."

Chalara squinted her eyes at the fool. *If this is true, then there is no one truly in charge here. Lord Moloch is taken and Lord Mulciber is captured.* She felt a surprising tug at her breast. Her baby let out a lusty grunt. She looked down and saw the little one had latched onto a breast on her own. The baby was suckling. *Suddenly you are full of life and have started eating.* She looked at the bloody stone knife in her other hand and started to realize what was happening. *You are your father's daughter.*

She turned to the dead body on the altar. She set the knife aside and unceremoniously shoved the body off the other side and onto the floor of the temple. It landed with a heavy thud. She turned to the priest and beckoned him closer. He took a hesitant step forward. She motioned to the acolytes to approach and they stepped forward as well.

She spoke clearly and forcefully, pointing at the fumbling man. "You are a priest of the gods. Your temple is almost destroyed. You have not guided your people well. The gods have deserted you." She paused and turned to the crowd below where the two terrified deserters were still being held.

She said, "I am the wife of the god, Moloch. I bore him his son. I have here his daughter, who I bore three days ago at the start of this flood. In your presence, I name her Melka. I will rule here, now. I will be priestess here, now." She turned back to the stuttering man. Blood dripped from his lip where she had struck him.

"And you will be the next sacrifice to the gods." As if on cue, the acolytes grabbed him. "Put him on the altar."

Before the terrified man could react with anything more than incoherent grunts, the acolytes bent him backward over the stone platform, lifted his legs up onto the surface and Chalara lifted the dagger over him. Her baby sucked greedily at her breast and a smile crossed her face for the first time in days.

"Your life now serves one greater than yourself. I take from you all ..." she continued the sacrificial chant and slammed the stone knife into the priest's chest. He screamed and blood gushed from his already open mouth and pulsed from the wound. Chalara felt the babe jerk and bite her nipple. Chalara's smile twitched with the pain, but she knew the child would live now. The baby seemed to grow in size and squirm and twist with added energy. *I can train her later not to bite, but at least she will live now. This is what my daughter needs. The energies of the dying used to feed her father, Lord Moloch. Now they will feed her.*

Chalara pushed the body of the priest off the altar. It landed on the other victim's body almost soundlessly. She motioned to the crowd below the altar.

"Bring those two deserters to me. They left my son when he needed help and he died. They left me when I was in labor and needed help and I almost died. They left my baby when she was being born and she almost died. The gods are hungry now. It will take much to remove their anger from us. Now these two will die."

The two men shrieked in terror as they were dragged down the aisle toward Chalara's bloody knife.

CHAPTER 2 – AT THE NECROPOLIS

"In search of this new world whom shall we find sufficient?"
— John Milton, Paradise Lost

The Present

"Hello. What's this?"

Henry Travers moved up and lightly flicked the small broom across the dirt. *Is that a metallic gleam? Perhaps more gold?* He leaned forward again, making sure not to obstruct the lights that illumined the dig site. He was working late this evening, but didn't mind the long hours. Henry finally, finally had found his niche and loved what he did. *It took me bloody long enough!*

He used the hand broom to sweep away more dirt into a dustpan which he placed on the screen for later sifting. *We mustn't lose any small artifacts.* He needed to break up a bit of the packed dirt before the little broom would do much more good, so he took a dental pick in hand and started loosening some of the clods around the item. *My dentist would be horrified to know to what uses we archaeologists put dental tools.* He smiled at the private joke.

He moved the additional dirt away and looked carefully at the object that was partially uncovered. *Not metallic, I'm quite sure. Then what is it? Bone maybe? Stone? No and no, it looks almost translucent. Perhaps volcanic glass? It looks carved, with possibly some designs around this top edge. Carving glass would be tricky in the Eneolithic period.* He used his smallest dental pick to loosen some more dirt. The item was round like a disk or the top of a cylinder, perhaps four centimeters in diameter. He pulled additional dirt away from the center of the object.

He spoke under his breath, "Hello again. It looks to have a hole in the center of the disk. Hmm."

A male voice spoke out very close to Henry's ear. "Perhaps a spool of some kind. Or something that would go on a necklace."

Henry jumped. "Professor! You startled me. What are you doing out here at this time of night?"

The older man continued to peer over Henry's left shoulder at the dig site. He spoke with a fluid command of English, but with the musical accent and rhythm of his native Italian. "I came to see why you were working so late." He nodded toward the item in the dirt. "Now I see why. You've photographed and recorded locations?"

"Definitely." Henry said shortly and turned back to his work, trying to ignore the man still leaning over him. Professor Paolo Russo seemed to have no conception of personal space and Henry felt the man was always too close to him whenever he was in the vicinity. In conversation, Russo leaned in too close. In greetings, he was always embracing, and on the dig site, well. *One should not be so close that others can tell one's preferred brand of olive oil.* Henry sighed.

He carefully removed more packed soil from the object. Periodically he swept the loosened dirt and moved it to the sifting screen. More and more of the item came into view. It was longer than he'd expected. Henry's pick scraped against something else nearby that was very hard. *That felt like bone.* He shifted away from the first item to uncover this new find. If these were human remains, it could be some of his more important work in this excavation.

Professor Russo backed away, but found a folding canvas chair and located a place nearby where he could sit and observe Henry's progress. Neither Henry nor Professor Russo spoke for a while as Henry concentrated on the new find.

Henry worked steadily, carefully, yet with great energy and slipped into a deep state of concentration. He dug methodically, using the picks when needed, removing debris with broom and dustpan. He seemed to know what needed to be done without thinking, and felt like he could almost picture what would be uncovered before it was revealed. *I've found my niche at last. Dad will be relieved.* Henry lost all track of time and experienced again that deep sense of immersion and awe that he often felt during the unfolding discovery of a lost segment of the past.

Henry finally stopped and assessed what he had done. He tipped his head from side to side and spoke out loud. "Now there's something you don't see every day."

Professor Russo's voice broke the silence, almost too loudly, "You certainly don't."

Startled, Henry looked over at Professor Russo and felt confusion. The Professor had been joined by the group of grad students that were assisting at the dig. *What are they doing out here so late? No wait, what time is it?*

The professor saw Henry's confusion and interrupted. "Henry, you've been at it all night. Here, have some coffee." Professor Russo held out a cup. "Tell us what you have here."

Henry looked around and had to agree that it was already morning. *Where had the time gone? Well Henry, you know that don't you? There's where the time went.* He turned back to the dig site. There she was and she was brilliant.

"Um, well, Professor, as you know, I got going last night, and though it was quite late, I couldn't bear to stop. I'd found the first piece of necklace and then you came by to check on me and that was when I ..."

Professor Russo broke into Henry's verbal onslaught. Paolo laughed and said, "Henry, perhaps you should start over and from the beginning! We have not been here with you every step of the way during the night! Here, take a sip of that coffee while you gather your thoughts. I will ask a few questions of our students to test their powers of observation and then come back to you in a moment."

He motioned to one of the female students while indicating the dig. "Now, Maria. Look at the dig where Henry has been working during the night. What is your first assessment of what he has found?"

Maria Conti spoke confidently. She wore work coveralls like the other graduate students and had her hair tied in a long, dark braid that trailed from a broad hat. She wore sunglasses against the growing morning brightness. She also spoke with a nearly musical cadence. "*Professore*, I see what appears to be a newly uncovered grave site. It is one that has human remains that are richly adorned with gold and other items of jewelry. The upper torso has been revealed very expertly." She smiled at Henry.

"Agreed. *Signore* Travers has done his usual excellent work. What else do you see?" said the professor.

She said, "This grave appears to be consistent with some of the other sites here in Varna, except this one has many larger items. I believe this to be a rich find. There are pieces that appear to be golden necklaces, rings, bracelets, flat medallions and chains. I think I see golden beads. I don't know what to make of that cylindrical object that is resting in the ribcage."

"Very good," said Professor Russo. "Henry, what do you think of Maria's summary?"

Henry stuttered, "Um ... very good. It was ... um ... a smashing job of description. I mean, good. It was quite good." Henry blushed. *How can I be blushing? I'm thirty years old!*

Russo asked again, "Henry, what do you make of the cylinder that Maria noted?"

Henry looked away from Maria and the slight smile on her face. "Well, well, um ... as you can see, the skeleton is laid out in an elaborate style with many items of gold. Most of the items make sense in their positioning with respect to the remains. The rings are on fingers, the bracelets encircle wrist bones, etc. The question is what about this cylinder?"

Henry continued, "Actually, I found the top of the cylinder first, before the bones. As you can see, it is approximately seven centimeters in length and four centimeters thick." He paused. "Anyway, the cylinder was resting down between the bones of the ribcage, but it looks like it had just settled in there after burial. The priestess' remains are remarkably intact…"

Professor Russo interrupted, "You say priestess? Why? The pelvic bones haven't been uncovered yet. Also, most of the female remains we've found in Varna have not been laid out and arrayed like this one. That tends to be closer to the way the male remains are found."

Henry answered, "True, true. Though in the oldest ones that we've found most recently, the females are arrayed in like fashion to this one. In these particular remains," he motioned to the skeleton, "in the chest, the length of the sternum is too short to be male. Also, by the shape of the skull, especially the smoothness of the forehead would indicate female remains. Of course, these characteristics are not definitive, so the angle of the pubic arch in the pelvis will need to be measured to provide a cross check."

The professor smiled, "Very good. But you also said, 'Priestess', not just female. Why assume the priestess caste when we have indications of later graves where the occupants were likely male priests?"

"I believe this grave is older than any previous graves. We determined early on that this newly excavated portion of the Varna Necropolis would be older than anything found to date. Also, the earlier excavations in this portion of the cemetery have all proven to be female. The biggest kicker is the jewelry. Look at these two medallions, for example. The two are solid gold, heavy and threaded to fit on a substantial necklace chain. The first of the two carries the familiar bull symbol, that of their god. The second carries a new design not seen before: that of a flame and what looks like a hammer or an axe. I believe these medallions would indicate the remains belong to a high religious official."

Maria spoke, "But you started to mention the cylinder?"

Henry paused again. *Get a grip, Henry. She can't help it that she distracts you entirely too much.* He said, "Yes, the cylinder. Besides the medallion with the flame and hammer, the cylinder is the real find here. It seems to be made of some translucent stone or jewel, but there are raised carvings all around the outer surface of the cylinder. I haven't yet had time to take an impression of the surface."

Maria interrupted, "Is it a cylinder seal?"

Professor Russo said, "Good question, Maria. Henry, for the other graduate students, refresh their memories on the subject of cylinder seals…"

Workers at the excavation site had been collecting around the graduate students to see what had been discovered during the night, but some noise began at the outer edge of the crowd and Henry didn't have a chance to respond to the professor's request. The commotion and shouting accompanied a thin man with a narrow face and dark, bead-like eyes. He pushed his way through the group and spoke insistently and stridently, "What is going on here? If there has been a discovery, why was I not informed? What are you hiding?"

Professor Russo stepped to the man. "Master Balev, I didn't know you had arrived yet today. Welcome. Come see what Henry has discovered at the new excavation site of the older graves."

Balev said, "Nonsense. You know the rules. I am the government's antiquities representative here and must be told instantly of each and every find. There will be no looting of this site while I am in charge. This is one of the richest ancient sites in Europe and there is too much gold here to allow out-of-control work. There have been too many instances of items mysteriously disappearing from here, probably to wind up in the black market. I will shut down this operation if I have to!"

Russo went to the man and took him by the arm. "Krastyo, Krastyo. Let me explain. With my permission, our own Henry Travers worked all through the night and we just arrived to find that he had made some wonderful discoveries. Let us show you."

Krastyo Balev shook his finger in the professor's face and said, "Russo, this is going too far. You should have told me there was work going on last night."

"I know, I know, Krastyo. It is my fault. Let Henry show you what he has found. Henry, tell us of the cylindrical jewel and what it might be used for," Professor Russo said.

Balev glared at Henry Travers as if to say, "Well?"

Henry said, "Um, we found a small cylinder that is seven centimeters long and four centimeters thick. It seems to be made of a translucent jewel or stone and have raised carvings all around the outside of it. It may be what is known as a cylinder seal. If so, it could be two thousand years older than any found to date."

Krastyo Balev looked irritated and said, "I am not familiar with this term. We do not see such items around here. What is a cylinder seal? Why is it called that?"

Henry said, "Because the ancients would sometimes take hot wax and pour it on the fold in a parchment or scroll and roll the cylinder over it, leaving an impression from the cylinder and sealing the document. If the design or picture on the wax seal were broken, it would be obvious that the document had been opened. Equally often, these impressions would be made by rolling the cylinder in soft clay. Cylinder seals were used by those in high office, for example, kings, princes or priests. The oldest ever found before dated from about 3500 BC. This one is two thousand years older than that based on the nearby graves which we have already dated." Henry said.

Balev smirked, "Who would have been this king or prince? There are no records of such prehistoric kings here in Varna."

Henry said, "In this case, likely not a king, but possibly a religious leader and ruler. Ancient peoples expected their rulers to also be their religious leaders. We may have found the grave here of one of the original high priestesses of the ancient city of Varna. And with that kind of power, she would have ruled them like a queen as well."

Professor Russo broke in. "Henry, you say the cylinder has carvings on it. Is it a language or a picture of some kind? And how would these people have carved such a substance? They had stone tools and copper, possibly bronze. Would that have been enough to carve something made of jewel or volcanic glass?"

Henry warmed to the subject. "It's a really crucial question, professor. I don't know <u>how</u> it was carved. Possibly with a tool made from the same type of jewel? I don't know. As for the carvings themselves, from a first glance, they don't appear to be a picture of any kind. It would be typical of cylinder seals, to have a tableau engraved on them, I mean, but this one looks to have some diagonal lines, no, more like chevrons and dots on it. Perhaps it's just an ornamental design, but it might be writing of some kind, too. That would be terribly interesting if we found writing here. We've not seen writing of any kind in the Eneolithic time period. Written language here would likely predate all other evidence found elsewhere as well."

Maria jumped in and said, "*Che bello!* You would have found the earliest known examples of written language anywhere!"

Professor Russo chuckled. "Henry, Maria, let's not get ahead of ourselves. This has just begun."

Krastyo Balev said, "I will need to take this cylinder into my care immediately. Such a possibly valuable item must be secured."

The graduate students look shocked. Maria's brow knitted and she said, "No! That is not the way it is done. First, we examine, photograph, analyze …"

Professor Russo held up his hand. "Master Balev and I will work out the details of the item in question. Henry, carry on please. Everyone, get to your tasks. Maria, assist Henry if you would. He's tired." Russo took the protesting antiquities officer by the arm and led him away, nodding sympathetically at the scolding the smaller man administered to him.

Henry exhaled in relief. *That Balev character is really starting to get out of hand. I am so glad that Professor Russo has to deal with him. I wouldn't want the professor's job.*

Maria stepped up beside Henry. Though her eyes were covered by sunglasses and he couldn't see her expression, her tone of voice sounded sympathetic. "Balev is such a nasty fool. I wouldn't be surprised if the missing artifacts he mentioned were his own doing."

Henry was startled, "Not really! You don't mean that."

Maria said, "I do! Nothing he did would surprise me. One of the other students, Angelica, told me the *porco demonio* had tried to *palpeggiare*," she stumbled over the English word and offered, "he tried to fondle her, to feel her up. She told him to get away and he threatened her to keep silent about it, but she told me just to be safe. He is bad news."

Henry was appalled and shook his head. "He sounds like a beast."

Maria's expression was fierce for a moment and then she calmed herself and said as if using high courtesy, "Exactly, *signore*. The man is a beast."

Henry wondered what was going on in Maria's head. He said, "I hope the man hasn't been untoward to you."

She frowned, balled one fist and held it in front of her face. She said firmly, "He tried once. I dealt with him." She relaxed her expression and changed the subject. "Now what can I do to help? We need to take advantage of the coolness of the morning before things get too warm."

Henry said, "I'd like to get the rest of the skeleton unearthed. Um … also, we need additional measurements and photographs. I'd also like to get an impression of that cylinder just in case Balev confiscates it."

Maria said, "I will go get some things for an impression and a cast. I'll be right back."

Henry said, "Thanks so much. I'll be right here, then." Henry turned back to the dig site and began taking more measurements and photographs. Before too much time had passed, Maria was back with a sack containing some trays, casting compounds, moist clay and in her other hand a plate full of food.

Maria handed him the plate and said, "Here. Take a few minutes and eat this. You've been at it all night and haven't stopped once. I'll prepare the clay and casting chemicals while you take a little break."

Henry said, "Um, that's very kind. Thanks so much." *I am hungry.* She'd brought him mostly standard local breakfast fare but with a little extra. A sliced cucumber, some buttered bread, a chunk of cheese, a hard-boiled egg, some olives and slices of melon and even a piece of honeyed pistachio baklava. *This is quite a large breakfast, actually. Where did she find that baklava? Very nice.*

He dug into the plate of food. He briefly looked up and noticed that Maria had her sunglasses off for close-in work and was looking at him occasionally and smiling. She was quite striking with her long braided black hair and large, dark eyes. She wasn't exactly beautiful, but definitely attractive with a very sweet smile. Henry mentally shook himself. *Now, imagine if she'd just heard my thoughts. She'd probably charge over here and take me by the throat. No, that's not right. She'd only do that if I'd really insulted her. Instead, she'd probably say, 'So I am no beauty? You, signore, are no prize, either. I've seen better looking rubbish collectors.'* Henry tried again to concentrate. *Stop letting your mind wander, Henry.*

She was preparing the clay for the cylinder impression and multitasking to get the casting chemicals ready for the three-dimensional negative image of the artifact. *I can't multitask. I wish I could, but it's only one thing at a time for old Henry.* He shoveled in the rest of the food and disposed of the plate. He went over to the table where Maria was working.

She said, "I wish I'd been here last night when you found the priestess. It must have been very exciting." She continued working while they talked.

Henry said, "Oh, it <u>was</u> exciting. I completely lost all track of time. I couldn't believe it was already morning. I got going and couldn't stop. I can't imagine doing anything else besides this. It's so exciting."

Maria smiled brilliantly as if understanding him completely. She said, "You are so right! I read an article recently that referred to the state of mind we get into when we are engrossed in something. It said when a person is being challenged to the edge of their ability in something they enjoy, they can lose track of time and forget themselves in the activity. That state of mind is called, 'Flow.'"

"Um, that is an interesting concept. I like the term 'Flow,' too. I didn't know you read outside of the archaeology field. You have broad interests?"

She lifted her eyebrows as if surprised and said, "Can't I enjoy learning about other fields? I find that kind of thing interesting. True, I don't have the background to understand all of it, but I find it helps broaden my mind and stay open to other possibilities."

Henry felt defensive. "My apologies, Maria. I didn't mean to imply you shouldn't be reading other things…" He trailed off.

"It's nothing," she said, suddenly seeming mollified.

Henry hesitated, unsure of his ground. He felt he might be walking through a verbal minefield. He finally tried to choose a safer topic. "Don't you find it fascinating that one's frame of mind can make time seem to go away? I wonder what that means about our minds? For example, why is our perception of the passage of time so subjective, so mutable? Have you read anything about that in the field of neurological research?"

"No, but it does sound interesting," Maria said. "There, the clay is ready for an impression. Let me finish preparing this casting compound and get it into a tray. Would you like to make the clay impression?"

"Yes, certainly," he said. Henry put gloves on and carefully took the cylinder in hand. He inspected it for dirt or debris and found a few flecks which he removed with his ever-present hand broom. With the artifact ready, he moved to the tray full of clay that Maria had prepared.

Henry lightly set the small cylinder on its side on the clay and pressed firmly, rolling it out along the flat tray until he was certain he had made an impression of it all the way around. Maria took it from him in her gloved hands and began cleaning it for the casting.

She spoke as she examined it. "Henry, what type of mineral is this? It does appear partially translucent and a type of light blue. I don't see any obvious crystalline structure or impurities. What do you think it is?" She poured the thick casting gel into another small tray.

Henry said, "I don't know. I'd like to send it to a lab for testing, but I'm quite certain we'd never get permission from our antiquities officer to do that. We'll have to do what we can here. Do you know any spectroscopy?"

Maria said, "No, but I believe that Angelica has some geology background. Maybe she can help us identify the type of mineral this is." She finished preparing the tray and then pressed the cylinder on its side halfway down into the gel. "That will need to set a little. I'll prepare the tray for the top half." She smiled and said, "I wonder if dentists know that we employ the same substance they use for taking castings of teeth?"

Henry said, "I don't know. I was just wondering yesterday about the dental picks we use. Someone thought first of using dentistry techniques, but who was it? An archaeologist with a dentistry background, I imagine. Come to think of it, some good archaeology gets done by people with mixed backgrounds. My dad is a geologist but does archaeology as a hobby. He got me interested in the field and it helped me finally find my niche. Good thing he did, I suppose, or I'd still be undecided in my profession." He motioned at the clay impression he'd made with the cylinder. "What do you make of this? Does this pattern strike you as rather odd?"

She took the first tray of partially set casting compound with the cylinder and flipped it over onto the second tray. She set a timer, took off her latex gloves and looked at the clay impression that Henry had indicated. It appeared to be a series of chevron-like lines and circular dots. There was also a vertical line that ran from top to bottom. There were six dots, four in the top half and two in the bottom half. The dots all seemed to be positioned between the lines, but at various vertical positions. The entire picture struck Henry as highly organized but without any discernible meaning.

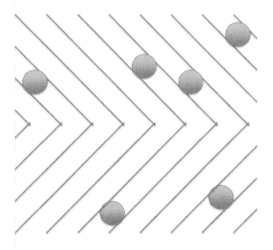

Maria said, "Did you roll the entire cylinder on the clay?"

"Yes, absolutely. Strange, isn't it?"

"Very," she said.

"Well, we will just have to ponder it further, won't we?" said Henry.

Maria's face went dead serious. "Yes, we will. And, I accept."

Henry's face wrinkled in confusion. "I beg your pardon. I accept? Accept what?"

Maria said, "You said that we should ponder it further. I accepted your suggestion. It is a date, then. When and where?"

The abrupt change of subject left Henry disoriented. "What? Why …?"

Maria laughed merrily. "You should see your face. I was joking with you. Don't worry, you didn't ask me for a date. Unless you _were_ asking me for a date …?"

Henry thought he understood her hint and blushed again. "Oh! Um, well. That would be super. I mean, yes. Um." Henry stuttered to a halt. He inhaled and said, "Let me start again. Maria, would you like to have dinner with me tonight? There, I've said it." He dropped his eyes and took a step back, a grimace starting to cover his face and he backpedaled verbally. "Sorry. No need to let me down gently, I thought I'd just get it out there and say it …"

Maria gave him a glorious smile and said, "All is well, _signore_. Of course I would love to have dinner with you. But first, we finish here with this cast and unearthing as much of the priestess as we can. Then, after lunch, you must go off to your apartment to get a nap. I don't want you snoring during dinner. Where shall we go to eat tonight?"

CHAPTER 3 – COUNTERMOVE

"But neither self-condemning; and of their vain contest appeared no end"
— John Milton, Paradise Lost

Dmitri Slokov's ship-to-shore call finally went through and he almost shouted with impatience when the voice on the other end answered.

"Alexi. This is Dmitri. Listen to me." Dmitri looked around the small communications room where he stood holding an old style telephone handset to his ear. *What a squalid wreck. Why did this ship have to be the one that rescued me? I have to be careful. Their radio man can overhear everything I say.*

He continued, "Alexi. I am on a ship named the *Legend*."

Alexi Slokov answered, "I thought you were on the *Lucian*. What are you doing on another ship?"

Dmitri said, "Just listen to me. I need you to get in contact with the *Lucian* and tell it to turn around and come back for me. I left the *Lucian* to go to the *Fortuna*." He kept his eye on the radio operator while he spoke, "But something terrible happened on the *Fortuna*. It sank and I barely made it off the ship alive. I was pulled out of the water and rescued by the crew of the *Legend*. The *Lucian* has sailed off and I need it to turn around and come pick me up off of the *Legend*. I am calling you from the radio room of the *Legend*. Do you understand what I've said?"

Alexi paused as if trying to assimilate all of the meaning behind what his brother had told him. "I understand, brother. You escaped from a shipwreck and you need our tanker the *Lucian* to return for you. Is that all?"

"No, there are two more things. One: I need a helicopter. The one I was on went down with the *Fortuna*. Second, I need to find out if Mercy Teller survived the *Fortuna* disaster."

"You're talking about the Rodica woman? Tresa's daughter?"

"Yes. I need to find Mercy Teller. I want her addresses, emails, cell phone numbers, anything. I want to find out if she is still alive. If she is, I may want to contact her. Once I get aboard the *Lucian* I will call you again. Hopefully by then, you will have the information I need. We'll discuss what to do next when I speak with you then."

Alexi said, "I'll put our people on tracking her down. Can you send me the *Legend's* current position and communication information so the *Lucian* can get in touch with it?"

Dmitri put the radio man on the phone and soon Alexi had the data he needed and had hung up. Dmitri fumed at the delay. His phone was no longer working after his dunking in the Black Sea, so he had to rely on the *Legend's* radio system. Besides, this far from shore, he wouldn't have found a signal anyway.

Dmitri flinched in pain. His broken arm had to be tended to by a doctor soon. The crewman on the *Legend* that had tended to him had basic emergency medical knowledge and had only been able to bandage Dmitri's cuts and burns and splint the broken limb. The man also gave Dmitri some painkiller, but it was not doing much good. Dmitri wanted to get to his own doctor quickly. As soon as the *Lucian* picked him up and he was able to get on the helicopter, he'd have it take him to Bucharest where his very first destination would be to his doctor.

Now I've got to wait, probably several hours before I can be on my way back to Bucharest. This is maddening! His thoughts turned back to those last moments on the *Fortuna* when Janos' man Rakslav had killed Dmitri's hired gun, Vasya. Janos had shot Dmitri's helicopter pilot and the chopper had crashed, sweeping Dmitri off the deck of the *Fortuna*. He'd blacked out for a few moments but regained consciousness when he hit the water. Nearby ships had seen the smoke from the *Fortuna* and had come to give aid. That was when the *Legend's* crew had fished him out of the water.

Everything is turning into a disaster. The Russian was killed by Janos' bodyguard, Rakslav. I don't know what happened to Tresa's daughter, Mercy. As far as I know, Parasca escaped and is still alive. I need to find out somehow if Parasca survived that disaster. If, in spite of everything, he died, I might be able to finally sleep well for the first time in almost forty years. I need to get my people on it right away to find out if he has surfaced somewhere. Let's see, if I were him, where would I go? To Bucharest? It's possible. There will be lots of fires to put out at his corporate headquarters because of the sinking of the Fortuna. His insurance company is going to want answers. In fact, they may want to try to salvage the ship. Hmm. I need to think about that some more.

Where else could he go to ground? The only other place I can think of is his Greek island. He could go there and try to remotely put things back together. It's a good thing I have some contacts there; they'll let me know if he shows up.

I need to get the full story of the Fortuna disaster to Alexi, but I've got to get over to the Lucian so I can speak to him freely. I couldn't tell him anything earlier in case that radio man overheard me, but I've got to prepare him. If Parasca or any of his people survived, PetroRomania may try to accuse me and my company of piracy or worse. They may try to tie us up in a big legal fight. Alexi needs to mobilize our legal team to file suit first if possible or a countersuit if not. What would we file suit about? In the short-term, it doesn't have to be true, it just has to sound plausible. If we can hit first, then any suit they file will just look like retaliation. Alexi and I will come up with something.

But what happened to Mercy? Could she have survived that disaster? Parasca said she was probably dead. How would he know that? Was he just making wild claims, trying to scare me? Please, let her be alive. If she is, maybe I can still find her. I wanted so much to see her. Her picture reminds me so much of her mother. She's Tresa's only child and all I have left of Tresa except for … wait a minute. Hmm.

I've got to get some of my people to dig into PetroRomania's systems. They've already broken into them before and installed those 'back-doors' the hackers always talk about. I need them to find some contact information for Mercy. If there is any way at all I might be able to get in touch with her I need them to do it. If I had an apartment address in Bucharest or the United States, maybe a phone, an email address, or some other way she might check in, I might be able to reach her. If she made it off the Fortuna, I think I have just the way to get her to contact me back. She'll have to respond if I let her know she's not alone.

CHAPTER 4 – RETALIATION

"Untamed reluctance, and revenge, though slow, yet ever plotting"
— John Milton, Paradise Lost

The small submarine broke through the surface of the Black Sea and Janos Parasca breathed a sigh of relief. *I'm near the shore now with only five percent left on the batteries. It took all night.* He opened the hatch and breathed the salty sea breeze. *And fresh air at last.* He looked across the breakers to the beach and muttered to himself. *I've got to get as close in as possible, though I will still have to wade up to the beach through these waves. Do I have enough charge on the sub batteries to make it?* He looked at the solar panels on the outside roof of the sub. *Those won't help me much. They take too long to charge anything.* He cursed his bad luck. *My phone will not work if I let it be submerged in water, so I can't chance getting wet if I want to use it. I can't tell where I am. Do I have a cell signal yet?*

Parasca pulled out his phone and checked. *Finally, I have some reception! I'll try calling now.* Parasca's phone quickly picked up a Turkish network, though not a strong signal. *I must be fairly close to a town.* He dialed the international number for PetroRomania's headquarters in Bucharest and waited through the multiple clicks indicating call routing. Finally, the PetroRomania corporate number for the security department rang. On the second ring, a human operator answered.

"PetroRomania Corporate Security. How may I direct your call?" the operator said.

"I am Chairman Janos Parasca. This is an emergency call. Put me through to the department head on duty."

"Sir, I beg your pardon. Would you repeat your name once more?"

Janos Parasca snarled at the operator. "This is Chairman Parasca. If you do not connect me through to the department head on duty in Corporate Security, I will have you fired immediately."

The operator seemed to sense from his tone of voice that he was serious. With a few clicks, his call was routed to another line. *I never needed to know anyone's numbers before. My secretary would get people for me. She's dead and I haven't gotten an adequate replacement yet. Rakslav Gachevska always took care of the security part of things for me and he is probably dead now. That helicopter crash swept him and Dmitri Slokov both over the side of the Fortuna.*

"This is Corporate Security, Officer Alex Lacusta speaking. How may I assist you?"

"This is Chairman Parasca. Do you understand what I just said and who I am? Repeat back to me what I just said. Who is speaking to you?"

The man's voice changed markedly in tone. "Chairman Parasca, I recognize your voice. Chief of Security Gachevska spoke of you often. How may I help you?"

At last, someone who is marginally competent. "Officer Lacusta, I have been on our oil exploration ship *Fortuna* and our company has suffered a grave loss. The ship was damaged and sank and I escaped but many lives have been lost. Your superior, Rakslav Gachevska, was with me on the *Fortuna* and was swept into the sea. He may be dead." Janos Parasca changed to a very severe tone. "Officer, I ask again, do you understand what I have just said? I need you to acknowledge what I have told you to make sure you understand me."

The man sounded calm and matter of fact. "Yes sir. You said the *Fortuna* was sunk and there has been grave loss of life. You said that my superior, Director Gachevska, may be among the casualties."

Parasca said, "Good. Now listen further. I have just this moment made it to shore and have only now been able to call anyone. I think I am on the coast of Turkey but will consult a map on my phone as soon as I hang up. Take my phone number down." Parasca called out his phone number and continued, "You are to send a text message to that number right now while I am waiting on the line. Do not hang up. If we are disconnected, you are to call me back and continue calling until you have reached me again. Now send a text message to the number I just gave you."

A few seconds later, the security officer said that he had sent a message. After ten seconds, Parasca's phone vibrated with the receipt of the message. *Good. Rakslav didn't hire an idiot.*

Satisfied for the moment, he said, "Here is what you will do. Write these things down. First, I need a helicopter to come pick me up. Contact the Transportation Department head, Serban Ciorbea, and tell him to personally call me at the number I gave you. He will need to arrange for a helicopter to pick me up no later than two hours from now. I will give him my location after I've had a chance to consult a map. If I am in Turkey as I suspect, the helicopter can come from Istanbul and take me there." He had the man read back the order. Then Parasca proceeded.

"Second, I need the head of the legal department, Bognan Antonescu, to call me as soon as possible at this number as well. There are lawsuits to file and matters of legal ownership to begin work on immediately. We will also seek damages for willful destruction of the *Fortuna* from Dmitri Slokov's company, Intercon Transport. We may also face lawsuits concerning the casualties on the *Fortuna*."

"Third, you can do this for me immediately from your place in corporate security. Get a list of all employees, contractors and subcontractors that were on the *Fortuna*. They should all be presumed missing and possibly dead until we can conduct a thorough investigation. Any inquiries about these employees should be handled by the legal department and corporate security. You are to also have the HR department flag all of their employment records. Pay special attention to locating one of our employees, the geologist Mircea Teller. Check on whether there have been any reports on her whereabouts."

Parasca continued, "Fourth, I need the fleet operations department head, Michel Luca to contact me to mount immediate salvage operations at the site of the sinking of the *Fortuna*. I will tell him what is to be salvaged and what is not."

"Lastly, I want the head of research, Dr. Caba Ozera to call me. He must call me personally, not one of his staff. I have a very, very important message for him. This last instruction includes you as well. After I speak with him, you will need to let Dr. Ozera have access to my executive offices where he will need to retrieve an item from my personal art collection. He will be using the item in his research. As acting head of security, you have the key to the door of my executive suite, but not the code to open the room where I keep my collection when I am not there. Here is the code." Parasca called out a nine-digit passcode and described the item that he should allow Dr. Ozera to remove from the art collection.

"Now read all of those instructions back to me." After hearing the recitation and being satisfied, Parasca said, "Officer Lacusta, I have entrusted you with a list of very critical responsibilities. I stress to you now, these tasks are of supreme importance. If you carry these out quickly and correctly, I will reward you personally. If you hesitate on these tasks or do not complete them, you will be dismissed. Again, do you understand?"

"Yes sir. I will get to work on these immediately. If problems arise, would you like me to contact you at this number?"

"Yes, though I may be in transit between locations. Send me text updates. Only call if there is a problem you cannot get resolved."

"Yes sir."

Parasca hung up and started guiding the sub slowly closer in to shore. He kept an eye on the blinking warning light for the batteries. *That's not the battery charge I'm worried about though. The big concern is if I will have enough of a charge on my phone.* He looked at it and saw it had fifty five percent left on the battery. *That had better be enough. I have a lot of calls to take right now.*

Though the network connection was not the best, he consulted his phone's mapping software and found he was on the western side of the Bosporus. *There isn't a city on the Turkish coast here. The closest town is one on the Bulgarian side of the border.* Saray was the closest Turkish town and that was inland by twenty or thirty kilometers and 125 kilometers from Istanbul. *My people might be able to get a helicopter from Saray, but it might be quicker to just get one directly from Istanbul.*

I still can't believe what happened aboard the Fortuna. He looked at the sword that rested across the other seat in the mini-sub, feeling amazement at what he had seen. *I've always wondered if there was something else beyond this reality: otherwise it would be difficult to explain my abilities. Since I first touched that stone knife recovered from that ancient grave site, I've been able to see the past by touching things with a history of blood. I suppose I always knew that I had unique abilities, even paranormal, but ... supernatural? No. Even after what I've seen, there must be some logical explanation. But is there ...?*

Parasca shuddered at the memory of the release of the monstrous Moloch that the *Fortuna* had brought up from the bottom of the Black Sea. *The creature had been trapped in that box for over seven thousand years, and yet it revived!* Not only had it revived, it had laid into the crew of the *Fortuna* and Dmitri Slokov's invading mercenaries. It had torn people apart, flayed them, roasted them alive and even eaten them.

The creature had captured Parasca and Rakslav. It had enthralled Rakslav with some kind of mental force. Rakslav had acted like he was hypnotized and did whatever the monster had commanded. *It wasn't able to control me mentally, but it tortured me.* The thing definitely had supernatural abilities. It had smashed Parasca's face with a blow from its hand and shattered Janos' jaw and splintered his teeth. *Then it grabbed me and made my jaw whole again and regrew my shattered teeth. It healed me in moments. It levitated me in the air. It snatched my gun out of my hands from a distance. If that is not magic, then it is so close to magic that it makes no difference.*

Parasca didn't know how to explain any of what he had seen. He didn't understand how the creature had survived millennia of imprisonment or how it had been able to do what it did. *Maybe that is what is really meant by the religions when they describe a demon. But why has no one ever seen one of these things before? Maybe they had seen them but didn't survive to tell about it. Or maybe those that did survive were driven insane or knew they would be mocked and ignored so they kept silent. I need to keep that in mind. I mustn't show any mental cracks.*

Janos Parasca continued waiting on board the mini-sub. A few minutes later, he started receiving phone calls from his corporate lieutenants. *The security officer is doing well. If he keeps this up it could go nicely for him. With Rakslav probably dead, I may have found someone to promote into his spot.*

The first of his people to reach him was Michel Luca of PetroRomania's fleet operations. Parasca immediately launched into a series of instructions.

"Michel, listen carefully. The *Fortuna* has been sunk. I will work with our legal group to hold those that are responsible to account, but I need you to mount an immediate salvage operation. I will send you the coordinates I took from the location where the *Fortuna* went down."

Michel said, "You want the *Fortuna* raised? That may not be possible to do quickly. These things take much time and planning."

"No, I do not want the entire ship raised. That would take too long and the ship took severe damage before it sank due to some … terroristic activity, so its major worth now may be only in scrap metal. Except, that is, for what I want salvaged. I need a quick extraction team in there to pull out two items that were on the deck of the ship when it sank."

"Only two items?"

"Yes, but one is a very heavy metal box about two and a half meters high by two and a half meters wide by six meters long. You will need a crew and salvage ship capable of lifting between seventy and eighty metric tons from around three hundred meters deep. The second item is a small metal disk less than two meters across. I need this effort begun immediately to retrieve the two items. Tomorrow would not be too soon."

"Janos, can I ask what is so special about these two things? They must be very valuable. The cost of this will be huge."

"Cost is not important to me in this matter. Speed is the most important thing. These things are made of a new kind of metal that is tremendously valuable. PetroRomania must own that metal. These two items are some of the only samples in the world. We must retrieve them before anyone else gets to the site of the *Fortuna*. For all I care, you can even call those salvage people that righted that cruise liner that tipped over on its side near Italy. I do not care how much this salvage operation costs. Just make this start happening immediately. Find out now, and by that I mean today, what can be started instantly. This is your top priority. You must cancel all meetings, appointments, everything and handle this."

Parasca ended the call and waited again. *Is Michel asking too many questions? I need to watch him. I don't want him turning on me or alerting authorities. Michel hasn't balked before, but I need to be careful and keep an eye on him. Of course I didn't tell him the other reason the salvage must begin now. That sarcophagus, Moloch must be back in it, and it must never be opened again. If Moloch escapes from it, he will come after me, I know it.* Parasca had a frightening thought that sent chills through him. *What if Moloch isn't inside that box? I only assumed he is because I stopped hearing his raging thoughts in my head. Before I lost consciousness and Rakslav carried me from the moon pool, it was obvious that Mercy was going to try to get Moloch back inside it. What if she did not force him back into it? Could she have killed him? No, I don't think that's possible. A thing that won't die without air, food or water for over seven thousand years simply can't be killed. He can't be dead, and if he's out he'll know I didn't try to free him again. He warned me about trying to evade him. He'll be after me and if he catches me, I'll be lucky if he just kills me. I don't think I'll be lucky. I saw the sarcophagus closed again when I took the mini-sub down to retrieve the sword. I assumed Moloch was in it. He must be. Please let him be in it.*

Parasca felt sheer terror at the thought of falling into the monster's hands again. He couldn't shake a feeling of dread and was startled when his phone rang again. It was his head of research, Dr. Ozera. After briefly describing the situation with the *Fortuna*, Janos Parasca launched into his directives.

"You are to go to my executive offices where security officer Lacusta will meet you. He will let you in and then take you to the inner room where my personal art collection is kept. There is a display case with a small metal dagger with a dark, glossy wooden handle. On the box, it has an engraved label that says, "From the *Fortuna*, found in an undersea tar whip." You are to remove that item and its case and no other items. Take the knife to the company research laboratories. You will remember this item from earlier in the year when we had some metallurgical tests run on it. Your team did some work to determine its crystalline structure and hardness. Now I want you and your people to figure out how to make more of this metal. PetroRomania needs to understand its properties and how to make it commercially. This is urgent and I want you to delay all other research. Put all of your best people on this task and move everyone else off of any other projects so they can assist as needed. Develop an economically feasible way to manufacture this metal and do it immediately."

"Mr. Chairman, of course I will do what you say, but may I ask to what use you plan to put the metal?"

Parasca felt impatient with the question. "What difference does that make?"

The scientist replied, "You said you wanted my people to figure out how to make the metal commercially. That means it will have to be made economically and the economics of any manufacturing process depend on how much the end product can be sold for. The price that can be gotten for a product depends on who will buy the product and for what purpose. So, what do you plan for this new metal? Will it be sold as a replacement for structural steel? If so, the economics and production processes will go one direction. Will it be targeted at tubular goods such as pipelines? That would aim us in another direction. It all depends on the planned uses…"

Parasca jumped in. "I am losing my patience, Dr. Ozera. Do not yet concern yourself with the target audience for any products. This is not a new cell phone we are talking about here. We are talking about a revolutionary new metal that may have many uses. Your first task is to understand how it can be made. Then make some. Then make a lot more of it as cheaply as you can. Then we will decide how to scale up for different uses. Is that clear?"

"Yes, Mister Chairman."

Parasca hung up. *Academics! What maddening nonsense. If I wanted a lecture on economics, I'd have called my financial officer. I'm going to have to push that one or he'll get bogged down in writing research papers for publication. I don't pay that department to develop new theories. I want applied research that I can turn into money, not ivory tower pig slop. We must find out how to make more of that crystal steel, and quickly.*

He looked again at the sword. Did he dare touch it again? The feeling of power that he'd known when he touched it was almost overwhelming, but he knew that he could not yet control the thing. *I don't want to kill myself. I have to go slowly. As soon as I get to my island retreat and get some rest, I'll concentrate on learning how to handle that thing.*

He was giving the crystal dagger to his researchers to study it and learn from it. There was another reason as well. *It's not just for making and selling metal. It's also for power. That metal somehow stores the energy of the dying. I saw the vision of how it was forged with the deaths of thousands of people. If we can make more of it, I'll be able to store more life energy and use more of it. I need to learn to use it safely like Moloch did when he forced my rebellious daughter Mercy to heal herself of her injuries.* He felt his face where his old scars used to be before they were healed. *I just keep feeling younger and younger. Already I feel as good as I did almost twenty years ago. I can't let that go. If I can get my strength and youth back, it would be worth more to me than all my wealth. I might even get other appetites back as well.*

Parasca's phone rang again. *This security officer Lacusta is very good. The entire headquarters building must be hopping.* He answered his phone.

"Janos Parasca speaking."

"Bognan Antonescu here. I've got some insistent idiot named Lacusta in the security department demanding that you wanted me to call you at this number. He says the *Fortuna* sunk. Is it true?"

Parasca smiled at the head lawyer's annoyance. "It is true and I did want you to call. The *Fortuna* has been sunk. That is what I wanted to talk to you about. I want you to fire off some lawsuits against Dmitri Slokov's company, Intercon Transport. They sank the *Fortuna*. There have been many people killed and hundreds of millions of Euros in damage."

"What? Are you sure?"

"Bognan, I wouldn't be talking to you if I weren't sure. I was there on the *Fortuna*. Dmitri's company had some people on the ship posing as subcontractors. I believe they set explosives off and scuttled the *Fortuna*. He also sent some armed mercenaries onto the *Fortuna* and tried to seize it before it sank."

"How do you know Slokov was involved?"

"Dmitri arrived on another ship named the *Lucian* that pretended it was rendering aid to us when the explosions started. The pig flew over us on a helicopter before the *Fortuna* sank, and was trying to gloat over me. His helicopter crashed and he was swept overboard. If he's still alive, I want him bankrupt. If he's dead, I want his company for my own. If I can't have it, I want it destroyed. Check and see if the *Lucian* is registered to Intercon Transport or one of his other companies. I've contacted Michel Luca in Fleet to begin work on some salvaging operations, but if Dmitri's alive, it's his neck that I really want."

"This is going to take time, Janos. InterCon Transport won't take this lying down. They'll fight back. Is there any written proof? Maybe some letters or emails? Are there sound or video recordings that were taken? Do you have any pictures of Dmitri on the *Fortuna*?"

"Bognan! The ship sank. Any proof went down with it. If you want emails or other electronic foot prints, get some of our IT people looking for evidence of hackers in our systems. But be clear on this: I want Dmitri out of business. He committed piracy against my ship and I'm not stopping until we strip him of everything!"

"Janos, I'm just telling you it won't be an easy thing to prove unless we have something tangible backing up our story like email traffic or video. No court will rule for us just because our ship sank. It will be hard to convince a judge or jury to give us the win simply because we lost a ship. There will have to be proof." Antonescu paused and then jumped at an idea. "Didn't you say Luca in fleet operations is going to lead a salvage effort? That might help us. Get some of the divers they use to examine the *Fortuna* site and take lots of pictures. If they provide us with photographs that show explosive damage, it would be a point in our favor. Oh, and have them look for anything else that might be proof, like bullet-riddled bodies. That might help our case."

"Now you're starting to think like the Antonescu that I know. Call Luca and tell him your ideas. That's all for now."

"Wait, Janos. The *Fortuna* was an oil and gas exploration ship, right? Did it have any oil on it besides the diesel fuel it would have used for its engines? Was there anything in its storage tanks?"

"There may have been. They had liquefied a large quantity of tar with steam prior to being sunk. That liquefied tar was probably still in the tanks when it went down. Why do you ask?"

"Because of the environmentalists! That tar could be leaking from the *Fortuna* now. We could have the world's press down on us in hours once word gets out we own a sunken ship that's leaking. They'll be showing pictures of tar on beaches and dying birds. What a nightmare!"

Parasca sneered, "I don't care one bit about that. Let them weep and wail. PetroRomania is privately owned. I have no stock exchanges or shareholders to keep happy. Let the press complain."

"But the politicians will be all over this in a moment if there's a large leak!"

"I pay the politicians enough. They'll keep quiet, and they know what will happen if they don't. Call public relations and warn them to be ready in case this story hits the wires. Now get on it."

As he finished the call with Antonescu, Parasca saw that a voice message was waiting for him from Serban Ciorbea. He didn't bother to listen to the message. He just used the call back option and had Ciorbea on the phone in a minute.

"Where's my helicopter?" Parasca demanded. Even with the hatch open, and outside air coming in, he wanted out of this mini-sub.

Ciorbea said, "I know you're on the Turkish coast, but as soon as I know where you are specifically, I'll have a chopper on the way. Where do you want to go from there, Istanbul?"

"Yes, and when I get there, I want my private jet to meet me and take me to my island. Here is my location's latitude and longitude coordinates according to what the mini-sub says." He sent the data.

"Got it. I'll get the helicopter on its way to pick you up. As soon as I know when it will be there, I'll send you a text to let you know. I'll also get your jet on its way to Istanbul to meet you and take you to your island."

Parasca hung up. A minute later, he got a text from Officer Lacusta that all of the tasks he been assigned by the Chairman were under way and there were no problems encountered so far. Parasca smiled slightly. *This man will be useful to me, I think. He needs to receive a generous bonus right away. Now, if he can be cold-blooded when necessary, he could make a good new security chief. Actually, to be as good as his old boss Rakslav, Lacusta will need to handle blood whether it's hot or cold.*

At that thought, Parasca's slight smile grew a little bit wider.

CHAPTER 5 – DIRECTION

"And from the shore they viewed the vast immeasurable abyss"
— John Milton, Paradise Lost

Mercy said, "We're close to shore now. What a relief that we had enough of a charge to make it this far. Let's open the hatch and you can try calling in to headquarters."

Her face took on a look of concern. "I feel nervous about this, Jack. Surely by now, headquarters knows about the sinking of the *Fortuna* last night. It's probably a madhouse of confusion there as they try to find out what happened and who was on the ship. They don't know who may have survived and who didn't. If Parasca or his man Rakslav survived, he may have sounded an alert to be looking for us. This call could bring down attention on us we don't want."

Jack said, "I don't think there's much downside here. If they know we're alive, they might give us help. As far as anyone there knows, we're still employees in good standing. But just to be safe, I won't let them know who is calling at first, until we know a little more. This call will be a test of what kind of reception we might get."

She said, "All right, but I'm still nervous that they'll be able to know it was you calling. When you called me back in the US, I saw your name come up on my phone."

He said, "You saw that in Manhattan because that was my US phone. This one is the phone I use in Romania and I have caller ID turned off on the account. It just felt like a little extra privacy that I wanted. I'm glad now I exercised that option." Jack asked about her concern. "What do you think might happen when I call in?"

She said, "I don't know. Parasca might have survived the *Fortuna*. If he did, who knows what that crazy man will do? I know he tried to kill me and had allied himself with that monster, Moloch. He was cooperating with it on human sacrifices! If he's alive he might try to get his hands on us again. I for one don't want anything to do with him."

Jack understood that Mercy was referring obliquely to her relationship to Parasca. She had only found out yesterday that Janos Parasca was her biological father. That was a heavy burden to bear considering how she had already hated the man. Now with the events of the last twenty-four hours, she'd almost have to be fanatically opposed to him. Jack stood up from his chair in their mini-sub and opened the outside hatch. The morning sunlight flooded in and they heard the sound of sea gulls. Jack climbed the short ladder until his head and chest were outside. He breathed deeply and let out a long sigh. He took his phone in hand and saw a weak signal. It might be possible to get a call through. He keyed in a number and waited.

A voice answered in Romanian, "PetroRomania. How may I direct your call?"

Jack replied in the same language. "Please connect me to Jack Truett."

"One moment please." There was a long pause and then the call was put on hold. A minute went by and the call rang through to a phone.

"Corporate Security. This is officer Lacusta speaking. Were you inquiring about a PetroRomania employee named Jack Truett?"

Already on his toes, Jack said, "Yes. If he is not available, I'd like to leave a message for him."

Lacusta said, "Mister Truett is currently unavailable. Could I have your name and number please?"

"Certainly." Jack paused only momentarily and then rattled off the name of the manager of his apartment complex in Bucharest. He gave his own cell phone number but inverted several digits.

"Thank you. As I said, Mr. Truett is unavailable at the moment. I'll connect you to his voice mail."

The call clicked through again and Jack's voice announced in Romanian and then English that he "… was away at the moment, please leave a message after the beep."

Suspecting it might be picked up by someone other than himself, Jack left a message in Romanian, "Mr. Jack Truett, this is the manager at your apartment complex in Bucharest. Could you please call the office about the plumbing work order we spoke about a few weeks ago? I have an update for you. Sorry to call your work number but I've tried several times to reach you at your apartment and haven't been able to catch you."

Jack hung up and went back down the ladder.

Mercy said, "So you had to leave a fake message. I heard. What happened?"

Jack said, "Yes. I left a fake message. But they did something I wasn't expecting: they forwarded my call directly to security. The security officer tried to take my name and number and I gave him fake information. It could mean a couple of things. It could mean that they know the *Fortuna* sank under questionable circumstances. It could mean they are keeping tabs of all inbound and outbound calls for employees or contractors that may have been involved."

"And it could mean that Parasca left special instructions in case there was anything for us. They could be trying to catch us."

"True. We just don't know at this point."

Mercy shook her head as if irritated at a buzzing insect. "This part almost makes sense in a way. It's kind of what you would expect for a corporate disaster with the public relations department trying to lock down information and having to refer all matters to the legal department. But what does it mean that they sent your call asking for Jack Truett directly to corporate security?"

"I don't know, but it sounded ominous," Jack said.

Mercy said, "Jack, I don't know what we're supposed to do now. We survived the *Fortuna* disaster and I'm glad for that. But there has been so much else that happened, how do I assimilate it all? And now, we find out it's not even over, not really. Now if we show our faces, we could be in trouble somehow. What if PetroRomania tries to put the blame for the *Fortuna* sinking onto us?"

"I don't know how they'd do that. The ship is sunk and with it all of the data we collected. Those crystal steel artifacts are gone too, as far as I know. Moloch's back in his sarcophagus and that's at the bottom of the Black Sea. Just because I called into the office and they routed my call strangely doesn't mean that they're trying to blame us for something."

Jack continued, "We do need to think about where we're headed next. I won't work for Parasca again, that's for sure. In fact, after what we've been through, I think I've learned that I'm not going to go the corporate route any longer. I've been kowtowing to higher-ups for too long and it's been bad for me. I've made too many compromises and pushed my own principles down much too long. If anything, I need to go the entrepreneurial route now." He looked at her and arched one eyebrow. "You're not looking for new employees in your company are you?"

Mercy laughed, "That would be great, Jack. Sure, we could both work out of my little company. We could get contract jobs, true, but it's just that," she paused and looked at him shyly, "I don't want to be headed in a different direction from you anymore. I might have an assignment in one part of the world and you might have one in another. After what we've been through, I don't want to lose what we have."

Jack took her hand. "I promise you we will not lose each other again. As soon as we get back to the United States, I'm going to put an engagement announcement in the Dallas Morning News. I want the world to know that we're getting married and you are off the market."

She smiled and said, "Good. Your eligible bachelor days are over too. There will probably be a lot of brokenhearted women over that, too."

He played along with the joke. "Well then, they'll have to get over it." They both smiled. Mercy's expression changed to worry.

"Jack, I still can't come to terms with the whole supernatural element of what happened over the last few days. Yes, I knew since I was a teenager that I was stronger than most people. I had to hide it. I knew I heard those demonic voices, but I never thought of them as something outside of me. I thought they were in my mind and that I was crazy. But now I find out that I'm not even entirely human. The DNA test Hayden had run on us all showed that I'm some kind of hybrid and that I'm distantly related to Moloch, to say nothing of having that evil monster Parasca for a father. I also know that the voices are not just in my head. Moloch called those voices the 'unbodied'. And what about that creature Moloch? It had supernatural powers. That is absolutely undeniable. We all saw what it could do. Jack, what has happened to our world?"

A look of pain crossed her face. "And think what happened to poor Hayden! I can't believe he was killed. Smashed into a wall by that giant like he was a rag doll. He must have died instantly. What about Hayden's family? I remember he once mentioned his son in graduate school. I know he was married for over thirty years and he and his wife lived in the UK. How can he be dead? What a tragedy. Someone has to tell his family."

Jack said, "Mercy, I don't know what to say about all of those things. I'm the kind of person that always takes things the way they are, so if this is the new world in which we live, I say let's figure out how to survive in it. Up until a few days ago, I didn't believe in the supernatural either, but now, I can't deny it. I saw a lot of the things you saw. I saw Moloch revive after thousands of years of being entombed. That does not fit into the tidy non-supernatural world view I had a few weeks ago. I saw him levitate things and I heard him in my head, forcing me to be perfectly still, paralyzing me. Mercy, I never had voices in my head before like you've suffered with all your adult life, but if that is a tenth of what it has been like for you every day, then I don't know how you stayed sane. Now I know what it's like to have voices in my head and I am so sorry you had to endure that alone."

She reached over and squeezed his hand. "So what's next?"

Jack checked the mapping function on his phone and found their location. "We're at the Bulgarian coast, almost to a town named Burgas. Do you speak any Bulgarian?"

"Just a little that I picked up in Romania when I lived there," Mercy said.

"I think we should go into town. They may not have a rail connection here, but I'll bet we can catch a bus toward the Romanian border.

Regardless of whether Parasca survived and is after us, I want to get back to Bucharest to collect some of my stuff and some emergency cash."

"That's a good idea. I want to get to my apartment in Bucharest too and pick up some things. After that, maybe we should try to get back to the US. I won't feel safe until we're well away from Parasca and his people." She smiled at him. "Also, when we get back to Dallas, you can put that engagement announcement in the paper. You know, I haven't seen your folks since we were in graduate school together. You'll have to reintroduce me to them."

Jack looked uncomfortable and said, "Well, I'm not real close to my folks these days, so it's probably not necessary." Mercy looked at him questioningly. He continued, "I'll tell you about it later. It's complicated."

She pursed her lips, nodded as if determined to return to this discussion later. Then she hesitated as if just remembering something. "Jack, we don't have entry visas into Bulgaria since we left Romania through the port of Constanta. When we try to cross the border into Romania, what if the Bulgarian authorities check and find out that they don't have records of us entering the country?"

Jack said, "I say we just tell them what happened at the *Fortuna* and how we just got to shore. They can't blame us for being survivors of a shipwreck. If nothing else, we can call the American embassy. We both have our passports, so we should be okay. I've got my wallet with some credit cards so I can buy bus or train tickets when we need to. From this map it looks like we need to get a ride from Burgas to Varna and then from there we head to the port of Constanta across the Romanian border. Once we get to Constanta, we can catch a train into Bucharest and get our things."

Mercy said, "I think we'll be at the most danger from Parasca or his people in Bucharest. We'll need to be careful when we get into the city and try to go to our apartments. Oh, and just remember to use personal credit cards, not any corporate cards. They might be able to track where we've been by those transactions on a corporate card."

"I think you've been watching too many spy movies, but I get it. I'll put that piece of corporate plastic in credit card jail. They could probably also track us on our personal card usage, but only if they had people in the government or the banks in their pay."

Mercy guided the mini-sub in as closely as possible to shore. *I didn't tell him the other reason I want to get back to my apartment in Bucharest. I want my medicine. All of the supply I took on board the Fortuna is at the bottom of the Black Sea. The voices haven't come back yet, thankfully, but just in case, I've got to have those pills. It makes my skin crawl to know that I've been hearing demonic beings speaking to me all these years. It's like I was mentally raped every day for the last twenty years. I can't bear the thought of them getting inside my head again. The pills never stopped the voices entirely, but they helped me cope with them for years. If those things ever start attacking me again, I've got to have a backup plan and those pills are it. I should just tell Jack. I guess I don't want him to worry about it, though. Old habits of living with secrets are hard to kill. Just tell him.*

She said, "Jack, I need to tell you something."

"What's that?"

"I want to go back to my apartment in Bucharest to get my pills."

Jack said, "What pills?"

"I need to get my anti-psychotic pills. I never told you about them before. They're the ones that helped hold off the voices for all of my adult life. I've been taking them for over twenty years now, though this is a newer formula than what I first started with. I want them just in case the voices start jabbering again."

Jack was concerned. "Are you afraid that's going to happen? I thought you didn't hear them anymore."

"I don't hear them right now, but I find it hard to believe they won't be back. In case they start at me again, I need to have that medication."

Jack looked worried. "Sure Mercy, no problem. We'll go to Bucharest and pick up your medicine. That way, if you need it, you'll have it."

Mercy said, "That's not all Jack. I also need to tell you that I was just now struggling with keeping this need for my medication a secret from you. I've been so habitually secretive about these strange qualities of mine, that out of habit I almost kept this a secret from you too. I'm sorry. I need to let down some of my walls." She had an expression on her face that blended both sadness and hopefulness.

Jack looked serious. "You're right. Old habits are hard to break. I was just thinking about my tendencies to over-compromise and try to keep things calm and even-keeled at all costs. Those are good qualities sometimes, but they've gotten me into some problems as well. I've been that way for years, since I was a kid, as a matter of fact, and I've never told anyone about it. It's not a real pretty time in my life. It fits in with what I said a few minutes ago about my parents. I'll tell you about it sometime. Anyway, I understand problems with habits of thought. Thanks for telling me though."

A large, broad smile spread across his face. "Hey, this is a good sign. I think we're really going to make it work this time. You just broke through and told me something you would have kept secret before. I promised to tell stuff I've not talked about before. Are we getting wiser with age?" He smiled.

Mercy had a rueful expression on her face and shook her head slowly. "Trying to lighten a serious discussion with humor again? You have a tendency to change the subject when stuff gets uncomfortable. Besides, my age has nothing to do with this. In fact, let's talk about something else."

Now I'm changing the subject. She chuckled in spite of herself.

CHAPTER 6 – INNER THOUGHTS

"Oh, how glad I waked to find this but a dream!"
— *John Milton, Paradise Lost*

After bringing the mini-sub in to the narrow beach and running it aground with the last dregs of charge in the batteries, they anchored it as best they could and waded the rest of the way in being careful not to let any phones, electronics or passports be submerged. Using his phone map, they headed up to a dirt road running parallel to the beach and Jack pointed them south toward the nearest town. They looked along the road and saw that just across from them was another body of water. It looked to be a narrow tidal lake or basin.

"This road, if you can call it that, looks like it's built up on top of a long sandbar that separates the sea from that tidal lake. If we head south from here, in about a mile, our dirt track should turn into a paved road. Then there's a resort beach area and lots of buildings before we get to Burgas a few miles further on. I'll bet we can find a bus in this resort town and maybe an ATM machine if we need cash. We may not even need to go into Burgas. I want to buy some clothes and get out of these beat up work coveralls. I'll bet we can find some more casual resort wear and blend in better, too."

"Jack, I've got to get something to eat. I'm famished."

Jack said, "Okay, we'll see if we can find something at the resort."

Mercy said, "Jack, you don't understand. I really need to eat. It's another thing about me I haven't told you. You think I just have a healthy appetite. That's not the half of it. I absolutely must eat ten thousand calories a day or I start getting shaky. I can feel it coming on. I've got to get food in me and

I mean quick."

Jack looked concerned. "When did this start? Maybe you've got some kind of …" Jack grasped for words, "…illness. Have you told a doctor?"

Mercy pursed her lips. She said with exasperation, "Jack! I don't have a parasite like a tapeworm, if that's what you're hinting at. My appetite isn't a disease. It's my strength and speed. It takes a lot of energy. I get real woozy if I don't consume a lot of calories continuously, and it's not really something I wanted to discuss with a doctor. It would set off alarms and people would have started testing me and monitoring me. I didn't want that."

"All right. We'll get food here. That'll be the first priority."

They walked along on the dirt road and came to the outskirts of the town and saw cabins and bungalows set side by side all along the widening beach area. There was a paved road with a parking lot.

Mercy read the letters on a sign and said, "We're in Bulgaria alright. The sign uses Cyrillic lettering and I don't have a lot of Bulgarian vocabulary. If we have trouble communicating, I can try Romanian or even Greek. They might understand something." Her stomach growled audibly. She looked around them. "I don't see any shops yet. Let's keep walking."

They walked along the road past the beach cabins and soon came to a small shopping area. They went into a little market and when they found out that the store accepted Jack's credit cards, Mercy stocked up on high energy food bars, candy bars, and anything else she could find that was compact and high in calories. She gathered up food like she was someone who'd just been released from a concentration camp.

She managed to communicate well enough with the cashier to explain that they had just gotten off of work and arrived here and needed to find out where they could buy some more casual clothes. The clerk directed them to several stores a quarter mile closer in to the center of the resort area. After a short walk where Mercy ate as much as she could, they arrived at one of the resort's stores. Soon she and Jack were outfitted in more casual clothes. Jack wore comfortable shorts and a t-shirt that had the words, "Black Sea" on it in Bulgarian. Mercy surprised Jack by getting some short-shorts, a top that was midriff and cleavage-baring, a wide brim hat and sunglasses.

Jack's eyes shot open and his eyebrows went up. "Whoa. You look great, but that's not your usual conservative style. This is a side of you I haven't seen in many, many years."

She smiled and with a pleased expression said, "I wanted to blend in with the tourists. Look at the women around here. Anyone that has anything to show is displaying a lot of skin. This was actually the most conservative outfit I could find that looked good. Can you handle it, Mr. Truett?"

He laughed, "Sure, but I don't know if my eyes can stay where they're supposed to all of the time."

"You can look all you want, but when we're talking, remember to make eye contact occasionally, too. Besides, I like knowing you're looking at me that way."

Jack said, "You'd better watch out. I've still got red blood in my veins. I can only take so much temptation. Anyway, we'd better keep moving and find that bus. We need to get from here to Burgas and then on to Varna and the border with Romania."

They found their way to an ATM, got cash and with several more delays got to the proper bus stop. They managed to get to Burgas and discovered they'd need to take a bus to Varna. Several hours later, after boarding the bus and getting settled, Jack quickly fell asleep.

Mercy looked fondly at him. She wasn't sleepy yet and was still massively hungry even though she'd been eating constantly since the resort town by the beach. She kept eating and eating, downing candy bars, nuts, dried fruit, energy bars, salty snacks and several Coca-Colas they'd bought as well. *I don't care if people stare at me. I have to fuel up. With my metabolism, I need every bit of this. It's afternoon and I'm not even half way to eating what I should have and I hardly had anything at all yesterday on the Fortuna. I don't care if these people think I'm a pig. I'll never see any of them again.*

Her mind wandered as she finally started to relax and settled in against Jack's softly breathing frame. Turned loose, her thoughts drifted back over the last twenty-four hours. Some of the memories almost burned. She felt her breath catch as she remembered Hayden. *He was such a wonderful man. He tried to get between me and that monster and got killed. Killed. It's so horrible. And when he died, a burst of energy ran into me and gave me the boost I needed to hold on and fight Moloch.*

She looked at the palm of her hand. *If I concentrate, I can still see that tiny blue thread running from the center of my palm and off into the distance.* She remembered how she'd acquired the thread. *When I had that dream or vision or whatever it was, I was in the throne room with the Counselor and that butterfly-like creature landed on my hand. It dissolved and sank in and left that thread behind. When I was in the throne room, the other end of the thread trailed away into a small pool of water there, though now it trails away into the distance in front of me no matter which way I turn. How does that work? Ever since then, I can feel energy trickling through it and into me from that thread. Originally, I used the energy from this thread in the fight with Moloch, and when Hayden died, it boosted my energy tremendously, but what should I use the energy for now?*

More importantly, what am I supposed to do with my entire life now? Can I ever go back to what I was doing before? Probably not. I'm a hybrid, half-human, whatever that means. It's not like there is a big call for people like me. My abilities might be some use if I were in a military role, but that has no attraction for me. If only I knew something about what it means. Maybe I should ask the Counselor. Asking for answers from that one used to cost me. I'd be knocked unconscious for twenty-four hours, but now it just drains me and makes me feel weak-kneed. And, there's been nothing but silence from the Counselor since we closed the lid on Moloch yesterday. I wasn't expecting a medal, but is it too much to ask that I at least get a debriefing?

Now that's another strange thing. I had this vision and the Counselor was in this throne room place with all of these fantastically-shaped attendants around like it was a Lord of the Rings *convention. Was that dream imagery that my mind made up? I've never been a religious person even though my adoptive parents were, but that throne room scene was almost mythological in some aspects. The Counselor gave me this task to recapture Moloch and gave me this little thread of power even though it knew that it wasn't giving me enough to turn the tide of the fight in my favor. It knew how strong Moloch was but sent me anyway. Did it know that Hayden was going to sacrifice himself to save me and that his death would give me the energy from his sacrificial actions? I have so many questions.*

Jack twitched a little and Mercy saw his eyes move under his closed lids. *He's dreaming. He sure goes to sleep fast and hard.* She continued looking at him and tried to just listen to his breathing. *In and out. So peaceful. How can he even sleep? I'm exhausted and still feel so beat up, yet I can't sleep. What am I supposed to do? My mind is racing, but there he is asleep sitting up in a bus. Wow. I wish I could do that. Jack has always been the kind of person that accepts things however they are and adapts to them, rather than what I do. I have all of these expectations about the way things ought to be. I bump up against things because I think they shouldn't be that way. Jack goes along, adapting. I don't do that well.*

Jack inhaled suddenly and shifted in his sleep. *I wonder what he's dreaming about? If I could listen in, would it be like one of my own dreams?* A thought occurred to her. *I wonder if I could use that same power that Moloch forced me to use in healing myself? He made me go into a trance state and concentrate on the bullet wound and expelling the bullet and forcing energy into the tissues to speed up the natural healing. I know that visualization method also helped me keep the unbodied out of my mind.* She shivered at the memory.

She studied Jack's face and made a decision. She closed her own eyes and imagined descending that familiar long staircase, going deeper into a trance almost automatically. She moved further and further down the mental staircase and saw a door. In her trance-state, she put her hand on the door handle and shifted to visualizing Jack's sleeping face and held the image.

She opened the door and stepped into another space unlike any she'd experienced before. It didn't look like anything she knew. It wasn't a room or a chamber and it wasn't someplace open to the sky above. It seemed more like she was contained in a dark globe exactly large enough to fit her. If she'd been able to touch its inner, invisible surface, she might have expected it to have a flexible, stretchable skin. In that tiny space though, she felt that she had no hands, limbs or body. Her perspective shifted and she felt like she'd been looking through the wrong end of a telescope. She now felt she was a miniscule thing inside a large space and she was instantly surrounded with distant voices, noises and fleeting glimpses of pictures and scenes that flashed into existence and as quickly disappeared.

With a jolt she recognized glimpses of her own face in some of the pictures that flashed into being and then winked out. She heard a distant conversation that seemed to be running on fast forward. As if on a movie screen located far away, she saw a tiny scene of Jack and herself speaking, though on that one, she couldn't hear any distinct words. She realized what she was experiencing. *This is Jack's sleeping mind.*

Mercy felt queasy, almost sick as a realization hit her. *These are his private, unrestrained, subconscious thoughts. There is no telling what I could see here. He could dream about anything: subconscious fears, desires, hungers, lusts, anything. His conscious mind is not in control. He could experience terrifying nightmares or childhood trauma. Jack cannot stop anything that happens in this place. It can't be right for me to be here and hearing and seeing this.* She struggled to release the trance and found it surprisingly difficult.

She fought to get away, but she suddenly found herself on what appeared to be the front row of an audience before a brightly lit stage where a man and a woman were screaming at each other. The man shook his fist in rage at the woman who stood her ground, pointed a long-nailed finger and shrieked back in a frenzy of hate. Whatever the two were saying was incomprehensible. It sounded almost as if roaring winds were pouring from their mouths. Mercy heard a voice suddenly speak to her from the chair next to her.

Mentally jumping in surprise, she turned and saw the speaker was a young boy of perhaps nine years old. Mercy said to him, "I'm sorry, I couldn't make that out. What did you say?"

With eyes full of sadness and almost endless despair, the boy spoke to her. "I said they're at it again. They always get this way eventually, no matter how they promise."

Mercy felt extreme confusion and disorientation. *Where am I? How did I get here? What is this we're watching? In fact, who is this child?*

The couple continued raging at each other. The man threw his hands up and marched up to the woman as if to strike her. The woman jutted her jaw towards the man as if daring him to hit her.

The boy continued, "She hates him. He despises her." The boy hung his head. "There's only one way to get them to stop." He sniffled and Mercy realized he was crying. The boy stood up from his seat and walked toward the stairs leading up to the stage.

He stepped onto the stage and said to the man and woman, "I'm here now."

The two adults snapped their gazes toward him and their expressions changed to ones of hungry, even ravenous delight.

"At last you're back, sweetheart," the woman said. "We've missed you so much!"

The man said, "Well, buddy! Glad to have you back. How was your day?"

The adults didn't seem to notice that the boy was weeping. Up on the stage, he walked slowly, inevitably toward them. The adults kneeled down with open arms and beckoned him on.

At the last moment before the child got within arm's reach of the two adults, Mercy saw their eyes change and glow with reddish inner light. Mercy shouted in fear, "Watch out!"

The two adults leapt at the boy and pulled him down to the floor with them, their hands locking onto him with steely grips. Their lips parted and she saw a poisonous stream pour from each of their mouths, retching onto the child who lay pinned and writhing in pain in their acid bile.

Mercy felt paralyzed in terror for a moment but then leapt to her feet. She called to him, "I'm coming!"

The tableau on the stage froze for a moment as if caught forever in a photograph. The only thing that moved on the stage was the boy's head which turned and looked at her in the audience. The burning acid smoked on his skin. The unmoving vice-like hands held his arms and shoulders. The two monstrous adults loomed over him with maniacal expressions and red eyes.

He said, "You can't help. No one can. This is the only way to make them stop."

The still scene shattered into frenzied movement again. Mercy lost sight of the boy beneath the slavering adults.

Mercy dashed to the stage steps to get up there and help the child. She bounded up the stairs and leapt onto the stage, but the scene was gone and the actors were nowhere to be seen. A jittery chill ran through Mercy. Other scenes, pictures and voices swirled nearby.

Mercy snapped back to the realization of where she was. *I came to look in on Jack's dreams. I have to get out of here.* She tried to calm herself mentally. *Jack can't control this place, but I can still control my mind if I have the strength.*

With great effort, she forced herself to not pay attention to the voices and pictures and let them flow past her. She pried herself loose from the quicksand of Jack's dreams and visualized herself approaching a wall. In the wall she saw a door, walked to it and opened the latch. She stepped through, closing it behind her. She was on a landing on her familiar staircase again.

She mentally relaxed and thought. *I shouldn't have done that. Somehow, I know it could have turned out even worse. It's almost like a part of my mind could have become detached and been left behind in there. Is that rational? I just know I shouldn't ever try that again, at least when he's asleep. Maybe I could try if he's awake and gives me permission. But after seeing that glimpse of his dreaming mind, do I really want to know what goes on in someone else's head? Mind reading might not be such a good idea after all.*

Mercy opened her eyes. Jack rustled again at her side and opened his eyes sleepily.

"Hey," he said drowsily. "I had an awful dream."

"I know," she said. "I know."

He closed his eyes again and drifted back into sleep. Mercy sighed and looked at him. *Jack, Jack. What happened to you when you were growing up?*

CHAPTER 7 – CRYPT

"Into utter darkness, deep engulfed,
his place ordained without redemption, without end"
— John Milton, *Paradise Lost*

In spite of himself and all his efforts to concentrate, Henry's mind kept wandering back to his dinner last night with Maria. *What great food and conversation that was. Of course, the wine helped relax us both. My, but she is undeniably smart and witty; I had no idea. Attractive as well, and she seemed to be genuinely enjoying my company. That is a shocker. Henry, my boy, you must be on your best behavior. A woman like that in this field is as rare as a unicorn. Don't mess this relationship up before it barely gets started.* A grin spread over his face. He shook his head and tried to get back to work.

Professor Russo and a full crew of graduate students were working on the priestess' burial site that Henry had unearthed the day before, measuring, recording positions, cataloguing and photographing. It was one of the happier occasions on a dig like this and one where everyone was excited and busy. There was a sense that behind any pebble a discovery might be lurking. At Professor Russo's suggestion, Henry was working at the new adjacent site about four meters away. The older man wanted to give the other graduate students with less dig experience a chance at the priestess and was supervising them.

Henry's eyes wandered over to the Professor's group and saw Maria. Just then, she looked up, caught sight of him, smiled and gave a slight wave before turning back to the work and Professor Russo's instruction. Henry's heart felt like it skipped a beat. *Steady, Henry. Back to work.*

He looked down at the rectangular hole where he stood. *This is about where we expect the next grave site to be, if it continues following the same pattern as the previous burials here at the Necropolis. But, we've hit nothing so far.* The sod had been removed several days before along with the first meter of dirt to get down to almost the same depth as the nearby graves. Nothing had been discovered yet in spite of the meticulous care that had been taken in sifting each scoop of the soil that had been dug out of the ground. This morning, Henry and another man had spent the time slowly digging into the dirt with small hand shovels and trowels. The other fellow was on a break, but Henry continued working and thinking.

Too bad Dad isn't here to see this. He'd be fascinated. It's a good thing his amateur interest in archaeology was contagious to me or I'd probably still be acquiring degrees, floating from one field to the next. Henry continued trowelling dirt away from the hole which was now a meter and a half deep. He stood and his head and shoulders came above the edge of the hole and he looked back again at the professor's group. They were all still working busily.

Henry dumped some more dirt onto the screen mesh. Back and forth he moved from dirt to screen, with time again seeming to fade from his consciousness. *Dad started in geology but puttered with archaeology as a hobby. I started in art history of all things and then moved into ancient history. Finally I ended up here. I was missing something in my other studies. Oh sure, I was interested, but they didn't hold my attention. I didn't daydream about art history work or ancient history. So glad I tagged along with some of Dad's hobby efforts.*

Henry's trowel hit something hard. He worked around the edge of it with automatic care, being cautious about scratching or marring anything that might be there. It was just an irregular rock. Henry removed it and continued digging. *When I was growing up, we'd take vacation trips to places like this and he'd work as a volunteer at dig sites. When I got old enough to help, they let me work with him. It wasn't until just a few years ago on one of those volunteer digs we were working that I realized my art history and ancient history studies might fit perfectly with archaeology. Dad asked me, "Well, what do you dream about doing? You seem very happy doing this. Maybe you should think about archaeology."*

Henry's trowel hit something else hard. He started again searching for the edge of the object, gently probing, moving further away from the initial point, but still feeling something hard. *Hmm. This is bigger than just a rock.*

"Have you found something?" Maria's voice interrupted his thoughts.

Mildly startled, Henry looked up and saw Maria on the edge of the excavation, kneeling and looking in at the place where Henry was down on hands and knees probing.

Henry smiled and said, "Yes, in fact, I've probably found an even bigger rock than usual. I'm just looking for the edge of it." He kept probing with one hand and waved expansively at the hole in which he crouched with the other hand. "Here is my new domain. 'Look on my works, ye mighty, and despair!'"

She recognized his reference and smiled mockingly, "Oh. In that case, *signore* Ozymandias, I will back slowly away from your domain."

He laughed. "Doesn't all this dirt inspire you to poetry? Well, never mind." He stopped as he found something with his probing. "Here, now. This might be an edge." He began clearing dirt away starting at about a half meter from the initial spot where he'd found something.

Maria said, "Do you need some help? I can come down there with you. Our group is taking a break."

Henry was still moving dirt along a lengthening edge, "Please do. I'd appreciate the help."

Maria landed lightly in the pit and kneeling beside him started working in the opposite direction. Bit by bit, they troweled dirt away and located a smooth, hard edge. Henry's length of edge was straight and continued all the way into the vertical dirt wall of the pit. Maria's length of edge was straight and then turned suddenly at ninety degrees and became a corner about a third of a meter from the opposite wall.

"Henry, look at this. You've found something very large here. It continues around this corner." She said.

He shifted over by her and the two of them continued feeling for the edge as they uncovered more and more along the long end of the pit. They found another corner and traced it all the way back to the opposite end of the dirt wall where it disappeared.

"Very odd. I'd swear this rectangular edge we've uncovered is stone and I didn't find any seams so perhaps it's a single large one."

Maria said, "Perhaps an altar stone, or maybe a sarsen stone like those upright ones at Stonehenge."

"Wouldn't that be exciting, now? Perhaps a top lintel stone like they think was originally on top of the sarsens. Shall we see if we can uncover some of the stone surface?"

Maria smiled brilliantly. "Yes. *Assolutamente!*"

Henry grinned back, noticing a dirt streak on her chin. He said, "Here, let me get you a handkerchief for that little smudge..." he pointed to his own chin so she would understand what he intended and started to fumble in a pocket with what he suddenly realized were his own very obviously filthy hands.

Maria laughed merrily and raucously. "Heal thyself doctor! You are as dirty as a little *scugnizzo*, an urchin, a beggar boy. Do not try to clean <u>my</u> chin! And you'll need more than a handkerchief for yourself, you'll need a bath, or maybe a fire hydrant."

Henry blushed, realizing it was true. He looked sheepish and she laughed heartily and shoved him playfully on his shoulder. She said, "Yes, yes, my little *scugnizzo*, let us clear away the top of the stone, but no cleaning up for us yet. There is much more dirt to come."

Henry chuckled ruefully at himself and motioned with his hand to the dirt. They went back to their work and began uncovering more and more of the large, flat rectangular stone. The part inside their pit seemed to be two and a half meters wide by one and a half long, but was certainly longer than one and a half meters because that was merely where it met the dirt wall of the pit.

Henry said, "We'll need to widen this pit and find out just how broad this stone plate is."

They cleared away more and more of the dirt from the top of the stone and after some time at it, they were about to pause for a breather when Henry used his hand broom to sweep away a small pile of remaining dust.

"There's something else here Maria, in the center of this portion. Look." Henry finished brushing away dirt to uncover a design.

Maria said, "It looks like…it looks like the metal medallion that came from the priestess' grave. The one with the hammer and flame design."

Henry said, "I believe you're right." He stood up and stretched. He saw the lowering position of the sun in the sky and checked his watch. "Look. The day's practically gone. We'll have to stop. Hold on. What's this?"

Henry pointed toward the Necropolis' main building complex which was well away from the current dig site. Walking briskly in their direction was the Bulgarian antiquities officer and Professor Russo was right behind. The thin man was obviously agitated and marched to the edge of the hole that held Henry and Maria.

Krastyo Balev's face held a sneer and he said, "There he is again, working without supervision. And this time, he has an accomplice." He pointed at Henry and Maria as he turned to the professor who had just joined him. "Russo, this is absolutely unacceptable. Who knows what items they have made off with? I am going back to my office to review your University's agreement with the antiquities department of the Bulgarian National Museum of History. I will be recommending that they rescind your permission to continue here unless this stops immediately."

Professor Russo said, "Now Krastyo, these are my two top young researchers. Doctor Travers has completed his PhD and is working with us on his postdoctoral research. Maria is a doctoral candidate who will be completing her PhD within the year. They are young and enthusiastic about the work and would never endanger any Bulgarian antiquities. Look at them. They have been working unceasingly all day and now and they have uncovered a design on that stone monolith that Henry has unearthed. I personally guarantee they have not allowed any artifacts or treasures to be removed from the site."

Balev shook his fist at Russo, "You westerners are always looting us, admit it! There is a huge black market in relics coming out of Bulgaria. A dealer in black market antiquities was caught at the Frankfurt airport just last month with over sixty kilograms of ancient coins from Bulgaria that he was smuggling to the United States."

Russo said, "We are not smugglers or black marketers. I have a suggestion, Krastyo. You are stretched too thin with all of your responsibilities. Why not bring in an additional security officer to watch the dig site during the day? We already have one that watches at night. Add one during the day that you trust and you'll feel so much more at ease with what is going on. It will reassure you that nothing untoward is happening."

"Impossible. We have no budget for such an expense."

"But I'm sure the University would be glad to fund the cost of such a security guard. After all, we don't want any of our hard work to be stolen or vandalized either."

Henry and Maria had been watching the exchange between the two men. Henry was looking at the professor and saw out of his peripheral vision that Balev turned his head. Henry glanced in the man's direction and noticed the other man was looking at Maria as if he recognized her. Henry did not like the look in the Bulgarian's eyes. He saw from Maria's face that she didn't like it either. Her eyes looked disdainful and her lips were pinched together in such a way that Henry knew she was biting back a response, forcing herself to be silent.

"That may be the only way we can permit you to stay." Balev pointed at his narrow chest. "I must select the security officer though." Balev insisted on the requirement as he walked away. Before he left, he took one last quick glinting look in Maria's direction. She puffed out her breath in agitation and crossed her arms over her chest.

"*Porca miseria!* That man disgusts me." She said. "I think I will start carrying a rock hammer with me just in case I need to beat him senseless. He's always sneaking around trying to catch me or one of the other women alone." She spat in the direction he'd gone. "If there is any stealing going on, I guarantee it is him. In fact, he's probably only mad that we are still here because we are preventing him from looting the site. Pig!"

Henry brushed dirt off of his hands. "I do wonder about that man and all of his hostility. Perhaps you're right and he is looking for items to loot. You were right earlier. I am definitely as dirty as a street urchin. I need to clean up and it is getting late. By the way, how did the replica of the cylinder seal turn out? I'm afraid Mr. Balev will take possession of the original and we'll never see it again. We'll be very glad you made that copy from the impressions you took."

Maria had calmed herself and said, "It looks very good. I made the copy from a liquid plastic that I put into the molds and then joined the two halves once the plastic hardened. Would you like to see it?"

"Definitely. How about at dinner? Would you like to join me again? That is, I mean, after I've cleaned up."

"Yes, *Doctor* Travers," she emphasized the title as if teasing him about Professor Russo's earlier conversation with Balev. "I would like to join you again. Will you come by my apartment in two hours to pick me up?"

Henry smiled, "I certainly will. You know I'm not a big one for titles." He assumed a straight face and said, "You can call me 'Doctor Henry' if you like."

She harrumphed in mock disgust and laughed. "How about just 'Henry'? Would that be good enough for you?"

"Yes. How does one say it in Italian? ... '*Bella Donna*'? Is that the expression?"

Maria blushed unexpectedly. "You think I'm pretty? How kind of you." She planted a light smudge of a kiss on Henry's cheek. "I will see you in two hours." She lightly climbed up and out of the pit and headed away to the main building. Henry's hand went to his cheek and he was left with his happy but confused thoughts.

* * *

The next morning, Henry and Maria began carrying out the plans for the dig they'd discussed over dinner. The rest of the huge stone plate with the hammer and flame symbol needed to be uncovered. Russo had obtained approval for the additional security guard from the University and then had received permission from Balev to proceed with the larger excavation effort around the stone plate area that Henry and Maria had been working on the day before. By early afternoon with a bigger crew and many shovels, Henry and Maria had uncovered another two and a half meters of the rectangular stone plate's length. By end of day, they had finally exposed the remaining outline of the whole thing and uncovered most of the stone itself.

Henry said, "A single piece of stone, six meters long by two and half meters wide with the hammer and flame symbol repeated over and over again. How amazing. And one additional feature..." He kneeled over the center right side of the stone. "... a circular depression about four centimeters across."

Henry put his face closer and brushed more dirt away from the depression. From his tool pouch, he took out a dental probe about the length of his hand and began testing the depth of the depression, picking out flakes and small clods of dirt. He removed more and more debris.

"Seems to be a circular hole," Henry said.

Maria was right next to him on the rectangular stone plate. She whispered, "Henry, doesn't it look like the cylinder seal might fit into that hole?"

He looked up at her with a questioning expression. *Why is she whispering?* He said softly, "Perhaps..."

"What are you looking at? What are you doing there?" Balev's suspicious voice cut through their whispers. Henry and Maria straightened up and stood.

Henry said, "Sir, it looks like besides the 'Hammer and Fire' designs, there is a circular hole near the middle right edge of the stone plate."

"What is it for?" Balev said.

"I'm not sure yet, sir. We need to see how deep the hole is. Just theorizing here, but it might have been a socket for holding something upright." Out of his peripheral vision, Henry caught sight of a small nod of Maria's head. *She approves of my misdirection.*

"Professor Russo," Balev said turning to the older man abruptly, "what is the purpose of a large flat stone rectangle like this in a cemetery? Why is it here?"

The professor stood near Balev. He said, "Krastyo, we don't know. This is unlike anything else we've seen here. Everywhere else in the Necropolis, there have been ancient graves, hundreds of them. This large stone is out of place compared to the rest. Henry, do you think it could be a cenotaph?"

Henry said, "Hmm. It's possible, I suppose. The only markings are the repeated hammers and flames, though."

Krastyo Balev spoke impatiently, "What is a cenotaph?"

Maria answered Balev's question but did not look at him. "It is a memorial to someone not buried at the same spot. They are sometimes found in cemeteries to remember someone interred elsewhere." Her face was turned to Russo, but was calmly expressionless, as if she were purposely ignoring Balev and trying to make them all aware of it. Professor Russo arched an eyebrow sardonically, seeming to be aware that Maria was snubbing Balev.

"Maria is right," Henry jumped into the verbal fencing match. "Cenotaphs are memorials without corpses. You can see many of them around the world. In Westminster Abbey in London, you'll see cenotaphs side by side with burial spots. Chaucer is buried in the Abbey while William Shakespeare and John Milton are buried elsewhere, but their names are memorialized there even though their remains lie in other places."

Henry continued, "If this is a cenotaph though, I don't know who or what is being memorialized, unless the hammer and flame symbols stand for some individual or group."

Balev walked over as near as he could get to the circular hole that Henry and Maria had been examining. His eyes narrowed and he walked back to Russo.

"Professor, let us go speak about the new security officer and a few other items I would like to discuss."

* * *

Professor Russo's expression showed his disgust and frustration. He said, "Balev has confiscated all of the relics from the Priestess' grave."

Henry and Maria looked at each other. Her lips were pinched together slightly and her eyes narrowed. She said, "I knew that man would do something like this."

Henry asked, "Everything has been confiscated? Even the medallions?"

Russo said, "Everything, including the medallions and the cylinder seal. The bones are locked up. I don't know where he's taken the other items."

Maria looked like she'd bitten into something rotten. She muttered something to herself.

Henry stifled a smile. *I imagine that was a choice and very profane insult in Italian.* He said, "Thank goodness we have photographs, measurements and impressions then."

Maria casually moved one finger to her lips. Henry wondered for a moment if she was trying to tell him something. *Oh. She wants me to be silent. Shut up Henry. Say no more.*

Professor Russo didn't notice Maria's body language message. He continued. "Yes. It is very good that we have all of the documentation. We simply must do the best we can without them. Now the two of you should be done for the day. I suggest you clean up and rest."

After the professor had gone, Maria turned to Henry and with a fierce expression said, "The pig is at the trough now and will eat everything. I saw him looking at the cenotaph and I think he made the connection between the cylinder seal and that hole. That's why he confiscated all of the artifacts."

Henry said, "But we don't know if there is a connection between the hole and the cylinder seal yet."

Maria said, "But he thinks there may be, just as we do. The man is prowling. We must be careful. Everything we find must be recorded in every way possible, because once he sees we've recovered something, we'll never see it again."

"You're right of course." Henry said.

After they cleaned up, they met for an inexpensive supper and split a liter of red wine. Afterward, they sat sipping small cups of dark, strong coffee. Maria took something out of her purse and set it on the table between them.

"Look at this. What do you think?" She asked.

Henry picked up the small white item and admired it. "What a beautiful replica! It looks like a perfect copy of the original cylinder seal we found the other day. This is fantastic work, Maria!"

She lowered her eyes and smiled deprecatingly, "It's not the same color, because of the epoxy I used for making it, but I am certain of the shape. It's good."

Henry held it up to the light and said enthusiastically, "It certainly is!"

He looked more closely at it. "What do you think these parallel chevrons and dots mean? I can't imagine going to the trouble to make something like this just for the sake of abstract art and I studied art history. Then again, the more I think about it, there are many historical examples where people seemed to have done just that: gone to a lot of trouble to do incredible art just for art's sake. Still, in this case, I don't know."

Maria said, "I don't know either. I feel we're missing something."

Feeling relaxed from the end of the day's work, they set out walking back to their apartments. The Varna Necropolis was located in a small wooded area near the center of the city and not very far from the lake. It was one of the world's premier archaeological sites that lay within a modern city's limits. Their apartments were not too far from the ancient cemetery and they passed close to their work on the way back from supper.

Henry walked, holding Maria's hand. Maria was telling him about her schooling. Somehow, Henry found himself interested and that surprised him. *Have I ever been interested in someone else's academic history before? Maybe I'm finally 'growing up' as my mum used to say. Yet everything Maria says seems to be fascinating. I just cannot believe how easily we've hit it off. Henry, you've landed on your feet this time. A girl like this doesn't come along very often. In fact, for me, they've never come along. How can you hold on to this? You've got to do this right and not muck it up. You know you're falling head over heels for her.*

They walked past the Necropolis site, close to the trees near the new section of the dig. Maria stopped talking and peered ahead. She pointed and said, "Look. Someone is out there talking to the night security guard." She stepped closer and said, "It's Balev." The two of them watched as the guard walked off in another direction. Balev moved closer to the priestess' grave and cenotaph site where the confrontation between them had taken place earlier that day. Balev seemed to descend down into the hole where the cenotaph's excavation site was. Startled, Maria and Henry looked at each other and both started walking quickly toward the last place they'd seen Balev.

They saw a torch beam ahead and to the right of the site and Henry realized someone else was running to the dig. *That electric torch is going in the opposite direction as the guard was headed. Who can it be?* Maria and Henry picked up their pace and broke into a run. Then they identified the other person running to the cenotaph site: Professor Russo.

Maria started to call out to him, but Russo motioned to them to remain silent. In one hand, he carried a torch. In the other, he held a small video camera. Henry and Maria ran up and Henry remained silent, but motioned questioningly to the camera. Russo pointed to the dig site and handed the torch to Henry to carry. He realized what the professor intended to do. *He's going to try to capture video of Krastyo Balev at the cenotaph. If we catch him making off with artifacts or doing anything he shouldn't be doing, he'll be through here.*

They approached cautiously through the ancient graveyard and saw a flickering light from the pit of the cenotaph. *Balev's got a torch as well.* Professor Russo motioned them to slow and he readied the camera. *I hope he makes sure to deactivate the flash and sets the camera to work with low ambient light. He won't get any footage if it's set not sensitive enough or if that bright light goes off in Balev's face.*

Russo moved forward with the camera up and Henry stepped up beside him with one hand on the older man's arm. *I don't want him to fall over the edge of the pit.* From where he stood next to the professor, he could see from the screen that the camera was working well and recording mode was on. Henry's fears about the flash at least were alleviated.

Russo, Henry and Maria stood at the lip of the dig site and saw below them that Balev's back was toward them and he was kneeling at the edge of the stone cenotaph near the circular depression Henry and Maria had discovered earlier. Balev appeared to be busily digging, then took something from a pocket and tried to insert it into the stone. They all heard an audible click followed by a bone-deep rumble.

All around the edge of the stone, dirt and dust shot out and away from it in a furious outgassing of what appeared to be a dark fog. Balev coughed and rolled off the edge of the cenotaph and came up still on hands and knees beside it in the dirt. A deep grinding sound like the rolling of a mountainous mill wheel came from the stone and one edge lifted upward by two centimeters in a sudden wrenching movement. A second, larger dark cloud billowed out from the seam around the stone. To Henry, it smelled like the rot of a long-dead bog.

Balev coughed painfully and played his torch over the surface of the shifting cenotaph. His eyes went wide in the flickering light. The rasping, grinding sound continued and the stone plate shuddered upward another bit, lurching and throwing dust aside. Balev's torch traced the dark fog that moved toward him and the thin man edged back from it. The grinding stone plate lurched upward again, and something deep under the earth groaned as if under tremendous strain. All at once something gave way and the stone swung upward in a single movement, pivoting as if on a massive hinge, only stopping at vertical with a jarring crash. It was a door six and a half meters long by two and a half wide, and a black pit was open where it had lain moments before.

Balev stopped coughing and his torch beam moved to the edge of the dark opening. The man climbed up on two unsteady feet and moved closer to the edge of the black rectangular doorway in the ground, probing into the darkness below with his light. In its beam, Henry and his two companions saw glints of metal and traces of indistinguishable white. Balev edged closer to the lip, continuing to point the light into the cavernous opening. With movement that seemed to indicate he'd made a decision,

Krastyo Balev stepped to one end of the rectangular opening and took a descending step into the darkness.

Henry wanted to shout out a warning, to cry out that this man should not be the first to discover what lay below, when Balev took his second step and his feet seemed to go out from under him. He crashed tumbling downward, screaming as he fell.

Professor Russo lowered the camera and Henry leapt down into the excavation pit, followed closely by Maria. Russo climbed down more slowly. Henry and Maria ran to the edge of the opening where they'd seen Balev moments before. Henry turned on his torch. He saw a gigantic stone stairway descending into the earth, strewn with moldering skeletons, loose and detached bones and reflective pieces of metal. At a landing some distance below, a cursing Krastyo Balev was sprawled, one arm grotesquely broken with a knife-edged shard of white bone sticking through the bloody sleeve of his shirt.

Balev looked up into the light of Henry's torch and screamed in fear, pain and rage. "Help me! Get me out of here and away from this!"

CHAPTER 8 – PLEA FOR HELP

"Under what torments inwardly I groan"
— John Milton, Paradise Lost

The suffocating darkness tightened around him. He strained against the lid a short distance above his chest, pushing with all of the strength that would have formerly cracked stone. The metal plate above him moved not a hair's breadth. The lingering traces of smoke and lack of oxygen constricted his throat and burnt in every corner of his lungs. *No air! No air! How can this be? Not again!*

His consciousness pulsed in and out in waves, seeming to swell and fade. For moments he felt aware and awake and a few seconds later, his mind seemed to be screaming at the end of a long tunnel. His chest heaved in and out, trying to strain the rapidly dwindling oxygen from the air in the sarcophagus. An incredible weight seemed to be crushing down on him, its pressure increasing and threatening to flatten him. *There's no air!*

After the lid had slammed closed he'd been tossed about inside the small rectangular chamber. He'd felt himself falling as if his prison were sinking beneath waves, rolling, rocking and tumbling in its descent. It had thudded to a stop and he'd rolled in the pitch blackness to a stop, gagging, choking and with sparks seeming to flash in his sightless eyes.

The floor of the sarcophagus was sticky with the unburnt heavy oil that had filled it before his entrapment. There were pieces of bones from some of his victims that still remained in the oil. Most of the bones had been reduced to mere fragments in the violence of his escape efforts. He could still smell the odor of charred flesh and marrow, but the act of inhaling the scent from the depleted air caused him agony. He involuntarily twisted into a curling mass of pain, his gut churning in acid torment. Chains seemed to be encircling his chest in an ever tightening band.

His pulse raced faster and faster as he tried to move the dwindling oxygen ever more quickly to the depleted cells in his body. His head throbbed with each heaving thud of his laboring heart. He heard a roaring, clanging sound in his ears.

Of a sudden, dizziness overcame him and Moloch felt he was rising, twisting and turning like a leaf in a whirlwind. He gasped for breath with no relief and gasped another breath, faster and faster. There was a stronger burning, fiery feeling in his chest.

He seemed to see himself from above, looking down into the imprisoning sarcophagus. He saw the straining muscles in his legs and arms where his giant form pushed and kicked against the lid, trying somehow to open that which would never open. He saw his massive fists pounding at the ceiling of his inescapable jail cell.

A human being would have long since given in and expired. One of the half-breed hybrids that were descended from him would have lasted much longer, but would have finally slumped into eventual unconsciousness and death would have followed at long last. With one of his rank though, and cursed to this deathless body, he could not die a physical death and therefore could suffer almost limitless pain. *The mortal fools always longed for endless life, envying those that were immortal. What they never understood was that the curse of immortality meant the possibility of endless death as well.*

For the thousandth time, he cursed his imprisonment on the Earth and this body. *Oh, to be one of the unbodied, never tied to the torment of the physical, roaming free in their restricted realm.* Thousands of years ago, the countless other minor angelic beings that had also been betrayed by Lucifer and defeated by Michael's host hadn't rated the punishment reserved for the likes of Moloch, Mulciber and the other turncoat Archons. The inferior ranks of rebels had been stripped of material form and locked into a small corner of this noxious plane. They were unable to leave and unable to thrive though able to move freely albeit in a dark sensationless void. They preyed upon the human minds that intruded into this extra-dimensional space, drawing dark energy from their torment and anguish.

Fighting through his mental fog, he raged at Heaven, Earth and all realms in between. *Focus your mind!* He screamed mentally at himself. *Try again to open the latches!*

Moloch drew his scattered thoughts, blocked a fraction of the sweeping undercurrent of agony wracking his body and concentrated it all into a solitary line of thought. *Open the latches.*

He visualized the sarcophagus, just a little longer than he was tall and not quite half that in width and breadth and mentally pictured the outside of the box. There were three latches that secured the lid on the outer edge. If they were released, the lid could be opened from the inside, and he would be able to escape. He aligned his mental energy, drawing from all of the death drafts he had consumed over the last day and focused it into a beam of motive power. In his mind, he moved it like a lance, probing at the lid of his prison, seeking a crack, a crevice, some slight imperfection in the crystalline steel of the sarcophagus that he might use, might influence, perhaps even nudge. There was nothing.

He redoubled his energies and remaining strength, ignoring the convulsions he felt in his physical being. *I have to find a way to do this.* Doubts seemed to echo distantly and say, "You weren't able to escape the first time, and you will not escape today." *I have to!* The beam of mental energy moved against the inside lid of his cell. A reddish glow began in the lid where he aimed it, but remained small and contained.

This cursed metal! Though he tried again and again, the energy would cause a small amount of heat, but with only the amounts of energy he could call upon presently, he could not melt the crystalline steel. Moloch knew that his cell was fashioned by Michael because only an Archon-level empowered agent of the Creator could have wielded as much energy and resources as were required to construct an object of this size from the metal. Moloch knew from his years in alliance with Mulciber what it took to make the metal and he also knew of the shortcuts that his devious ally had developed to give the two of them the ability to use the crystalline steel in spite of being cut off from the Creator's power. Mulciber had also discovered that the metal could be used to store energy, which was why it absorbed the power Moloch directed at it. He wanted to move and release the outer latches from a distance, from the inside of the box, but the metal absorbed energy rather than allowing its passage. *No, I can't be trapped like this again!*

Moloch was determined to try until his mind was gone, possibly for the last time. *What hope of sanity do I have if I am lost in this way again?* He gathered every shred of power he could muster, releasing his hold on every bit of energy he normally needed; even that which he used to keep the pain at bay. He dropped his barriers to control and compulsion, even the feeble screen that he used to keep the unbodied from interfering with his thoughts. He launched all of the power at the crystal steel barrier. *If only a miniscule amount can get through, I may be able to free myself.*

He held a mental probe for what seemed an eternity, pushing with all of his remaining mental power to penetrate the wall of metal. His consciousness again seemed to pull away from his body, divorced from his physical form. He almost believed that he floated above and could see his body below, though he knew that there was no light in his cell. His mental probe failed. *Nothing. If only I had more power. If only someone could help me...* He pushed again, in a final, teeth chattering effort. *Nothing. No, no, no ...*

His mind floated in the agony of suffocation and his sense of disembodiment increased. He thought he felt his body recede further and further away from his mind, but knew it was only an illusion; his soul was forever trapped in that physical form that could suffer pain, agony and injury, but not death. *I've failed...failed...*

He thought he heard a distant, tentative voice speak, "Great one?" The voice had echoes in it of pleading appetites and miserable longing.

His sluggish, slowing thoughts staggered, as if preparing to fall into deathly quiet. *What was that? Get away, gnat.*

"Great one ... Lord Moloch, you said, 'If only someone could help.' I would help you, if I knew how."

Moloch's thoughts slid further down into fading darkness. *It must be one of the unbodied. I dropped all of my barriers and one of those parasites slid in. Begone, pest.*

"I heard you call... I know you despair. I am not one as high as you yourself, doomed as I am to trap and torment the humans, but I was there when we were all cast down. I remember your first fight against Michael and his armies. I remember seeing your struggle against him and his only cause of victory being the great Sword of Banishment that he carried. I remember when we lower ones were torn from our incorruptible bodies and cast into this planar prison. I remember it all."

Moloch's thoughts echoed feebly. *I remember... I remember...*

The voice continued, "Then let me help in some way. Give me a task. I have no calling except torment, no purpose except temptation, no accomplishment except deception, no work but confinement, no striving except hunger. Give me something to do again, if only to carry a message..."

A message...

"Yes, Lord Moloch. Give me that. I can do it for you. I will carry a message for you!"

A message... a message; carry this message. His mind guttered to a halt, stuttered like a dying candle flame and surged again for one last moment. *Tell Mulciber... tell my followers ... I live yet... I escaped for a while ... help me escape this prison...*

Moloch lapsed into twisted, undying unconsciousness in the charred darkness of his sarcophagus. For a moment, there seemed to be the sense of a fleeting presence in the smoky cell at the bottom of the Black Sea, one that was not bound by physical walls. The sensation was there for only a moment, then it was gone, moving away, upward and toward the north.

CHAPTER 9 – A GREATER MASTER

"Better to reign in Hell, than serve in Heaven."
— John Milton, Paradise Lost

Rakslav Gachevska was a huge man, but somehow managed to move quietly and with speed. He ducked around a corner and out of sight of two approaching crewmen on the *Lucian*. He grumbled to himself. *I need to find someone my size.*

He had fought the Russian on the sinking petroleum exploration ship *Fortuna*, killed him and then been swept off the deck of the ship when Dmitri Slokov's helicopter had crashed. *Lucky for me, I was just banged up and smacked around. Much better than what I did to the Russian.* Rakslav had swum the distance to the *Lucian* and had ridden the anchor chain up as the tanker pulled away from the *Fortuna*. He had spent the next couple of hours hiding. *Now I have to blend in. It isn't easy for a man my size to blend in.*

Rakslav was six foot two and two hundred and eighty pounds of muscle. His chest was massive and barrel shaped. His head was dome-like and scarred from his years as a street tough in Sofia. When the Russians had pulled up roots and left Bulgaria, Rakslav had left Sofia as well, but not to go with the Russians. He had moved to Bucharest. As far as he was concerned, there was nothing keeping him in Bulgaria and the women were better looking in Romania.

Once he had set himself up in Bucharest, he'd drawn the attention of some of the local authorities with his brutal but efficient tactics. One night a man named Janos Parasca from the Romanian Securitate had stepped into Rakslav's path and made a deal with him. Rakslav Gachevska never really understood why he'd agreed to the deal that day and taken up with Parasca, but he told himself that it had just felt like the right thing to do at the time. Rakslav had become Janos Parasca's right-hand man and enforcer and moved up along with him. When the government of Romania imploded and Parasca left the Securitate and went into business for himself, Rakslav had gone along. When Parasca had made successive moves to take over larger and larger organizations, Rakslav had been there, pushing people around when needed, eliminating roadblocks when necessary, killing people that wouldn't get out of the way. For every year since he'd been with Janos Parasca, it had felt like the right thing to do. *Until now. I'm through with Parasca for good.*

On the *Fortuna*, Rakslav had encountered the monster Moloch and his world had completely changed. Rakslav had never believed in the afterlife or anything having to do with religion, but after living through the disaster on the *Fortuna*, his worldview had been swept out the window. There was more out there than Rakslav had ever realized. He had seen the proof and had even felt it inside his own head.

Rakslav crouched behind some storage containers. *I've been ducking and hiding for hours now, waiting for my chance. I've got to find someone my size soon.*

On the *Fortuna*, Parasca's people had opened a giant metal sarcophagus that the crew had raised from the bottom of the Black Sea. In the sarcophagus, they'd found a gigantic mummified creature that had been sealed inside for over seven thousand years. They'd thought the creature long dead, but it had revived somehow and started preying on the crew of the *Fortuna*. The creature was a giant monster named Moloch and was more than five meters tall. *How can there be something over five meters tall? It was more proof that I didn't know everything I thought I knew.*

Rakslav had seen the monster when they'd opened the sarcophagus and after it revived. He'd even encountered the demonic thing when trying to escape the ship with Parasca. They'd been headed across the deck of the *Fortuna* to reach one of the mini-subs so they could get away and they'd run into the newly awakened monster. It had paralyzed Rakslav and the others, killed the ship's security officer by peeling off all of the man's skin and somehow seized control of Rakslav's mind. It had dominated all of their minds except Janos Parasca. In some way, he'd been able to partially resist the demon. *Mind control! I always thought that kind of talk was nonsense, but it was true. I couldn't move a muscle without permission from it. I could see and hear, could understand what was happening as if I were watching myself from a distance, but it controlled me completely. I couldn't take a single step that it didn't want me to take. It let me live in order to serve it. It was pure power.*

While Rakslav had become its servant and was completely controlled by it, Parasca didn't want anything to do with it and would certainly have left Rakslav and the rest behind if he could have gotten away. Parasca had been reluctant to obey Moloch, but finally he'd been cowed by the demon when Moloch had punished and tortured him sufficiently. It had levitated him in midair and later, Rakslav had seen it smash Parasca's jaw and then heal it in moments, even making shattered teeth regrow. There was no doubt. This being, Moloch, had demonic magical powers. It could read minds, could heal, could paralyze with a thought. Rakslav had finally found a god worthy of worship.

Parasca, on the other hand, was someone that Rakslav could do without now. *How can Janos Parasca compare to a being like Moloch? How can anyone?* Parasca had resisted Moloch repeatedly in spite of the creature's power. He'd had to be tortured by the demon to do as it demanded. Whenever he'd had a chance, Parasca had tried to evade obeying. He had gotten away from Moloch as quickly as possible after Rakslav had rescued him at the end of the fight between Mercy Teller and the demon. *Mercy Teller must be some kind of demon herself, though. She fought Moloch powerfully! If I hadn't been so far under Moloch's control, I might have been able to help him. It wasn't until Moloch's control of me dropped that I came to and saw Parasca. I grabbed him and carried him away from the fight, but he was not grateful and seemed happy to abandon Lord Moloch. I don't feel any loyalty to Parasca anymore, but I will follow Lord Moloch. He got into my head. He controlled me. He could read my thoughts. He commanded me to bring him victims for sacrifice. That is the kind of power I can respect.*

Rakslav paused in his reflection. He heard a single set of steps approaching. He ducked behind a stack of crates a few steps away and hazarded a look back at the corner where he'd been hiding. The steps came closer and Rakslav saw a large, heavyset man in work coveralls come around the corner carrying a coiled cable over one shoulder. He was walking straight toward Rakslav and his hiding place.

The man stopped in front of the crates and reached to flip a latch on the lid of the one closest to him. In an instant, Rakslav moved with smooth grace and swept from behind the crates, came around and stood just behind the man. The worker's hand came in contact with the latch but stopped in mid-movement.

Rakslav's huge fingers closed around the man's neck and squeezed with vice-like power. The man clawed at his throat and pulled at the choking fingers, but Rakslav did not budge and held the man's windpipe closed. The big man kicked backward and tried to twist around. He punched backward and thrashed, but Rakslav held his windpipe pinched shut. The man's fight abruptly slowed and stopped. The man's bulk sagged and his legs went limp. Rakslav released him slowly to the deck and checked the man's pulse and breathing. *Good. Not dead yet. Don't want him to soil his work clothes. I need them.*

Rakslav pulled the man's body behind the crates and stripped him of his coveralls and cap. He checked the man's ID badge that was clipped to the right vest pocket. Rakslav grunted. *Good only so long as no one looks too closely at the picture.* He pulled the coveralls over his own clothes. *The fit isn't good, but will do. At least my clothes dried out some in the time since I got aboard.*

He checked to make sure that no other crew members were nearby and dragged the man nearer to the railing. With the sea beckoning below, Rakslav needed to dispose of the body. He couldn't afford to have the man regain consciousness and call for help. Next to the railing, Rakslav bent over to lift the man. There wasn't enough clearance under the railing to just roll him into the sea, so Rakslav would have to lift him up and over the railing before dropping him to the water below. He leaned down to take the man by one arm but stopped. The man was twitching.

Rakslav leaned away from the body and saw the twitching intensify. The man's body was shaking and vibrating rapidly. *Perhaps I did choke him for too long. Looks like he's going into convulsions.* Rakslav moved a step back and watched the body with mild distaste.

The man's tremors became more and more extreme. His arms thrashed and shook and the man's head flipped back and forth from side to side. The man's bloodshot eyes opened suddenly, staring sightlessly into the distance. The man coughed and retched and then finally lay quiet. A long, sighing breath eased out of the man.

Rakslav backed further away, a disgusted expression on his face. He waited for the man to inhale again. There was nothing. The man's chest did not move up or down. Rakslav waited another minute and then moved closer and took the man's wrist. *No pulse. Alright, now I can dispose of the body.* Rakslav heaved and pulled the limp corpse by the arm up to his shoulder, just enough to get him up and over the rail.

In mid-lift, the corpse's head was near Rakslav's shoulder. He heard a sound and stopped lifting. *What was that?* A soft smacking noise came from the place where the corpse's head would be if Rakslav were facing it. He turned his head to look.

The dead man's head was lolled to one side, his eyes staring blankly, but his lips were moving, lightly smacking together as if preparing to taste something. Rakslav's skin crawled and he felt a chill ripple from his scalp down to his chest. *What is it doing?* The corpse's lips smacked louder and then they shifted to a more complicated motion, with the cheek muscles exhibiting spasms and the upper lip and lower lip seeming to move independently. The lips writhed as if under uncoordinated direction and a thin stream of bile leaked from the thing's mouth. Rakslav couldn't look away from the horrible sight. He felt a panicked thought rise in his mind like a scream. *Throw it over the side!*

He lifted it higher and had the body only a hand's width away from the tipping point where he would be able to push it over the rail. The thing's chest heaved in a gasping breath and wheezed air out through its twitching lips. It sounded at first like a garbled mumbling, but it repeated itself over and over. Transfixed in revulsion and horror, Rakslav finally made out the sounds.

The dead thing was repeating in a hoarse mumbling whisper. "I live yet... I escaped for a while ... help me ... I live yet... I escaped for a while ... help me escape this prison ..."

Rakslav looked at it in terror and wonder. The thing gasped in another breath. Its eyes were open but bloodshot and milky at the same time. *This thing cannot be conscious!* Its rubbery lips pulsed and bounced as if being jostled.

The mumbling whisper continued. It said, "Tell Mulciber... tell my followers ... I live yet... Tell Mulciber... tell my followers ... I live yet..."

Taking more breaths, it repeated the two phrases several more times and then finally stopped with a wheezing exhale. The lips continued pulsing and twitching for a few moments, but slowed down and stopped at last. Rakslav stared at the dead, motionless face and waited for several minutes. Finally satisfied, he flipped the body up and over the rail and watched it drop into the sea. He waited and watched to make sure no 'man overboard' alarm was sounded.

He leaned over the rail and stared at the already distant point where the body had splashed. *That man was dead. I am certain he was dead. Yet, some power moved the mouth of the corpse. The Lord Moloch must have sent me a message. 'Tell Mulciber, tell my followers that I live'. I am one of those followers. And Moloch still lives. 'Help me escape this prison'. He must be trapped again in that sarcophagus and it must have sunk with the Fortuna. Somehow I must rescue him, get him out of the sarcophagus and release him from that confinement permanently.*

* * *

After cleaning up remaining signs of the struggle with the workman and disposing of the cable the man had carried, Rakslav stepped cautiously away from the section near the anchor where he been hiding the last couple of hours. He pulled his cap brim as far down over his face as he dared and walked toward the control tower section of the tanker *Lucian*. He heard a two-whistle alert sound through the ship's public address system.

A voice came over the ship intercom, speaking in Romanian. "This is the captain. We are executing a tight turn. We are going back to the last position of the *Fortuna* at fourteen knots and will rendezvous with the merchant vessel, *Legend*. Chairman Slokov is alive aboard the *Legend* and will come back on the *Lucian* as soon as possible. Prepare the helipad for an incoming chopper within the next few hours that will take him back to Romania. Repeating..." The captain of the *Lucian* detailed the message again.

Interesting. He escaped from the crash of his helicopter and the sinking of the Fortuna, but it was Dmitri's men that attacked the ship and sent it to the bottom in the first place. He admitted to Parasca that the Russian was working for him. I may just need to stay close to Dmitri. Perhaps I can make sure he does not survive much longer.

Rakslav stayed out of sight for the time it took to return to where the *Fortuna* had gone down. He noted that while returning for Dmitri, the ship was moving at a much faster speed than it had previously. *The captain is not worried about burning more fuel when his boss is waiting.* Dawn was breaking by the time they made it back. Soon, they were near the *Legend* and Rakslav saw a launch put away from it and approach the *Lucian.*

Slokov must be on that launch. Below, Rakslav saw a portly man with an arm in a sling climb slowly out of the launch and up a short ladder. *Dmitri's onboard and it looks like he was injured. I wonder if I can get close enough to kill him? No, it's not the right place. Perhaps I can get close enough to overhear plans? I may not have much time with a chopper on the way. Speak of the Devil…*

Rakslav heard a rhythmic thump, thump and knew a helicopter was approaching though he hadn't seen it yet. He gave up trying to get closer to Dmitri below deck and started up the outer stairs of the control tower toward the helipad. On the way up, he considered his options. There weren't many to think about and he couldn't count on being able to deceive the rest of the crew for very long. He reached the top of the stairs on the control tower. The sounds of the chopper were louder and he looked up to see it closing in to land on the ship's helipad.

A door opened on the landing below Rakslav and several men stepped out. One seemed to be dressed as the captain of the *Lucian* and two others wore uniforms of officers. The fourth man was Dmitri Slokov. He was rapidly firing orders to the other men. Rakslav backed away from the edge so he could hear but not be seen.

* * *

"Get me a phone, now. Mine was ruined in the sea water when I fell in." No one seemed to know what to do about his request and finally Dmitri cursed at them in frustration. The captain and his men shifted uncomfortably.

"Wait." He held up his uninjured hand and pointed at the captain. "Just give me your phone."

The captain again looked confused. Slokov continued insistently, "Yes, I mean your personal phone. Take it out of your pocket and give it to me." He waited impatiently for the man to take a cellphone from his pocket and hand it tentatively over to him.

Dmitri took it and said, "I need to speak with my brother Alexi and I must do it before I board that chopper. You don't need this phone as much as I do. Order yourself another when you get to shore; as of now, this one is mine. Now excuse me, I would like to speak with my brother." The ship's officers stepped back inside and left Dmitri outside. He put his back against a wall and sighed. He tried several times unsuccessfully to get the phone working while muttering to himself about the phone's volume.

Finally Dmitri dialed Alexi Slokov, keyed a button to set the phone's speaker on and started talking to his brother.

"Alexi, this is Dmitri. This stupid phone doesn't work right, so I've got you on speaker. There's nobody else around. I'm on the *Lucian* again. The chopper has landed and I'll be boarding it in a few moments. When I get to Bucharest, I will have my driver take me to a doctor first. I am crazy with pain right now because my arm is broken and I have to have it tended. After the doctor, I will go to my home and rest for a few hours. Oh, and send my secretary to my home. I will tell her what else to do to get things moving."

Alexi said, "Dmitri, slow down! You sound feverish."

Slokov bulled ahead and continued, "You must set in motion a salvage operation. Put Petr Ivanov in charge of it and have him get a team together quickly. He always smashes things through for us. There are some very valuable things that sank with the *Fortuna* and we must get them first before PetroRomania gets people there. The salvage team will need heavy lift capability."

"What? Brother, that is not easy to do. How deep is the water? How heavy is the material? How big is the object? Salvage operations are expensive and you have already cost us a lot of money with this adventure. How much is this new scheme of yours going to set us back?"

Dmitri said, "Listen to me! PetroRomania will try to accuse us of piracy or sabotage or terrorism, I don't know which. We need to get our legal people moving. Parasca's lawyers will try to tie us up in a big legal fight, but our people are better. We beat Janos before when we held up his purchase of the *Fortuna* and now, our team needs to file suit first."

"What would we claim in a lawsuit, that they got in our way when we boarded their ship? That they tried to impede us when we set explosives on the *Fortuna*?" Dmitri snorted, but Alexi pushed ahead, "Yes, I know some of what happened on the *Fortuna*. Let me ask you, Dmitri, do we have to keep calling these men security consultants, or could we call them what they really are and say, 'mercenaries'?"

"I'm not joking, Alexi. Don't push me about those security men. We needed them. I just barely survived the madness on that ship. I'm still stunned that Parasca's man, that big hulking Rakslav, killed our Russian contractor. And no, I don't know what lawsuits to file yet, industrial espionage or something else. It doesn't have to stick; we just need to get in the first punch. Our legal team will think of something. After I get my arm taken care of, we'll figure out with our lawyers what to do. The first thing though, is to get that salvage operation going. Remember, I told you that Parasca's people found something at the bottom of the Black Sea. It was so important that he was willing to repurpose an entire exploration ship away from its original mission to find oil. It's that new metal that they found, that new kind of steel. I know that there was a giant box of it on the *Fortuna*. We need to get that thing for ourselves. It will make us all rich. That's what we need to salvage before PetroRomania can get to it."

Alexi said, "Dmitri, we're already rich. We don't need that."

Dmitri said, "Don't argue with me on this, Alexi. We may not need it, but at the very least we have to make sure that Parasca and PetroRomania don't get it. So we have to get it first and deny it to them. The salvage needs to start. Can you get our people on that right away?"

Alexi sighed with what sounded like resignation. "Yes, brother."

"Then that is good. The other thing is this, were our people able to find out Dr. Teller's contact information like I asked?"

"Yes. I have some cell numbers for the USA and Romania, several email and instant message addresses and some apartment addresses and land line numbers. Can I text them to this cell number?"

"Yes, but also send all of that information to my work email address. As soon as I get better access to the internet again, I'll pick it up from there."

"Alright. Now, Dmitri, that is enough. You are hurt. I can hear the strain in your voice. Get on that helicopter and get to your doctor. I'll get in touch with a salvage company. The nearest to the *Fortuna* site would probably be in Varna, but I'll find out if there are any others that are in transit or maybe just finishing up salvage jobs. They might be closer and able to get to the *Fortuna* more quickly than Parasca's people. Go take care of yourself. I'll send your secretary to your house. Go."

Dmitri's voice softened, "Little brother, you are good to me. Forgive me for being the bully again."

Alexi sounded tired and exasperated. "Dmitri, I think sometimes you are insane. Plus, you drive me crazy, but we are blood. Take care." He hung up.

* * *

Rakslav heard the sound of a door opening below.

Dmitri said, "I am through with my call. I don't want your piece of garbage phone after all, but I do need to copy down some information coming in on a text message that will arrive in a moment."

Rakslav heard the buzzing of a phone vibrating from an incoming message. "Ah, there it is. Give me that pen in your pocket and a piece of paper to write on." There followed a pause where Dmitri could be heard scratching something out on paper.

Dmitri said, "Here, take it. And, delete that text: it is private." Rakslav imagined Dmitri waiting as the flustered captain fumbled with the phone, deleting messages under Dmitri's watchful eye.

Seemingly satisfied, Dmitri said, "Now I will leave with the chopper. You take this ship to Varna and get back to your regular route."

Rakslav didn't wait to hear Dmitri's footsteps coming up the stairs. Rakslav went rapidly across the helipad past Dmitri's waiting chopper, down the opposite outer stairs and heard Dmitri's helicopter take off a few minutes later. He found a hatchway down and looked for a place where he could hide for a few more hours. He found a storage locker with cleaning supplies.

From the look of this ship, they never do any cleaning. This will be a safe place to hide for a while. He pondered what he had overheard of Dmitri's conversation with his brother Alexi.

How interesting. I think I will stow away until we reach Varna. If Dmitri's people are mounting a salvage operation to bring up the sarcophagus, the Lord Moloch will surely be in it. I must be there when he is brought up to make sure he is released. I also need time to think this through. I must plan this out, but I know the first thing to do will be to get on the crew for that salvage operation. Perhaps at Varna I can get on the ship. I know some tricks that might defeat their security procedures.

Rakslav thought about the departing helicopter. *And why did Dmitri want contact information for Dr. Teller? Does that mean she survived the wreck of the Fortuna as well?*

CHAPTER 10 – DREAMS

"This uncouth dream, of evil sprung"
— John Milton, Paradise Lost

After Mercy and Jack rode the bus to the Bulgarian port city of Varna and made connections, they headed on a separate bus to the Romanian border. After the crossing, they planned to continue on to Constanta and then to catch a train to Bucharest. Mercy ate most of the rest of their supply of snacks and felt sleepy. *I'm losing weight, I can feel it. I'm not getting enough to eat, especially for all of the energy I've been expending. It's a curse for which I can expect no sympathy from anyone.*

She noticed that Jack had already nodded off again and she looked at him with concern. *He's a man that stays in shape, but he doesn't have the physical resilience that I have. We're so exhausted after all we went through. One more day and I'll be back to normal, if I can get enough food, but he'll need more time than that.* She looked at Jack and noted numerous scrapes and bruises. *We were really banged up on the Fortuna.*

She felt herself becoming sleepier and finally gave in, resting her head on Jack's shoulder. After a minute she was snoring softly.

* * *

Mercy was at home. It felt like her bed, it smelled like her house. She lay in bed in her pajamas, enjoying the feel of the soft, warm flannel. She looked at the curtains on the window above her. *Those are my curtains. I picked them myself.* On the wall across the room, she saw pictures of herself with her high school friends, pictures of herself in the school band and pictures of herself with her parents. There was her desk with her school books piled high. *I have to get to my homework. I've been putting it off and I don't want to be late turning anything in.* There was a knock at her door.

"Mercy? Are you awake? It's getting late." It was her father's voice.

"I'm awake, Daddy." Mercy rose from bed and noticed she was already dressed. *When did I get dressed? I had my pajamas on, but when did I put these clothes on? I can't remember. Oh, well.* She walked to the door and opened it. Her father stood in the hallway outside her room looking like a big friendly bear.

"How did you sleep, sweetheart?" He asked and opened his arms wide for a hug. She was as tall as he and she hugged him, her chin fitting perfectly on his shoulder.

She said, "Fine, Daddy. What are we doing today?"

"It's time to go see your doctor again. That older woman; the one you like."

Mercy felt her heart abruptly sink, her good mood vanishing like smoke. She said plaintively. "No, Daddy. Not another doctor visit! They never make me feel any better."

"We have to keep going to these visits, Mercy. The doctor is just helping you. Those voices you hear won't go away by themselves. You have to stick with it."

Mercy's heart pounded. She felt threatened. She also felt mad. *I don't want to go see that old witch! She's always asking me questions. I don't want to talk about it anymore. What good has it done to talk, talk, talk, for all these months? The voices are always there. Even when I take the medicine, they still scream at me all the time. The only thing the medicine does is make them be not as loud.*

Fearful and angry, Mercy balled her fists. "I don't have to stick with it! I don't want to anymore. The doctor isn't helping me, no one is helping me!" Her voice rose to a shout. "You and mother aren't helping either! Why do you keep punishing me?"

Her father looked concerned but said calmly, "Mercy, no one is punishing you. We love you. You're just sick. Did you take your medicine today?"

Her anger grew like a giant wave. She heard a roaring sound in her ears like the surf crashing in a storm. In that sound there seemed to be thousands upon thousands of voices shouting, calling, imploring, begging and screaming. Many of them spoke. *Mercy, listen to us. He's not your father. She's not your mother. They're all lying. No one is who they seem to be.*

She was terrified and her hair felt like it was standing up at the roots. She looked at her father, Edward Teller, and suddenly hated the sight of him.

"I'm <u>not</u> sick and I won't take my medicine now or ever again! Do you hear me? You and mother are trying to poison me. You don't love me and you never did."

Edward Teller shook his head sadly but spoke insistently, "Mercy, that's not right and you know it. We do love you and just want to help. Now don't be like this. You're a sixteen year-old young lady now and need to act your age. This tantrum is not you. You're acting like a five year-old."

Mercy shouted, "Don't call me a baby and stop treating me like a child! I hate you! You're always punishing me for things I can't help. Leave me alone!"

Her father said, "Mercy, that's enough! Stop it. You're upsetting me and …"

A voice called from downstairs. "Edward, what's going on?" It was Mercy's mother.

Mercy said, "Now look what you've done. You woke up the witch."

Edward Teller's eyes narrowed and he said, "Mercy, that's an awful, hateful thing to say about your mother. She has done more for you than you can ever know."

"I don't care! You're not my real parents anyway!"

Her mother had come up the stairs and was standing behind her husband with one foot up on the landing to the second floor hallway where Edward Teller stood. She said, "Mercy, stop saying such terrible things. I know you're upset, but it's just those voices that are really making you feel bad. If you don't take your medicine, those horrible things just get worse and worse. You need to behave yourself and do what you're supposed to do and take your pill. Here."

Mercy's mother held out a hand and opened it palm up. In the center of the hand was a little white disk. Mercy stared at it with hate. A chorus of voices shouted inside her. The Jailor's voice spoke loudest. *It's poison! Don't take it. They want to kill you or trap you.*

"I don't want it! I won't take it!" The pill in the palm of her mother's rock-steady hand shifted and rolled. It flipped over and uncoiled into a tiny, chalky-white snake the size of a worm. She screamed and felt her blood freeze. The worm hissed and grew larger in her mother's palm. Mercy shouted, "Look out!" But neither her mother nor her father moved or even seemed to be aware of the now softball-sized albino snake coiling and rearing up in Martha Teller's hand.

Mercy's mother moved closer to her, the hand holding the snake coming ever nearer. She spoke with a soothing expression on her face. "Mercy, you know you have to swallow it. This will help you cope with the voices, but you have to take it. Now."

Mercy was overcome by a feeling of panic. The snake hissed and its red eyes seemed to bore into her. *I won't swallow that snake! How can she even think I would? That's the proof. She and this man aren't my parents. My real parents wouldn't try to get me to eat a poisonous snake. They are imposters. I've got to get away.*

"I won't!" She jumped forward and shoved her mother to one side. The woman caught hold of the bannister and did not fall but Mercy heard the sound of the breath being knocked out of her and Martha Teller slumped to one side, clutching the rail. Mercy's father reached out to catch his daughter's arm, but at the first touch on her, she instinctively jabbed her elbow back at him in an upward angle.

Mercy's elbow caught Edward Teller in the neck and his eyes bulged. He tried to gasp, but couldn't. The moment seemed to freeze and then time's clock ticked again at an agonizingly slow rate. Edward Teller's eyes rolled up in his head and his legs went loose. He toppled over backward and tumbled down the stairs in a slow motion roll: crashing with his limbs splayed and ineffectually flopping until he smashed onto the entryway floor and stopped abruptly at the base of the front door.

The roaring in Mercy's ears was like a freight train. She heard screaming laughter in her mind from legions of voices. Distantly, she heard her mother shouting, "Edward! Edward!" Mercy's mind felt like it was shattering and she heard another voice calling to her, a voice from somewhere else.

"Mercy."

* * *

"Mercy. Wake up. You're having a nightmare." Jack's voice sounded very distant and muffled, but jarring.

What? Who is that? Jack? Mercy opened her eyes and felt like she was in shock. *What just happened to me?* Tears came to her eyes involuntarily and she groaned with the disorientation that she always experienced with vivid dreams. *Oh, no. Daddy. I can't believe I had another dream about the day he died. I guess I'll never stop suffering for that. And that would be only right, too.*

The countryside rolled by outside the bus window behind him. Jack put his hand over hers and said, "Pretty bad, huh?"

"You have no idea," she said groggily. She shook her head, trying to get some clarity back.

"You want to talk about it? Go ahead, tell me what your dream was about." Jack said.

Mercy shook her head. "Trust me, you don't want to know. It was just stupid nonsense like all dreams."

Jack smiled reassuringly. "You know better than that, and really, I do want to hear about it. I'm not half bad at interpreting dreams. I've had more than my share of frightening ones, so I've done a lot of reading about dreams and their meanings. Tell me about it. Humor me."

She looked at Jack and a thought occurred to her. *Maybe I should start by telling Jack some of this. There's still a lot I haven't told him. In the past I would have thought, 'No way, because I'd have to tell him about the voices and all my other quirks too' but now, that's moot. He already knows all of that stuff. But I still feel myself being reluctant, almost wanting to say, 'I don't want to burden him.' That can't be right either*

72

anymore, though. I can't treat him like he's some fragile little person that might break if I say the wrong thing. We can't have a life together if I have to constantly be hiding stuff from him. How could I even keep track of all of it, of what I was hiding and what I wasn't?

Jack smiled knowingly. "Take your time. You're wondering if you can bring yourself to tell me. I get it. I've been fighting with myself about that kind of thing too. I've said to myself, 'What can I tell Mercy without making her want to run away screaming?' That's what you're thinking about your stories, aren't you?"

She smiled in spite of herself and said, "True, but I don't think you really have much to worry about along those lines. I'm the one that's been half-crazy most of her life. I doubt you have much in the way of deep, dark secrets."

Jack's expression changed to a slight wince for a moment and then he recovered his steady, calm demeanor. "You weren't crazy; you were under siege by those disembodied voices. Besides, every one takes damage in life, Mercy. No one gets through unscathed. Part of surviving to adulthood involves taking blows, hits, whatever you want to call it and almost everyone has a past they don't want to discuss. Some people have things they *have* to keep secret, like *you* do. Other people have things they just *want* to keep secret. Like *I* do."

Mercy felt a jolt of emotion, almost like a shock that had jumped from Jack to her. It was full of feelings of shame and apprehension as well as determination; a mountain of determination. *What was that? Did I feel something from Jack just flow to me mentally?*

She said, "I didn't mean to make light of anything you've gone through."

Jack said, "It's alright. You didn't, but it makes me realize I do need to come clean. But, you first. You were going to tell me about your dream."

Mercy smiled ruefully and said, "Was I?"

"Yes, you were." Jack said. His pleasant expression remained in place but his voice was firm.

Mercy sighed, "It's not that I don't want to tell you, it's that I've kept things secret for so long for so many reasons, it's habitual for me now. In the past, if it was about my voices, I didn't want people to know I was psychotic. So I wouldn't tell that to anyone but a doctor and I'd only tell them so I could get prescriptions for medication. If it was about my strength, speed or appetite, I didn't tell anyone because I didn't want the freak factor to become known. That would have caused so many complications."

"And if it was about nightmares, why wouldn't you want to tell anyone about that?" Jack prompted.

She sighed with exasperation. "I just now started to say 'because it's no one else's business!' but I caught myself. For my dreams it was more like avoiding humiliation. I don't want people to know what I've done and still have nightmares about."

"I can see that." Jack waited patiently.

He's just going to wait me out on this, I guess. But he's right. If Jack had a superpower it would be patient relentlessness. Well, he said he wants to marry me, and he's as serious as can be. She frowned and blinked slowly as if coming to a big realization. *So let him know all of it. If he can handle it, then it's meant to be. If he can't handle it or starts getting cold feet, then it's better to know now than later.*

Mercy made her decision, took a deep breath and watched Jack closely while she began to talk. She wanted to know as soon as possible how he handled what she said, in case she needed to back off.

"Alright. In my dream just now, I was reliving the day my father died. It was one of the worst days of my life and something I never want to remember, let alone relive. The worst thing about it was that I killed him. By accident, it is true, but I killed him, nevertheless." She related the entire dream sequence to him and did not spare herself in the retelling.

At the end of the story, Jack was silent for a minute then asked, "So, all of that in the dream really happened that day, or was it embellished by your subconscious?"

She said, "Most of it was very close to reality. He really died and yes, he fell because my elbow hit him in the neck. We had this gigantic argument and my mom joined in and tried to get me to take my dose of antipsychotic drug. The only part that was over the top in the dream was what happened after that. Mom didn't try to feed me a snake; it was actually only a pill, but the rest of the dream wasn't an exaggeration."

Jack nodded. "Dream imagery can be pretty distressing. Snakes in dreams are a kind of archetypal symbol, like a recurrent theme. They could point to your perception of evil of some kind. Freud thought they were phallic symbols and a snake in a dream had to do with sex in some way. Of course, Freud thought everything was about sex. One thought is that in a dream when something changes into a snake, it might mean that you perceive an attempt to corrupt you or compromise you in some way. That would be understandable given the trauma you experienced from the onset of the voices in your teen years. So, in your dream, you felt like you were back to being sixteen?"

Mercy said, "Yes, my bedroom was like when I was in high school, my parents looked like they did back then and I was acting like a teenager." She muttered and shook her head. "I wouldn't want to be that young again for all the money in the world! The racing, uncontrolled emotions and overreaction; it's so humiliating to know I was once like that. Teenagers are notorious for irrationality and over-the-top angst, but why did I have to have such a flare up when my more-than-human strength and speed were also starting to manifest? That was also when I started to experience my super-hyped up metabolism."

Jack said, "You didn't really understand until later what was going on, did you?"

Mercy laughed, her face covered in a fatalistic expression. "You're kidding, right? It really wasn't until this week that I started to understand some of what was going on. And a lot of it I still don't know. I mean, come on, Jack. There's all of this stuff about universal languages and demons and angels and me being not quite all human. What am I, caught in the middle of some ongoing supernatural war? If so, am I a pawn or some other piece on the chessboard? Will I ever know? Could I even understand my part if someone told me?"

Jack nodded and said, "I know that all of that is 'way beyond our pay grade' as the saying goes, but back to the dream. You see yourself as responsible for your father's death because you bumped him and he tumbled down the stairs and died?"

Mercy said, "How could I think anything else? He died because of me and his death just about killed my mom. It was a year before she was halfway back to normal. That is probably the worst thing I've ever done in my life. I can't undo it and I can't make it better. I can't even say I'm sorry. Daddy is gone and so is mother and I can't tell either of them how sorry I am."

Jack said, "Your mother knew it was an accident. I'm sure she didn't hold it against you once she got over the shock."

"I know. I know. But that almost made it worse in some ways. She was so sad. And for the rest of her life, too."

"Is this the first time you've had a dream like this?" Jack asked.

"No, I've had these dreams about Daddy falling for over twenty years now. You'd think I'd be over it, but there must still be something going on in my subconscious that wants to drag this out every so often to chew over again and beat me up about. I dream this every few months. The twist with the snake was new this time, but the rest was pretty standard."

"But didn't you tell me about another dream that had your father in it, the dream about the Counselor in that throne room scene?"

Mercy said, "Yes, my father was in there, but that was different than the dream I just had. In the dream from which I just awoke, it was a memory of him. It was Edward Teller as I saw him when I was sixteen on the day he died. In the vision I had of the throne room and him leading me there and talking to me, it was not a memory. It was like he was there in the present, and knew what had been happening with all of us on the *Fortuna*. That vision was not me remembering him; it was me interacting with Edward Teller as he is now, in that different plane of existence."

"The afterlife?"

"Jack, it has to be. My father really did die when he fell, but he also really spoke to me in that place where I met with the Counselor."

Jack said, "I know, it's just ... I never expected to be confronted with the reality of the supernatural like this."

Mercy said, "Me either. And what part does the Counselor play in this? In that vision I had, the Counselor sat there on a throne in a massive chamber. There was a constant procession of fantastical beings going in and out and the Counselor seemed to be speaking to some of them before talking to me. There was that sphinx-like thing that was the size of a bus. If it had spread its wings it would have been as big as a passenger jet. Daddy said it was a cherubim."

Mercy continued, "I have to believe it was really him there with me in that chamber, and I know it wasn't just a dream because that was where I got this energy." She looked carefully at her hand and could still see the bluish power thread leading into it. "You can't see that, can you? It's a neon blue thread that comes out of my hand and connects me to one of those pools of power that was in the vision. I can still see the thread, going off into the distance and I can feel power coming to me through it."

Jack looked at her hand as if searching. Finally he shook his head. "I can't see it, but I have no doubt it's there if you say it is. I wish I could see it, but even though I don't, I believe you. I saw too much the other day on the *Fortuna* not to believe you about this."

Mercy said, "Thanks for trusting me. I'm convinced this power is as real as the clothes on our backs. I've got to learn more about how this energy works, what I can do with it and what I can't. I know I can heal myself. Moloch forced me to learn that. I wonder if I could heal someone else, like maybe curing all of your cuts and bruises?" She put a gentle hand to his cheek. "Though I wouldn't want to try that without a better understanding of anatomy. I wouldn't want to accidentally hurt you."

Jack said, "I remember the monster paralyzing me and Hayden. Do you think you could do that? That might be useful if we ran into Parasca or some of his thugs."

Mercy said, "Perhaps. I just don't know how. I remember Moloch spoke a single word like 'halt' and you two just froze. Maybe I can figure out how that worked, but that word he used wasn't English. I think it was in that ancient, universal language he spoke and we somehow could understand. It's hard to recall the exact sound. I'll try to remember."

"Could you use that new power to read thoughts?" Jack asked.

Mercy said slowly, "Yes ..."

Jack raised his eyebrows questioningly and said, "I think I hear more details wanting to come out in your answer."

She sighed, "You do. Jack, I heard your thoughts earlier today. I need to be straight with you on this. You were dreaming and I caught snatches of your dream."

Jack's eyes went unfocussed for a moment as if he were replaying a memory. His expression turned bleak. "Did you see the dream about me and my parents?"

She felt embarrassed and said, "Yes. I'm sorry, Jack. I tried not to but I couldn't get loose from your dream until it was over. I'm so sorry."

He held up his hand reassuringly. "It's alright. That's kind of a relief after all. If you saw that, you know my life growing up was not ideal, but I'm not complaining. A lot of people had it rough when they were young. At least I didn't get physically abused."

"Jack, you were emotionally abused. It's just as bad. If your parents were always fighting like I saw in your dream, and the only way to make them stop was to put yourself between them, that was abuse."

"I try not to think about it. They hated each other and as soon as I left home, they broke up and divorced quickly thereafter. I think I was a child in that dream you might have glimpsed. Did you see the part about them fighting and then jumping on me? " He looked and saw her nod. "They didn't really attack me physically when I was a child. I was treated more as a messenger between the two of them. They couldn't talk without being absolutely vicious to each other, so they'd tell me things to tell the other. Then they'd attack me as the messenger and send me back with abusive comments for the other."

She put her hand on his lightly, looked in his face with concern and said, "That sounds horrible."

"I won't sugar coat it. It was a bad place to grow up. On the other hand, I came out of it with an ability I'd never have had to develop otherwise."

"What's that?" She asked.

"I became a really good negotiator and mediator. I had to. I developed the ability to see the world from another person's point of view and finally got to the place where I could shift at will from advocating for one person to being the champion of someone else. I can convince, cajole and compromise, but I wouldn't have learned that without them." He paused and frowned, his eyes looking downward.

Jack finished with emphasis, "But I still don't want anything to do with either of them. They were selfish, cruel people. I don't hate them anymore, but I am still angry at them. I don't understand them and don't want to either. I don't want to waste any more of my life thinking about them or spending time with them."

He looked in her eyes and squeezed her hands tightly. She squeezed back just as hard. *I can take it Jack. I'm very strong. Lean on me a little. You can, you know.*

He said, "Isn't it ironic that you grieve for the parents you lost and I grieve for the parents I never had? You would give anything to be with yours again, while I would give anything to never see or hear from mine again. What does that say about us? What does that say about me?" He squeezed her hand again and stared out of the bus window, watching the countryside roll by.

Mercy felt a buzzing and for a moment could not figure out what was causing it until she realized it was her phone vibrating. She reached for it, drew it out of her pocket and looked at the front of the phone.

"What is it?" asked Jack.

"It's an incoming message. What could this be about …?" She said.

She entered the passcode for her phone and opened up the message application. She read for a moment, looked shocked and reread it. Jack watched her with increasing curiosity.

Jack said, "You look perplexed and shocked at the same time. Who's the message from?"

Mercy said, "You'll never believe it. I don't believe it myself."

"Oh?"

"It's from Dmitri Slokov, the Chairman of Intercon Transport. I think he was the one that the Russian guy worked for and the one who sent those pirate mercs onto the *Fortuna*."

"What? Why would he send a message to you? Trying to strike up a friendship since he didn't succeed in getting us all killed on the Fortuna?"

"It's crazy, I know. But that's not the worst part. Wait till you hear what he says."

"Well, tell me!"

"He says, 'Your grandmother Sonia is still alive and I can put you in touch with her. Contact me at this number. Dmitri Slokov.'"

* * *

Fevered, chaotic thoughts clattered through him like a clicking insect. His thoughts gnawed unknowingly at pieces of scattered memory, intermittent and incoherent. The thoughts were sluggish, sometimes taking minutes or hours to form and pass on through his trapped and dazed mind. There was a fleeting image of a giant sword, wielded by a sinewy hand. Another thought held a glimpse of chains that were wrapped around him. He was suspended before the vengeful face of the Archon, Michael. He saw a flash of lightning and rain. There was a massive earthquake sundering earth and letting in an ocean's worth of water. He was thrown into a metal box that closed until darkness engulfed his world. There was a fluttering memory of rumbling thunder like a mountain falling. Over it all was a layer of pain, unending and choking. There was an eternity of pressure and coughing, and more pain. There was the weight of a thousand boulders on his chest. *Was this death? But he couldn't die! They wouldn't let him think or be free. They wouldn't let him design, build or experiment. And now, they wouldn't let him die. I can't die and I can't live.* A slow wondering question breached his consciousness like something from a deeper, older world. *What am I: here in this grave, caught between life and death?*

Eternally uneasy sleep smothered him, giving no rest and no escape. Another dream image ran across the chaotic stage of his mind, that of a skeletal figure, its hands cupped at the sides of its emaciated face, calling out a warning of some kind. An echoing sound seemed to come from it as if from far away. It sounded like a cry of torment. A slow, longing thought rustled through his mind like a breeze over a desert. *I wish I could cry, but there are no tears for me and no moisture at all. There are no tears left in me. There are certainly no tears being shed for me. Oh, for a drink of water.* The dreamer tried to swallow in his sleep, but the parched muscles would not move, could not even cough. His mouth felt as dry as bark.

The voice sounded again from the skeletal figure on his mind's stage. *What is it saying?* The actor cupped his hands around his thin face in a makeshift megaphone and shouted. Still the sound came from a vast distance. The dreamer heard snatches of words.

The actor shouted distantly, "I live yet... I escaped for a while ... help me ..." The dreamer despaired. *Someone lives. If only I could die, but I am cursed to unending life.*

"... help me escape this prison ..." *Would that I could escape. There is no escape.*

"...Tell Mulciber... tell my followers ... I live yet..."

The dreamer trembled in shock. Chaotic thoughts rolled through him. He nearly regained consciousness. *Mulciber. Tell Mulciber I live yet. What?* He struggled to concentrate. *I am dreaming. I'm caught in a dream. I must awaken.* He tried to force consciousness, to break through the membrane of sleep. He willed himself to rise from the deep water of the subconscious.

The skin at the surface of his thoughts seemed to stretch. He felt the layer thin out and he regained a portion of his senses. He thought he could smell a thick moldering taint to the air. He reeled away from it mentally. *Not that. Oh, for a drink of water.* He felt his mind give way, falling back again into the deep. He swirled in a maelstrom and was swept spiraling downward. His thoughts were lost in a scattered void.

Only one thought remained. *Mulciber! I am Mulciber!*

CHAPTER 11 – INNER CHAMBER

"And many are the ways that lead to his grim cave, all dismal"
— John Milton, Paradise Lost

Maria called, "Henry! Come look at what we've found now!"

"Hmm?" Henry looked up questioningly from where he was examining a skeleton lying prone on the long stairway leading down into the earth. Maria waved enthusiastically. She and several other students were moving a portable photography setup that also tracked geo-locations. It worked even underground once it was calibrated to a known location. She pointed at the floor of the landing further down the stairs. Henry waved back.

"What is it?" He called.

"This skeleton may be the remains of a craftsman. These look like tools in a pile next to the bones. This might be a stone hammer and that could be an awl. Perhaps this is a chisel. It looks to be made of a different stone than the hammer. I don't know what these other things might be."

Henry said, "Make sure to get good pictures from all angles before anything is touched. We need to record the locations and orientations of everything before any of it gets disturbed. I'd better finish up with this poor fellow before I move down there to look. Can you point me to it later?"

Maria said, "I can. And don't worry. We will get pictures of everything."

Henry resumed his study of the prone skeleton. The great stairway from the surface that they discovered yesterday evening when they'd followed Balev had turned into a gold mine. *Well, not literally, I suppose. There are a few little pieces of gold here and there, but mainly it is a treasure trove of archaeology. There also has to be a really frightening story about what went on here.*

The 'Grand Staircase' as he'd come to think of it, opened at the surface where the huge stone door had been latched shut. As soon as they'd got lights down into the pit, Henry had wanted to look at the mechanism that had kept the door shut and yet had allowed it to swing open as soon as the lock had been tripped.

There weren't any gears, cables or pulleys as Henry had at first thought. There was hardly a mechanism at all. It was a big relief to Henry because he couldn't imagine how the builders of this would have managed to keep a complex mechanism functional after thousands of years. In fact, there was only the stone door with its underside counterweight and the hinges. The door was intentionally unbalanced on the underside with the heaviest part of the stone object just on the far side of the thick stone hinge. As soon as the latch of the lock mechanism had been released, the stone tried to right itself and the topside of the door swiveled up, pivoting on the smoothly rounded stone hinges at the edges of the door. The heavier counterweighted underside found its more natural position downward by causing the rest of the door to pivot upward.

The trickiest part besides the sheer weight of a stone this size was probably the stone door's lock. That too however had, upon examination proved to be a relatively simple design. It had an uncomplicated latch that would be released when a cylinder of the right size was pushed into it. With the latch tripped, the counterweight's rebalancing effort opened the door. *This is truly a singular and ingenious design. It's like something the Egyptians might have engineered, but a few thousand years earlier. Henry, this site is proving to be an absolute treasure house. I could probably spend my entire career here, researching and writing papers and still not get to the bottom of everything.*

"Henry, we've really done it this time. We really have." It was Professor Russo and his voice sounded cheerful.

Henry looked up at the older man and smiled, "I believe we have, Professor."

"So what do you think we have here now, a subterranean tomb complex?" Russo said.

"I think so. It's almost Egyptian in the way it was done. Not the architecture, of course. The artistic designs in the stone down here seem consistent with the jewelry we've found. The stone mechanism appears to be consistent with the artistic and tool capabilities of the time, though I am so impressed with that counterweighted door. Ingenious."

He paused, took a drink of water from a bottle at his belt and continued. "By Egyptian, I'm referring to the style of ritual murder of so many retainers and workers. Just surveying this stairway, there seems to be at least a dozen separate skeletons. From their possessions, some, maybe half, appear to be soldiers."

"How so?" Professor Russo asked.

"Well, it's the spears. Of course, their clothing has long ago decayed away or been eaten by insects. It's the copper spearheads for the soldiers and stone tools for the workmen."

"I thought those looked like stone hammers and axes."

"Yes, and Maria's group down there may have found a chisel. Imagine the work it would have taken to fashion this stone door with hand tools. Amazing."

"So you think that when the important personage was buried down here, they immediately shut in all of the workmen and some soldiers too?" Professor Russo said.

"Actually, no. I don't think they just shut them in. These skeletons show signs of violence. They are scattered from the very top to the very bottom of the Grand Staircase. Large, extreme breaks in bones are common and it doesn't look like the work of the little teeth of underground rodents. There are at least two decapitations and several skeletons show partially shattered ribcages like might be seen due to stabbing injuries. I think these people were violently killed and then left in here. Or perhaps they were shut in and then slowly killed each other off. Either way…" Henry trailed off.

"… it would have been a very bad way to die." The professor finished Henry's thought.

"That was my thinking as well and why I said it seemed almost Egyptian in scope."

"I see your point," said Russo.

Henry said, "Professor, what about the bottom of the stairs? We haven't got that far I know, but the hallway continues on at the base of the stairs. There looks to have been a partial collapse of the roof, but I think the hall continues beyond that. Do you think it might be the main burial chamber? I mean, if this is a larger tomb complex."

"We shall see, won't we?" said the Professor.

Henry spoke in a lower, more confidential tone. "With Balev healing from his injury, we stand a good chance of making some rapid progress, don't you think?"

Professor Russo winked at Henry. "I do. In fact, why don't we get some lights and continue down the stairs? Let's look at the hallway and see how safe it is."

They took some electric torches and carefully picked their way down the stairs, being cautious not to disturb any of the bones or fragments on the broad stone steps. They went down to the first landing that was more than twelve meters below the surface and stopped. Maria and Angelica halted their photography and waited on the professor who seemed to be considering something.

"Yes, Professor Russo?" said Maria.

"I am thinking. Maria, can you detach that camera easily from that tripod mounting? I know we use it especially for low light environments. I wonder if you would be able to quickly free it up and come with Henry and me. We are going to go further down and examine the rest of the passageway. I want to see if it leads to another chamber.

"Of course," said Maria. She set to work detaching it with Angelica's help. After a couple of minutes, camera in hand, Maria proceeded down the second flight of stairs with Professor Russo and Henry. All of the cataloging work was currently taking place above the landing, so the three of them had only their own lights to navigate by.

They made it to the bottom of the stairs without incident. Henry examined the remains as they went. *By the number of tools and lack of spearheads, these skeletons seem to be entirely workmen now.*

At the bottom, there were no more skeletons. The hallway was clear of bodies or scattered bone as it stretched ahead. Henry felt puzzled. Something seemed strange about the situation.

"Why are all of the dead on the stairs? Why are there none down here?" Maria asked.

Russo said, "It does seem odd. Why would people die on a stairway rather than a level hallway? Perhaps they were killed and then their bodies were carried to the stairs. I can't see the logic in it, but that might explain it."

Maria said, "I can explain it and I don't like it."

Henry frowned and turned to face Maria. "Why? Is there something bothering you about this too? I can't quite tell what is confusing me ..."

Maria's dark eyes glinted in the dim, reflected radiance from their electric torches. Her face was troubled, almost worried. She said, "The bodies are on the stairs because they were trying to get out when they were killed. They were trying to get away from something."

Henry felt a chill and looked down the tunnel to the cave-in. His stomach twisted into a knot.

Professor Russo said, "Hmm. Maria, you may have something there, but let's hold onto that thought. Shall we see what is down the hall here?" Henry and Maria both nodded, eyes bright with excitement and nervousness.

Another twelve meters away, the passage was partially blocked by several large stone boulders and rubble that appeared to have fallen from the ceiling. The three archaeologists picked their way carefully through and around the debris and found beyond them a large opening six meters tall and two and a half meters wide. They slowly walked to the doorway, held their torches out and looked through into another large chamber.

The room was triangular in shape. The doorway in which they stood was in the middle of one leg. The long, diagonal hypotenuse side was opposite them and approximately thirty meters in length. The ceiling was at least nine meters above the floor. The torches they held revealed many more skeletons in their flickering beams. All across the triangular area before them, dusty bones covered the floor.

On the diagonal wall to their left, there was a long section that looked like some kind of untarnished metal, similar to stainless steel in appearance. Another section of that wall was discolored and cracked but was decorated with pictures and tableaus. Some of the paintings depicted animals and one large picture showed a bull's head.

They walked into the room in complete silence, stepping between bones, fragments and entire skeletons. More decapitations were evident and they saw more tools but caught no signs of spears or spearheads. Henry shook his head in disbelief. *No weapons in sight; this is another killing floor with even more victims than the stairway.*

As they approached the wall that reflected back a metallic glow from their torches, Maria caught sight of something on it and approached it more quickly than the other two. She raised her torch and studied a portion of the wall with a rectangular inset. She shook her head in confusion and blinked her eyes heavily. She opened them wider and leaned nearer to look more closely. She finally spoke.

"*Architetto?* This makes no sense! Professor, what does this mean?" Her voice held some hint of fear, but mainly called out a sense of dismay, almost of despair.

Both Henry and Professor Russo leaned in to examine that portion of the metal wall. Henry tried to make sense of it, but couldn't find words to capture all of his confusion. *What am I seeing? This defies all logic!*

The professor spoke in utter confusion. "The English translation would be, 'Architect of the Abyss,' but it is written in Italian. How can anything down here be written in Italian?"

Maria immediately started talking very quickly in the same language. Henry caught snatches that he was sure had to be curses. She waved her hands and arms and sputtered in disbelief.

"How can this be? This *ancient tomb*," she sneered, "cannot be ancient if it has writing in modern Italian!"

Henry looked at her intently, "I don't follow either of you. It looks like English to me."

Maria turned and stared at him as if he had made a comment which was both absurd and insulting at the same time. "Of course it is Italian! You think I can't read my mother tongue?"

Henry pointed at the first word in the rectangular plaque. "What word is that?"

Maria and Professor Russo both spoke at the same time and said, "Architetto."

Henry said, "To me it looks like the English word, 'Architect.'"

CHAPTER 12 – CORRUPT

"Yet from that sin derive corruption, to bring forth more violent deeds"
— *John Milton, Paradise Lost*

Krastyo Balev lay in his bed in a gray hospital room with two other patients, one who was snoring and the other who was whimpering loudly and ostentatiously. A fourth bed in the room was unoccupied. Balev wanted to hug his broken arm close to his chest, to cradle it, but couldn't because he was anchored to supports that kept the shattered limb from moving. He winced at the memory; his arm had been horribly mangled and had required surgery to put it back together. They'd told him that the bone fracture had lanced through his flesh and had splintered all throughout his arm. *As if I hadn't known that already!* It had required extensive cleanup and stitching of the skin and they'd had to install metal pins inside the remaining arm bones to hold it together. They'd also put in metal pins that penetrated from the outside through the flesh and down into the bone to keep everything steady. He had come out of the anesthesia a short while ago, but the ache was only slightly dulled by the painkillers he'd received. He caught himself grinding his teeth in discomfort and forced himself to stop. He tried to turn his attention elsewhere. His conscious roommate at the other end of the room groaned very audibly in a nearly theatrical quality effort.

Balev snarled, "Shut up! Do you think yourself the only one in pain? Be quiet!"

The man paid no attention and moaned again, perhaps even louder than before.

Balev cursed the man under his breath and took in hand the nurse call button. *I won't put up with this. I'll get out of here or get him moved to another room. Besides, I want more painkillers or I won't be able to sleep at all.*

While he waited on the nurse he thought about the dig site. *Russo and his students probably think they can do whatever they want now that I am in the hospital. They think with me here, they'll go wherever they want, dig wherever they want and take whatever they want, but that dig is mine. I've got to do something about them. They can't get away with tricking me into opening that stone door.*

The nurse arrived. She was sturdy and blank-faced. She put on a skeptical expression as if it was a disguise she assumed through long practice. She said simply, "What?"

Balev frowned, pointed and said, "That man is disturbing my sleep with all of his moaning and groaning. I want to be moved to a private room. I can't get any rest in here with all his cowardly whimpering. And I need more painkiller."

She pursed her lips as if assured and certain that she had been correct in her initial assessment. "There are no private rooms in this hospital. You have to stay here." She turned immediately and was halfway out the door before Balev could react.

He said, "Wait! Then move him to another room. I won't be able to sleep at all with his noise."

At that instant, the other man called out. "The pain! I can't stand it! Help me, help me! Oh ..."

The nurse had already assumed a totally blank face once more, but at the other patient's groan, her expression cracked with a little smile. She looked like she was starting to enjoy this part of the exchange.

She spoke, "There are no other rooms for him. They're all full. He has to stay here too."

"Well, move him to another bed in a different room. Trade him for some quiet patient to put in here. I can't stand the man's constant pleading and begging and wailing."

The nurse's smile broadened. "Why would I do that? Why would I switch him to another room and disturb other patients when I can leave him here with you? You two deserve each other."

Balev sputtered, "I'll report you to the hospital management and to the doctor. You can't do this to me!"

The nurse's smile broadened even further into blatant malevolence. "That will be amusing. I'll make sure and tell them that a patient is upset and wants to file a complaint against the hospital and the nursing staff. Of course, the nurses that take care of you while you're here will also be thankful for your complaints. I'm sure it won't affect their care for you at all. Whenever your food is delivered I'm sure it won't be raw or contaminated in the least and will always be exactly what you requested. I'm sure that when you need pain medication, the nurses will make sure it will be strong enough and won't be too delayed. I'm sure that when you need to move your bowels, the nursing staff will be there to assist you and clean you up. Eventually."

She moved closer to the loudly moaning man and pulled his bed out of its position in the room. In a few moments she had rearranged the four beds and placed Krastyo Balev right next to the groaning man.

Balev's face was livid. "You can't do this to me! I'm with the department of antiquities! This is outrageous!"

She chuckled and said to him, "And just like this man," she indicated the groaning patient, "You'll be happy that you took the trouble to file a complaint." She smiled brightly and said, "I'll see if I can find any more painkiller for you. The hospital has been running low on it for some time." She laughed as she walked from the room.

Balev lay in misery. *I will have her job.* There was a knock on the door.

Balev shouted over the groaning from the other patient, "Who is it?"

Professor Russo entered, looked over the room and pulled the only chair over to Balev's bed. The injured man said suspiciously, "What do you want?"

Russo settled himself and took a folder of documents and photographs out of a briefcase. He said, "Krastyo, I need to tell you about what we've found at the tunnel you discovered."

Balev noted that the professor was attributing the new site's discovery to him. *He is trying to curry favor with me. He is a lying thief. He'll be trying to loot my artifacts before I can stop him.*

Russo continued, "I've brought photographs of the Grand Staircase and the Grand Hallway too." Russo placed some pictures on the small bedside table. Balev glanced at them suspiciously.

The professor continued, "I know you are incapacitated at the moment, but we've taken these pictures of everything just as we found it. I need to show you these things and let you know about the next room beyond the Grand Hallway."

Balev assumed a lofty expression and said, "You wouldn't have found any of this without me. You'd still be scraping at the surface graves above if it hadn't been for my inspiration and determination."

Russo raised an eyebrow, but continued on. "Krastyo, at the end of the Grand Hallway, we found a partial cave-in and beyond that an archway opening into a chamber. It had many more bones and skeletons on the floor. It also had a metal wall. We have no theories at present for how a metal wall came to be there at the site. Here is a photograph of the wall." He held up a photo of the wide expanse that took in the entire wall from edge to edge. Part of the wall appeared to be metal and the rest to be decorated plaster of some kind. Russo held up a picture that included a detailed shot of a smaller area on the wall.

"What is this?" Balev said as he took the picture in his uninjured hand.

Russo said, "It is a plaque on the metal wall. The wall there may contain a door because we have found a rectangular seam that would indicate a possible opening." Russo looked cagily at Krastyo Balev and said, "What do you make of the plaque? We wanted to get your opinion about it." Russo watched him carefully.

Balev had been squinting at the photo in irritation. "It says, 'Architect of the Pit', so I assume one of your vandalizing students wrote on the door in Bulgarian. They have very poor handwriting since I almost couldn't make it out. I've warned you about your students and their careless ways. Now one of them has defaced an ancient monument of some kind. I'll have your job for this, Russo!"

Professor Russo looked even more concerned. He took the photograph and rotated it until it was upside down and handed it back. Balev looked at it and squinted again, then gasped. "What trick is this? Even upside down it says, 'Architect of the Pit.' Is this some kind of optical illusion?"

"We don't know what it is yet, Krastyo, but I do know that it is not the doing of one of the students. I was there when it was discovered and I can tell you that it reads the same in every language we have tried. To those who grew up in Italy, they read it as saying 'Architect of the Abyss' in Italian but English-speaking students claim the plaque is written in English. Bulgarians claim it is written in Bulgarian and Greeks and Romanians claim it is written in those languages. Krastyo, we have found a sample of writing here that at the same time defies and includes all known languages. This plaque looks like it contains writing made from some kind of universal language that anyone can read in their own mother tongue! This plaque is probably the greatest archaeological find of all time. It is greater than the Rosetta Stone and greater than King Tut's tomb. This find will rewrite all of the history books. It is unbelievable."

Krastyo Balev looked at Russo like he was some kind of madman, but after a few moments of studying his face, realized the bigger man believed what he was saying. Balev's thoughts started to race. *He really believes this. This picture proves what he says and the fool has brought it to me. To me, the perfect one positioned to make a killing on the information. What an idiot.*

Balev said, "Who has seen these pictures?"

"You and I, Henry, Maria and three other students that we asked to see if they could identify the writing."

"Anyone from my department? Any of the security guards?"

"No," Russo said.

Balev said, "Good. Russo, I want you to investigate this further, taking all pictures and positioning information possible, but the new security guard must be present at all times until I can get out of here. I will call him to let him know he must shadow you at all times and be present whenever you or your students are in the dig site. Do not attempt to fool me in this, Russo. You and your team must also maintain confidentiality on this. The more people know, the more likely we'll suffer from looting by the unscrupulous, so we must have complete and total silence on this find. No one must speak of it."

"I understand," the professor said. He packed up his things and left. Balev had retained the photographs and flipped through them.

This is a magnificent find. I'll be able to make a fortune on this if I engage the right buyer. What was that wealthy collector's name? Oh yes, the Romanian businessman, Janos Parasca. He will certainly be interested in this treasure trove. He'll probably buy the whole lot for his collection, every bone, every spearhead, every medallion and especially that plaque.

But what should I do about the Professor and his students? They know about the site. Russo, Travers and Maria also know that I was out there in the middle of the night trying to get into the site before anyone else. I can't have that and can't leave them with that knowledge. I think an unfortunate accident is about to occur. Too bad the site was already prone to cave-ins. But then, they deserve to be buried close to the artifacts they love so much. Once I've taken my pick.

Balev started to smile at the thought but winced at the pain in his arm. He reached for the nurse's call button but thought better of it and drew back his hand. *Maybe I'll just live with the pain for now. The sooner I'm out of here, the better anyway.*

His roommate groaned loudly and piteously. Balev gritted his teeth and reached for the phone. *First, I'll call the security guard and get him to bring me something I can use to create and send an email to Janos Parasca. After that, my next steps will be getting out of here as soon as possible and back to the dig site. I've got work to do before Russo and his students start spreading rumors or removing objects.*

* * *

Rakslav Gachevska had found it: a small room with a computer that some of the crew had been visiting. *It must have an internet connected computer for the crew to use.* Rakslav needed to get into his email and send a message to certain people within PetroRomania to let them know what was going on. He needed to make sure that things were still under control, but more importantly, he needed to get hold of some key contact information. He had no loyalty to Parasca anymore, but he had built up too many contacts within and without of the shadier parts of Romanian society to chance not having them at his fingertips. One in particular was the head of the Dock Workers Union in Constanta. If the man had contacts in the Bulgarian Dock Workers Unions, Rakslav's job of getting on board the salvage ship might become a lot easier.

Rakslav stored his personal confidential data in an encrypted folder that he kept out on the Cloud in a personal account. If he could get on the Internet at this computer, he'd retrieve some of that information, write down a few phone numbers and check his PetroRomania email. By then, the *Lucian* would be closer to Varna and the beginning of the Varna salvage operation.

Rakslav went to the door, used his keycard like he'd seen the rest of the crew doing and heard the lock in the door click. Rakslav opened the door and walked in. He saw the computer that had been visible from the doorway and saw a second one that hadn't been visible from the door, but which he had suspected might be there from the size of the room. It had a crew member sitting at it with his back to Rakslav.

Rakslav sat down in front of the unoccupied computer and confirmed his suspicion that the ship's network was secured and would require a login ID and password. *Now I'm glad there's someone here and I won't have to wait until someone else shows up.*

Rakslav got up, took two steps over to the other man in the room and said in his native Bulgarian, "Excuse me. I'm new to the crew. How do you log on to the computer network and get to the Internet? I want to check my email."

The man grunted and turned around. He looked up at Rakslav and pointed at his name tag.

"Didn't they tell you anything? Your login ID is the same as your employee number on your badge. Your first password is probably 'password' or something like that. They should have given you the information before you left port. What department are you in?" The man looked at Rakslav's name tag again. "Hmm? Engineering. That's weird. You're new and you have the same name as someone that's already on the crew." The man looked at the picture on Rakslav's badge, shook his head in confusion and looked up at Rakslav's face. "Hey, what is going on…?"

The man's question was interrupted by a hand at his throat. Rakslav calmly squeezed. *This time, I have to be more careful.*

"I'm going to need your computer for a while. You're going to sleep." Rakslav jerked the man to his feet, moved him a bit to the right and slammed the back of the man's head into the wall. The fellow went limp and slumped to the floor. Rakslav checked for his pulse and nodded in satisfaction, took the man's belt and tied his arms behind his back with it and stuffed a wad of paper into the man's mouth. Rakslav went to the door leading to the outside and jammed a chair into it so it wouldn't open.

Rakslav sat down at the other man's computer and within moments had an Internet browser open. Rakslav downloaded some contact data from his cloud account and after figuring out the printer in the room, printed off a couple of pages. He logged into the PetroRomania internet email portal and scanned through the messages, not bothering with anything trivial. He printed off a couple of pages of things he'd want to think about. He was about to start composing a message for his man Alex Lacusta when he saw another email with a strange entry in the subject line. Rakslav opened that message and saw that the email hadn't been directed to him, but to Chairman Parasca. As head of corporate security, Rakslav had set up an email agent to copy him on all external emails sent to the Chairman. The email said:

To: Janos Parasca, Chairman PetroRomania
From: Krastyo Balev, Department of Antiquities, Bulgarian National Museum
Subject: Priceless discovery found at Varna. May be written in universal language. Contact me.

Chairman Parasca, I thank you for your patronage in the past. Perhaps you do not remember me, but I have acquired exquisite objects for your collection in the past and thought you would want to know about the fabulous discoveries that have just been made within the past day at the Varna Necropolis archaeological site.

While excavating a grave, my team has uncovered a large, deep chamber with many skeletons, articles of gold jewelry, weapons and tools. These are all newly discovered and may be of interest to you, but the amazing prize of which I write is entirely unique and to my knowledge has never been found at any other location throughout the world.

The item I am referring to appears to be a large metal door that has a plaque with lettering on it that reads "Architect of the Abyss" in several languages. This would be unusual enough even if the item was just another Rosetta Stone, with a single phrase written in multiple languages, but it is not. The plaque is only written in one language, but is readable in their mother tongue by anyone that looks at it. In some unknown way, the lettering on the plaque appears to each reader as if it were written in their own native language. The plaque seems to be written in a universal language that is readable by all.

Such a find, as you know, would be of incalculable commercial value, without even considering its archaeological value. I am sure however, that only a collector of your renown would truly understand the priceless nature of this object. It and the other items will be of particular interest to you I am sure, and that is why I have contacted you. Please respond at your earliest convenience to let me know should you decide you would like to proceed with acquiring any or all of these recently discovered items.

I have not sent word of these valuable artifacts to any other collector because I knew that you would want first choice. I am proud to extend this privilege to you and would be glad to provide you with photographs. If your interest is as great as I think it will be, I know you will want to conduct a site visit for you and your people to determine the best ways to dismantle and transport such items.

Please let me know as soon as possible how you would like to proceed with this acquisition.

Yours humbly,

Krastyo Balev, Department of Antiquities, Bulgarian National Museum

* * *

Rakslav Gachevska reread the email and thought. *This fellow is trying to hawk a contraband antiquity to Janos Parasca. It's from a newly discovered crypt and has a plaque with a phrase written in a universal language. That sounds exactly like the marker that was on the sarcophagus of Lord Moloch that read, 'Imprisoned Until Repentant'. Everyone could read that in their own language as well. This one says 'Architect of the Abyss' and it's on a giant metal door. I wonder if the metal door is made of that same crystal steel from which the sarcophagus was constructed? If that is the case, my next guess is that someone like the Lord Moloch with the title, 'Architect of the Abyss' is inside it. Very intriguing. This ship is bound for Varna and Varna is where this Necropolis and this discovery are located. Perhaps I can rescue Lord Moloch from his captivity and also unite him with this 'Architect' in Varna. So many possibilities. First, I'll send a response.*

To: Krastyo Balev, Department of Antiquities, Bulgarian National Museum

From: Rakslav Gachevska, Director of Corporate Security, PetroRomania

Subject: re: Priceless discovery found at Varna. May be written in universal language. Contact me.

As Director of Corporate Security, I want to thank you for your offer of assistance with the archaeological find you mentioned in your letter. Chairman Parasca receives many inquiries and emails of all kinds which are routinely filtered through me and my department.

This message is to inform you that Chairman Parasca will very likely be interested in the new find you describe. You should therefore immediately restrict all access to the site, preserve it in pristine condition and do not allow any information concerning this find to leave your facility.

Chairman Parasca, as a collector of ancient artifacts of all types, will expect your utmost discretion in this matter. You will be contacted in the near future concerning a site visit to verify the nature of the artifacts you describe.

Sincerely,

Rakslav Gachevska, Director of Corporate Security

cc: Janos Parasca, Chairman PetroRomania

* * *

Rakslav finished up with the computer and considered his best options on body disposal. They would be too close to shore soon to toss someone else overboard. He frowned at the senseless form. *Perhaps you can just stay hidden a while longer.* Rakslav removed several cords and cables from the other computer and tied the still unconscious man more securely and improvised a better gag. He studied the door mechanism and opened it to the outside. When he was certain no one else was around, Rakslav stepped outside, twisted and broke the card reader on both sides of the door, then slammed it shut. The door would not be easily opened. *That will keep him locked up for quite a while.*

CHAPTER 13 – FIRE AND STEEL

"Or arm...with stubborn patience as with triple steel"
— John Milton, Paradise Lost

Janos Parasca scowled at his hand where a drop of blood welled up from a cut. He set the straight razor aside and turned his full attention to the small wound. He concentrated on the slice in the skin, willing it to close, willing it to heal over. Nothing happened except that the blood continued flowing. It welled up into a small pool as he strained his mind at it. *Nothing! What am I doing wrong?* He relented and spat out a disgusted oath, sopped up the blood, cleaned the wound and bandaged it. He glared at the sword that lay on the table next to him. *What am I missing? I feel the power in me when I am near that thing. I feel it wanting to race from me, but I can't seem to direct it to do anything at all.* He slammed his wounded hand down on the table and cursed. *I will get this right. I will learn how to do it. If Mircea can learn it, so can I. But for now, I will put this aside. I need to see how my people are doing on their assignments.*

Parasca reached for his cell phone and before he could dial a number on it, the phone rang with another call coming through. He looked at the face of the phone to see who was calling and frowned. *He'd better not be calling to waste my time. I've just about had enough of his foolishness.*

He started the call and said, "Janos Parasca here. What do you want, Ozera? Make it quick."

Dr. Ozera said, "Mr. Chairman, we've had a significant development with the artifact you asked us to analyze for commercial potential. It is a very significant development."

Parasca did not feel impressed and said, "What does significant mean to you, Dr. Caba Ozera? Significant to me would be a profit of a half-billion Euros. If you aren't talking about numbers at least that large, then go back to your computers and lab equipment."

94

Ozera seemed undeterred and said, "Mr. Chairman. I am talking about something that is <u>extremely</u> significant. The crystalline steel dagger you asked my team to analyze is amazing. The substance it is made of is superconductive!" Ozera spoke triumphantly and waited for a response.

Parasca said simply, "So?" *What is this bookworm prattling about now?*

Dr. Ozera's voice took on an impatient tone. He said, "Mr. Chairman, superconducting materials are extremely valuable. The metal of the dagger is superconductive at high temperatures and will cause a revolution in the power industry!"

Parasca said, "What are you talking about? What good does this do me? I run an oil and gas company, not a power company. What use is superconductivity to me? Make some sense, man." *I really need to start looking for a replacement for this jackass.*

Ozera said, "Chairman Parasca, let me start again. My enthusiasm is getting the better of me. First, the commercial possibilities: you mentioned a profit threshold of a half-billion Euros as required to gain your interest. If we can make this crystalline steel in commercial quantities, the profit from it could be a thousand times that. The profit potential is nearly astronomical."

For the first time in recent memory, Parasca felt interested in something Dr. Ozera had to say. "How so? How does this metal being a superconductor make profits like that possible?" *Maybe I won't have to fire him yet if this is as good as he says.*

Ozera sounded relieved. He said, "A superconductor can carry massive amounts of electricity without any heat and without any loss. Much of the electricity generated around the world today is wasted simply because it has to travel in copper wires. A significant portion of the electricity is lost through resistance in the copper and becomes waste heat. A superconductor on the other hand, has zero resistance. Not just low resistance, but zero. That means that if we are able to manufacture crystal steel wiring for the world's power generation needs, we could save a large portion of the world's electricity from being wasted. Economical superconductive wire and cable would change the face of the earth. It could be worth billions, even trillions of Euros."

Parasca was intrigued but still skeptical. "As I said, PetroRomania is not a power company. I run an oil and gas company. What good is this to me?"

"Think of it this way, it would allow us to diversify. We could license this technology to large international corporations like General Electric and receive huge amounts of royalty fees."

Parasca felt deflated. "So that's all it is good for? Wires for electricity?"

"That is just the beginning. This crystalline steel is not only superconductive; it is that way at normal temperatures. This metal isn't like previous superconductors which only work under extremely expensive hyper-cold conditions. This steel doesn't require liquid helium, liquid nitrogen or even water for cooling. My team has run thousands of amps through it at no resistance at all at room temperature. The metal is not even warm afterward. Mr. Chairman, this is world-changing! This substance is going to start an entirely new industrial revolution."

Parasca grew impatient. "My question again is: 'What else is it good for besides wires?'"

"With this metal, companies could make super powerful magnets that would change many industries. MRI machines could be miniaturized and made portable and cheap. Batteries could be manufactured that would make electric cars practical for the first time. Superconducting batteries could power an electric car for thousands of kilometers, not the dozens of which they are now capable."

He took a breath and continued, "Right now, power cannot be stored efficiently so any that is not used immediately goes to waste. Superconductivity like this makes it possible to store power for entire cities. No more blackouts. Renewable power like solar and wind could become much more economical because these batteries could be used to store the power they generate for use later. The list just goes on and on."

"My scientists are calling this the world's first 'pyrophilic' superconductor. By that, they mean that heat does not faze it and it is still superconductive at high temperatures. And since the metal is superconductive at room temperature, it doesn't need to be chilled to nearly absolute zero. Because of this, there is no expense for cooling and the material doesn't become brittle like other superconductors that have to be cooled in liquid helium. Because the metal isn't brittle, it can be used in situations where magnetic stresses cause problems: we'll be able to make massively powerful motors that will be nearly perfectly efficient; we'll be able to make vehicles that use magnetic levitation. This kind of superconductivity and the super magnets it makes possible might make it easier to produce viable nuclear fusion generators. It's just astounding the many uses to which a metal like this could be put. I have only scratched the surface. We could use it for power generation, power storage, saving energy, and making technologies more practical and cheaper. The mind boggles."

Parasca said, "Hmm. This is beginning to sound interesting. So you believe that it has many possible commercial uses. I had thought that its structural strength would be the main selling point, but it appears to have other possibilities as well. What progress have you made in manufacturing it?"

Ozera said, "We think we have an approach now that could work. We discovered the superconductivity properties when we were running crystalline analyses and looking at test results. The microscopic structure of this material is very unique. It is made from a dense matrix of carbon graphene nanotubes filled with iron atoms chained edge to edge. Because of that analysis, we think the best way to duplicate this structure is to try to grow it like crystals are grown."

Parasca said, "You lost me. Grow it like what?"

Ozera said, "Like a crystal. The metal of the crystalline steel dagger that you have us testing is in a crystal structure. Crystals are a type of matter that grows into its shape based on its atomic properties. We have examined the details of this material and have decided to develop a way to expose it to a superheated gaseous form of carbon and iron. We hope that the atoms of iron and carbon in the hot gas will latch onto the crystal structure of the dagger and propagate it into larger and larger crystals."

Parasca's voice grew icy cold. "I didn't understand much of what you just said, but I think I heard you say you want to use the dagger and put it into a gas of superheated carbon and iron. If that is what you said, I want to tell you this: if you harm that dagger, I will personally kill you. I will cut your throat with my own hands. Do you understand me?"

Ozera seemed to pick up on the other man's tone of voice and said, "No, no, Chairman Parasca. We will not harm or scar it in any way. We merely want to try to grow an invisibly small crystal at the very tip of the point of the dagger. If you give your permission, we will expose only the tiniest portion of the tip of the dagger to the hot gas mixture. If we can grow one microscopic crystal on the point of the dagger, we can remove it using a laser and then grow more crystals from that seed we harvested. We want to grow a seed crystal and then use that for further work. If we can grow that crystal, the rest of our work will be possible without touching the dagger again."

Parasca asked, "You want to expose the point of the dagger to hot gas so you can grow a seed crystal. After that you would cut off the new crystal with a laser. None of this will harm my dagger. Is that what you are saying?"

"Yes, Mr. Chairman."

"You do understand that the dagger is almost eight thousand years old and is some of the only evidence of an ancient and rich civilization? You also understand that this artifact is irreplaceable and that the item is the one and only of its kind in the entire world? With that in mind, are you still asking permission to perform this procedure?"

Dr. Ozera paused as if considering his options, then answered, "Yes, Mr. Chairman. The procedure should be safe for the artifact. Once we finish, we should have in hand a seed crystal from which we can grow unlimited crystal steel in the future. After that, the dagger can go back to your collection, no worse from having been used."

Parasca said, "And you are willing to bet your career on this? I won't even remind you of my threat to kill you if you botch this and harm my artifact."

"Yes. I believe this is the best approach. I will stand behind the method I've described to you. We need that seed crystal. Once we have it, we can proceed with greater speed. We'll be able to try various methods to accelerate the manufacturing process and try to make different versions of the steel. We'll be able to try making superconductive wire, try to grow the crystal into different shapes and test for tensile strength in different configurations. We'll be set up to test for many further applications of the metal, but first we need to grow a seed crystal from the dagger. That is the key."

Parasca said, "Be quiet for a minute and let me think." Ozera stopped talking.

If I give the go ahead for his team to try this and they fail, at worst, the dagger could be destroyed. It would be the loss of an irreplaceable artifact, but it wouldn't be a disaster since I still would have this sword made from the same metal.

I also should be able to salvage that sarcophagus and would have tons of the metal there, though I never want that tampered with. I don't ever want to take a chance on that demon Moloch being released. He would immediately read my mind and find out I could have opened the latches on his sarcophagus with the mini-sub and released him at the bottom of the Black Sea, but didn't. I am certain that even the pressures at three hundred meters under water would not kill that creature. It's obvious to me now that nothing can kill it. I don't want to think about what he would do to me once he found out I could have let him out and didn't. He would probably kill me eventually, but there is no guarantee of that. Maybe he would torture me and then heal me over and over again just for the pleasure of keeping me alive to continue torturing endlessly. Parasca shuddered.

Parasca spoke again, "Alright. Go ahead and try this method. I want to be notified as soon as you are about to make the attempt to grow the seed crystal. Call me back then and not before." He hung up on Ozera and turned back to the sword.

Parasca made another call and received news that the salvage operation would be starting within the next two days. *Not as soon as I would have liked, but still faster than I expected.* After finishing that call he thought again of the healing technique he was trying to decipher.

I've got to learn how to heal using the way Moloch forced Mircea to learn. I remember he told her to concentrate on letting the body heal itself. He said the body knows how to but needed the influx of power to speed the healing process. Hmmm. Influx of power ... maybe that is like the way I used to feel energized when I would kill people. Or perhaps it is like the burst of power I felt when Moloch killed his victims on the Fortuna. Maybe that is what the flow of energy feels like. I somehow need to let the power from this sword flow through me like that.

Parasca looked out the large windows of his island home and scanned the Aegean Sea. His house sat on a cliff fifty meters above the sea. *What to do? How do I draw power from this sword in the same way I draw it from someone that is dying?* He made a decision, picked up a small silver bell and rang it. Within seconds there was a knock on the door to his office.

He said, "Enter." The door opened and a male servant came in a few steps, bowed and waited.

Parasca continued, "Go find Mr. Karras and tell him I want to speak with him. That is all." The servant bowed and left, closing the door behind. Parasca arranged his thoughts and decided he wanted to appear cold and in command to his head of household security. *Always take on whatever demeanor and appearance it takes to make people do what you want. That is the easiest way to get these stupid fools to do as I desire. It is like donning a costume. The actor plays a part, but the audience never knows whether they are seeing the actor or the role he plays. Put on a persona: that is the way to manipulate people into doing what you want. And people are so easily manipulated.*

A few minutes went by as Parasca studied the ocean through the broad picture windows. Finally, he heard a knock at the door. "Enter." He said again.

Damon Karras came into the room, closed the door, bowed and waited.

Parasca walked closer to him and spoke forcefully. "I need you to find another 'guest' for me."

Karras stared straight ahead, "The same kind of person as before? You want someone from the mainland that will not be missed?"

"That is correct. This time, I'd like it to be a woman. Can you do that?"

Karras hazarded a look at Janos Parasca and then hastily looked away. "The woman ... should she be of a certain age or ..." he stuttered and resumed, "... or appearance?"

"She should be an attractive adult woman, clean and healthy." Parasca smiled. "I am feeling energetic again. Do you take my meaning?"

Karras swallowed and said, "Yes, sir."

"She should be unattached. Look among the tourists on the mainland for someone travelling alone who seems adventurous. Wear your uniform to appear like an official. Ask to see her passport then tell her that she is on your list of people for whom there is a message from her embassy. Hold onto her passport but offer to take her to the embassy. Once you get her in your car, offer her bottled water that has already been laced with that drug you always use. When she is unconscious, bring her here. If she will not cooperate, find another suitable woman. Do not return without a woman that meets my criteria: attractive, clean and healthy. Do you understand?"

"Yes, sir."

"Go then." Karras turned and left the room.

Always before when I had him bring me a 'guest', I was not particular, as long as the guest was alive when they got here. Now he is uncertain about my intentions and was surprised that I wanted him to bring me a woman. Let him wonder about me. He sees that I look younger than I did. Let him speculate. His hands are so dirty with the many he has procured for me through the years that he cannot reveal me without revealing himself.

Parasca looked at the sword on the table. *I will unlock the key to using this power because I must learn how to use what is stored in this sword. This time, with the woman he brings me, I will use her to try to understand the flow of energy from her as she expires. I will concentrate on learning how the energy acts and how I might manipulate it. Perhaps if I am fortunate, other passions will reawaken in me as well.*

Parasca picked up the straight razor again and positioned his arm for a cut. *In the meantime, until she arrives, I will continue trying my own methods of mastering the healing skill.* He slid the blade along his arm and began slicing.

CHAPTER 14 – OFFER OF REUNION

"Abide united, as one individual soul, forever happy"
— John Milton, Paradise Lost

Mercy and Jack left the bus at the border crossing at Vama Veche. They had transferred to a smaller minibus for the final leg to the border and found themselves in a crowd of tourists going from Bulgaria to Romania. Mercy spoke to a Romanian woman in the customs line with them and asked about the size of the crowd.

The woman said, "It's the music festivals this time of year on the beach in Vama Veche. I'm going to hear some of the bands myself. Lots of people come in from both Bulgaria and Romania to hear the music."

The crowd worked in their favor. The harried guards at the checkpoint waved most of the mob of people through, only superficially looking at papers. When they saw Mercy and Jack's American passports, they were waved through without a second glance. Mercy felt relieved. *That was easier than I expected.*

After they made it into Vama Veche, they went to another bus station, caught an outbound to Constanta and settled in for the short trip. It was a fairly direct drive to Constanta, but the minibus would make several stops on the way and so would take more than an hour. Jack looked at the Romanian newspaper that he'd picked up in Vama Veche.

Jack said, "Look at this." He pointed at the paper. "It's an article about the *Fortuna*. The headline says, 'Lost at Sea'. They claim to have no idea what caused it to sink and it says, 'PetroRomania officials had no comments to make about the loss of the ship'. Uh oh. The article says a salvage operation may be gearing up to 'recover unnamed valuable items from the wreck site'. I don't like the sound of that."

Mercy looked over at the paper in alarm. She said, "Jack, what if they bring up Moloch's sarcophagus? That would be a disaster!"

"My thoughts exactly. If he gets out again and onto dry land, Heaven help us all. I've been thinking about all that happened and I am certain that one of the only reasons he didn't do worse damage is that he was trapped on that ship. If he gets to the mainland, he could kill people right and left and cause untold chaos. No one would understand the threat because they wouldn't believe what they were seeing at first. If he gets his bearings and digs in, things could go very badly for a lot of people." He shook his head at the terrible prospect. "You said he can be injured, but can't be killed, right?"

"I know, it sounds crazy. I don't know how much of our fight you could see from the crane, but the damage he took was unbelievable. The only reason I could stand up to him at all was I had the shield which absorbed a lot of damage and I also had all of the life energy that Hayden gave up for me." She pressed her lips together, fighting back grief. "After he cut through that steel pipe I was using to try to kneecap him, I rammed it all the way through him. It knocked him back for a few moments, but he was right back up. I stabbed him with that stone knife and opened his side up like a gutted fish. That didn't stop him either."

She said, "He said he can't be killed. He said it is part of the curse he bears being trapped in a physical body on earth. He suffers, but does not die. If he escapes again, he'll be less disoriented about what is going on and harder to deal with. There is no way he would be caught in that sarcophagus again. We have to stop them from opening it up."

He asked, "Do you think Parasca is behind the salvage operation?"

Mercy said, "Who else could it be? He was that monster's disciple on the *Fortuna*. He and his bodyguard Rakslav were acting like that thing's priests and bringing it victims for sacrifice. I saw Moloch eating a charred human thigh! I can't believe how evil that thing is and how monstrous Parasca and Rakslav were for serving it."

She continued, "That salvage operation must be Parasca's doing. I can't imagine there were many other survivors. I don't see how he escaped at all, actually. The last I saw of him was during that fight with Moloch, but I lost track of him. I guess he ran when he realized the ship was going down."

Jack said, "We need to decide what, if anything, we can do about the salvage operation. Should we warn the authorities? Would they believe us? What would we even say? 'Hello, Government of Romania, I need to report a demon trapped in a sarcophagus.' That kind of warning would not get us very far. It might even get us locked up."

He said, "And, we also need to think about something else. Have you decided what you're going to say to Dmitri Slokov about his offer? We'll be at the train station in Constanta in a couple of hours. You've got between now and when we arrive to decide what we should do. In Constanta, we can either rent a car or take the train to Bucharest or wherever you want to go, but we need to have a plan by then."

Mercy shook her head. "I feel torn up about this, Jack. I've got to get my medicine in Bucharest in case the voices start coming back. They've only been gone for a couple of days and that dream I had about my father's death reminded me how horrible the voices were. In the dream, they were back in full force. I know it was only a dream, but sometimes I'm aware of just how thin a barrier there is between those voices and me. I know that if my mental barrier fails for even a moment, they'd be back in my head. Jack," She grabbed his arm tightly, "I can't stand the thought of them coming back."

"I know, but think: perhaps that barrier you have is not so fragile as you fear. It doesn't require your constant concentration, for example. It stays up while you've slept, hasn't it?"

She seemed surprised at the question and reacted almost hopefully. "Yes, it has, now that you ask."

He put a hand on her shoulder and winced at what he felt. "Here," he said gently, "Turn to the side and let me rub those shoulders. You're as tight as a drum." She smiled slightly but turned her back to him and let him massage her shoulder muscles. She was very tense and he had to work hard to get some of the knots out. She gradually relaxed and released some of the tension holding her. His hands gripped her shoulders tightly but felt very good to her.

At last, she felt more relaxed and looked over her shoulder at him. She said, "That was really nice. You're hired. When can I have my next appointment?"

"I aim to please, ma'am," he said with a smile. "I think I can work you into my schedule very easily."

"Good." She sighed and leaned back into him. He held her close.

At last she said, "Jack, if my grandmother Sonia is still alive, I want to see her. She would be in her eighties at this point and may not have much time left. She took care of me during one of the hardest times in my life. Parasca's Securitate took me from my adoptive mother in Bucharest and just dropped me on Sonia. She took it in stride and actually welcomed me. She said she was overjoyed to know she had her granddaughter back again that she had thought was lost forever. She taught me the Romanian language and got me through my first years at Polytechnic in Timisoara where she taught chemistry. I owe her a lot."

Jack said, "I see that, but don't you think this is just some kind of trick by Slokov? Why should he know about Sonia and even if he does, why should he want to help you meet with her?"

She said, "Realistically, I do think it's probably a trick of some kind. On the other hand, I don't know what Slokov's game is, but I know he is rabidly opposed to Janos Parasca for some reason. Maybe he just wants to use me as some kind of pawn in his chess game with Parasca, but somehow I think that isn't it. Do you remember on the *Fortuna* when those mercenaries caught us in the geology lab and wanted me to come with them?"

"Yes. I remember you went into your 'Wonder Woman' mode and took them all down before Hayden and I could even blink." Jack said. There was a distinct tone of awe and admiration in his voice.

She snuggled into him and smiled. "Wonder Woman? Is that what you think of me? That's nice." She touched one of his hands that still rested on her shoulder. She said, "Anyway, those men had orders to bring me back to their ship 'as an honored guest'; I think that was the wording they used. They had a laminated picture of me that they used to identify me. It was creepy, but they did say, 'honored guest'. Why would Dmitri send mercenaries to retrieve me in that way? If he just wanted me as a pawn against Parasca, it doesn't make any sense to do it that way, and if he'd wanted me out of the way, a man like Dmitri would have just had me killed, not brought to him as an 'honored guest.'"

Jack said, "I remember that incident. It did seem strange. Maybe there's more going on between Slokov and Parasca than just competition for market share in shady business dealings. It sounds like they might have a long history of being at each other's throats."

Mercy paused to collect her thoughts and widened her eyes in sudden understanding. She put both of her hands before her as if holding a globe between them and said, "Listen to me for a minute while I puzzle through this. Stop me if I miss something."

He said, "Okay."

She spoke in a low, clear voice. "We know that Parasca was in the Romanian secret police before the fall of the communist government in 1989. I was interrogated by him myself prior to that when I was in Bucharest and he had separated me from my adoptive mother. Parasca was also my biological father. Tresa Rodica, my biological mother, was Parasca's mistress back before I was born."

Her emotions were still held in check vocally, but Jack could tell it was getting hard for her by the way she moved one hand back to her shoulder and took his hand that was still resting there. She squeezed it hard and continued, "According to what Parasca let slip to me back on the *Fortuna*, he had pressured Tresa to have multiple abortions. In those days, abortions and contraceptives were illegal in Romania because the communist government wanted as many babies born as possible, probably to keep filling the ranks of the workers. Abortions had to be obtained on the black market. The last time she went to a back alley abortionist, when she was pregnant with me, the police burst in on the illegal abortion doctor before he could carry out the procedure. The doctor was tried and convicted. She was arrested and held in prison where I was later born."

"Apparently, Parasca knew all about this and just let it happen because he wanted my mother Tresa, to 'learn a lesson.' She must not have wanted to return to Parasca, because she killed herself in jail." Her voice clouded and turned husky. She whispered, "Tresa Rodica committed suicide." She paused to get her feelings under control.

After a few seconds, she swallowed deliberately and said, "Of course, I didn't know most of this while I was with my grandmother, Sonia. And, I didn't find out until a few days ago that Janos Parasca was my biological father. But, I did know at the time from what Sonia said about my mother Tresa that she had been going through a rebellious streak for several years. Grandmother once said to me, she didn't understand why Sonia took up with those types of men. She once said, 'one of them wasn't too bad, but that last one was a nightmare.'"

Mercy said, "That we know. Now I'm going to speculate. What if Parasca and Dmitri knew each other all the way back to prior to my birth? We know Parasca was involved with my mother. What if Dmitri was the one Sonia was referring to when she said about the men Tresa had been seeing that, 'one of them wasn't too bad?' In other words, what if Janos Parasca and Dmitri Slokov were rivals for my mother, Tresa Rodica?"

Jack said, "That might explain the bad blood that Dmitri Slokov carries for Parasca. It didn't make sense that the man would go to such bloody lengths just for a business rival. There had to be more to it than just being competitors. The situation between the two of them looks like a serious revenge scenario with Dmitri Slokov being Captain Ahab and Janos Parasca being the White Whale, Moby Dick. Slokov seems to be totally, unreasonably motivated by revenge and a desire to destroy Parasca." Jack paused and remembered something. "You know, the *Fortuna* was tied up in legal proceedings for quite a while before PetroRomania finally got hold of it. I will hazard a guess that Slokov was behind that, too."

Mercy said, "It also might explain why he holds me in high regard in spite of never having met me. It would explain why he had his mercenaries looking for me to get me safely from the ship. He wants to protect me because I am Tresa's daughter. If he was planning on sinking the *Fortuna* all along, he didn't want Tresa's daughter hurt, so he had his mercenaries looking for me."

Jack said, "So where does that leave us?"

"If these guesses are right, it means that Slokov might really know where my Grandmother Sonia is. If Slokov is still obsessed about what happened between him and Parasca over my mother, Tresa, he could have kept track of Sonia. It could also mean that he isn't trying to use me against Parasca, but is trying to contact me because I am Tresa's daughter."

Jack said, "I see that, and it all sounds plausible, but what if we're wrong about why he is a rival of Parasca's? What if he knows that Parasca is your father and is just assuming it would hurt Parasca for you to be captured by his enemy? What if Dmitri is trying to lure you in with a story about Sonia and just wants to hold you hostage, thinking it would be a poke in the eye for Parasca?"

She said, "No, it doesn't make sense. For someone as ruthless as Slokov, if he was trying to do what you say, he would just kill me and drop my corpse in Parasca's lap."

He said, "Well, maybe that is exactly what he plans to do. Maybe he sent those mercenaries to capture you for that very purpose."

She said, "Again, it would be overkill for someone just trying to distress Parasca. There is more to this bad blood between the two of them than we know yet. My gut tells me that on this message about Sonia, he is being genuine."

Jack said, "But is it safe to risk everything on a gut feeling like this? Didn't you tell me about this Counselor figure that all your life you thought was just another voice in your head, but just happened to be the one that wasn't evil? Not necessarily good, just not evil, and of which you could ask questions? You said that you could ask it questions but it would knock you out for twenty four hours. Before we make some big momentous decision, why don't you ask it a question?"

"I don't think it would put me under for a day anymore. The last two times I heard from the Counselor, it didn't knock me out. Maybe it had something to do with all of the energy I was getting from the deaths on the *Fortuna* and soaking up power from that sword and shield. But if contacting the Counselor did make me pass out, I can't chance that happening on a bus! How would you explain carrying an unconscious woman off of the bus?"

Jack said, "So, wait until we get on the train from Constanta to Bucharest. Or if we decide to rent a car instead, wait until then to ask the Counselor."

Mercy said, "Jack, I almost feel reluctant to ask the Counselor for anything anymore."

He said, "Why?"

She seemed puzzled. "I don't exactly know, but I just do."

He said, "It can't hurt to ask a question, can it?"

She looked at the glowing blue thread trailing away from her hand. It was irrefutable evidence to her of the connection between her and the Creator's power, though only she could see it. She said, "I guess not. I have this line of energy connecting me to that throne room. And I have a strong feeling that it will be enough to do what I need to do and certainly enough to keep me from lapsing into unconsciousness."

"Good. We're almost to Constanta now. When do you want to try contacting the Counselor?"

"Let's catch a train to Bucharest. That leg of our trip will take around seven or eight hours to get us there. If I'm knocked out, just stay on the train until I wake up, though I don't think there's a real danger of being out too long because I'm stronger than I was, but just in case… if I'm still out and they try to run us off the train, just say I'm drunk and carry me off."

He smiled. "Alright, but I don't think I've ever seen you drunk. I'll bet you're mean when you're blasted."

Her eyes flared with mock indignation, but she grabbed him and pulled him close for a passionate kiss. After a minute, another passenger gave a low wolf whistle. Mercy let go of Jack and looked over at the man that had whistled. He was carefully staring ahead and avoiding her gaze. She chuckled and she and Jack settled in for the final few kilometers to Constanta. The minibus dropped them right in front of the main train station and they quickly bought tickets for the next train to Bucharest. Jack purchased first class tickets that entitled them to a separate compartment so Mercy would have a place to rest undisturbed if she fell unconscious while attempting to contact the Counselor.

Once they were on the train from Constanta to Bucharest and the train had departed the station, Jack settled in to keep watch over Mercy.

Mercy went through her now familiar process of mental relaxation. She visualized descending a long stairway, fell deeper into a trance state at each step downward and finally entered into a completely separate consciousness.

* * *

Rakslav loomed over the desk of the mousy man in the shabby office at the Port of Varna. The burly head of the local dock workers union stood beside Rakslav. The union man clenched a ham-sized fist and pointed one sausage shaped finger into the face of the Port of Varna official.

The burly said, "You <u>will</u> put my union safety officer on board the *Vlad!* Some of my men will be working on her and they tell me she is on the way to that wreck, the *Fortuna*. That ship was used for petroleum exploration. There might be oil or gas in the water at the site and that could be a great danger to my men. I don't trust the safety people already on that ship. They will only be looking out for the ship's owners and they won't care about my men. You either put my man here on the *Vlad*, or the dock worker union will walk off the job. Every ship in port will be stuck, unable to load or unload. The port will have to be shut down. Is that what you want?"

The port official looked pained. His voice had the whining quality of a child being assigned extra homework. "It's not the proper procedure. We can't just force someone onboard a ship without all the right forms and approvals."

The union man said, "There's no time for that. I say he goes on the *Vlad*. If you don't give him the papers to do so, I shut down the port. It's that simple."

Rakslav looked into the eyes of the frightened official and said, "Lives are at stake here. I need to be there in order to ensure things are done properly. You wouldn't want to stand in the way of safety, would you?" Raklsav took an envelope out of his pocket and slid it across the desk. The man looked massively relieved and moved the envelope quickly out of sight.

The little man said, "Now that you put it like that, I understand perfectly. Come back in thirty minutes and everything will be ready."

The union man said, "Make sure it is. I can have my men on strike in five minutes."

He and Rakslav walked out of the office and into the open air of the port. The sounds and smells of large machines were everywhere. Rakslav put a hand on the other man's shoulder.

He said, "My friend, you are a genius. I owe you."

"It is nothing. When we were still on the streets, there were many times that you watched my back and kept me alive. Now, I return a little bit of the favor."

Rakslav said, "You are sure I can't give you something for your trouble?"

The man motioned to a nearby food truck. "You can buy me some lunch over there. There is time to grab a bite while we wait for that idiot to stamp your authorization to board the *Vlad* as Union Safety Officer. You like that new title that I just made up?"

"I like it. Let's eat. Then I need to get those papers and get on the *Vlad*. That is one ship I cannot afford to miss."

CHAPTER 15 – BENEATH THE SURFACE

"A bright sea flowed of jasper, or of liquid pearl"
— John Milton, Paradise Lost

Mercy saw a door at the base of the stairs. She turned back to look behind and realized she was in the familiar bedroom of her childhood. She saw again the pictures on the walls, the pennant showing her high school's mascot and her desk with stacked school books. She wondered at the sight, but somehow knew she was not dreaming. *I'm conscious, but in a different state. This room is real, with all of the right colors and textures as if brought back to life by my memories of it.*

She heard a knock and turned back to the door.

A familiar voice came through the door and said, "Mercy, are you there?"

Her heart leapt and she opened the door. Her father stood in the hallway, a peaceful, broad smile on his face. Mercy fell on him with a hug.

Words rushed from her and she said, "Daddy, I am so, so sorry about everything. I'm sorry I was selfish and cruel and spiteful and ..."

He patted her head and just listened as she talked. After a time, she ran out of words and he kept holding her until she finally felt calm once more.

At last she said, "Are you real? If I let go of you, will I awaken and realize this was all a dream?"

He said, "Sweetheart, sometimes what we experience is a dream and also at the same time, real. Sometimes, dreams are the only way we can experience true reality. Our minds aren't big enough to understand it all otherwise. And, I won't disappear, not yet."

She released the hug, pulled back and looked at him. He seemed as she remembered him, apparently not a week older since his accidental death on that awful day.

"Why haven't you aged? Or is that a silly question?"

He looked back at her and said, "It's not silly, but the answer isn't simple. This place is hard to describe, but it would be accurate to say it is another plane of existence. There is something about human beings that survives after the biological body is dead. That part flows into this place and is why you find me here. This plane is much more mutable than the physical plane from which we came on Earth. The more powerful the mind, the more it molds the structure of this plane. Smaller minds, like mine and yours can mold small areas such as the way you are molding the room and this hallway to look like our old house."

He continued, "Your mind also molds how I appear to you." He smiled and his face shifted, the age lines disappearing, hair regrowing in a moment so all traces of baldness disappeared. He looked to be about twenty-five years old. "But, now you see how I would appear to myself. Even in life, as people age, they often still visualize themselves as younger and are shocked to be reminded of their age when they look in a mirror. I probably appear to be in my mid-twenties, don't I?"

There was a note of awe in her voice. "Yes. It seems strange. I never thought of you as this young."

He laughed. "You never <u>saw</u> me when I was this young. Not many children would remember their parents as young." His face changed back to middle-age. "There. I relaxed my image so yours would win out. Does that seem better?"

She said, "Yes, but that makes me nervous. It makes me think that nothing is stable here and that I am still dreaming."

He said, "The Earth that we came from and know of is a place of material things, of matter and physical laws. This place also has matter and physical laws as well, but it is more strongly a place of energies and power and mind. Here, the matter is very obedient to the mind. On Earth's plane of existence, matter is not so obedient to thought. There, only the strongest, most powerful minds with control of great energies can manipulate matter and physical forces. It is why the supernatural is so rare on Earth that many do not believe it exists at all."

He said, "You are not dreaming, but are glimpsing another place. You are like a fish, still submerged in water that has ventured up to the very top, the last inch of liquid. That fish can see through the liquid ripples into the air above. That fish can see things moving and flying overhead. It can hear dim sounds echoing around it in that thin layer separating it from the world above."

"When you put yourself into this trance state, you were moving your mind right up to the interface between your physical plane of existence and this plane of energies and light and mind. You can see into this realm as if through that last inch of water. Many people on earth have experienced something of what you are feeling now, but you have one additional advantage over all of them. They are like fish near the surface, but you are more like an amphibian. You can cross through the interface."

Mercy said, "What?"

Her father said, "A young tadpole grows legs and eventually can break through the water and crawl up onto the lakeshore. It has lungs that start to breathe the air of the world above the water, but then it can move back into the water. From then on as a frog, it lives in two worlds, in the water and also on the land. It draws its oxygen from the water or the air, whichever it happens to inhabit at the moment. This is also your advantage."

"You can live on both sides of this planar barrier. Your trance state brings you to the interface between the Earth's material plane and your mind brings you across the barrier, completely into this plane. You have this advantage because of your ancestry. Because you descended from the fallen ones, your mind is capable of crossing the barrier. I'm told it is something that often takes a long time to learn for someone like you. I could never learn it because I didn't have that distinct ancestry, but you, my dear adopted daughter, had it, though your mother and I didn't know it."

Mercy said, "Is mother here too? Is everyone here?"

"Yes, your mother is here. Now that you can travel here, she will want to come to you. We thought it would be easier on you if one of us came to you first and helped you understand. As for your question on whether everyone is here, I can say that yes, all minds transition to this plane, but not all minds can understand it or accept it. There are many dark minds that find themselves here, turn inward and shrink to almost impenetrable points. They refuse to communicate or interact. We continue to hope that someday they will open themselves up to the rest of us, but we don't know if this will be possible."

She said, "Father, I came here to speak to the Counselor. Can I do that?"

He said, "I came here to help you understand the answer to that, which is, 'For you, not now.'"

"What? Why?"

He said, "I don't know why, but I can guess."

Mercy said, "I don't understand! Why would the Counselor do that and refuse to talk to me? It helped me the last time I came to it. It always gave me an answer to my questions before, even when I thought it was just another of the many voices in my head."

He said, "I don't know this for certain, but here's what I suspect: you're to find your own way for a time. The Counselor does not want you too greatly dependent on its advice or direction. If you turn to it at all times in many areas, you will wait before acting and hesitate before doing what needs to be done. It trusts you and your heart. It wants you to do your best and act as you believe you should act. Of course, you will make mistakes and err, sometimes you will act for the wrong reasons and sometimes you will act selfishly. But, the Counselor values the best efforts of those that are trying and believes that in the long run, the best results are achieved by beings that act from their own best knowledge and wisdom."

"You have to be joking. I don't know what I'm doing."

He said, "I think you know enough. You know of this place and the beings here. You know that there is more to existence than meets the human eye. You know that on Earth, there are creatures like Moloch that can cause great damage if left unchecked. You know that part of your task is to meet that challenge, whatever it entails. I think it is enough."

"Is it alright to say, I'm afraid you and others here seem to have a higher opinion of me than I have?"

He said, "And that is another reason why you are right for this gigantic effort. Those who think themselves equal to great tasks are often after glory and are the worst ones that can be given the work. On the other hand, the humble can sometimes feel themselves unequal and prove otherwise. You are capable, have proved yourself capable, but are nervous about the next task. You may not succeed, but you are ready."

Mercy persisted. "I came here to ask the Counselor about a proposal from an evil man. He has offered to put me in touch with my grandmother Sonia. What should I do?"

He said, "Mercy, if the Counselor won't speak to you about this, how can I?"

Mercy felt frustration building. "But I need advice. It's why I came here."

Her father held a peaceful expression and answered, "Did you come here for advice? Do you need it?"

She sighed in exasperation. "Daddy, you are really irritating me! Why can't you answer my question?"

He laughed and waited.

She gave up and sighed. She shook her head. "You and mother were always like this; just as stubborn as mules. You're still like that."

He said, "I know. I can't advise you about your question, but I can tell you this: Moloch was not the only being imprisoned on Earth for reasons of rebellion. Be aware and alert. Now you must return."

"I don't want to leave. You said I can live on both sides of this interface between the planes. I want to stay longer," she said.

"Your young man is waiting and grows concerned. Go back to him, but remember you can return again when you feel it to be right. The next time, others will want to spend time with you. Come back again."

She felt him recede and his face seemed to waiver as if seen through ripples. *It's that metaphor he used of being in the top inches of water near the surface. I see him as if I am sinking back beneath the waves. My mind is supplying the images that make sense to me.*

"Goodbye, Daddy."

His voice sounded very distant and muffled. "Goodbye, sweetheart. We will speak again."

* * *

Mercy opened her eyes and reoriented herself. She was in a train compartment and her muscles ached slightly. *I've been in one position for too long.* She willed herself to sit up. Jack shifted next to her.

"Mercy, are you alright?"

She said, "Yes, I'm fine. Where are we?"

"We're arriving at Bucharest. We'll be at the station in ten minutes. You've been unconscious the entire time. Want to talk about it?"

She said, "It's not what I thought would happen. I didn't talk to the Counselor. Dad intercepted me and said that for now I couldn't speak to the Counselor. I have to make my own decisions and that would be good enough. He said the Counselor trusted me to do what I thought was best. I guess that's good news and bad news." She told him the rest of the dream.

Jack said, "Strange. So, he had no advice about the communication from Dmitri?"

"No, in fact he said if the Counselor couldn't give advice, neither could he. Oh, and he said, I could return again and others would want to speak to me then. I think mother will be one of them," she said.

Jack pondered and said, "You really have some kind of window into the afterlife, don't you? I never would have accepted that as credible just a few weeks ago."

She shook her head. "I don't quite know how to say this, but here goes. Now that I've spoken to my father twice, I think that place is not at all the kind of afterlife we've heard people discuss before, but in some ways it seems to be better. I always rejected and felt uncomfortable with some of those ideas before. No, it's more like mother and father have relocated to a distant continent, but I can still reach them if I need to. I know they're alive and it's a big nuisance to speak with them, but still possible. Does that make any sense?"

He said, "I think so. Go on."

"I asked him if everyone goes there when they die. He said something odd in answer about all minds transitioning to that plane, but not all of them being able to understand it or accept it."

She narrowed her eyes in thought while trying to grasp what it all meant. "He also said that there were many dark minds that came there but they turned inward and shrank to tiny points. They refused to communicate or interact with the others there on that plane. The way he talked, it's almost like people's souls moved there but some of them couldn't handle it, were too depraved, or refused to accept it. They imploded inward. Isn't that strange?"

Jack said, "I'm going to have to think about that. It doesn't sound like any idea of Heaven or Hell I've ever heard, but maybe I'm wrong."

Mercy said, "I don't know. I've never been a person with faith like Hayden, but maybe what my father described represents an underlying truth. Anyway, since we are going to get no advice from the Counselor, I say we go to our apartments in Bucharest, gather anything we need like my medicines and then contact Dmitri. I do want to see my grandmother Sonia. Let's just be careful with Dmitri and try to figure out what his game is and not let him trap us."

He said, "I think we can do that. We'll stick together in Bucharest, though. Let's not do something stupid like getting separated."

She said, "Absolutely not. I don't want to lose track of you, Jack Truett. I'm not letting you out of my sight."

They picked up some more currency at an ATM at the train station, bought more food and another newspaper and caught a taxi. Their first stop was Jack's place to pick up his money, some clothes and car keys. They went to the parking garage level in the subbasement, loaded everything into his car drove out of the underground and onto the streets of Bucharest.

The next stop was Mercy's place. It was a corporate apartment that PetroRomania leased for its executives and it had been assigned for her use for the first six months of her assignment. At the door of her apartment, she pulled a card key from her wallet and slid it through the electronic lock. The light turned green and she opened the door.

Mercy had only lived in the furnished apartment a matter of days so it still seemed new and unfamiliar. The lights were all out so she flipped them on and looked into the first room. It was sparsely but expensively decorated and spotlessly clean. There was a lingering odor in the front room. *Is that air freshener? It reminds me of the smell of all those hospitals I stayed in when I was younger. Ugh.* She felt a chill run up her spine.

Jack said, "We may have just missed your maid service. That smells like cheap artificial pine scent."

"I don't know what a maid would have been doing in here. It's been a couple of months since I was here so there can't be any recent messes to clean unless someone else has been camping out here. Since I wasn't going to be here a lot at least at first, I didn't think I needed the apartment at all, but thanks to you, they allocated it to me anyway. Let's go get my medicine and get out. This place was never home to me, I just slept here for a few times. It's as soulless as a hotel room."

Mercy walked through the bedroom and then into the bathroom. She opened a medicine cabinet, took a medicine bottle in hand and turned abruptly back into the bedroom. Jack saw a look of confusion come over her face and she stopped and raised the bottle to her eyes. Her expression showed increasing concern and then alarm. She rapidly removed the bottle top and poured a few pills into her hand.

Jack asked, "Mercy, what is it? What's wrong?"

She said, "There are way too many pills in this bottle. I took half of my meds with me on the *Fortuna* and lost them there when the ship sank. This bottle is too full. Let me look at the pills themselves. They look the same shape, size and color…"

She looked at the pills carefully and cross-checked the code stamped into the pills with the code listed on the bottle. She gasped. "Some of these pills have the wrong code on them…" She poured the pills carefully onto the dining room table and sorted them. Jack sat down and helped her. After some time, the two of them looked up at each other. Mercy's face was bleak.

She said, "A third of these pills have the wrong code stamped in them."

Jack said, "Maybe it's a generic substitute with a different code but the same dose of drug."

"This prescription was for the same name-brand drug I've been using for years to keep the voices in my head in check. I got it from the same pharmacy and doctor I've been using all along. If they'd needed to do a substitution they would have told me."

He said, "Then maybe it was just a mistake. The druggist put the wrong pills in your bottle."

She said, "If they'd done that it would have been all one kind or the other, not a mixture. Besides, I'm sure this bottle had a third less medicine in it when I left it here two months ago. Someone put different pills in here that are the same size and color as the other pills. Why would someone do that?"

Jack took the bottle and put all of the pills back in it and walked it back into the bathroom. He put it into the medicine cabinet and closed the door. He went back into the kitchen and took her hand. He spoke very softly to her.

"We need to get out of here right now…"

Before they could move, there was a knock on the door.

CHAPTER 16 – TRAP

"Caught in a fiery tempest, shall be hurled, each on his rock transfixed"
— *John Milton, Paradise Lost*

Mercy's face flushed with the realization that they'd been caught. *How'd they know we were here? Oh. I used my cardkey to the apartment. What an idiot. It was a dead giveaway.*

Jack said, "It might be someone that was notified when your room was opened: probably someone from PetroRomania. Can't be the police, I don't know of anything we've done that would be considered illegal."

Mercy said, "I'll get the door. They won't be expecting me to act, so if I need to, I'll take them out." Jack's eyebrow lifted at her. She smiled grimly, "Non-lethally if possible."

The knock sounded again and she opened it. A man in a PetroRomania Corporate Security uniform stepped in holding a cellphone to one ear. Mercy thought he looked vaguely familiar.

The officer held the phone slightly away from his mouth and said to her, "Good day, Doctor Teller and Vice President Truett. It is good to see you both well after the disaster on the *Fortuna*. We didn't know if either of you had survived the sinking of the ship." The man stopped speaking and put his other hand to his forehead as if he had forgotten something. "Oh, I am so sorry, I should have introduced myself. I am Officer Alex Lacusta of PetroRomania Corporate Security. I normally report to Director Gachevska but not yet having heard from him, I now report directly to Chairman Parasca. Welcome back to Bucharest."

He took the phone away from his ear and held it out for Mercy to take. She held back, reluctant.

Lacusta said, "It is alright. The call is for you. It is Chairman Parasca. He wishes to speak with you."

* * *

Mercy felt shell-shocked but took the phone, gritted her teeth and spoke in a hiss. "What do you want, you monster?"

Parasca said, "Now, now dear daughter. Let's be civil. No need to be insulting."

Mercy didn't say a word. She let her classification of him stand and waited for him to speak. It almost felt like a requirement of honor that she not dirty herself by breaking the silence. Parasca waited as well, but finally spoke out after an eternity seemed to pass by.

"Well, you must have never learned normal civil courtesies while growing up in America. We will go on then. Mircea, we have an interesting past history you and I, but it doesn't have to be a determinant for our future."

He paused, but she persisted in silence. He continued, "There is much work to do now and I want you working for me. You can name your own pay. I will start the negotiations by offering you five times your last salary."

Mercy spoke in an icy-cold tone, "You must be completely psychotic and out of touch with reality. I don't work for PetroRomania anymore and certainly not for you. I learned how you really felt about your employees when I saw you offering them as human sacrifices to that demon Moloch. He was eating your people. You and 'Director Gachevska' even helped him. 'Monster' is too good a word for you or Rakslav. You have less conscience than a poisonous snake. Of course I refuse your employment offer."

Janos Parasca spoke from the other end of the line, "Now, now. Who can explain the actions of that being Moloch? Rakslav and I did what we had to do to survive. Don't judge us for the actions it compelled upon us. We were merely following orders."

She scoffed, "Said the Nazis to the judges at Nuremberg. I repeat, I will not work for you."

He said, "Mircea, you had better reconsider."

She bristled at the repeated use of her legal name and said, "Why? Why should I?"

Parasca said, "I have the sword. I recovered it from the wreck with one of the *Fortuna's* mini-subs."

Mercy felt a wrenching in her gut. She said, "Janos, you don't know what that thing can do. It's dangerous."

"Oh, but I do know. I saw much of the fight between you and Moloch. I also saw before that when Moloch forced you to learn to heal yourself. I know this sword has a thousand lives worth of power stored in it. I know that it only takes a small amount of that power to do the most miraculous things."

He paused and his tone abruptly changed. She couldn't seem to recognize the inflections in his voice at first. He said, "Mercy, I have lived a difficult life, but I'd like to make some amends if it is still possible for someone like me. I want to learn how to use the power in the sword for healing. If I could learn to heal the way Moloch taught you, I could finally do something worthwhile perhaps. It might not be much, but it would be a start."

She said, "What?" *He sounds almost sorry for what he's done. He must be mad to think I'd be fooled by him like this.* "You want to use the healing power? I don't believe you. There would be nothing in the world more out of character for you than that. You're just trying to manipulate me into thinking that you've had a change of heart. You must be insane to think that would work. Either that or for you this is just a game. You must think we're just chess pieces to be moved about; that we're pretty stupid. So now you try putting on another of your acts in hope it will change things between us. It won't work, and I won't teach you anything about healing."

His voice grew very cold. "Then, this conversation is over. Please give the phone back to Lacusta."

"Gladly." Angry, she flipped it to the security officer.

The man took the phone, held it to his ear and said, "Yes?"

He apparently heard a short response from Parasca, ended the call and put the phone away. He stepped further into the room and closed the door behind him. "Chairman Parasca informed me that for both of you, your employment with PetroRomania has been terminated. Please leave this apartment immediately and do not return." He turned to Mercy and said, "I will need the cardkey that you used to open the door."

She looked at him cagily, but looked down and reached into a pocket to take out the card. As she was glancing away, she heard a sudden gasping intake of breath from Jack. She looked back up instantly and saw that Lacusta was pointing a large pistol at her. An arcing electric current sparked at the end of the square barrel and made a crackling sound. Before she could move, she heard a loud popping noise and all of her nerves felt on fire at the same moment. She collapsed and hit her head on the floor. In another moment, she heard crashing sounds that seemed to be taking place a great distance away. She twisted and writhed on the floor in what seemed like a world of fiery spasms. Her body felt completely out of her control.

The feeling of fire finally receded but Mercy lay twitching involuntarily with violent pulses running randomly through her. If the muscles in her body could have shouted, every one of them would have been shrieking from agony and exhaustion. She heard sounds of a fight and managed to open her eyes and look, though she couldn't move her neck in a controlled fashion. She saw that the apartment had been transformed into a wreck within the last few moments since she fell. Glass shards lay on the floor from a broken mirror. A china cabinet lay on its side. The dining room table a few feet away was overturned.

Jack Truett and Alex Lacusta moved into her view and she saw Jack's mouth was bleeding and an eye was swelling shut, but he had a chair in his hands and swung it at Lacusta. The security officer ducked but not enough and a leg of the chair crunched into his shoulder. Lacusta fell back with a grunt of pain and almost came within reach of Mercy's limp form. *I couldn't grab him if my life depended on it. My muscles are useless.*

Jack swung the chair again, this time to bring it down on Lacusta's head, but the man rolled away. The chair slammed into the floor two feet from Mercy. *If only I could do something! My muscles have all turned into a twitching jelly. I can't even speak. I only have my sight and my mind, but what can they do right now?*

Lacusta rolled back to his feet and grabbed at the chair, almost pulling it from the other man's grasp. Jack pulled back hard and the two of them tumbled over the dining table with the chair between them. Mercy could see glimpses of their struggle. She felt proud of Jack for fighting so hard, but he wasn't trained and probably wouldn't be able to last much longer. *This Lacusta guy will eventually get the best of Jack unless we're very lucky. If only I could help.*

She caught sight of a long, narrow glass shard on the floor near her face. *It looks almost like a dagger. I'd stab him with it if I could, but I have no control over my body, only my mind. I wish I could move that glass like I moved that bullet when I was shot on the Fortuna.* She felt a mental jolt of realization. *Idiot. Yes, why don't I move the glass like I moved the bullet?*

She heard pounding sounds and Jack's voice cried out in anger and pain. She heard him gasp like he'd taken a heavy blow. She blocked all of the sounds of the fight out of her mind. She looked at the glass and moved herself quickly down the mental staircase and through the relaxation and centering exercises she had often used. With eyes open, she looked at the glass shard in front of her and mentally pictured the blue energy lifting the glass. With immediate responsiveness, it rose one inch above the floor and stayed there as if resting on solid rock. She saw the blue energy curling around it as if blown by a slight breeze. *Rotate the point away from me, come closer, rise to six inches above the floor and get ready.* The glass dagger obeyed without wobble, the blue energy coiling around it.

She heard Jack yell as if he'd been hit by a heavy load and he and Lacusta came into view with Jack staggering. The officer had a blackjack in one hand and swung it at Jack. Jack pivoted but the weapon hit him in the left shoulder. Jack winced and staggered backward against a wall. Lacusta stalked forward, raising the weapon to strike again and this time it looked like he was aiming for Jack's head.

Mercy shouted mentally. *Now!* The glass shard turned and pointed at the security officer's back. It shot forward in a line so steady it was as if it were attached to a steel rail. Blue energy trailed behind it like jet exhaust. The point of the dagger stabbed into the back of Lacusta's jacket, penetrated it, went through his shirt and undershirt, into his skin, slid between his fifth and sixth ribs, punched through the right lung from the back, sliced between the fourth and fifth rib at the front, exited through the skin and stopped with two inches sticking out the front of Lacusta's chest.

The man gasped and dropped the blackjack. He looked down at the bloody glass sticking out of his chest, seemed to be about to ask a question and sank to one knee. He paused for two seconds on that knee and slowly toppled over on his right side, gasping painful, shallow breaths. Jack staggered to Lacusta, picked up the weapon and stumbled to Mercy's prone form.

Jack's face had taken a bad beating. He had swollen, bloody lips, a black eye and blood running down his scalp. One arm seemed limp and useless. He bent down to her, keeping one eye on Lacusta. Mercy looked at him, but the best she could manage was a slight fluttering of her fingers. He looked around and grimaced at the wreckage.

He said through swollen lips, "We really have to get out of here now."

Jack disconnected the stun gun's darts from Mercy and pocketed the blackjack. He kneeled and carefully pulled Mercy up and draped her over his good shoulder, holding onto her with that still functional arm. He slowly rose until he walked with her to the door. He opened it carefully and looked up and down the hall. There was no one in sight. He carried Mercy out into the hallway, closed the door behind him and walked to the elevator. They rode it down to the basement level. Jack walked slowly to his car, and painfully knelt with her, leaning her against the side of the car. His face was flushed and blood dripped from his chin. He was breathing hard.

He opened her car door and lifted her carefully inside and belted her in. He got into the driver's seat, gasped in pain as he buckled himself in, coughed and leaned out the door to spit out a mouthful of blood. They pulled away and he drove for five minutes before pulling into a small parking area in front of a market.

Mercy said feebly, "I think I'm snapping out of it. Thank you, Jack. I'm sorry I was no help."

Jack said, "No help? What do you call stabbing him? I didn't see how you did it, but I know it had to be you. It certainly wasn't anything I did. I think I was at my limit. One more hit with that blackjack and I'd have been done."

She said, "I stabbed him. I couldn't move any muscles after he hit me with that stun gun. But I could still think. I remembered how I'd had to mentally remove that bullet when I was shot on the *Fortuna*, so I saw a long shard of glass and mentally stabbed it into him. I didn't mean to kill him, but I didn't have time to figure out anything else."

"You levitated a dagger shaped piece of glass and stabbed him with it from a distance. All with just your mind. Wow."

She said, "Jack, maybe we should call an ambulance for him. He might still be alive."

He said, "My first inclination is to say, he deserved it. But I guess you're right. He didn't try to kill us, just render us helpless. I wonder why?"

Mercy walked slowly and carefully to the market from where they were parked, found that they had a public phone and placed a call for an ambulance. She gave the person on the other end of the line her apartment address.

When she returned to the car she got in, turned to Jack and said, "Now I'm determined to contact Dmitri Slokov. I don't care how bad he is, if he's against Parasca, that's good enough for me right now."

She found Slokov's text message and replied to it: "This is Mercy Teller. I am interested in seeing my grandmother, Sonia. Let's discuss. Send a message with details on when and where to meet."

A few minutes later, she received a reply: "Good. We should meet tomorrow in Timisoara at 10am. I will take you to her after we meet. I am sure you have many questions for me. I will explain all details when we meet. Address follows." A separate message arrived a few minutes later containing an address.

She said, "Timisoara. Huh. She decided to stay in that city even long after she must have retired from the university. It will be strange to return there. I haven't seen it in over twenty years." She turned to him and said, "I'm just warning you, Jack. I have lots of intense memories from that time. This is not going to be easy."

Jack shrugged, wiped his bloody face and showed a slight smile with his swollen lips. "Nothing is easy for us. This is obviously a high-maintenance relationship. But really, you're warning me of intense memories? Is it any more intense than all of this?" He waved a hand in the air to indicate their predicament. She nodded and gingerly raised a hand to his swollen eye.

He said, "With one eye out of action like this, I have no depth perception. If you are stable enough to drive, it's undoubtedly a good idea for us to switch. I'll probably get us into a wreck if I continue driving. The question is, do we want to drive to Timisoara or take the train. It's over 500 kilometers. Frankly, I think neither of us is up to driving a long distance, so I would prefer to take the train. We could get a sleeper car and be there in the morning for this 10 o'clock meet up with Dmitri." Mercy nodded in agreement and she set off driving back to the train station.

Jack sank back into his seat, closed his eyes and flinched from the pain in all of his cuts and bruises. He shook his head in disbelief. "So we go to meet Dmitri Slokov, the man who had the *Fortuna* sunk. I guess that means we're committed now."

CHAPTER 17 – RELATIVES

"How glad would lay me down as in my mother's lap.
There I should rest, and sleep secure"
— John Milton, Paradise Lost

The train to Timisoara took Mercy and Jack around the western end of the Carpathian Mountains, and Mercy thought the view was still full of beautiful scenes, but she sighed. *I just wish I could spend some time enjoying it.* In their sleeper cabin, Mercy had Jack lay down so she could examine his injuries. She lightly touched his battered face and studied him. His right eye was tightly shut with bluish-black bruises. The right side of his mouth was swollen and the lip was cracked and puffy. He had lacerations, welts on his shoulders and chest and ominously, it looked like he might have broken ribs and a partially dislocated shoulder where the blackjack had struck him.

He said, "I'm a mess, aren't I?"

She said, "Yes. You're really mashed up." She smiled tenderly at him. "You took a huge beating from that man of Parasca's. Thank you for doing all of this for me. I'm sorry he caught me off guard like that or I would have helped you. Parasca must have warned him to take me out of commission first."

Jack said, "Hey, what kind of man would let his fiancé get attacked like that and not try to beat the guy down? He had it coming. I just wish I'd been more effective. I'm in pretty good shape, but I don't know anything about fighting except for basic scrapping that I learned during my summers as a roughneck when I was in college."

Mercy was surprised. "You were an oil field roughneck?"

"Yeah, as you can imagine, once I got out from under my parent's thumb and went to college for my undergraduate work, I didn't really want to go home for the summer breaks so I got a recommendation from one of my engineering professors and got a job as a roughneck. It was hard, dirty work with long hours. But it paid real well for a guy my age and I got lots of good experience working in the down and dirty part of the oil business. I went back every summer and made enough between that and my scholarships to finish college owing very little on my student loans."

She said, "I'll bet that's one of the reasons why the men on the rigs and crews on ship respect you. You understand their work and have been on the drilling floor with them. They like to know that the executives over them have had real world experience."

He said, "It's true. People in the trenches hate it when 'suits' show up on the rig. That's what they call the executives who come to a drill site all dressed up in fancy coats and ties. It means work stops while all of the money men get their little tour. The roughnecks trash talk them behind their backs and say 'the poor men in suits have to put on hardhats that tend to mess up their hundred dollar haircuts.' They say you can tell from their soft hands that the only kind of dirt they ever handle with their manicured fingers is a little mud from picking up a golf ball. When I worked as a roughneck I did get a taste for the real life the men in the field lead."

She nodded, "I've seen the way rig crews look at 'suits' when they come for their tours. So you got in a few brawls during those years?"

Jack said, "I did. Nothing epic, mainly some fights in bars after work. Once, when we got off shift some of us went together for pizza and some college football players at the next table thought they'd play a stupid joke on our foreman and tripped him when he was bringing some beers to our table. That broke out into a huge fight between the roughnecks and the punk footballers. Some of those kids must have been linebackers, but even though they had a lot of beef on their side, they did not have real working muscle. We pounded them and ended up getting arrested for disorderly conduct, though thankfully no one got seriously hurt. We all chipped in and paid for the damages at the pizza place. It was worth it to see those punks get some pay back."

Jack stopped talking, shut his eyes tightly and sighed. Mercy asked, "Are you still in a lot of pain?"

He said, "Yes."

She said, "Hold still. I'm going to see if this works the same way on you as it did on me."

She moved quickly into her trance state and tried to envision his injuries. It didn't work at first. *Hmm. I can't do it in the same way I can envision something happening in my own body. I guess that makes sense. But I was able to catch sight of his dreams the other day. Maybe I can use the same approach here.* She moved down the mental staircase in her trance-state as she had done before entering Jack's dream. At the bottom of the stairs, she put her hand on the door handle and shifted to visualizing Jack's injured face and held the image. She mentally opened the door and was slammed by a wall of pain.

She felt a tremendous gnawing ache in her face, shoulders and chest and saw a disorienting sight: she was directly facing herself. *Ah. I'm looking out through Jack's eyes and seeing myself. How strange. I don't look fresh as a daisy either. Wow, his face hurts horribly; the rest of him too.* She felt a strange sensation and sensed Jack's jaws move and heard the sound of his words from inside his own head. *How different his voice sounds from in here!*

He said, "Mercy, are you in my head? I feel really strange, almost disassociated from myself."

She started to speak, but changed her mind and shifted her approach. She tried speaking mentally to him.

She said, *"Jack, I'm in here with you. Can you hear me?"*

Jack said out loud, "I heard that, but your lips did not move. Your voice is in my head! Is this what it felt like when you heard voices? How did you keep calm? This is too weird for words."

She said, *"I don't know if it's the same, but I'm here. I can feel all of your pain now and I'm going to try to see what I can do to help."*

She was able to visualize and mentally sink down into his hurt tissues. She released a small trickle of the power into his swollen lips. It seemed to have no effect at first, but she visualized the swelling starting to recede and imagined a soothing, cool compress on the site. She released more energy into the wound. She felt the blood flow pick up.

Jack said, "That feels a little better. Whatever you're doing, it's helping."

Mercy opened the flow of power to as much as Jack's body would take. She felt the energy wash through him, pooling in three main areas, his face, his shoulder and his ribs. She opened herself to the blue thread of life energy and seemed to see it pour into him, soothing the swollen tissues, speeding up the flow of blood, knitting flesh and frayed ligaments. Finally, she felt the flow of energy slow down as if his body had taken all that it could accept at the moment. She pulled her mind back and sensed his thoughts had slowed down into a peaceful rhythm. She realized he was in a dreamless sleep. She detached from him and felt her consciousness flip and return to her own head. She opened her eyes and looked at him.

He looked much better and he was certainly asleep. She sighed, relaxed on her own couch near him and quickly fell asleep herself.

* * *

"Hey sleepy head, want something to eat?"

Mercy opened her eyes heavily. She looked confusedly in the direction of Jack's voice. He was sitting up and gently shaking her by one shoulder. He looked well again. He pointed out the window.

"We'll be in Timisoara in an hour and a half. If we hurry, we can get some breakfast in the dining car before we reach the station."

Mercy roused and sat up. "I need to take care of some business first." She went down the narrow hall in their train car and into the little bathroom that was no bigger than one that would be found on an airplane. After using the facilities she checked herself in the mirror, doing the best she could. *I look hideous! I've got to get some basic supplies soon, like maybe just a hairbrush to start with.* She went back into the hallway and found Jack waiting for her.

They got a table in the dining car and ordered a large traditional Romanian breakfast. Mercy realized she was starving again and decided to eat her fill no matter what people thought. They had bread with feta cheese, cold cuts, cucumbers and tomatoes. There was a large dish of scrambled eggs and lots of strong, Turkish-style coffee. Mercy ordered fruit juice and yogurt as well.

Between mouthfuls, Mercy said, "I need to tell you about the time I spent in Timisoara so you'll understand some of the dynamics in play there with me and my grandmother."

He said, "Alright."

She said, "I told you already about how I came to Bucharest with my adoptive mother after I finished high school. I was still an emotional wreck from the voices, the trauma of losing Daddy and all the rest, but mother thought it would be a good idea for the two of us to get away. When a opportunity opened up for the business that Daddy had founded and that mother was now running, we went to Bucharest to see if mother could get a deal made with the Romanian government to provide them with the low-tech farm equipment Daddy's company made and distributed."

"Once there in Bucharest, things quickly went sour and before I knew what had happened, mother had been arrested on some trumped up charge of spying on the Romanian government. Ceausescu was still in charge and his secret police, the Securitate, was going strong. Janos Parasca was an officer in the Securitate and interrogated both me and my mother. Now that I think about it, I realize that he had probably figured out that I was his biological daughter even then, because when I was being questioned, the Securitate thugs showed me my Romanian birth certificate. I remember it said 'Mircea' Rodica on it. Later, when I was at the Technical University in Timisoara, people in the Admissions department would ask me why I had a boy's name on my birth certificate. In Romania, 'Mircea' is a male name. What could I say? I don't know why my birth certificate had a boy's name on it: probably just some typographical error. I became very glad my American parents had Anglicized my name to 'Mercy' so I didn't have to put up with that kind of questioning from most people. It's also why I get irritated when people who know Romanian and know my real name, like Parasca, insist on calling me 'Mircea'. I am Mercy."

"Anyway, I was taken by the Securitate to Timisoara to live with my Grandmother Sonia. Thankfully, she spoke some English so I didn't completely drown. From the first minute I saw her, she was kind and gentle with me. She knew something of what had happened in Bucharest and was outraged by the brutality of the 'thugs', which is what she called the Securitate."

"After a couple of months there, I had begun picking up the language and she got me enrolled at the Polytechnic University where she taught chemistry. I was interested in the sciences and took up studies in geology. That life lasted for about two years until the winter of 1989 and the Romanian Revolution."

"The whole country had been groaning for decades under communist rule and Ceausescu's dictatorship. He had practically destroyed the economy of the country by selling and shipping away almost all of our agricultural and manufactured goods to other countries. Rations were short and almost everyone was hungry. It was a really dismal place to be in those days. Strangely, Timisoara was in some ways the epicenter of the Romanian Revolution that year."

"The people were fed up and students at the university were as fed up as any. The match that lit the fuse was a strange one, though. There was a small church in Timisoara that had a young pastor who spoke out against the government. Ceausescu's people accused him of inciting ethnic hatred and got his church's bishop to remove him from his post. He lost the right to his parsonage apartment. He refused to leave for his new assignment out in the country and wouldn't be silenced. Members of his church encircled him and refused to give him over to the authorities. My grandmother Sonia was a member of that small church."

Mercy was done with the first meal and after she had finished all of the remains, she ordered a second round and kept eating until that had run out as well. All the while she continued telling her story to Jack.

"Eventually a large gathering of students joined the church members to defend the pastor from the government. The mayor and local party officials came and tried to take him in. The government started calling troops to quell the crowds and it broke out into riots with people being shot and killed by the government forces. The mobs raged through Timisoara and finally, the government troops retreated."

"The riots spread through the countryside of Romania and into other major cities and grew larger and larger. It all climaxed in Bucharest with a crowd of fifty thousand Romanians encircling Ceausescu's palace. The dictator tried threatening them and cajoling them, but it was obvious that he had lost control, so, terrified, he tried to flee. He and his wife were caught while trying to escape and put before a hasty tribunal. They were convicted of genocide and executed by firing squad."

"I was with that group of students from the university that defended the pastor and I was with them when they marched through the streets of Timisoara and were shot at. I almost died in Timisoara when the police shot at the crowd so I only heard later how it all ended. I had been hit in the neck and my boyfriend Stefan was shot and killed. I spent a month in the hospital after the riots recovering."

"My grandmother Sonia nursed me back to health through the aftermath of the revolution. When things settled a little bit, she got the attention of some of the new local officials and told them my story about how I'd come to Romania with my adopted mother and was an American citizen. The new government was keen to establish good relations with the United States and so located my adoptive mother who had been in a Romanian jail the whole time. The new government granted mother's release and we were both received by an American delegation and taken back to the United States."

"After getting back to the U.S., I lost contact with my grandmother Sonia and got involved in college again. Mother died the next year and my life was in turmoil, so I didn't reach back out to Sonia as the years passed. I really want to see her again and hope it isn't too late. I want to have some time with her before she passes on, but I know she is very old now. I don't know how her health is, but I hope she still remembers me. Jack, what if she's senile or has Alzheimer's? I don't know if I could stand it."

Jack put his hand on hers. "You can stand a lot and you already have. Still, I can only imagine how you feel and it must be horrible. I wish I'd had a good relationship with any family member that I could look back on positively like you do. You've had a lot of hard things in your life, but I'm really glad you have some good memories of family. Not all of us have that."

Their waiter came by and looked at Mercy with what appeared to be some small amount of awe. "Would Madame care for anything else to eat?"

Mercy looked at him without embarrassment and said, "Nothing right now, thank you."

The waiter walked away from their table, shaking his head in incredulity at the sheer volume of food that Mercy had consumed. Jack smiled and paid the waiter well, giving the man a very nice tip.

Jack looked back at Mercy. She held one hand six inches above a water glass. She said, "Watch."

The glass floated smoothly from the table to her hand without sloshing or spilling. She held the glass and said, "I'm getting better at this. I wonder if there is a mass or size limit. Worth a test or two, don't you think?"

Jack said, "Yes it is. It definitely is worth some testing."

CHAPTER 18 – BETRAYED

'For neither man nor angel can discern hypocrisy,
the only evil that walks invisible"
— John Milton, Paradise Lost

Maria said, "Henry, what do you think of this plaster and the painting on it?"

Henry Travers looked up in confusion. He had been examining the plaque that showed the 'Architect of the Abyss' script in the universal language and couldn't quite understand her question. "What did you say, Maria?" His distraction showed in his face. *I wish I could notify some of my colleagues back at the university about this! Absolutely stunning. This will turn the field of linguistics upside down, but only if I can get the word out. Instead we're under radio silence and can't communicate with anyone. All because that twit Balev had to go fall down and break his arm. I wonder how a person becomes as twisted as he is?*

She looked mildly irritated and said, "Henry, look at me. Your mind is a thousand miles away. Look in my eyes so I know you are really listening. There." Satisfied that he was looking at her and she had his attention, she repeated her question then said, "This bull painting looks almost out of place to me compared to the other depictions, and this plaster! It makes no sense. Why plaster over part of this beautiful metal wall or door or whatever it is and then paint a bull head on it?"

"Another mystery, I suppose. Perhaps they were covering up something, a flaw in the metal maybe, or an earlier bit of art that they didn't like anymore. I think there is more we don't know about this place than what we do know. The important thing is that we unearth and reveal all that we can, and of course, write and publish all we can. Then, other people can build on what we've done and develop theories that explain it. The crown jewel here is this plaque. What do you suppose is meant by the words,

'Architect of the Abyss?'"

"You mean 'Architetto' of course." She smiled and shook her head, still amazed by the mutable script. "It is so wonderful, so unexpected. Maybe the reference to the 'Abyss' is the key. Could it be referring to an early deity in the vein of the god Vulcan? Some ancient myths had builder-gods like him that lived in the underworld and were always forging things out of metal. Of course, this crypt complex would all predate Greco-Roman mythology, but that strange writing might be referring to a proto-myth, especially since we found the hammer and fire symbol painted here on the plaster as well." She pointed at the design.

"Now there's a thought: Vulcan, the god of fire." Henry said and waved his hand to encompass the underground complex. "We need more clues to start grasping all of this. They've started excavating that new side tunnel on the landing of the Grand Staircase: perhaps there will be some more paintings or another plaque like this. If we could find more examples of this writing, it would help so much!"

Professor Russo walked over to the two of them and put his hand on Henry's shoulder. His face looked serious. "Henry, there was a phone call for you back at the operations center. They've been trying to contact you. I think you need to go call back."

"Why, is anything the matter?" Henry felt concerned.

"I think it may be. The message said to call your mother in London. It also said the message was about your father, Hayden Travers. Henry, I pray to the Holy Mother that it is nothing serious. But if it is, know that we are here for you." Professor Russo said.

Maria stepped up beside Henry and put her hand on his arm. Her face showed concern and empathy. "Henry, do you want me to come with you?"

Henry felt stunned. He said, "No. I'll need to call mother and find out what has happened. I'll come back and tell you when I know something."

Henry walked quickly from the chamber and toward the Grand Staircase. He made his way up the stairs and past the team working at the landing on the new side tunnel. There seemed to be some kind of loud discussion going on between the new security guard and the workers there. As Henry stepped past, some voices were raised.

One of the students pointed at the guard and said, "You can't do that!"

The guard said, "Yes I can. These orders come from Mister Balev."

Henry ignored the fracas. *I can't be concerned about that right now. They'll have to work it out themselves.* He climbed up the rest of the stairs and came out above ground. He stepped away from the site to a more secluded place and pulled out his phone. His mind was whirling and he found it hard to think. There were messages and voice mails waiting on his phone, all apparently from London. He didn't stop to pick them up but dialed while he walked away from the people going in and out of the dig site. He stepped off by himself.

A woman answered his call. "Yes?" The voice sounded unsteady.

"Mother, it's Henry. I got a message that you'd been trying to reach me. Is something wrong? The message said something about father."

She said, "Henry! Thank goodness. Something horrible has happened. The exploration ship that your father was on in the Black Sea has sunk. The authorities say there were reports of fire and possibly explosions. Your father is missing! Henry, I'm so worried. What if he's hurt or worse?"

"What? Are you sure? How did you find out?"

"Someone from his company called me and said they'd gotten word from the higher ups in the corporation. They said they didn't have anything definite yet to report except to say that he was among the missing. So far they've only found a handful of survivors. Henry, what am I going to do? Your poor father! I can't believe it." She started sobbing. "Henry, Henry! What am I to do?"

Henry fumbled for words while his heart sank. "Mother, I'm stunned. Of course, I'll come home to you as quickly as I can. Let me think, what do I need to do first? I'll have to go tell my professor what has happened and get excused from the work here. He will be very understanding, I'm sure. As soon as I know, I'll call you back and tell you when I can get there, but I'll have to find out what I can work out with the airlines here in Bulgaria. Mother, did you hear me?" Henry felt tears coming to his own eyes and blinked them back.

His mother cried in despair, "My sweet husband! His ship is sunk and he's missing. Perhaps lost at sea. Oh, how can I bear it?"

Tears rolled down his cheeks. He swallowed hard and said, "Mother, I'll get there as soon as I can. Can you hang on? Can Aunt Margaret come and stay with you for a few days? I don't know how quickly I can get there. But it shouldn't take more than a day."

It sounded to Henry that his mother was able to pull herself together a bit and said, "Yes, Henry. Margie is here already. I called her first thing. She is sitting right next to me. I didn't want to tell you until I knew something for certain, but Margie told me you needed to know. She's right of course. I'm so sorry to take you from your work, but I would so love to have you near me just now."

"Of course, mother. I'll do just that. I'll get there as quickly as I can. As soon as I know my travel plans I'll send you a message." He spoke to her for a few more minutes, spoke to his Aunt Margaret and then hung up. He stood still, his stomach in knots, his mind whirling fruitlessly.

Maria's contralto voice carried to his ears softly. "Henry, I am so sorry."

He turned and saw she had come up from the dig site and had walked to within a few paces so as not to invade his privacy during the call. She stepped closer and said, "What has happened? Can you tell me?"

He gulped and told her in a flood what his mother had said and how his father was missing. He told her that he'd need to take some leave for a time and go back to be with his mother. "I have to help her through this. She and I will have to prepare ourselves for the worst I fear, because father may not be coming home again."

She took his arm and led him to a nearby group of unoccupied folding chairs where they could sit. She faced him and leaned in close, holding his hands. "What can I do? Is there anything? I will do anything I can to help you."

Henry felt numb and as if nothing was quite real or as it should be. He slowly shook his head. "I need some time to absorb this. I don't know what to think." He talked to her for a few minutes, rehearsing the details his mother had given. "I can't believe it. How could a modern industrial ship like that sink?"

She said, "Take your time. It is always hard at first to accept something terrible."

He shook his head slowly and finally stood. "I can get my head together while sitting at the airport waiting for a flight, but first things first. I need to go speak with Professor Russo and tell him what has happened."

"Henry, I can tell him if you just need to go. Or I can help you make travel arrangements and take you to the airport. I want to help if I can."

"I know, and thank you." He hugged her tightly. "I need to go tell the professor myself. But if you want to help me with the travel part of things, that would be very nice. I'm not thinking clearly and you might just save me from making a costly mistake."

She squeezed his hand and kissed him lightly on the cheek. He led the way back down into the dig and down the staircase. The group by the side tunnel at the landing had broken up and a yellow caution tape had been strung across the opening to the new dig area. The security guard from earlier stood just inside the opening and behind the yellow tape. He watched Henry and Maria as they walked by and continued down the rest of the staircase.

"I wonder what that is all about?" He said to Maria.

"I don't know, but I heard him saying something about a directive from Balev when I came by a few minutes ago. That pig again. What is he up to now? I thought we'd get some peace from him at last with him in the hospital, but I guess that would be too easy."

They came to the main chamber and found the Professor. He was speaking to some of the people that had been up on the landing at the new side tunnel.

"Professor," one of the students was saying, "the guard chased us all away and said that the new tunnel site was restricted by directive from

Krastyo Balev! It makes no sense. Balev hasn't been down here to see anything. How would he know if an area needed to be restricted? Oh and the guard said Balev was on his way and would be here soon."

Professor Russo held his hands up as if trying to calm the crowd and told the group, "Personally, I hope Balev does come. I currently have to make out a daily report of all activity and take it to him at the hospital. Every day I have to review what has been done and go through a checklist with him of every item found and every photograph. When the side tunnel was discovered, I had to review that with him too, but I don't know why he is restricting access to it. We haven't found the end of it yet and there haven't been any artifacts found in it that I know of. As far as we know, it might be an unused part of the complex or even just a tunnel that was made for storage purposes. I will speak to him about it when I see him next. Until then, we have to wait."

Russo looked at his watch and said, "It's getting late. Wrap up what you were doing and go back outside. It's nearly time to stop for the day."

As the last of the students and workers left, Henry was finally able to get the professor alone for a few minutes. He told Russo of the call with his mother and how he would need to leave Varna to return to her in London.

Russo nodded sadly, "I was afraid it was bad news. Why is it that good news can wait until evening, but bad news always demands immediate attention? Certainly, Henry, you must go to your mother. Maria and I will keep things going here until you return."

"Thank you, professor. I'll just gather a few of my things, my notes and such to take with me." Henry started to move away but stopped. The security guard that had been watching the site of the new side tunnel came up toward them.

The guard said, "Professor, I have a message for you from Administrator Balev." He handed a paper to Russo.

The older man raised an eyebrow, took the paper and read it. He said to the guard, "Do you know what this says?"

The guard said, "Yes. Please come with me, all three of you. Administrator Balev waits above at the upper site."

Professor Russo raised an eyebrow and objected. "Krastyo Balev has arrived? Why has he left the hospital so soon? And why has he come at the end of the work day? He could just as easily have come tomorrow morning. And besides, Henry here has experienced a family emergency and needs to depart immediately to go to London. Maria and I can go meet with Balev, but Henry needs to leave."

"No. Administrator Balev's instructions were clear. He said that the three of you needed to see what was discovered today in the side tunnel. I know you haven't been in that tunnel today because I was there the entire time. I sent him the information myself as I watched the workers. These are the instructions he gave me to carry out when he arrived. Mister Travers can leave for London after he and you and the woman speak with Administrator Balev."

Maria bristled at being called 'the woman' and raised one hand to point at the guard. Her lips pursed and Henry could tell the man was about to get his ears singed.

Henry spoke quickly to Maria and said, "Let's just go with him. The sooner we get this done, the sooner I can be on my way." She stopped, inhaled deliberately and nodded assent.

Henry quickly gathered a couple of items from where he had been working earlier and they followed the guard out of the crypt chamber and up the staircase. At the landing, the guard moved the yellow caution tape out of the way and motioned them in. Before stepping into the passage, Henry looked up and down the staircase and noted that all of the other students and workers had gone. He remembered Russo's instructions to the group and looked at his watch. *I've lost track of the time again. Everyone else has left for the day.*

Henry stepped into the tunnel and came face to face with Krastyo Balev. The thin man had a large cast on the broken arm and wore a cumbersome sling on one shoulder as well as a bulky bag on the other. He looked at Henry coldly and waited for Professor Russo and Maria to notice him as well. *What is this all about?*

Henry said, "Mister Balev, I just received word from London about a family tragedy and need to return there as soon as possible."

Balev said softly, "This won't take long." He looked satisfied and said no more until they'd been joined by the other two.

Professor Russo said, "Now what is this about, Krastyo? What is so important that it cannot wait until tomorrow? Mister Travers needs to leave due to a family emergency. And why did you leave the hospital early?"

Balev said, "Never mind that. Come and see what is so important." He motioned for the three to lead the way. He let them pass and then spoke briefly to the guard who stayed behind at the entrance to the tunnel.

The passage was a little low for Henry so he bent his head as he moved into the tunnel. Lights had been strung along the floor and the ceiling and the passage was just wide enough for a single-file group. From what he had heard of the find the day before, the opening at the landing had been closed off by a shaped stone that fit like a door. Once that had been moved, this passageway had been evident. Henry saw there were some small pieces of rubble on the floor, but the tunnel was otherwise amazingly intact.

He walked carefully down the straight passage, cautiously avoiding hitting his head on the ceiling. Maria stepped after him, the professor came third and Balev followed at the back. The passage went straight for about fifteen meters or so and then turned a ninety degree corner. Henry moved around the corner, went ahead for about nine meters and came to the end of the passage.

The corridor ended in an apparent rock fall that blocked the way. Henry went to the piled rocks and looked. Without turning back, he said, "Is this where the item was found that you mentioned?" He heard Balev grunt assent.

"What am I looking for? Wait, maybe this is it..." Henry knelt down to examine a large flat stone at the base of the rock fall. There appeared to be some designs on the rock. *Are they painted or cut into the rock? I need more light here.* He took a high-intensity torch from a pocket and shined it on the stone. Maria and Professor Russo moved in close to see what Henry had found.

There was a carving of a figure cut into the surface of the rock. The stone was flat on one side and irregular on the other so Henry looked up at the ceiling to see if the stone had fallen from there. He scanned from the ceiling down to the floor and turned back to Maria and Professor Russo.

"This stone looks shaped on only one side, so I would guess that it was part of the wall or ceiling. All of these stones appear to be shaped on one side."

Maria said, "What is the design there? Is that another of the bull symbols?"

Henry said, "It looks to be a female figure holding a bull symbol in one hand. It looks more ornamented than the others we've seen, perhaps except for that one on the plaster."

Russo said, "And what is that second symbol?"

Henry said, "I can't make it out clearly. The carving shows her other hand holding something, perhaps it's a small rod. If that is a rod, it has a diagonal pattern…"

Maria said, "Henry! Like the cylinder seal? Does that look like the cylinder seal?" Maria pulled her backpack off and rummaged through a pocket. She pulled out the cast replica she'd made a few days earlier. "Does it look like this?"

"Henry said, "You're right. That's it. The bull symbol is in one hand and the cylinder seal is in the other. The third symbol on a medallion on her chest has the standard hammer and fire symbol, what Maria and I've decided should be called 'Vulcan.'"

Professor Russo chuckled. "Have you now? I don't get any say in this?" He turned to look behind him. "Krastyo, what does the Bulgarian Antiquities Department have to say about that? Krastyo? We've found the rock with the priestess and symbols. Krastyo?"

There was no response. The Professor shined his torch back down the passageway to the corner and there was no sign of anyone. He spoke louder.

"Krastyo! What exactly did you expect us to do other than examine this stone briefly?"

There was still no response. The professor frowned and straightened up. "Now where has he gone?" He said.

* * *

Krastyo Balev stepped out of the passageway and past the yellow tape. He looked at the security guard and motioned for him to leave. The man immediately turned and headed back up the Grand Staircase and toward the world above. Balev stayed, watching the man exit. Balev backed to the far side of the landing on the staircase away from the ancient passage. He opened the shoulder bag he carried and took out a small device with one large button and a selector switch with positions labeled one through four. He seemed to double check a separate device labelled with the number four that lay inside the shoulder bag. He pulled out and examined the thing's unattached wires as if wanting to make certain of their condition. Satisfied, he turned back to the small handheld device and its button. *It is amusing that an innocuous thing like this can be used for activation. The specialist guard I hired assured me it was better than a cell phone which would have difficulty getting a strong enough signal down here. He said this simple switch box would work fine.*

From the passage, he heard what sounded like Professor Russo's voice calling his name. *Let him. I'm done with them.* He set the selector to the 'one' setting and pressed the button on the device. An explosive thump sounded in the passage. He switched the selector to the 'two' setting and pushed the button again. What followed was another concussion. *That would be the first one at the inner corner and then the second around the turn in the corner. The third impact should be very close to the Grand Staircase landing to completely shut the opening to the passage. The fourth hopefully won't be needed, but now for the third one.*

He switched to the 'three' setting and pushed the button. There was no explosion or concussion, but dust from the previous explosions continued billowing out of the side tunnel in a large cloud. It momentarily obstructed Balev's vision and he backed away from the dust all the way to the far wall on the opposite side of the landing. The floor started shaking under him and his heart sped up. *I tried to set off the third explosive but it didn't seem to go off and now the floor is shaking. What is happening? Why is this trembling going on so long?*

Something pelted Krastyo Balev on the shoulder and something else hit his good arm, and he lost hold of the device he'd used to set off the detonators for the first two explosives. Balev's heart felt like it had jumped into his throat. The lights stationed through the Grand Staircase flickered off, but a second later came back on. The rumbling grew louder and Balev saw more rocks falling from above. His hand went to his mouth in terror as he saw a huge crack open in the wall above the now collapsed entrance to the passageway. The crack ran upward for twelve meters straight toward the counterweight that held the stone door open. Balev looked up above to the night sky that was visible through the opening. He heard a splitting and wrenching sound followed by a thunderous crash. All of the lights went out and stayed that way.

It thundered like a mountain of stone was sliding down and he saw that the night sky had vanished in the darkness above. Endless projectiles rained down on him. He tried to dodge, but with all of the lights from the stairway out, he couldn't see what he was trying to avoid. A large object struck his cast and he screamed in agony. *My arm! It feels like it has been broken again!* More rocks crashed down on him. He crouched down and tried to cower against the wall. Something heavy struck him and he heard a loud, throbbing ringing in his head. He lost consciousness.

* * *

There was a loud booming sound from around the corner behind them and the floor and ceiling lights went out in a moment. The floor trembled and Henry lost his balance where he had been kneeling. He fell to the side but caught himself with his hands. Chunks of rock rained down from the ceiling. One struck a glancing blow to Henry on his shoulder. Dust flew through the air. He coughed almost uncontrollably and thought he heard two more people distantly coughing.

He thought he heard Maria cry out in pain. He shouted her name but the noise of rumbling and crashing around them was too deafening to make out even his own voice. He reached in the direction of her cry and at first felt only rock and rubble. He scrabbled frantically to reach her and touched flesh. *It has to be Maria! Please God, don't let her be hurt.*

The rumbling continued at a subsonic level, felt rather than heard. There were booms and thuds and the floor continued to shake for a while. After what seemed like a very long time, the noise and shaking stopped and the only sound was coughing.

I've got to stay calm. I can't help anyone if I'm in a panic.

Maria's unsteady voice spoke. "Henry? Are you alright?"

He said, "Yes, I think so. I was hit on the shoulder but I think it just glanced off. With all this bloody dust though, I can't see a thing. You aren't hurt, are you?"

She said, "I took a knock in the head and something smashed me on the leg and foot, but I don't think anything is broken. I think my scalp is bleeding but I don't know how bad it is. I'm covered up in dirt and small rocks. The floor and ceiling lights have gone out. I can't see anything and I can't find my torch."

Henry tried to feel for his torch in the total darkness with both hands. He couldn't find anything and started to feel within himself a welling of panic.

"Professor Russo! Are you there?" Henry called. There was no answer.

She said, "Henry, what can we do? We need to find a light somehow. The professor must be hurt. We need to find him."

"I can't find the torch I was holding prior to the rock fall and from what I can feel, this part of the passage has changed from what I remember a few minutes ago." *Think, Henry, man! Think! Wait, my phone!* He struggled and got one hand into his pants pocket and found his phone. He pulled it out and pressed the button on the lower middle side of the front panel. It lit up and filled the tunnel with dim light.

Henry instantly felt claustrophobic and was almost sorry he'd found the phone. There was a dusty haze in the air. He spotted Maria and moved to her. The floor was piled high in rocks and dirt and the passage seemed much more constricted than it had. The regular ceiling had been replaced by a jagged surface that showed that many of the ceiling and wall stones had fallen.

Henry helped Maria dig out and checked her in the light of the phone's face. There was a trickle of blood on her forehead so she probably had a small cut on her crown somewhere under that thick hair. She had some large bruises developing on her arms, left thigh and foot, but she could move, albeit painfully. They both looked back and couldn't see any sign of the professor.

"Henry, I don't see him." Her voice sounded grim.

He said, "We need to look for him, though. The last I remember before the explosion was him trying to talk to Balev."

Maria said, "Balev could be buried in here with us. I'd almost forgotten about him. What do you think caused the cave-in?"

Henry said, "I have no idea. Our first priority is to get out, of course. After that we can worry about what went wrong."

Henry crawled on hands and knees back into the passageway, calling Russo's name. Henry heard a low moan and zeroed in on the sound. In the dim light, he made out the professor's prone form, almost entirely covered in a mound of dirt and rocks. Henry and Maria crawled to Russo and cautiously brushed aside the soil and tossed away the rocks. Soon, they had uncovered Russo and sized up the situation: Russo was unconscious and injured badly. He had a broken shoulder, a shattered wrist and multiple lacerations on his face and neck. He was covered in large welts and bruises and bleeding from multiple small sites and probably had internal injuries as well.

"He needs help." Henry looked at the face of his phone. "Of course, there's no cell signal in here. If there were, I could be sure there was a rescue team out there working to free us. As it is, we'll just have to trust that they are there. At least we have the light from this phone."

Maria said, "I also have my phone, but it doesn't have a full charge."

"Let me see about the condition of the rest of the passage." Henry crawled and ducked through the rubble and turned the corner that went back in the direction of the Grand Staircase.

He stopped and looked at the rocks piled floor to ceiling. He felt stunned and could hardly believe what he was seeing. "Maria, there is no passage around the corner anymore. It's completely blocked." He turned back and looked at her, his face bleak. "We've been buried alive."

CHAPTER 19 – LESSONS

"But what if better counsels might erect our minds,
and teach us to cast off this yoke?"
— John Milton, Paradise Lost

Janos Parasca looked at the crystal steel sword and at the homeless beggar that his local security officer Damon Karras had brought him. *When is he going to get me a woman that I can practice on? I'm tired of these derelicts that he brings me. Still, I've been successful at learning some things with them.*

He nudged the derelict's body with a toe. *Dead. Hmmm. I need to be more careful in the ways I use this sword. I wasted almost all of that escaping life energy.* He remembered the way the man's death had felt. In Parasca's eyes, the man had glowed with an aura of reddish light that grew brighter as his torment increased. At the last moment, the man's life had vanished and Parasca had felt the familiar rush of power that came like a burst of sunlight. This time there had been something different.

I actually saw the energy burst. It built up in his body and then at the last it seemed to implode and I saw it recede as if through a hole. There was a back-flash of energy and that is when I felt the power flow to me. I felt the backwash, but most of the energy flashed through that hole in space. That must be what Moloch referred to when he spoke about the soul transitioning to another plane. It leaves the body container and moves to that other place. In the transition, it leaves a trace of energy behind and that is what I was able to absorb. I also felt the sword absorb some of that last flash. When I hold it, I can feel that it contains slightly more energy than before. I wonder if there is a way to capture more of that energy?

Parasca stalked around the room, waving the sword. *More importantly, what can I do with the energy stored in this thing? I still haven't been able to use it to heal like Mircea was taught to do. Maybe I'm not capable of doing something like healing. It's not exactly in my personality in spite of what I tried to trick her into believing.*

Parasca shook his head at the botched results of that attempt to trick and capture Mercy and Jack. His security man Alex Lacusta had succeeded in stunning Mercy and rendering her helpless, but before he'd been able to do anything else, Jack Truett had jumped him and the two men had fought. Somehow, Lacusta had been stabbed with a long shard of glass in the fight and had almost died. Someone had called in an ambulance and they found Lacusta almost dead from loss of blood. He was recovering from the wounds now, but it would be a while before Parasca saw that man in action again. *A pity, he showed promise too.*

Parasca turned back to his thoughts of using the power. *What else did I see the monster do besides healing my broken mouth when he nearly crushed my face? He used the power to flay that man alive on the Fortuna. He read my mind, and he suspended me in the air. Perhaps healing is just too hard for me to learn and I could try one of those other uses of the power.*

Parasca concentrated on entering a trance state like he had known the monster taught Mercy to do, but each time he tried, he couldn't maintain his concentration and the trance slipped away. *Relaxation techniques just don't work for me! How am I going to do this? What was I doing when I perceived the energy aura around that dying man?* Parasca continued trying to think through the experience.

I didn't concentrate and try to go into a trance. I just let myself feel it, let myself enjoy it as if drinking an excellent glass of wine. I allowed myself to relax and fall into the flow of it. That's it! It's like when I sit back and study one of the pieces in my collection. I just let myself experience the sight and smell, the texture and feel of it. If there are memories tied to the object, I allow them to roll through me. I let it happen. That's what I need to do here.

Parasca sat down and held the sword across his lap. He allowed himself to experience the touch and texture of the sword and the story of its making. The feel of the deaths that went into it flowed through him. He relaxed into the enjoyment of the possession of it. *I own it and no one can take it from me! No one takes what is mine.*

In a flash, he saw the energy again pulsating in the sword like a red heartbeat. It washed over him and he felt absorbed in its flow. He felt energized and alive. He saw a reddish thread that lead from his hand into the sword and saw a trickle of energy moving through that thread into him. He experienced the energy. *I own it. It is mine. No one takes what is mine.*

He let the power flow into him through the reddish thread and felt more alive than ever. He felt youthful and powerful, capable of almost anything. He thought about the thread and accepted and embraced it. The thread seemed to widen and thicken into a cord and the energy flowing into him increased proportionally. He felt so much power that he wanted to hurl it in balls of energy, but didn't know how. *Try to lift something with it. I need to release this and let it flow through me and into something.*

He looked at the derelict's body and saw that there was no unified life energy aura around it any longer, though he did sense something like a sizzling, almost a bubbling sparkle coming from it. He looked closer and found that his eyesight was greatly enhanced while in this state. He could see the dead body at an almost microscopic clarity. He realized that he must be seeing tiny bursts of dying energy from the very cells of the dead man. *As his death progresses, I see the fizzing of individual cells giving up their miniscule life energy. His death is now echoed a trillion times over by the death of each cell as he decays. How marvelous.*

With the clarity of his vision and the swelling surge of power in him, he thrust out his arms as if to carry the body. The dead man's corpse rose into the air. Power crackled from Parasca and he held the body aloft from a distance. Exultation filled him. *The power is mine now to use, and no one takes what is mine.*

CHAPTER 20 – MEMORY

"That day I oft remember, when from sleep I first awaked"
— *John Milton, Paradise Lost*

The train pulled into the station in Timisoara and Jack and Mercy quickly disembarked. Mercy made a stop to buy some essentials at a shop in the station and visited the restroom to freshen up and brush her teeth. They caught a taxi to their meeting with Dmitri and on the way settled into a few minutes of quiet reflection. Both were lost in thought and they took advantage of the time for some silence. Jack took her hand and held it gently, but said nothing.

Mercy pondered her past life and the changes she'd been through in the last few days. *I can hardly believe I used to live here in Timisoara. What a long time ago. I was a completely different person then. I was traumatized, but still so naïve. I knew so little, but then, do I really know that much more now? Who am I really, even now? I'm the illegitimate child of a horribly evil man, but the adopted daughter of a wonderful man and woman. Both of them are gone, but now I know, not really. They've moved on to the next life... and I can see them and talk to them. I'm some kind of supernatural amphibian, able to exist in two realms, this earthly one and, what ... the afterlife, the realm where they now exist? I've spoken to my deceased parent! It's too much. I think I'm going into mental shock almost. My mind cannot accept all of this. How much change and upheaval can a person experience before it becomes toxic?*

I've heard people say that change is a necessary part of life and that without change, there is no life. But I think the opposite must be true too, with too much change, life also becomes impossible. Plants sometimes outgrow their containers and need to be transplanted. That would be good and necessary change. But, if you start uprooting it and transplanting it every month, you'll kill it. Too much change can become toxic.

Is that what is happening to me? Have I outgrown my container and need to be transplanted, or have I been jerked around and uprooted so much that I am being destroyed? Is this healthy or poisonous?

I used to be agnostic and didn't think it was possible to prove or disprove the existence of God. Now I have experienced the supernatural. I carry this power and use it for things I wouldn't have believed weeks ago. I can heal myself and others. I can levitate objects and move things at a distance. I can read thoughts, enter into another person's head and look at the world through their eyes. Unless I have gone completely delusional and am actually hallucinating in an insane asylum somewhere, this is my new reality. The question is: is it a reality that I can get my mind around, can accept, can understand and find my place within it?

Many things I believed have been shown to be wrong. How can I mentally survive this crisis of belief? Does this mental turmoil get any better, ever? When will the unbelievable start becoming accepted and typical? I guess I'm going to need a new vocabulary. I can't even use the word 'unbelievable' anymore, because what does that even mean after what I've lived through?

Maybe I just have to keep putting one foot in front of the next, continue to walk and continue to act. She looked at Jack and he looked back at her and smiled. He squeezed her hand and went back to his own thoughts. *I like being able to just sit quietly with this man. There are times when words are hollow and inappropriate. I'm so glad neither of us feels compelled to fill necessary silence with chatter.*

This man too was agnostic. He never believed in life after death, or the supernatural. And, he hasn't had the benefit of experiencing this from my viewpoint, feeling the power and experiencing the touch of the divine, first hand. His is a secondhand experience, he sees me go through these things and exercise these abilities, but what must it be like for him? Of course with my new ability to listen in on his thoughts, I could learn what it really is like to be him, but do I want to? Wouldn't that be equivalent to breaking into his home like a thief, or even like a kind of mental rape if I invaded his thoughts?

This is not going to be easy for me or him. It isn't going to be one change and done. For me, I think I have to go through a long tunnel of fire. I will be burned and forged. It has changed me, is changing me and will change me further. It will make me into something different than I am now, but isn't that the point of existence itself? If we are not becoming something else, something new, then why are we here at all?

She looked at Jack again. *Somehow, I believe he is going to be my anchor to reality, to Earth. I'll be going where neither of us can understand now, but he'll be earthbound: I'm the one who is the amphibian. I'm the one that can cross the planar barrier, but Jack has to stay here. Until death, he can't leave this plane of existence. Whatever I become, wherever I go, he is going to be the person who will pull me back down and set my feet on the ground again. He won't control me; I will control me, but he will be a reference point for me, the way I know to turn to get back home. How amazing.* She looked at him and he turned to her. She lifted her face to him and softly kissed his lips.

The taxi pulled up to the address and Mercy saw that it was a beautiful grand building very much like a luxury hotel. It had an ornate but small sign by the door that said simply 'The Duchess.'

Jack whistled and said, "A stay at a place like this would get a business expense report turned down and rejected. I'd get in trouble if I booked travel to a spot like this."

The taxi was met by an immaculately dressed footman who, finding they had no luggage, escorted them to the entrance. Another employee opened the door and escorted them in. The interior of the lobby was classically decorated with antiques and beautiful crystal chandeliers and lighting. In spite of the obvious expensive décor, the overall flavor was still somehow one of extreme tastefulness.

Mercy said, "I didn't know places like this even existed in Timisoara!"

Jack said, "It was probably reserved to party bosses back when you lived here years ago. Wow! Look at all this."

A moderately tall man in his fifties, dressed impeccably, stepped forward and asked, "Doctor Mercy Teller?"

She said, "Yes, I am Mercy Teller."

He offered his hand in greeting to her and said, "I am so pleased to meet you, Doctor Teller. I am Alexi Slokov, Chief Operating Officer of Intercon Transport Corporation. I believe my brother Dmitri has been in contact with you concerning this meeting today. He has been so looking forward to this time with you."

Jack stepped forward and extended his hand. "I am Jack Truett. Until recently, the Vice President of Black Sea Exploration for PetroRomania."

Alexi said, "Ah, Mister Truett, what an honor! My brother and I have been following your career with PetroRomania with great interest. Perhaps we would be able to discuss possible business ventures with you in the near future?"

Jack replied with a friendly but cautious manner. "Perhaps. Today, however, I am accompanying Doctor Teller as a business advisor. Also, Doctor Teller and I are engaged to be married."

Slokov raised an eyebrow but did not miss a beat in his reply. He took Jack's offered hand and said, "What joyous news! And what a fortunate man to be wed to such a brilliant scientist and accomplished archaeologist. I congratulate you and your beautiful fiancé and wish you many years of happiness."

Alexi motioned with one arm to encompass the lobby of the grand building. "How do you like our magnificent Duchess?"

"It's gorgeous, but why is it called 'The Duchess?'" Mercy asked.

"Alexi said, "My brother and I gave it the name after we acquired it years ago. By that name, we meant she is old, classical, finely appointed, wonderfully cared for and beautifully maintained. We believe it is the finest retirement home in all of Romania."

"Retirement home?" Jack said. His voice carried notes of skepticism.

"Yes, Dmitri and I are the primary investors in 'The Duchess' and we have many wonderful residents living here. The medical care is finer than any hospital in the country. The accommodations are fit for royalty, the kitchen is as good as any five-star hotel in Europe and the staff is top-notch."

Alexi offered Mercy his arm. She hesitated at first, but took it. He said, "Shall we go to the Salon and meet with Dmitri?"

Jack said, "First, weren't we to visit with Mercy's grandmother, Sonia Rodica?"

Alexi said, "Of course. But before you see her, I know that you must have questions for my brother and me. Would you follow me, please?"

They walked across the immaculate lobby and to a large double door of deeply polished oak. A doorman opened the door and Alexi ushered Mercy and Jack inside the salon. The room was smaller than the lobby but very nicely appointed. It was filled with polished leather chairs and couches. A rotund man rose from his chair and approached. He was well dressed but did not wear a jacket, possibly due to one arm being in a sling. He stopped and looked at Mercy. His face filled with a look of wonder and admiration.

Dmitri Slokov said, "Doctor Mercy Teller? How wonderful it is to meet you at last! Please, may I offer you some refreshments?"

Mercy said, "Yes, thank you. I am thirsty."

A butler stepped forward and spoke to Mercy, "What would mademoiselle care for? May I bring a beverage, cheeses and pastries? Perhaps some Turkish coffee and liqueur or perhaps mademoiselle would like some wine or champagne?"

Mercy smiled and said, "Yes, bring the cheeses, pastries, Turkish coffee and liqueur. Would you gentlemen care for something?"

All of the other three agreed with her choices and the butler left.

Dmitri's eyes shone with pleasure. He looked at Mercy as a starving man looks at food. He said, "Doctor Teller, forgive me for staring. Your photographs do not do you justice, and I see so much of your mother in you, except that you surpass even her, if such a thing is possible. In my eyes, your mother was a great beauty and I loved her with all of my heart, but you have gone beyond her." He slowed down speaking and seemed to choke up with emotion. "Forgive me. I am overcome." He hurriedly sat down, his face red. He quickly gulped down a glass of water.

Alexi stepped into the silence, "Please pardon poor Dmitri. He has been injured as you can see, and he cared deeply for your mother, Tresa. Seeing you has brought back painful memories."

Mercy felt suspicious. *Are they trying to manipulate us like Parasca tried to do? I think I'll just do a little listening.* Mercy plunged her mind through its paces and within only a second, she could hear Dmitri's thoughts. *I'm getting so much faster at this.* His mind was in turmoil and he was feeling short of breath. He was thinking, *"I didn't expect this. The pictures of her are nothing compared to seeing her in person. So regal. So powerful. She is a goddess! Tresa, your daughter! I have no words! I must not scare her away, though. Look how she is studying me. I must win her trust. Curse that disaster on the Fortuna!"*

Mercy pulled her thoughts away from Dmitri. *He seems sincere. I don't hear any deception in his mind, but there are obviously things he is keeping close to his vest and not telling. I need to be careful around this man. He may be positively inclined toward me, but he owes nothing to Jack. Who knows, he might even try to use Jack as leverage against me.*

Dmitri seemed to compose himself and calm down. He motioned to the couches and noticed the butler entering. "Here are our refreshments. Please forgive me again; I am not usually such an emotional man. I was … surprised." The food and drinks were placed in front of them and they took a minute to get settled. Dmitri thanked the staff and they left.

Dmitri said, "I know that you have questions for me, so let me answer some of them immediately." He turned to Mercy and said, "Your grandmother Sonia is indeed here at the Duchess. I provide her with these accommodations out of respect for her and your mother, Tresa. Sonia does not really care for me, but she tolerates my money used in her behalf. She perhaps feels it is some recompense to receive care from one who used to be in the Securitate such as myself."

Dmitri shrugged. "We have all made bad career choices at one time or another, have we not? I used to be a low level officer in the Securitate back before the regime change. I didn't go far once I got on Janos Parasca's bad side."

Dmitri Slokov looked at Mercy earnestly. "I am not a good man. I am efficient, but not good. I do things for my own sake and for the sake of my family. Beyond that, I am not concerned. Anyone that hurts me or my family becomes my enemy. Janos Parasca, who I once called friend, hurt me and the one closest to me in the most serious way possible. He didn't do it by accident, but because he wanted a woman to add to his collection. He's always been about collecting things and people. He's always been about owning and possessing."

He continued, "It happened back when Parasca and I served in the Securitate together. I was courting your mother, Tresa Rodica. Your grandmother Sonia didn't approve, but tolerated me. Once, Parasca went with Tresa and me for a night on the town. I caught him staring and ogling her. When I told him to back off, we argued and he beat me up. He was always a powerful man."

Dmitri stared off into the distance as if watching the past play out. "Later, he reported something subversive that Sonia had said. Sonia was taken in for questioning and Parasca told Tresa I was responsible. She never spoke to me again after that because she thought I had informed and gotten her mother arrested. I found out later that she took up with Parasca. He got her pregnant several times and arranged for her back alley abortions until the last one that was interrupted by police. You were born out of that pregnancy and Tresa committed suicide in jail. It is all such a tragic story. All the more so because Parasca cared nothing for her really, he just wanted another trophy, like another stamp in his collector's book. When he was through with her, I don't think it bothered him in the least that she killed herself."

He lowered his gaze back to Mercy. "When I found out what had happened, I knew I could never rest. My hatred of that man has become the all-consuming passion of my life. If there is something that I can do to thwart Janos, no matter how large or how small, I do it. If I can make money at his expense, I do that too, but it is not essential."

He said, "I have some informers within PetroRomania and my computer people have successfully hacked Parasca's systems so I often know what is happening in his corporation. When the *Fortuna,* on its shakedown cruise, found the original dagger and giant skeletal hand, I knew that I needed to act. I had a specialist take away the fossilized hand and I still have that monstrous thing. When I found out that Janos wanted you for the job, I knew I had to put a man on the *Fortuna,* so I got my specialist onto the ship posing as a security guard. Don't you think that is wonderfully ironic? Parasca's security team was infiltrated by my spy."

"When you found the crystal steel sword and shield and then found the giant sarcophagus, I knew I couldn't let Parasca make off with all of that, so I acted again."

Mercy said, "Dmitri, I realize you and I are from different worlds and don't share the same moral values. I understand what you said about your history with Parasca, Tresa and Sonia, and your desire for revenge against him, but you do realize that there were several hundred people on the *Fortuna,* and most of them weren't even employees of PetroRomania? They were contractors, hired to do jobs and that is all. You were responsible for many of them being killed, were you not?"

Dmitri spread his hands as if in apology, "As you said, dear doctor, we are from different worlds. I do not usually go out of my way to kill people unless they deserve it. But, I do not worry myself overly about people who get in my way, either. I know this must be hard to accept, but it is the way I am. One does not learn to be empathetic in the Securitate. And when there is damage that I might do to Parasca, I cannot resist, and I do not try."

Alexi inserted himself into the conversation. "Doctor Teller, my brother can be blunt, but he speaks frankly to you. For him this is a sign of deep respect. He only speaks this way to close family or friends. He and I are survivors of the revolution that brought down the Ceausescu government. We have done things that most people would not be willing to do, but for us, it has led to this success that we share. We do not ask you to approve of us or condone what we have done, but we tell you these things so you will understand that we are sincere in our care for Sonia Rodica. She is your grandmother and the two of you are Dmitri's only remaining links to Tresa, long-departed."

Dmitri said, "As long as she lives, she will be well provided for. It is the least I can do."

Mercy felt revulsion for these men, but also a grudging admiration. *It is as if they follow a code, but not a morality. They are not even good in their own eyes, but they would never break their own self-imposed rules that loyalty and family come first. I don't quite know what to think.*

She said, "I think I understand somewhat. May I see Sonia now?"

"Yes, of course," said Dmitri. "Alexi will escort you to Sonia Rodica. Mister Truett, could I impose on you for some conversation while Dr. Teller visits with her grandmother?"

Alexi offered his arm and Mercy took it. They walked from the room and to an elevator. The attendant took them to the seventh floor without being asked. After a short walk down the hall, they came to a door and Alexi knocked lightly. The door was opened by a woman in a nurse's uniform. They entered the apartment and Mercy saw that it was an immaculate suite with several adjoining rooms. A neatly dressed elderly woman sat across from the door near a window with a beautiful view of the square below. She wore a simple light blue dress and a darker blue sweater. Her hair was white and short and she wore reading glasses. She set aside a book that she had been holding titled, "Chemical Processes and Case Studies" and stood up slowly from the chair.

"Doctor Mercy Teller," She beamed. "I believe I have received the answer to a prayer."

Mercy went to Sonia Rodica and hugged her gently. *She feels so tiny! I didn't remember her like this.*

"Granddaughter. I prayed I would see you again, and now I have. Come sit with me."

* * *

Dmitri Slokov turned to Jack Truett after Alexi and Mercy had left. Dmitri said, "She should have been my daughter. If not for Parasca's treachery, she would have been. I know the two of you are close. Let me give fair warning: you must <u>never</u> hurt her."

Jack let the threat roll past him. "Do you know some of what Mercy has been through? She has experienced some of the worst that life has to offer and yet she still stands. She is strong and has grown more so in just the past few weeks. I will not hurt her, but it is not what I can do to her that worries me. It is what Janos Parasca could do to her." Jack told Dmitri of the attempt to capture them at Mercy's apartment in Bucharest. He included Mercy's stunning by Lacusta, but blurred the end details of the fight by saying that they'd barely escaped.

Jack continued, "I don't know what Parasca thinks to do with Mercy even if he captures her. She hates the man and would never cooperate with him again. She knows he is her biological father, but she only despises him all the more for that fact. It must be for some other reason that he tried to capture her. If he wanted her dead, he would have had her gunned down in her apartment rather than have her stunned."

Dmitri said, "Maybe it has to do with the salvage operation he is mounting at the site of the *Fortuna's* wreck."

Jack looked up startled. He said, "So he is the one behind that salvage ship I read about in the papers."

"Yes, he's on his way, but never fear, I am beating him to the punch. My salvage crew will get there first. My brother has wrapped up a deal that gives us the first possible ship near the site. But never mind that for a moment."

Dmitri leaned in, "Come work for me. After all, you owe nothing to Parasca after the way he treated you and Mercy. He left you to die on that sinking ship. Plus, your knowledge of the oil business will be invaluable to my companies that mainly concentrate on shipping, but need to expand, possibly into oil field service. I know what kind of person you are and I know what kind of work you do. It is your ability to manage people that matters to me. Besides, I can see that Mercy respects you and cares for you. I know by the way she looks at you that there is no hesitation or reservation in her when she thinks of you. That is a sign of complete trust. If she trusts you like that, I know I can too. I won't insult you with a salary offer. Suffice it to say it will be much higher than your last salary for PetroRomania. Don't decide now. Think about it."

Jack said, "I will think about it, but you must not get your hopes up. Remember what Mercy said to you before she left. She has some respect for you, especially in the care you give to her grandmother, but she does not agree with your morality. I don't either. You had some of my coworkers killed. That shows me a value system that I cannot live with. You wanted Parasca hurt in payback for hurt he has caused you and yours in the past. In order to do that, you felt the deaths of bystanders on the *Fortuna* were a necessary evil. You believe that the end justifies the means. I do not subscribe to that world view."

Dmitri nodded and said, "You have courage to speak to me so frankly. That is another thing I appreciate about you, but maybe you are right: we can cooperate on some things perhaps, but we are too different in other ways. Let us leave it at that for now. Agreed?"

Jack said, "I agree that we should leave it at that for now."

Dmitri said, "Jack, tell me how you and Mercy met."

Jack felt confused at the change of subject and said, "Pardon me for asking, but why do you want to know?"

Dmitri shrugged and said, "I just want to understand you better."

Jack spoke with caution, not sure where this conversation was headed. "We met in graduate school. I was in petroleum engineering and she was in petroleum geology. Different enough that we didn't know everything about each other's subjects, but similar enough that we had regular contact."

Dmitri said, "Ah, that explains it. When my information from within PetroRomania indicated that Parasca was trying to hire Mercy, I couldn't understand how she would agree to the offer of employment, knowing some of her past experience with Parasca. I understand now. It was because she knew you previously and trusted you. I imagine that had a lot to do with her agreeing to join."

Jack came back at Slokov with his own question. "What do you expect from Mercy and me? You offered to reconnect Mercy and her grandmother. You must want something out of this. What is it?"

Dmitri said, "Again, you speak frankly. It tells me that you are not a man that conceals and has ulterior motives. I respect that." He sighed, "Not many people are this way with me. My brother Alexi, yes. One or two other people." He chuckled. "Sonia Rodica is like that as well." He narrowed his eyes and seemed to consider Jack.

Slokov finally appeared to settle mentally on what he would say. "Jack Truett, this is what I want from you and Mercy: to not work against me as I try to preempt Parasca from his salvage operations on the *Fortuna* wreck site. I also want Mercy to understand that her grandmother is safe and well cared for. I hope because of this, Mercy will learn that she can trust me ..." He hesitated and concluded, "... in some things at least. I hope that you and she will work for me at some point in the future, but that, as you were saying, may be a bridge too far to cross, at least at the present."

Jack said, "Fair enough."

Dmitri leaned forward and said in a low voice, "Jack, what really happened on the *Fortuna*? The reports that I got were sketchy and frankly too fantastic to be believed in some ways. What was in that metal monolith? Was there really a giant mummified creature in it?"

How do I answer? He is connected to all of this but would probably disbelieve the truth of it.

Jack said, "Dmitri, you wouldn't believe me. I saw it and I can't accept it even though I was there."

Dmitri said, "So it is true then."

"What is true?" Jack said.

Dmitri said, "Vasya, the Russian I had on the *Fortuna*, sent me a message and said the gigantic mummified creature revitalized and started attacking the crew. I didn't know what to think. Now that I see your response, I am beginning to wonder. Was Vasya accurate? Just tell me that."

Jack said, "He was. A monster came out of that sarcophagus and went on a killing spree. Mercy stopped it, re-imprisoned it in that steel box and we escaped on one of the *Fortuna's* mini-subs. It was the most frightening thing I've ever experienced."

Dmitri said, "Mercy re-imprisoned it? Mercy?"

"Yes, Mercy did almost all of it, though I helped by operating the crane to lift and close the lid of that box. There are some things you don't know about her and I cannot tell you. She is very capable in ways you would not believe. She will have to tell you more if she wants you to know. It is not my right to tell you more. Suffice it to say, that she should not be angered or betrayed. She can be implacable."

* * *

Krastyo Balev opened his eyes, but the darkness remained just as deep as it had with his eyelids closed. He felt splitting pain in his head, right behind his eyes. *It feels like I have a rusty metal blade lodged in my brain.* He grew more aware and felt sensation returning to his limbs, and that was very bad. Pain lanced up his arms and legs. His already broken arm felt newly, horribly hurt. *What if my arm has been completely destroyed beyond all repair? What if it has been amputated? I think I feel my fingers, but what if I just am feeling phantom sensations and the arm is totally severed?*

He tried to take stock of his situation, but in the dark, in the silence, it was difficult. Balev couldn't move his arms or legs, though he could feel the rocks and debris pressing on him. Ripples of terror ran in waves up his arms, onto his neck and over the back of his head to his scalp where his hair stood up. *What if I'm paralyzed? I can feel but not move!*

He tried to speak, but he found his mouth strangely dry. He coughed feebly and swiped his thick, unresponsive tongue around his mouth. It didn't want to move, and very little saliva seemed to come at his command. He croaked out some words that sounded more like a wounded animal than a human being, "Help me! Please help me!"

There was no response, no acknowledgment of his existence or his suffering. The silent dark seemed to absorb his anguish. The stillness of the crypt seemed to physically tighten around him. Balev started whimpering. *This is all their fault! Those criminals, trying to steal the treasure that was mine by rights! I know they were trying to steal from me. They wouldn't have been working behind my back all those hours if they hadn't wanted to steal from me. Oh, what will happen to me? What will I do?* He cried in loneliness and terror until he slumped back into an uneasy sleep, still unable to move or even shift his weight.

CHAPTER 21 – IN THE DARK

"For those rebellious, here their prison ordained in utter darkness"
— John Milton, Paradise Lost

Henry sat for a moment, the light on his phone illuminating the collapsed passageway. Maria looked at him, worry plain on her face. Professor Russo groaned quietly. Henry looked at his phone.

"The charge is at fifty percent. I'm going to adjust the brightness down to save the battery. Then, let's see if we can locate any of the torches we had before we lost them in the cave-in. Maria, could you check my backpack there? I have a water bottle in the side pocket. See if the professor will take a drink. I'll dig for what we lost."

Henry went back to the end of the passageway where they'd been when the tunnel had collapsed. *What caused that? An earthquake?* He set the phone on a rock so the now dimmer light would give him a little bit of clarity and he began moving fallen stones and dirt out of the way. Henry soon worked his way back to the very end of the passage and shoving aside a pile of soil, he found himself looking again at the flat rock with the three symbols.

"Alright, I'm at the end of the passage now where we were when the collapse started. I've found the stone we were examining when everything started caving in. It has the bull, the cylinder and the Vulcan symbols on it. I'm going to see if I can dig under some of this and find my torch."

In the cramped and claustrophobic tightness of the passage, Henry slowly shifted stones one by one, sifted through dirt and touched something hard with one hand. He dug around it and pulled out his torch. It had a large dent in the middle and the lens section looked crushed. He looked more carefully and found the thing had been completely smashed. Flipping the switch did no good. The thing was ruined.

He said, "I found my torch. It was ruined in the cave-in. Even the batteries look crushed. It's a total loss. I'm going to keep looking."

He felt around in the same general location and touched something else. He realized it too was cylindrical and felt a surge of hope, thinking he'd found a second torch. *I didn't think there was another one in here!* He kept shifting dirt and rocks away. A realization hit him.

"It's the copy of the cylinder seal you made. I found it." He said.

Maria shouted back, "Wonderful! Henry, I think Professor Russo is starting to come out of it. Can you come help me?"

He said, "I'll be right there." Henry carefully turned and made his way back to Maria and Professor Russo.

Maria held the water bottle to the older man's lips and he took a sip and coughed weakly. He said, "Maria, where's Henry? What has happened?"

She said, "He is here, don't worry. Both of us are here with you."

Henry said, "Maria is right. We're both here. We've been caught in a cave-in and you've been hurt. I'm going to try to find a way out if I can."

Russo said, "How long has it been since the tunnel collapsed?"

Maria said, "Not very long. It's only been fifteen or twenty minutes. Henry found the stone that we were examining when the cave-in started. He found the cylinder seal that I dropped there. Now he is going to search for the torches we had. We'll need them for light once our cellphones run out of power."

Russo said, "You're right, save the batteries as much as you can. If there is no signal down here, we can't use them to call for help. Without signal, they are just fancy torches that won't last long."

Henry said, "The passageway we entered from is collapsed at the corner. So far as I know, it is collapsed all the way from there to the landing on the Grand Staircase. I don't know how we can ever get out that way."

Maria said, "We will have to wait for help. Someone must be trying to rescue us." She stopped suddenly and gasped. "But what if the collapse hit the rest of the dig complex as well? Do you remember how long the shaking and trembling went on? All of the rest of the team had left except for us."

Henry's face took on a grim expression. "... except for the guard and Krastyo Balev."

Henry and Maria exchanged significant glances and her eyes squinted in anger. "That pig! He did this! He sent us in here to our deaths! I think if you search long enough in the collapsed tunnel, you would find evidence of explosives. That man has hated us from the first and now he has tried to kill us."

Russo coughed and patted her arm feebly. "Maria, we don't know that. We don't know that Balev caused this."

Maria said, "Remember when we walked in here past him? Remember what he said to Henry? Henry told him that he needed to leave to go to his mother in London. Balev said, 'This won't take long.' The vile man thought we'd be dead in a couple of minutes and that would be the end of it. He knew Henry would not be getting out of this tunnel. What a monster."

Henry remembered the exchange between himself and Balev. *If Maria is right, that entire conversation didn't mean what I thought it meant.*

Henry said, "I'm going to go back and look for anything else we might have lost in the cave-in ..." He looked at Maria and said, "... and I'll keep my eyes open for any evidence of wiring or explosives."

Maria nodded and turned back to Russo.

Henry returned to the site of the flat stone and dug through the rocks and rubble. Some were too big to move and Henry prayed that what he sought was not beneath one of them. He kept working without finding anything and turned back to the first stone. *Hmm. There was a little space beyond the stone that was open before the cave-in. Let's see if I can get back there and shift some things around. Perhaps something fell back there as well.*

Henry crawled in and began lifting and shifting rocks and dirt. He was covered in caked-on soil and could barely see in the illumination from his phone. *How long will that last as a light?* He came up against a large stone resting on the floor at the furthest back part of the passage. *I don't remember this being here before. It's too big to lift, but maybe I can roll it.*

He struggled with the rock and got his fingers under an edge. He lifted and pushed to try to get the stone rolling, but felt a fingernail tear. He yanked the hand away and looked at the torn nail. It was bleeding. Henry muttered, gritted his teeth and went back at the rock. He braced his feet against the side of the tunnel, put his back to the rock and shoved against the stone with all of the strength he had. The rock moved to the side and with it part of the back wall. Rocks and dirt tumbled onto him, bouncing off of him, bruising and battering him. His legs were buried in the slide and he found himself pinned up to his waist in rubble and dirt.

Maria shouted, "Henry! Are you all right? Henry!"

He coughed and waved away the cloud of dust. *I moved the rock and caused another collapse behind it. This is not good.* He shouted to Maria, "Yes, I'm alright. There was another slide when I shifted a large stone back here."

Henry wiped a hand across his face. Sweat was mingling with the dirt and his hand came away muddy. He felt a little bit of cooling as a small breeze moved over the sweaty place on his forehead. *I've got to dig myself out of this.*

Henry worked steadily and freed his legs from under the piled up dirt and stone. He crawled over to the place where the decorated stone had been and again wiped his brow of the muddy sweat. He felt a small breeze again on his forehead. *Wait a moment. A breeze? Where is that coming from?* Henry struggled to the spot where his phone sat, still shining its dim glow into the dusty air.

He took the phone and crawled back to the place where the secondary slide had just buried him to his waist. He held the phone up into the dusty air. *There it is. The dust is swirling right there from a breeze.* Henry lifted his hand and felt the breeze. He grasped the flat stone with the symbols and placed it directly below the breeze so he wouldn't lose the spot. He turned back in Maria and Russo's direction.

"I've found an opening. Air is flowing through it into our tunnel here. It may be a way out."

* * *

Henry worked for hours on the rock slide and managed to open the hole to about a third of a meter in diameter. They had to trade cell phones and only use one at a time for light, set as dimly as they could bear. He paused for a break and sat down on the large rock that had started the entire mini cave-in. Maria handed him the bottle of water. Henry felt its weight in his hand. *Only half-full. We need to conserve this.* He took only a small sip and resealed the bottle.

Maria said, "What's it like up there? Can you see anything through the hole?"

Henry said, "Not yet, but when I get at it again, I'm going to take the phone with me and momentarily set it to the high intensity flash brightness and shine it through the hole to see what is visible. I only want to do it for a few seconds because that will eat down the battery very quickly. I'm already down on the charge and it won't last for much longer. I don't want to be stuck in here with no light."

Maria said, "Henry, I should have asked earlier. Do you have a spare battery or a portable charger in your backpack? If so, we could charge up one of the phones."

He said, "No, I don't have any of that. My phone has a non-replaceable battery and I haven't ever sprung for the money to buy a portable cell phone charger. I've seen them and wanted to get one, but never did."

Maria said, "You have your laptop in your backpack, don't you?"

Henry hit himself on the forehead. "Yes. How stupid of me. It has a full charge and we can plug the phones into ports on it to recharge them. While they're charging we can set its display to dim and see by its light. I am so sorry. Why didn't I think of that?"

Maria smiled. "It's alright. It's hard to think down here trapped like this."

He nodded. "True. How is the professor doing?"

She said, "He's napping now. We need to get help for him. I'm worried. Henry, how will we get him through if that hole you're digging leads to a way out? He may not be able to move himself."

He said, "I don't know. One of us may have to go try to find help."

She looked alarmed. She spoke forcefully and insistently, "Henry, we will not get separated! I won't let you go off by yourself. You could get hurt and then no one could help you or the professor."

He held out his hands as if to reassure her. "That's not what I meant. I'm not insisting on leaving you with the professor. I will go for help if you want me to, but I won't if you want me to stay."

She said, "Alright. Good. I want all three of us to get out or all three of us to stay. No separating." She rose to go back to the professor but stopped and turned back. "Henry, I'm sorry. It's one of my recurring nightmares. All my life, I have had these awful dreams about getting lost and not being able to find my way back. Sometimes I'm separated from family, sometimes it's a group I'm with, but always, always, I can't find my way back. Usually the dream ends very badly for me. So, no separating. Alright?"

He nodded.

She said, "Now let me get your backpack and we'll use it to start charging up cell phones."

He said, "And I'll get back to clearing that hole and checking to see if anything is visible through it."

A few minutes later after he'd made his way to the top of the pile of rubble, Henry cleared enough room so that he could get a line of sight through the hole. He turned the phone to its maximum brightness flash setting and activated it. After the dimness of the last few hours, the beam dazzled him for several seconds even though it was pointed away from him.

He strained his eyes and let them adjust to the new increased light level. He peered through the hole from which the breeze came and tried to make sense of what he was seeing. *It's pitch black in there ... can just barely make out a far wall ... seems to be some kind of large chamber.* Henry raised his head as high against the ceiling of his collapsed corridor as possible to get an angle looking downward through the hole. *Alright ... there is a far wall ... it looks like another large room ... maybe similar in size to the chamber we already found with the plaque of universal script ... wait ... what is that?*

Henry slumped back in surprise and gazed off into the distance. He lost his concentration and let the brilliant light from the phone in his hand point idly up at the ceiling.

Maria voice sounded full of concern. She said, "Henry, what's the matter? What did you see?"

Henry jerked back to awareness, squinted at the brilliant light and fumbled with the phone until he got the light turned off. *I only have five percent left of the charge: got to conserve.* He sat in darkness for a moment.

Maria sounded even more concerned at Henry's failure to answer. She shouted, "Henry! Your light has gone out. Are you alright? What did you see through the hole?"

He spoke from the dark and said, "It's the main chamber: the one with the plaque and the plaster painting and the metal wall. We've found a way from this passage into the Grand Chamber. We're saved! We've almost made our way out. I turned off the light to conserve the last bit of its battery."

Maria asked, "It's the grand chamber? Did you say it was completely dark? Nobody is in there? But Henry, it must be already morning up above now. We've been at this for hours and hours. People should be back again working in the Grand Chamber. Where are all the people and why is it dark in there?"

Maria couldn't see his face, but she heard the concern in his voice when he finally spoke. Only three words came out: "I don't know."

* * *

Henry traded phones with Maria so she could get his nearly depleted one charging. He went back to the hole overlooking the Grand Chamber and dug and shifted rock. With renewed vigor and determination he pushed everything he could through the hole to fall into the room on the other side. He worked in dim light, gradually widening the hole. He enlarged it to half a meter in diameter and then a meter. At that point, the work suddenly became much easier and he concentrated on enlarging the height of the hole to a meter and a half. *There. Now any of us can crawl out.*

He looked down into the room beyond and scanned the condition of the space. *It's all like we left it when Balev's man came and got us. No one has been in here since ... and none of the lighting is on. What happened?* He held out the phone and studied the room. *There is rubble on the floor that wasn't there earlier. Maybe the tremors that collapsed our tunnel brought this rubble down as well.* He swiveled the light over toward the metal wall. *Something's different about the painting on the plaster. I can't tell what from this distance.* He decided to examine it as soon as he could get into the room.

He looked straight down from the hole to the floor below. *There's that large pile of rubble that we found when we first entered this huge chamber. Its three to four meters down and right below this opening. Hmm. How to get us down?* He studied the rock pile below and realized it had become enlarged by the debris he'd pushed out of their tunnel. *That's it. Keep pushing this material out and make a slope of the pile below. Then we should be able to get out.*

Henry and Maria spent a half-hour or so working to exhaustion and past, digging and pushing piles of rock and dirt out of their tunnel. It was Henry's turn again and he kept going doggedly, feeling thirst he'd never experienced before. *Don't want to use up the last water. Something else must be wrong, or there would be people in the chamber out there. There's no way to tell how long we may have to stretch the rest of that water. I'm healthy and able to survive a little thirst. Just keep putting your back into it, Henry. Clear the way.*

Sometime later, he stopped working, crouched on his hands and knees, panting and dizzy. His vision swirled a little around him. *Have to rest for a moment. Get my breath back.* Something touched his shoulder from behind. He twitched and glanced back over his shoulder. It was Maria.

She said, "Rest, Henry. I'll take over for a while. Here, have a sip." She handed him the water bottle. It looked like there were only a couple of sips left. He took a small drink that was only enough to wet his mouth a trifle. She worked for a while at the opening and then stopped.

Maria continued, "It looks like we've almost done it. I think the hole may be clear enough and the pile below high enough to make it out and down. Let me try to see if I can get down the slope without breaking an ankle."

Henry tried to protest, "No, let me do it."

She shushed him, "I weigh less than you, if you haven't noticed." She gave a momentary smile and a chuckle. She waved at him and said, "I'll be less likely to crash clumsily down and break a long, gangly leg." She saw him about to protest further and pointed a finger in his face.

She said firmly, "Don't argue with me on this, Henry Travers. You'll lose."

He relented and nodded. "Let me help then. You can hold on and I can help lower you down so you have less distance to cover."

She smiled, "See. That wasn't so hard, *Amore.*"

He smiled weakly back at her and shrugged. They moved the professor nearer to their opening into the other chamber. They decided that if they could get Maria into the other chamber, she might be able to get to some tools, shovels and rope. Then it could be easier to get Russo out and to safety.

Maria got positioned at the enlarged hole leading into the other chamber. She looked down to gauge the distance and was satisfied that she had a good chance to make it. She backed out of the hole with her legs going first with Henry holding both of her hands from within their tunnel. She climbed down and Henry simultaneously lowered her to the debris mound below. Her feet touched down on the pile and she shifted them until she seemed to have a firm footing.

From there it was much easier. Maria crouched carefully lower and made her way cautiously down the rubble pile. She stepped onto the floor and breathed a loud sigh.

Henry, looking down on her from the passageway above, said, "Fantastic!"

She pulled her partially recharged phone from her pocket and used it as a torch. She immediately began searching for tools or other useful items. She stopped suddenly, reached down and lifted an item and said, "Perfect!"

Henry called, "What did you find?"

She shouted back, "Someone left a bottle of water and it's almost full."

Henry said, "They already drank some of it? Is that sanitary for us to drink?"

She laughed loudly and it echoed through the chamber. She bent over double with hands on her knees and kept laughing. She said, "You're joking! We've been trapped in an underground collapse for almost a day, are parched and weak from thirst and you're worried if it's sanitary to drink a little water that might have touched someone else's lips?" She laughed again, but opened the bottle and took a very long and obvious drink from it. She shouted, "It's delicious! Want some?"

Henry felt himself incongruously blushing even under the dirt that coated his face. He heard a rustle from behind. *What a dummy I am. She's right, of course.*

Russo echoed his thoughts and said, "She's right, Henry. At the moment, drinking after someone else should be low on our list of concerns."

Henry shouted down to her, "I admit you make a convincing case, *signorina*. Yes, I believe we would like a drink."

Maria said, "Catch!" and threw the bottle up at Henry's outstretched hands. He caught it and gave the professor the first drink. He encouraged Russo to drink more and when he had, Henry took a long, satisfying swallow himself. *I have never tasted anything so wonderful in my life!*

Maria made a quick survey of the room and set a few items at the base of the rubble pile that lead up to were Henry sat with Russo in the tunnel above. She called out to him, "I've found a hand shovel and about ten meters of nylon cord. We may be able to use that to help lower the professor down from the tunnel. I'm going to look out and up the Grand Staircase and see if there is anything we can use there."

Henry watched her as she moved by the metal wall on her right and past the section that had been plastered and painted. She stopped and looked at the painting of the bull, a look of confusion on her face. She shook her head with apparent sadness and continued past it to the large archway leading from the room, the dim light of the phone in her hand seeming to illuminate a small circle of floor around her. She walked through the doorway and Henry could not see her any longer, but could still make out the outline of the archway that was lit by her from the other side. She was out of sight for a couple of minutes that seemed very long to Henry and then reappeared in the archway and came back to the rubble pile below Henry.

Maria said, "The cave-in was much more extensive than we thought. I could only get part of the way up the Grand Staircase, not even to the landing. There's rubble and collapse all along the staircase and much of it is inaccessible. It looks like the giant stone door is closed at the top so there is no exit to the surface. Electricity seems to be out everywhere. I didn't find anyone else or any bodies, but I only went about six or seven meters up the stairway before I turned back. I did find some more tools and more rope. I think we can fashion a sling with this and the shorter section I already found. We can use them to help the professor down the slope."

She climbed carefully up the mound of rubble and handed the items up to Henry. Over the next twenty minutes they managed to get the professor out of the tunnel and lowered down to the main chamber below. It was difficult, but doable. Henry exited the tunnel with an immense sense of relief. *Now all we have to do is get out of the main section of the crypt, but how?*

They got the professor situated and went over the crypt bit by bit, looking for anything that might help. Maria found a first aid kit and Henry felt like he had won the lottery when he found a case of half-liter water bottles. Henry felt almost moved to tears when he had a full bottle in his hands and was able to drink his fill. Maria found a small stash of granola bars that someone had left behind. The three of them immediately ate one each and drank more water.

Professor Russo said, "That tasted heavenly." The others agreed and they all rested quietly for a few minutes, pondering their next moves.

Henry said, "Now, I see we have an immediate issue to deal with, that of the professor's injuries."

Professor Russo said, "I'm in a lot of pain, but I don't think anything is life threatening at the moment. The bone fracture hasn't broken the skin, so even though the swelling is bad and it is painful, there is no need to worry about infection."

Maria said, "The first aid kit may have painkillers and even antibiotic pills. I'll check. Even if it doesn't, it will certainly have antibiotic ointment for treating wounds. If we can find a short piece of wood, we may be able to fashion a splint. Now that we have a little water, I can attend to the professor's wounds properly." She checked the first aid kit and found pain pills and antibiotic ointment. She gave him the pills and spent some time cleaning and dressing the professor's wounds while they continued to talk.

Henry said, "Alright, the next thing is getting out of the larger crypt complex. The power is out, and unless we find another torch, we'll still need to conserve our batteries, so we can't waste time. The water will last a day or two only, and we have no food except for these few snacks we found. We have to get out, but the question is how? The main stone door above is shut. Looking at it from below, I think the tremors shattered the counterweight mechanism so the door shut itself. We won't be able to open it from this side."

Russo said, "Can we get a message to the outside?"

Maria said, "Neither of us can detect any cell phone signal down here."

Russo said, "But what about up there? Right near the stone door? You might get some small signal through the stone. It's not made of a metal that would completely shield out the signal."

Henry said, "That is true. But it would require one of us to climb up to the top of the Grand Staircase over all of the collapsed section. Maria didn't go past the first six or seven meters. We don't know if it will be possible to get to the top and even if we do, if there will be any signal."

Maria said, "If only there were another way out. Some ancient tomb complexes had back doors for priests and workmen, but we didn't detect any back doors during our initial survey. We weren't allowed to let many of the students down here because of Balev's restrictions, otherwise we might have done a more thorough mapping of the complex."

Henry said, "We didn't find the side corridor we were trapped in until yesterday. There could be other undiscovered halls and tunnels." He looked up at the passage they'd left behind. "You know, I think I know why that is there now. Maybe it was a balcony overlooking the crypt area. All of the tumbled down rock piled up at the base of it might have been the balcony before it collapsed. That passage we were stuck in would have been the access way to the balcony."

Henry turned to the crypt, looked over at the metal wall and pointed. "And another idea just occurred to me. There's that. It looks like it might be a door. Remember how we found that seam in the steel all the way around that section? What if that is a door and there is a way out behind it?"

Russo said, "Would the ancients really build a doorway out of metal? They couldn't really work metals harder than gold and copper."

Henry said, "I don't know. We also don't know why they plastered over part of the metal."

Maria said, "Well, we don't have to worry so much about the plaster now. I forgot to tell you, but a large piece of it cracked and flaked off, probably during the tremors that shook this place half to pieces. A big chunk of the painted bull is now missing. I saw it when I walked by on the way to check out the Grand Staircase."

Henry said, "Really? I missed that. What's under the portion where the plaster is missing? Is there just more of the metal?"

Maria said, "Yes, but I didn't look that closely. I was in a hurry and didn't have much light. Want to go check it out with me?"

He said, "Sure, but before we do that, let's finish the discussion we were having: we don't know any other way out, and we think our only chance may be to climb up to the top of the collapsed section on the Grand Staircase to see if we can get a strong enough cell signal to call for help. Correct?"

Russo said, "Unless your hunch is right, Henry; unless that metal wall contains a door that might lead out." Russo looked over at Maria and said, "You know, I think I am going to start believing Henry's hunches. He seems to have a good nose for this kind of thing."

Maria said, "Come look at what happened to the plaster painting."

* * *

They stood in the dim light, examining the wall. Large chunks of thick plaster had broken away from the metal wall where most of the painting had been hours earlier. Many discolored broken pieces lay on the stone floor, but many also seemed to be shattered irreparably into a chalky dust. Of the painted bull's head, only one horn, and one side of the face and mouth remained on the wall.

Maria said "It is such a tragedy. At least we were able to take photographs of it before the collapse destroyed it."

Henry murmured, "So true. Hmmm. Look at the metal. What is this behind where the eyes of the painted bull would have been?" He leaned closer with the dim cell phone's light. "I can't quite make it out. I see these diagonal lines cut into the metal but I can't see things well enough ... I need to turn the light intensity up." He made adjustments to the phone, turned the brightness up and held the phone back to the metal wall.

Maria gasped, "Henry, watch out! Something moved, I saw it!"

Henry twitched his hand back, "I thought I saw something move too. What is it?" He held the light closer and aimed it down from above that portion of the metal wall.

Maria said, "There it is again! What is it, insects? It is like something is crawling on the surface of that part of the wall."

Something tickled Henry's memory, like an itch. *I've seen something like this before, but where? No, wait! What does that say?*

Maria said, her voice rising, "No, it is writing! It says, '*ma-le*' in Italian. Does it say 'evil' in English?"

Henry said, "It does. That's why we thought we saw something moving. It's more of that same crazy script we found days ago, that writing in the universal language. But why was it covered over with plaster?"

Maria looked at him, worry showing plainly on her face. "Why were they hiding this?"

Henry asked, "And hiding it from whom?"

CHAPTER 22 – FOUND

"And with impious hands rifled the bowels of their
mother Earth for treasures better hid."
— John Milton, *Paradise Lost*

The diver surfaced by the ladder of the salvage ship *Vlad*. He pulled his mask off and shouted up to the man leaning over the rail above. "The robot submersible is ready. They can take her down now."

The man by the rail raised a two-way radio to his mouth and said, "Take the drone submersible to two hundred and fifty meters and begin the search for the *Fortuna*." He received confirmation of the order, turned off the two-way and placed a call using his cell phone over the ship's network.

The voice on the other end answered, "Yes?"

"This is Petr Ivanov on the *Vlad*. The submersible is deployed. We are to look for the *Fortuna* first and then locate the large rectangular box that is between six and seven meters long, correct?"

Dmitri's voice sounded through the phone and said, "Correct. It resembles a metal container. Find it and bring it up. It will be heavy. There is also a round disk that is less than two meters in diameter. That needs to be brought up as well. You have the photographs that should help you identify the items."

Petr said, "Yes sir." He ended the call and walked away to direct his men. Petr had been assigned by Alexi and Dmitri Slokov to make sure the salvage operation went quickly and without a hitch. He looked around the deck of the salvage ship. It was large and completely unlike any of Dmitri's oil tankers. It was also vastly different from the exploration ships like the *Fortuna* had been. If anything, it reminded Petr of a gigantic tugboat with two massive cranes; one at each end. It had multiple huge engines and seemed to be covered in winches and cables except for the helipad at the stern opposite from the control tower at the fore of the ship.

It had been quite expensive, but the boss' brother Alexi had come through and delivered this salvage ship in record time. Apparently he'd located one that had just passed through the Dardanelles and into the Black Sea. It had actually been committed to another salvage operation, but Alexi had bought out their contract with the first client and now they were going after the *Fortuna*. After docking in Varna for refueling, it had picked up Petr and some other men, including that union safety officer that Petr didn't like. He was always snooping around, probably looking for something that would allow him to file a grievance for the union.

A man spoke behind Petr. "Sir, would you like to be present for the images when they start coming back from the submersible?"

Petr turned and saw it was the captain of the *Vlad* speaking. He nodded and said, "Certainly."

The captain led him back to the control tower and they walked up the steps to the bridge. Upon entering the room, they moved behind a technician who was controlling a computer. The man held the controls and watched his screens carefully, occasionally typing something on a computer. He wore a headset over one ear and a microphone near his mouth. He spoke commands into the microphone at irregular intervals.

The captain put a hand on one of the technician's shoulders and said, "Bertrand, how are we doing? How deep is the drone now?"

"The submersible is at two hundred meters; almost to depth. The lights are on and we don't see any ship yet, but the instrument package has detected a large magnetic anomaly. It must be all that metal from the ship, so I think we are close."

They watched the dark screen. The drone's two headlamps projected broad beams of foggy white in the dark water. One indicator on the screen showed an increasing number labeled 'depth' that went from two hundred ten to two hundred fifteen as they watched.

"How far ahead do the headlights illuminate?" asked Petr.

The technician said, "It depends on how murky the water is, but here it is probably showing ten to fifteen meters ahead."

The drone kept diving. At two hundred and fifty meters, the technician slowed the descent.

He said, "The magnetometer shows something large back toward the west. I see nothing ahead of the drone so I am turning and will try to locate the large mass of metal the instruments are sensing." The technician made adjustments and directed the drone with the joystick.

A knock sounded on the door and it opened. A big man in a hard hat, coverall and a name tag that read 'Union Safety Officer' stepped into the room and glared at them.

The union man said, "There is oil in the water outside. You need to implement high level fire safety precautions."

The captain's voice carried a strong note of irritation. "We know what we are doing. The fire crews are standing by at the ready. You don't belong in here. Get out."

The safety officer said, "I belong wherever I need to be in order to ensure the safety of the union men. You wouldn't want me to tell the dock workers union that you have been uncooperative, now would you? Besides, with that oil slick out there, we must be right on top of the target. Have you found the wreck yet?"

"The captain said, "That's none of your business. I don't report to you and I still don't understand why the port authorities required us to take you on. We've never had a safety officer like you on board before."

The man answered, "You do now."

The technician interrupted and said, "Found it. There it is." He pointed at the screen. It showed a grey-shaded expanse and the word, '*Fortuna*' on a wide, scarred metal hulk.

The man at the computer station said, "There it is, sir. I knew my little drone would locate it."

Petr said, "Good. Have you found the large rectangular metal box yet?"

The technician said, "I will maneuver the drone over to the sunken ship and circle it until I locate the items you are interested in."

The captain said, "While he does that, I need to reposition the ship to be overhead. If we are going to do any recovery, I need to be directly above the wreck." The captain gave orders for the ship to be moved.

The drone moved around the *Fortuna* slowly. Wide gashes in the hull were visible on the monitors. Also visible were a mass of cables with a dead body caught in the snare. The drone's camera zoomed in. The body showed multiple puncture wounds.

The union man said, "What are those, bullet wounds?"

Startled, the captain looked from the computer screen and over at the intruder. "Why are you still here? Get out of this room!"

The big man stared at the captain, shifted his gaze to Petr and raised his eyebrows as if the image on the screen were of great significance, then he turned and left the room.

After he had left, the captain said, "That one bothers me. There is no good reason for him to be on board, let alone in the control room. What will he report now that he has seen that?" He waved at the body on the screen.

Petr shifted his attention back to the wreck of the *Fortuna*. The ship lay on one side at the bottom of the Black Sea in approximately three hundred meters of water. The middle section of the top deck held the twin drilling derricks. That structure was bent and crumpled. The ship looked to have slid down an undersea hill before it stopped at the bottom of a little valley.

Of the four cranes that were originally on the top deck, only two were still attached. *Perhaps the ship had rolled over them as it settled.*

Petr saw something and spoke suddenly, "Wait! What is that?"

The technician shifted his grip on the joystick and the underwater video moved and re-centered on a portion of the sea floor about thirty meters from the ship, back up the side of the hill from where the ship had settled. The camera zeroed in on a box shaped like a shipping container. It was made of a highly reflective metal and was half covered up in silt from the sea bed.

The technician said, "The magnetometer is going off the scale! So that is what gave off such a strong magnetic signature."

"I don't care about that," said Petr Ivanov. "Get closer to it. We have to be sure it's the right one. According to the description I have, it should have a design on the top lid. There should be latches on one edge of the lid and hinges opposite the latches."

The drone got closer and Petr couldn't make out any design on the two sides that were visible from their approach angle, but he could see three slight protrusions along the top edge that might be hinges or latches. Alexi had sent pictures that were to help Petr identify the item he was seeking.

He said, "Move around to the other side. If those are hinges on the top edge, there should be a relief carving on the opposite face."

The drone moved over the metal container and circled around. The headlights cut through the silt-clouded water and shined onto the metal on the opposite face. The metal box lay on its side, half covered in silt. Cut into the metal on the other face was the design of a rampaging bull.

Petr said, "That's it. That's the one we need to bring up. Mark that location and then look for the other smaller piece. It's a disk of the same kind of material. It also has a design on one side and a handle-like arrangement on the opposite side."

The technician said, "If it's the same crazy metal, I may be able to locate it with the magnetometer." He adjusted some controls on the drone's interface and scanned.

A Klaxon blast came from outside the control room. Petr turned to the captain and said, "What is that?"

The captain looked concerned and took some binoculars and started to step outside when one of the crew came in, obviously looking for him.

"Captain, it's another salvage ship, the *Baltic Rage*. They're flashing a message to us that says, 'Back off. You are trespassing on the property of the PetroRomania Corporation.' What should we do?"

Petr Ivanov said, "PetroRomania has arrived finally? Captain, we are staying. We were here first and have first finder's rights. The *Baltic Rage* will have to settle for leftovers."

CHAPTER 23 – CLUES

"On bold adventure, to discover wide that dismal world"
— John Milton, Paradise Lost

Hours later, after studying the site further, discussing the possibility of climbing the rubble of the Grand Staircase and puzzling over the wall where they'd found the additional strange writing that had been under the plaster, Henry and Maria realized how exhausted they both were and decided they must try to get a small amount of rest at the very least.

Henry said, "I'm feeling almost drunk from exhaustion. You must be feeling just as badly."

Maria said, "I am, but I'll manage, just like you will." She lifted her chin as if challenging him to say something chauvinistic.

He said, "No need, no need to get flustered. I'm merely suggesting we sit down, both of us, and rest our eyes for a while. I'm not trying to be a macho pig or anything. We'll turn off the lights, conserve power and rest a bit. The professor is asleep and we're so tired, we'll probably hurt ourselves if we try to continue without getting a few minutes of down time. Besides, I think we've only got enough charge in the laptop to rejuvenate one more phone battery. We need to power everything down for a while and rest."

From beneath the grit and dust in her hair, she smiled tenderly and said, "*Amore mio.*" She paused and touched his lips with her fingertips. She switched back to English and said, "You are right, my love. I am pushy sometimes; I know that. I have to stop reacting to you as I have learned to react to others. You are different. Let's rest." She pressed herself lightly against him and kissed one of his hands then drew him down to the floor. She patted the space next to her and when he lay down, she curled up against him. "Turn out the light, dearest. Hold me."

Henry turned it out. *I will never understand why she loves me, but I don't have to.*

167

I am just so grateful that she does. Henry held her close. Within minutes, exhaustion took over and he fell into a deep sleep.

* * *

Henry walked into the kitchen of his parent's house in London. There was Mum at the kitchen table with a cup of coffee and Dad was standing at the stove cooking some American-style bacon. *Yes, that's just like old Dad. He loves his bacon.* The smell of the cooking seemed delicious. Henry said, "Dad! So good to see you back. I thought you'd be gone for a while longer." Something tried to nudge Henry's memory about his Dad. *What was it? Dad and a ship he was on? What am I trying to remember?*

Hayden patiently removed each slice of bacon from the pan and turned to Henry. He carried the plate to the table and motioned to Henry to sit down. Henry joined his parents and Hayden brought him a cup of coffee. Hayden touched his wife lightly on the shoulder. She turned her face up to him and smiled sadly. She squeezed Hayden's hand and set her cup down.

She stood and said, "I'm so tired. I need to go lie down for a while. You two boys visit."

Henry was surprised. His mother was usually the most social of people and it seemed unlike her to step away while Hayden and Henry were both in the room. He started to say something to her, but glanced up at his father in time to see Hayden slightly shake his head. Henry held back and watched his mother leave the kitchen, her shoulders drooping and sadness seeming to press her down.

His mother was gone and Hayden sat down across from Henry. He said, "She's very tired and has been through a lot. I've already spoken with her and she needs some time alone. The days ahead will be very hard for her as she grieves."

Henry said, "Dad, what has happened? What is mother grieving about?"

Hayden looked at his son, emotion starting to cloud his voice and said, "You know why, Henry."

Henry's throat tightened. He spoke with difficulty, "You're already gone, aren't you?"

Hayden put his hand on Henry's from across the table. Hayden nodded slightly and said, "There was a disaster on my ship. I helped a colleague to escape, but I didn't make it. Henry, your mother needs you. She will need your strength. Go to her as soon as you can."

Henry felt paralyzed. He wanted to say something, but words seemed to stick in his throat. He regained control of himself and as memory flooded back, managed at last to force out the words. "I was trying to go to her, I tried. But now I'm trapped. I don't know how to get out." Henry's eyes moved about uncertainly. He sought out his father's serious gaze and said,

"The Grand Staircase is in ruins and looks very treacherous. I'm afraid for us if we try to climb it. We're not trained for that kind of thing and will probably just get ourselves seriously hurt or killed."

He continued, "I can't imagine we'll be able to get a call for help out that way even if we do safely make it to the top of the collapse there. If help comes from that direction, it will have to be without us. And, if we just wait for help to arrive, we may die of thirst. Father, the situation looks bad."

Hayden said, "I know, Henry. You're in a tight spot. You have a lot of things working against you at the moment, but what do you have to work with? What do you know?"

Henry said, "We have only a small amount of power left and that means not much remaining light. We ate the last of the granola bars; there seemed no point in stretching that out. We have no other food."

Hayden said, "Yes, but what do you have? There's the remaining power for light, and what else?"

He answered, "We have water enough for a day or so, but we'll weaken quickly once that is gone. We can use extreme measures to conserve, and if I remember correctly, we could recycle urine once without damage. So we'll need to start collecting it. What a revolting thought."

"Yes, Henry. Now you're thinking. Obviously, you'll be in desperate straits before you can stomach that, but you'll do it if and when the time comes. What else have you got?"

Henry said, "We've got the tools, we've got the laptop, but that's almost dead."

Hayden said, "But what about Maria? What does she have?"

"Well, notebooks; and she's carrying the water bottles. We never were able to find the other torches. She has the cylinder seal replica she made. We have thoroughly explored the crypt complex and there is equipment and lights, but no power for them."

Hayden nodded knowingly. "What have you discovered about this place?"

He said, "The crypt complex itself, the strange writing that is readable in multiple languages, the shattered plaster painting that has sloughed off of the wall…"

Hayden said, "What has sloughed off of the wall?"

Henry said, "The painting on the plaster. The tremors from the cave-in shook it loose from the metal wall and that crosshatch pattern."

Hayden asked, "What pattern?"

Henry became impatient, "Crosshatch. I said crosshatch, Dad. Will you listen please? It's that diagonal pattern on the surface of the metal wall near that seam that looks like a door. We can't see all of it, but it shows diagonal lines going from the lower left to the upper right. It also shows other diagonal lines cutting across in the other direction going from the lower right to the upper left. It was all underneath the plaster covering with that large bull painting."

Hayden stared at Henry and appeared to be waiting for him to say more.

Henry said, "What? There was the bull painting on the plaster. It was a large painting, done in the same general size as the crosshatch diamond pattern that was on the metal behind it. Under the crosshatch lines there was that fragment of the universal language that says 'evil' in English. I think there's more to that plaque, but it is still covered up in the remaining plaster. I keep thinking that the crosshatch reminds me of something, almost, but I can't put my finger on it."

Hayden said, "Son, you have what you need to work this out. Be ready though, things are more dangerous than you know. You and Maria can make it through this, but it will be hard. She is a wonderful woman, Henry. Hold on to her."

Henry said, "But Dad, how do we get out? We're running out of water and power. We have no food. We have no way out!"

Hayden said, "There is a way out. Keep thinking. Think before you do anything. Your instincts are good now that you've found your calling. Just remember to think things through to their logical end. Follow the clues." Hayden's voice changed to a tone of tenderness. "Watch out for your mother and go to her when you can." His voice started to grow softer.

Henry said, "You're gone aren't you, Dad? Dead?"

Hayden's voice dropped down to a whisper. "Yes, Henry. Care for your mother. I'll not see you or her for a time now. Goodbye. I love you and I love your mother." His last words were slight whiffs of sound but still distinct. "Tell your mother we spoke. It will comfort her." Hayden's voice floated away. Henry felt his vision of the kitchen of his parent's home fade into mist.

* * *

Henry woke. The dream filled his head with its images of his father and his grieving mother. *So he's really gone. Is that the truth or merely my subconscious trying to cope with the bad news that I know is likely at this point? Dad's almost certainly dead in the Fortuna disaster, and I'm stuck here in this bloody cave, and my subconscious is wrestling with that reality. And how will I get to Mother? She's got to be near frantic with worry about me, unable to reach me, unable to get messages to me. I've got to get to her, but how?*

And what did he mean asking me all of those questions about what Maria and I have? Is that my mind's attempt to make me do inventory, to make me come up with something, some way of escape? Really, all we have are some tools, a dying computer and dying phones, some paper notepads and writing implements and the cylinder seal. As for the cave itself, there's a bunch of useless electrical equipment that has no power, the metal wall, broken plaster painting, the new universal language writing and the crosshatching in the metal. I wish there was another circular indentation in the metal wall where we could put that cylinder seal. Maybe we could use that to open the metal door and see if there is indeed a back door out of this complex.

Henry roused a little more and felt Maria next to him, breathing slowly in and out. *That's a nice sound. I like her breathing.* He didn't want to wake her, but he needed to get the cylinder seal and check on the last phone they'd left charging on the remaining laptop battery. He carefully extricated himself and reached over to where they'd left the phone connected to the computer. The laptop was indeed dead, but he took the phone in hand and pressed its button. Its screen lit up and indicated a charge of eighty percent. He immediately put it back into sleep mode, but not before making sure that all of its settings were tuned down to minimum power use. *We've got eighty percent. What a relief! If we use it wisely, we can stretch that for quite a bit of time.*

He sat back down in the dark, determined to use the light minimally. He felt for the backpack, but before he found it, his hand brushed by the cylinder seal. He picked it up and let his fingers run over it. He felt the raised lines on its surface and the bumps between the chevron lines. *The metal wall that was covered over by the plaster and the painting had diagonal lines. Could there be a connection?*

The only sound Henry heard was the breathing of Maria nearby and a little further away, the professor. The darkness was so complete it was almost a physical thing by itself, covering, coating and embracing them. It seemed to Henry's mind like an all-encompassing liquid that flowed into every joint and seam. It filled the space between them, filled the chamber they were in, even reached into their nostrils and through their open mouths. Henry shuddered at the thought of it draining into Maria's lungs and driving out all air, choking her in its night touch.

Henry shook himself, his skin crawled and he scolded himself. *I've got to put a stop to that kind of thinking right now. Darkness is a not a thing, it's the absence of light. You know that. Get a grip. Think about that cylinder seal again. The chevrons, that's where I was going with my thoughts. There's no connection between the metal wall's crosshatching and the seal's chevron design because ... why? What is crosshatching except diagonal lines that intersect? And what are chevrons except diagonals that meet at ninety degree angles? Hmmm.*

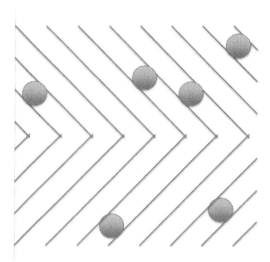

Henry held the cylinder seal in one hand and felt it with the other. *Definitely intersecting, diagonal lines, parallel to each other around the surface of the cylinder.* He felt the dirt in front of him with his free hand. It was fine and powdery. He took the seal and rolled it gently in the dirt, then tried to touch the impression. He couldn't make out any difference. *Perhaps a blind person used to reading braille could feel the differences where I'd rolled the seal, but I can't. I'll need to use the light to read the impression.*

He reached for the phone in his pocket but lost his grip on the seal and fumbled it. He tried to catch it before it fell, but dropped it in the dark. He muttered under his breath. *Now I have to use the light. I dropped the bloody seal. Can't lose that.*

Henry turned on the light, saw the seal and the impression he'd made in the dirt a minute earlier. *I messed up part of the impression with my fingertips where I tried to touch it.* He picked up the seal and laying it at the end of the rolled out impression he rerolled it and stopped, surprised. The impression hadn't been reinforced, it looked substantially different now. The dot-like impressions were placed differently and there seemed to be twice as many as before. He took the seal and stared at it and had a sudden revelation. *It's flipped. When I dropped the seal and picked it up again, I flipped it and rerolled it over the top of the original impression.* He looked at the impression in the dirt again and decided to start over.

Henry turned the seal in his hand and looked at it carefully. It still had only the dots, the chevrons on the surface of the cylinder, and one vertical line. *Let's try rerolling this and on the second try, lining up the vertical line.* He smoothed the fine powdery dirt with his hand and rolled the cylinder in it. He flipped the cylinder end over end, lined up the vertical line and rerolled it. The dot-like impressions now showed a distinct symmetrical pattern.

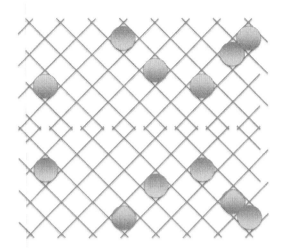

Henry heard rustling beside him and saw that Maria had awakened.

She said, "What's happening? What are you looking at?"

He said, "Sit up and look at what I've found. I don't know yet what exactly to make of it, or if it is important, but you should see it."

Maria sat up and looked over Henry's shoulder. He explained what he'd done and how he'd first made an impression and dropped the seal then rolled over the impression with the cylinder flipped. She looked at the double impression and frowned.

"It looks like a bull." She said.

Henry said, "What?"

She pointed at the double impression. "Look where the dots left their marks, it looks like the outline of a bull. Like the bull on the plaster painting."

Henry said, "And there are diagonal lines on the metal wall where the plaster painting of the bull came off."

Maria said, "We need to go over there and examine it more closely. Maybe the pattern that the cylinder seal reveals is a key of some kind to that metal wall. What if that is a door and this is the key to opening it?"

Henry said, "Then we might have a way out!"

They hurried over to the metal wall with the light and examined it further. *That script of the word "evil" just continues to unnerve me.* He said to Maria, "The plaster still remains over portions of this section. This part with the word in the universal script may continue under the plaster as well. The diagonal lines also continue under the remaining plaster."

Henry bent down to the ground, cleared away a space and mounded up some soft dirt. He rolled out the cylinder seal in the dirt, flipped the seal and rolled it again. The impressions lined up again in a formation of dots that resembled a bull's head.

Maria pointed at the dirt and then at the wall. She said, "That point on the impression would correspond to the point of the bull's horn here on the left. These dots match roughly with the left side of the bull's head. The dots on the right would be where the bull's head and horns would be if the plaster had not fallen off."

Henry said, "But look where the dots on the seal's impression fall between the diagonal lines. They could also correspond to the diagonals on the wall here. I wish I had something we could mark with like a piece of chalk."

Maria said, "No need for chalk. Just use one of these pieces of broken plaster." She handed him a chunk that had fallen to the ground from the wall.

Henry marked the corresponding places that the cylinder seal impression below seemed to indicate. For the ones on the right side where the plaster had fallen away, he placed them on the metal wall between the diagonal lines. For the ones that were on the plaster that remained, he marked very lightly, almost invisibly. He stood back and looked at the markings. All of the points together resembled a bull in outline.

Henry reached his left hand up and spread his fingers. "Huh. These points look like they could be pressed with the fingers of the left hand, except for the size of the thing. It would take a hand three times the size of mine for the fingers to reach this far. The same goes for the other side – these other points on the right could be reached with the fingers of a large hand. Too bad my hands aren't large enough."

Without warning or pause, Maria reached up to one of the spots on the metal wall that Henry had marked with the piece of plaster and pressed it. The portion between the two diagonal lines clicked in and stopped, depressed by about a centimeter. Henry jumped in surprise. Maria looked over at him with an arched eyebrow that seemed to say, "You liked that? Then watch this." She pressed another spot and then another. Soon all of the places on the wall that corresponded to the design revealed by the cylinder seal had been pressed. All remained pushed in.

Henry said, "That was awfully smart of you, but what do we do now about the plaster remaining on the other side? We can't push the corresponding spots on the other side with the plaster still in place."

Maria inhaled deeply, paused to consider and said, "I wanted to see what the rest of this script in the universal language said anyway." To Henry's horror, she reached up and started pulling away the remaining pieces of painted plaster from the wall.

* * *

They finished removing the last bits of the plaster. Henry still had a strong feeling of nausea from what felt like their willful desecration of the site. Maria shrugged at his distaste.

"I know, Henry. It feels wrong, but we have photographs of the original, and the largest area of plaster that was shattered was not our doing; it was caused by the trembling from the cave-in. Also, look at this. Now we can see the real writing in this amazing script."

What a bizarre experience! Henry read it out loud as soon as the letters stopped shifting in his vision. *How is such a thing possible? How can writing shift to match the language that I know?* He felt his hair stand on end as he read. "Evil Mulciber, killer of innocents, scheming ally of the foul monster Moloch. Judgment awaits you."

Henry continued, "Wow. What do you think this is? An incantation of some type? A warning?"

Maria said, "Perhaps it's a ward, invoking protection from evil. I think it's also a condemnation of a mythological monster, this Moloch and his ally Mulciber. Maybe they were a demonic pair of some kind in these people's pantheon of gods. Whoever made this wanted to keep Mulciber and Moloch away from here, because this is definitely not complimentary of either one of them. Maybe this is a shrine of some kind. Or like we originally thought, a burial site for some incredibly important ruler, king or priest."

Henry said, "The name Moloch seems familiar to me. Wasn't it some ancient Canaanite deity? And Mulciber: that seems to ring a bell too, but I can't place it. I need to look these names up. Well, let's finish this. We've got the plaster off, even though we may be condemned by generations of future archaeologists for destroying the remains of that ancient artwork. Let's push the rest of the buttons and see what happens."

Maria consulted the impression they'd made with the cylinder seal and pushed in the final spots on the metal wall over the inscription warning of Mulciber. The last button clicked into place with a sound like a dropping blade and then a thrumming vibration sounded. The floor of the Grand Chamber seemed to ring with the tone of a gigantic bass bell that continued humming and growing louder with each passing second.

Another sound echoed through the crypt, the thrum of a vast sliding lock mechanism swiveling into place and grinding into position. The metal seam on the top of the door cracked wider and a jet of fumes shot out. Henry and Maria cowered back from the opening. There was a blast of outgassing greenish vapors and the door to the crypt swiveled downward, fell open and crashed to the floor of the Grand Chamber. After the deafening sound of the opening subsided, Henry heard a slight sound of dripping, thick liquid from inside the crypt. In the dim light that he held, Henry and Maria could see a gigantic, gnarled and contorted form lying motionless within.

CHAPTER 24 – GATHERED THREADS

"Millions of spiritual creatures walk the earth unseen,
both when we wake, and when we sleep"
— John Milton, Paradise Lost

Mercy released Sonia Rodica from her gentle hug and said, "Grandmother, how did you come to be here?"

Sonia smiled cryptically as she sat back down and said, "You've spoken to my minders of course?"

Mercy looked behind at the door and saw that Alexi was gone. She assumed he had left her here, so she sat on the nearby sofa and said, "Do you mean Dmitri and his brother?"

Sonia said, "Yes. Those two: aren't they quite the pair? Of the brothers, I prefer Alexi. He is the more subtle. Dmitri is more to the point, so you can understand him more easily, and he has fewer hidden agendas. Alexi is the more courteous and I find the older I get the more I value courtesy."

She continued, "You asked how I came to be here. It is a long story, but the end of it is that Dmitri made a fortune after the revolution. He came back to Timisoara and found me still working at the university. I was cool to him, but he maintained minimal contact with me over the next several years. When I finally retired (I didn't have the energy to keep up with the class load anymore), I heard from him in the next year. He said he'd purchased the Duchess and wanted to offer me permanent resident status. When I asked him why, he just said, 'In honor of Tresa.' I refused at first, but after another year of barely surviving on my tiny pension and him pestering me every few months to change my mind, I finally relented. I think it is ironically appropriate that a former Securitate officer pays for my retirement, don't you agree?"

Mercy smiled sadly and leaned forward to place her hand on Sonia's. She said, "Yes, but I think it is small recompense for all they did to you, my mother and me."

Sonia's face hardened and she said, "It is no recompense at all. I miss my daughter every day, as I also missed you. There is no apology possible for what Janos Parasca did, and there is no forgiveness in my heart, may God forgive me. I have not found myself capable of forgiveness, even after all of this time. I know that it eats at me and I should forgive, but I still can't release my anger. Parasca stole Tresa and destroyed her. He treated her like a harlot and drove her to suicide. I cannot yet forget or forgive. Dmitri, on the other hand, had nothing to do with Parasca's evil. He cared for Tresa in his own way and was also victimized by Janos. Because of that, I allow him to pay for my upkeep, but I have no illusions that he is a good man. As far as I know, this may be the only good thing he has done in his life."

Mercy said, "I do not blame you for accepting his help or for your lack of forgiveness of Janos Parasca. I find myself in the same place. How is it possible to forgive such crimes? I cannot do it. I still find myself unbelieving when I remember that he is my father." Mercy hung her head and blushed as if in shame. "How monstrous!"

Sonia squeezed her granddaughter's hand and said, "I feared it was the case, but did not know for certain. Are you sure? There can be no doubt that he is your father?"

Mercy said, "None. A DNA test was done that revealed it as a certainty. I was crushed. I still am. I hate that man." She paused as if unsure how much she should say, but decided not to censor herself. "Knowing that he is my father feels like a permanently open wound that can never heal. I cannot escape it, I cannot change it. It is a truth that cannot be undone. I was sired by a monster."

Sonia squeezed Mercy's hand again. She said, "It is a heavy burden to carry." She looked at Mercy and said, "It is not something we can change by talking. Let us move on to something else. How is your adoptive mother in the United States?"

Mercy shook her head and said, "She has been dead for a long time now. When she and I were here in Romania years ago, you remember how she was imprisoned until after the Revolution. Finally, when relations were restored with the U.S., she and I returned to the United States, but she only lived for another year. That is one more of the evil things for which Parasca has to answer, the death of Martha Teller."

Sonia said, "He has much to answer for. If God is merciful, someday Janos Parasca will pay for all he has done." She looked closely at Mercy. "You look very healthy and strong. A little skinny, but tough. What have you been doing?"

Mercy laughed, "It is a long story, grandmother, but I am healthy and get a great deal of exercise. I may not look like it, but I eat a lot of food every day. You needn't worry about my health." Mercy took a different tack and asked, "Can you tell me some more about my mother, Tresa? What was she like?"

Sonia leaned back and put her hands together, intertwining her fingers. She said, "Tresa was a beautiful, gentle girl when she was young, but very stubborn. Even as a child, it was hard work for her father and me to manage her. She was very smart and active. She could eat, my, she could eat, but she never gained weight. As a girl she seemed like a starving sprite all of the time, snitching and stealing food from my kitchen and eating every crumb."

She continued, "I said she was stubborn. Shortly after she became a teenager her father died of lung cancer. He had been a heavy smoker and in those days, many people in Romania smoked. Tresa took it hard. Of course, I took it hard too, but I had to keep going somehow. She seemed to withdraw and become more and more distant. I know teen years are hard for anyone, but no one should have to lose a parent like that at that age." Sonia squeezed Mercy's hand again. She said, "You had to endure that too. I remember you spoke of how your adoptive father died when you were sixteen."

Sonia said, "Tresa continued to grow more distant from me and spent more and more time away with her friends at school. When she was ready to start at Polytechnic, I thought it might help her. She lived here at home to save money, but I hardly ever saw her. She would stay out to all hours of the night and I was very worried about her. I found out from one of her professors at Polytechnic that she had dropped his class and then found that she had dropped all of her classes. She and I had a big fight. It was after that, I think, that she started taking up with Dmitri and later Parasca."

Sonia continued, "It is such a sad thing for me to remember what a bad last few years she and I had. If we were together, it seemed that we argued. I tried to give her advice, but she would not listen. Later I realized that giving her advice was the last thing I should have been doing. All that time would have been better spent listening to her and trying to understand her. Of course, it was too late by the time I knew all of that."

She said, "After she was gone, I turned to faith. I started going to church, the same one that you saw me going to when you lived with me years later. It is strange what things lead us to God. For me it was the hurt and loss I felt at what had happened to Tresa."

Mercy said, "Why did you turn to faith for answers? Didn't you wonder why God had allowed such horrible things to happen?"

Sonia smiled gently at Mercy. "God didn't do anything to Tresa. It was Janos Parasca that did evil things to her. She made terrible choices and hurt herself, finally committing suicide. God didn't make my husband smoke himself to death. I even made bad decisions and alienated Tresa when I could have reached out to her. I could have tried to get closer to her and perhaps I could have helped her. God didn't do any of that. If you ask, 'why did he let those things happen?' I say, how could he not? The only way to have stopped me or my husband, or Tresa or even Parasca would have been to take away our humanity. It would have meant to take away our ability to make bad choices. I don't want a God that micromanages every choice I make or decision I entertain. I don't want a God that preempts every choice that every person on earth makes, negating every bad choice, only allowing good choices. That isn't a God. That is a fantasy. Such a thing is absurd. That kind of a God would be an infinite cosmic dictator, controlling every thought and deed, only allowing soft landings, never allowing mistakes or learnings from mistakes."

Sonia said, "I prefer to think of God as hard sometimes, letting us err, letting us do badly, while hoping we learn and improve. When God allows the bad in us and the random in nature, he also allows the good to happen. He allows us to be kind to others and to help others that are hurt. He is hard in some of the same ways I found myself being hard as a parent. And that hardness sometimes means to lose one's child." Sonia stopped talking and turned away to look out the window.

She said quietly, "It has been forty years and I still hurt. I still feel the loss. She was my daughter and I failed her, she failed herself, others failed her. She is gone and I can never talk to her or touch her. It is so sad." Sonia turned back to Mercy. "Do you still feel the loss of your adoptive parents? What was the name of that boy that you cared for; the one that died in the riots? Do you still feel the loss of him?"

Mercy said, "Yes, I still feel it. I still dream about him. His name was Stefan. He was my first real love. We met at Polytechnic when I lived here in Timisoara with you. During the run up to the revolution when the pastor at your church was protesting against Ceausescu's regime and they were trying to run him off, we and other students supported his efforts. When the marches started and the riots broke out and the police and the army started shooting at the crowd, Stefan was hit in the chest and I in the throat. I remember marching, suddenly falling and losing consciousness, but that is all. I didn't find out until later that he was killed." She paused and her voice grew very quiet. "I've lost so many that I love."

Sonia said, "But I heard from my nurse that you came with someone; a man. Who is he? Is he just a business colleague or is he someone special? Why did he come with you?"

Mercy said, "His name is Jack Truett. He is someone special to me. We met in graduate school years ago and were close then, but I was afraid and ended it. We have recently met again and I know now that I was wrong to break off our relationship. We have fallen in love again and are engaged.

When we are able to get back to the United States, we are going to marry."

Sonia said, "I am happy for you. You deserve some happiness." She looked carefully at Mercy and asked a new question. "Mercy, how did you get mixed up with Parasca and Dmitri? Something is going on and you haven't told me about that yet."

Mercy explained to Sonia about her job with PetroRomania and the sinking of the *Fortuna*. She told about Dmitri's forces and the attempt to capture the *Fortuna*. She told Sonia some about the archaeological finds that lead to her being employed with PetroRomania, but didn't know how far to go in discussing that, so she left out any and all of the supernatural aspects of the story.

Sonia was not fooled. She said, "That sounds like a heavily edited version of events. You left out a lot of things and I think you are afraid to tell me of certain others. I can well believe the whole destructive competition between Dmitri and Parasca, but it makes no sense to me why a man like Janos Parasca would divert an expensive ship like the *Fortuna* for archaeological work. He could have made money on it if he had used it for its intended purpose of oil and gas exploration, so why did he take the actions that he did?"

Mercy told Sonia about the crystal steel metal of which the dagger was comprised. She explained some of the nature of the metal that PetroRomania's metallurgists had been able to discover and mentioned some of its commercial possibilities.

Sonia immediately perked up. "You say it was composed of layers of carbon nanotubes with molecular iron in the tubes? Tell me more about that."

Mercy described what she knew about the metal, its hardness, mass and how Hayden Travers had used its magnetic properties to locate more of it on the sea bottom.

Sonia asked, "What about its electrical properties? Did you look into that?"

Mercy said, "No. We didn't have time to do much more than what I said."

Sonia said, "Such a pity. Carbon nanotubes have some amazing properties. I'm not an expert but try to keep up with the literature. More and more work is being done on carbon matrices and some very interesting things are being written about graphene. It's a form of carbon molecule only an atom thick but arranged in sheets. If you roll it into a cylinder, you get a carbon nanotube. Graphene has lately shown to be superconductive in certain situations. With the kind of structure you mentioned with iron running through the carbon nanotubes, I suspect that it might be even more superconductive. Are there any samples of this 'crystal steel' material? I couldn't do any experiments myself, but I still have some colleagues or students of colleagues that would like to run experiments on something like that."

Mercy explained that the only samples of crystal steel she knew of were the dagger, the sword, the shield and the sarcophagus.

Sonia said, "You say there was a large mummy in that sarcophagus? How large?"

Mercy said carefully, "It was extremely large."

Sonia looked at Mercy cagily, "There you go again! You're not telling me something that you know. You're afraid for some reason to tell me the full truth. Don't give me a vague description, girl! Be specific. How many meters long was the mummy or skeleton or whatever it was?"

Mercy grimaced and said, "Grandmother, you'll find it hard to believe. That was the only reason I was reluctant to tell you. The creature we found inside was five meters in length."

Sonia turned her head sharply and widened her eyes. She said, "Five meters? How long had it been dead? What was its condition? Now don't try to avoid telling me the full story. You'll find me to be difficult when data is being withheld. My students learned that lesson when I was their chemistry professor and it seems you've been away from me too long and have forgotten!"

Mercy sighed and said, "Grandmother, you'll have trouble believing the full story, I'm just warning you. It involves some things that I still have trouble believing."

Sonia said, "I'm not some fragile flower that will wilt under a little bit of sunlight! I've faced some tough times and unbelievable circumstances in my life. Just tell me what happened and don't leave anything out. I'll stop you when I'm satisfied."

Mercy smiled and dived in. This time, she didn't spare the details or herself. She told Sonia about Moloch and about the sword and shield. She described the fight on the *Fortuna* for the ship and the struggle at the end between herself and the giant creature Moloch. She told Sonia about the abilities she'd found in herself and decided to offer a demonstration.

Mercy looked around them to make sure that Dmitri's servants were nowhere nearby. The nurse had left them alone after the first few minutes and hadn't been back. Mercy saw no one else, so she asked Sonia if she might use her chemistry book to show her something.

Sonia said, "Of course," and started to hand the book to her, but Mercy demurred.

"Leave the book on that table, Grandmother." Mercy said.

Sonia took her hand away from the book where she had set it and folded her hands back in her lap.

Mercy held out her hand toward the book which was about six feet away. She went into her focused state almost automatically and gave a mental lift and push to the book. *Chemical Processes and Case Studies* rose up from the surface of the small table and then moved straight for Mercy's open hand where it stopped.

Mercy opened the book and flipped to its table of contents, turned her head to Sonia and said, "Shall I read to you, Grandmother? Where had you left off?"

Sonia laughed with delight and said, "Not necessary my dear! Now I need to tell you some stories about some of your ancestors. After what you told me, and what I just saw, they make a great deal more sense!"

CHAPTER 25 – VESTIGE OF POWER

"Hurled headlong flaming from the ethereal sky with hideous ruin"
— John Milton, Paradise Lost

Sonia said, "There are many stories of strange abilities, strange monsters and evil beings in this part of the world. Most of them are just that, stories. Some of those stories may have their basis in fact, I imagine. The stories of the vampires that come from these mountains and many other parts of the world probably have their original root in the disease called rabies. When the poor victims of the illness were bitten by infected and crazed animals, they too became crazed and sought out other victims to whom to spread the disease through their bite."

She said, "There may be other folk tales that were based on actual occurrences. Stories of tiny people, dwarves and giants could have come from the rare genetic anomalies that cause those traits in a very small number of the human population, while stories of werewolves and such could have come from deformities, hormonal disorders or diseases that sometimes occur to give people very frightening aspects."

She continued, "I say this to point out that there are rational explanations for many myths and legends that have been passed down through the generations. But, that does not explain everything." She smiled at the book in Mercy's hand. Mercy opened her palm and the book moved gently through the air over to Sonia. She took the book from the air and put it in her lap and patted it.

"This, for example." She looked down at the book. "There are other folk stories beyond those that coincide with the effects of genetic disorders, disease or deformity. They are the persistent tales of people with special abilities such as healing, telekinesis, extreme strength, incredible speed and endurance, mind reading, the reading of languages never studied, levitation, seeing into other people's dreams and controlling other people's minds."

Sonia said, "These tales persist across many cultures and have been assumed by most to be wish fulfillment stories; the longing for people to have godlike powers and capabilities. I have long thought there was more to it than that." She set the book aside on the table again. "There were stories my mother and grandmother told me as a child about witches that lived in the hills. For some reason, the stories always spoke of women that had these abilities, never men. I grew up knowing these tales and considered them cautionary morality lessons intended to graphically warn children of the consequences of disobedience, of wandering off alone, or of dishonesty. When I became an adult I found out from my mother that not all of the tales were fiction."

Mercy's grandmother continued, "She had a sister, my aunt, who had a small farm with her husband. In later years, it was taken from them and collectivized by the government. My aunt was an herbalist and midwife who practiced the folk medicine that many people utilized in more primitive times. In her last years, my mother admitted that her sister was more than she seemed and had achieved much greater success in her medical arts than should have been possible. My mother said my aunt could set bones in moments without cutting or breaking the skin. She could cause wounds to close in minutes. She could deliver babies that should have died. She never lost a single infant or mother in childbirth. Disease was beyond her ability to heal, but medicine requiring physical intervention or the speeding up of natural healing was her routine practice."

Sonia said, "My aunt was considered by the common folk to be touched by angelic power and they sought her out. She loved the people around and cared for them. When collectivization took place, many of the country people were forced onto state-run farms and my aunt and uncle were some of those. We never knew what became of them after that."

"Besides those stories of my aunt, my mother told me other tales of the women in our family, of grandmothers and great grandmothers back into the mists of time that were healers, fortunetellers, mind readers or witches. She had many of these tales. I believed few of them. Until now."

Mercy felt defensive. *I don't know what to say. Maybe I shouldn't have told her all of that, but what could I do? I couldn't lie to her.*

Sonia reached over to a small case on the table near her book and took it in hand. She opened it and took out a small locket on a chain. She held it out to Mercy.

Sonia said, "I want you to have this. It belonged to your mother, Tresa."

Mercy's eyes grew large. She looked at the piece of jewelry as if it were a priceless object. She said, "Grandmother, I don't know if I should have this."

Sonia said, "Who better? You have nothing from your mother except your life itself. She would want you to have it. Take it."

Mercy said, "Was it left among her things at your home?"

"No. It was with her to the end. Her father gave it to her and she always kept it with her. It was the only item of hers they gave me back from the prison where she died. They said she was allowed to wear it in prison and she died with it on. I want to give it to you."

Mercy felt stunned. Her hand reached for it, but not quite. Mercy hesitated. *This was with her when she died? It was with her when she killed herself? She must have worn it when I was born!* Mercy felt almost terrified of the locket. *What right do I have to have it? I can't know what she felt or what she went through. How alone she must have felt; how sad; how abandoned.*

Sonia saw her hesitation and studied Mercy's face. Sonia's expression softened as she seemed to understand some of the feeling racing through her granddaughter. Sonia rose slowly and carried the locket with her as she walked over and stood behind Mercy. Sonia put a hand on Mercy's shoulder.

"Tresa would be so proud of the woman you've become, of all you've accomplished, of all you are. Let me help you." Sonia took the locket's chain, opened the clasp and fastened it about Mercy's neck.

* * *

Mercy felt a mental jolt as the locket touched the skin on her neck. Pictures raced through her mind, crowding out the room where she and her grandmother were. Images flew by, some of modern times, some seeming to be from the past. She heard a sound that at first seemed to be of rushing water, but soon she heard individual sounds that resolved themselves into words. She knew she was hearing the speaking, shouting and weeping of hundreds, maybe thousands of voices all speaking simultaneously. She felt that she was falling into a circling maelstrom of scenes and sounds. Smells came to her, then textures as if she were experiencing these histories, not just remembering them.

She felt mental pressure on her as if from a waterfall of memory that pressed her under tons of cascading images. She struggled to put order to what she was experiencing, saw a glimpse of a younger version of Sonia and tried to concentrate on it. The rest of the memories pressing on her receded and her mind seemed to zoom in on Sonia. She appeared to be in her late forties and had an angry look on her face. She was wagging a finger and speaking in Romanian.

"Tresa! What are you doing? It is three o'clock in the morning and you have to work at the factory tomorrow! You've been drinking and look half dead. You think you can live like this? When are you going to grow up? You can't treat yourself so foolishly. You want to look like some used up tart before you're even twenty-five? Then keep it up! How do you expect …"

Mercy pulled back mentally from the scene. *I don't need to see an argument between Sonia and Tresa. I'll just disengage from that …* Another scene leapt to Mercy's mind and she saw a young man standing in front of Tresa.

She shouted at him. "You dare come back here? My mother is still in prison because of you! I was in jail for weeks until Janos got me out by pleading on my behalf. Then I find out you ratted on me to your captain, all to save your stinking skin!" She spat on him.

The young man seemed to fumble for an answer but couldn't get a coherent statement out. It was painful for Mercy to see. The young man finally said, "It's not like that. They forced me to talk. I couldn't help it." Then tears came to the man's eyes and rolled down his cheeks.

Tresa stormed back inside. The young-looking Janos Parasca had a smug look on his face.

Mercy jumped back mentally from the scene as if from a hot stove. *The emotions I feel from Tresa! She hated Dmitri at that moment, but if he was telling the truth earlier, the whole thing was a setup by Parasca to deceive Tresa. The man was, is and forever will be a monster.*

Mercy felt swept along by the flood of scenes. The images stopped again and suddenly she was in a starkly-lit gray room. She saw a guard, a medical doctor and a nurse. The doctor whispered something to the nurse and then bent over a sink to wash his hands. The nurse came to Tresa and roughly checked her for dilation. It was painful and humiliating.

She said, "She is eight centimeters, doctor."

The doctor said, "Close enough. Let's get this done. I need to be out of here as soon as possible. I hate these prison cases."

A labor pain hit and Tresa involuntarily stopped breathing as it seized her. She clamped her eyes shut and felt submerged in teeth-grinding agony. It went on and on like the worst, strongest and most painful cramping she had ever felt. Finally it eased up and she gasped for breath. She couldn't seem to get enough air.

The doctor's voice cut through the ringing in her ears. "We'll just do this with forceps. I can't wait any longer for her to dilate."

Tresa said weakly, "Can't I have something for the pain?"

The nurse said simply, "Shut up. Bite this." The woman stuck a piece of something that felt like hard rubber into Tresa's mouth.

The doctor was brutally rough and seemed to care nothing at all for the pain he inflicted on her or the baby. Tresa screamed nearly silently against the hard rubber that she clamped between her teeth. She felt horrible probing, rough hands and cold metal all at nearly the same time. She sucked in air through her nose as the next contraction began and with the muscles squeezing their strongest, she felt horror at the jerking tug that seemed to grab her by the inside of her bowels and rip all of her entrails out.

She shook her head from side to side at the agony, flinging hot tears left and right. Thoughts of terror rang through her. *They've killed me! I'm dying! They just disemboweled me. How long before I lose consciousness and wake in Hell?*

The doctor spoke and said only. "I'm done here."

Tresa felt something hot and sticky land on her chest. She managed to crack one eye open and saw a tiny crunched-up face with red, forceps-shaped indentations along the sides of its head. The baby cried feebly and plaintively.

The nurse's voice took on a cruel edge. "Your brat is a girl. Too bad, she'll probably end up like you now." She flipped a small, worn blanket over the child and turned away. She shouted, "Guard! Get her out of here and bring me whoever is next. The doctor doesn't need to be here for the rest of these scum."

Tresa fumbled weakly at the baby and began to weep in despair. She and the baby both cried. The baby opened its eyes and locked on Tresa's only a short distance away.

Mercy experienced vertigo as her mind felt pulled from Tresa's head and through and into Mercy's infant eyes, swirling into a looping dance, a maelstrom of falling and collapsing thoughts, circling back on itself from daughter to mother to daughter to mother, back in time, falling, falling …

* * *

Mercy woke up and groaned. Sonia's nurse sat on a chair in front of her and Sonia sat to one side, a look of deep concern on her face. The nurse checked Mercy's pulse and took her blood pressure. She asked Mercy how she felt and asked her if she could focus on the eraser of a pencil. She moved the pencil and watched Mercy's ability to visually track it. She checked Mercy's eyes for pupil dilation and went to a phone across the room. She placed a call and then left the room.

Sonia said, "Mercy, I am very sorry. I didn't know that you'd react so violently to the locket. You seemed to have a seizure of some kind as soon as I placed it around your neck. When I realized something was wrong, I took the locket off of you and called the nurse. Are you alright now?"

Mercy said, "I think so, but I feel so weak." Mercy suddenly remembered what had happened to her. A look of fear suffused her face. *Did I really just experience all of that?*

Sonia said, "Granddaughter, what happened to you?"

Mercy said, "It was memories. I felt all of Tresa's memories. Everything was there. I relived memories of her with Dmitri and Parasca and you… and I relived my own birth! I saw it from her eyes, experienced every bit of her pain." Mercy groaned from the memory. "She was all alone and terrified. I felt all of it."

Sonia looked at her and then at the locket. She closed her hand over it and reached for the small case in which it had been stored. She said, "I had no idea. I'm so sorry."

Mercy reached out gently for her grandmother's arm. "I saw more. At my own birth, Tresa looked at me as an infant and I felt like I was falling from Tresa's eyes to my eyes and over again and again. I plummeted through an unending spiral loop and saw myself going past decades then centuries and finally millennia. Somehow I knew I was watching memories go past from mother to daughter and mother over and over again, but with each second I fell, I moved further and further back in time. My mind dropped like a meteor out of the sky until I stopped at the bottom; at the end of all of the memories."

"I saw a woman give birth to a female child and slash the cord with a translucent metallic dagger. I saw her lose her grip on the knife and saw it tumbling end over end into a pit of tar. I saw a long reptilian tail sticking out of the tar, with the rest of the gigantic beast already submerged."

"It was the scene we found months ago buried at the bottom of the Black Sea, the huge crocodile, the sword and the shield stuck in the underwater tar pit. I think I saw the memory from some ancient great, great grandmother thousands of years ago when she was giving birth to her daughter."

"That must have been our family bloodline that I saw. That must have been the start of all of this. I saw the tar pit where we found the dagger itself. I saw the world as it was over seven thousand years ago!"

CHAPTER 26 – DISCOVERY

"So easy it seemed once found, which yet unfound
most would have thought impossible"
— John Milton, Paradise Lost

Janos Parasca looked at the phone, saw the number and answered it. The voice spoke and said, "Chairman Parasca, I have good news."

"What is it?" Parasca answered.

Dr. Ozera said, "Our idea worked. We were able to grow a seed crystal from the point of the steel dagger artifact that you loaned to us. We removed the seed crystal from the tip of the dagger with a laser cutter and have now grown a new filament wire from the seed crystal."

Parasca's voice took on a very menacing quality. "Did you damage my dagger? The answer had better be no."

The scientist hurriedly replied, "No, no. The artifact is unharmed. What we did to it is completely undetectable."

Parasca muttered, "It had better be. Now, what do I get for all of the risk you took with my irreplaceable knife?"

Ozera said, "We grew the crystalline structure from the seed into a two meter long monofilament thinner than a spider's web. We suspended the seed crystal from the ceiling of a sealed chamber and surrounded it in a superheated gas of molecular carbon and iron. The crystal began to grow downward from the seed as we hoped and we've created this amazing thread of the material. We've begun testing its strength and electrical properties and you will not be disappointed."

Parasca said, "Tell me more."

"We've tested its tensile strength and it is off the charts. We haven't yet tested it to destruction because we only have the one sample, but so far it surpasses steel and likely is stronger than just naked carbon nanotubes; it seems to be at or beyond the theoretical maximums for carbon nanotubes. We'll find out soon. We have sent large electrical currents through it and found it to be superconductive at high temperatures. Chairman Parasca, we have a breakthrough product on our hands."

Janos Parasca said, "Not so fast. How will this spider-web product be made into something useful? It seems something so thin would be impractical."

Ozera said, "Even by itself, this thread could be massively useful. As it is, it could be used as an industrial cutter that would slice through steel like scissors through paper. The edge on a cutter like this is only molecules wide and the strength of the substance far exceeds other known substances. It could cut through practically any material. But that would be a niche product to use it as a cutter."

Parasca thought to himself. *It could be weaponized. A blade made from such an edge would be nearly invisible. I need to think some more about that. It might be possible to license a blade like that to weapons manufacturers.* He spoke out loud to Ozera. "If not as a blade, what would be done with such a thing?"

The scientist said, "Create many of the threads and weave them together into cables. The cables could be used as conduits for electricity like I told you before. It would revolutionize industry worldwide to have mass produced superconductive cabling, especially of this strength. And speaking of strength, cable of this type could be made for support and construction uses. The toughness and flexibility of this cable would make it possible to create bridges and other structures that are unimaginable now."

He continued, "The Japanese have even been working on a concept called the 'skyhook.' It is a space station that would utilize a gigantic cable that would run from the surface of the earth out to a satellite's geosynchronous orbit. Elevators could move up and down such a cable from the earth to orbit for one percent of present costs to get freight and people into orbit. The Japanese haven't been able to get this concept off of the drawing board because there has been no material, no substance or theorized cable that could handle the massive stresses required. Until now. This invention of ours could make their vision possible. We are talking many billions of euros in possible sales for just that one application."

"Construction cables could be made from this, there could be power cabling, possibly super-powerful magnets, and all could be within reach now that we can make this tiny thread. Why, it could even be woven together into a fabric that would make regular clothing totally impenetrable to ballistic projectiles. A fabric made from this would make Kevlar completely obsolete for bullet proofing. Since the original dagger is translucent, it should be possible to make a fabric or composite that is transparent. Truly unbreakable glass might be possible."

Parasca said, "Good. Make more of this as quickly as possible. I want a practical, repeatable process that scales up to commercial quantities. Again, I repeat to you, I am not interested in pure research. I pay you for applied research. Learn how to make commercial quantities of this in cable form and then we can start demonstrating it to prospective clients that might be interested in licensing the material and the manufacturing processes. I don't have to tell you, do I, that all of your team's work needs to have patents filed that are defendable in international court? I don't want any others getting ahold of our work and then flooding the market with illegal copies."

"Yes, yes. All of our work is being documented constantly. We film everything and make sure all notes, documents, videos and backups of it all are stored on the PetroRomania secure network. We are being thorough."

"Good. Make this happen as you have said. Notify me of any developments good or bad." Parasca said. He lowered his voice into a threatening tone. "Dr. Ozera, I am watching how you and your team perform on this task. Don't think you can waste my time or resources. I expect results and you had better deliver. Do I make myself clear?"

Ozera said, "Yes, Chairman Parasca, you make yourself very clear. I understand my task."

Janos Parasca ended the call.

* * *

Ozera looked at the phone in his hand, an expression of contempt on his face. *Yes, Chairman Parasca, I am completely clear on the task I need to do. How I despise that man and his arrogant attitude. He has not the slightest understanding of science or its value. He spits on our ground breaking research. I have to put everything in terms that a five-year-old would find obvious and still he does not grasp the implications of what we have found here. If we were in academia, we'd be looking at Nobel prizes for our work on this. Instead, all he can think about is, 'what good is this to my oil company?'*

Ozera made sure the phone call was ended and looked at the computer on his desk. There on the screen, he saw a folder of all of the accumulated work of his team of researchers. Within the main grouping of all of the project work, he saw the subfolders he'd created for the team to put videos of their work, their documentation and notes, the experimental evidence and all of the data they'd captured from the trials on the material's tensile strength and its superconductivity. *It is all kept on the PetroRomania server network and backed up frequently.*

Ozera smiled to himself. *Yes, all safely captured and stored. Parasca has all of it, except for the copies of everything that is streamed through the back door to Dmitri Slokov's systems. Slokov's people in the PetroRomania data center take care of all of that. I can't wait until I and the rest of Slokov's people working in PetroRomania can get away from this hellhole of a place that Parasca has created. On that day, Parasca will find all of this information destroyed and all backups corrupted, while unknown to him, everything he has lost is safe within Slokov's systems. That is the day I long for. The sole downside is that Parasca will only know of his losses. He won't know how he was beaten and who beat him.*

Ozera pulled out his phone and opened an encrypted messaging service app. He sent an update message to Dmitri and closed down the app. *I'm not so stupid as to send a message to Dmitri through Parasca's systems. No one will be able to read the message I just sent except Dmitri.* Ozera closed his computer down, turned off the lights in his office and left. He wore a satisfied smile as he walked out of the building and past the PetroRomania security guard.

CHAPTER 27 – THE GIFT

"Lost happiness and lasting pain torments him"
— John Milton, Paradise Lost

Mercy saw that Sonia looked fatigued and realized she had to draw her visit to a close.

She said to her grandmother, "I know you need to rest. I've brought a great deal of upheaval to you today and I apologize. I know your normal days must be much more sedate. If you would still approve, I would like to have mother's locket. I will be careful, of course."

Sonia nodded, handed her the case, motioned at her book and said, "It is true that the most exciting thing that I usually do is read some scientific articles or books, but don't apologize my dear. I feel so glad to have seen you and to have a chance to get to know you once again."

Mercy said, "Still, I can see that you are tired, so I'll need to leave soon. But, grandmother, may I come to visit you again? Could I telephone you? I really value your thoughts in so many areas."

Sonia stood slowly again and walked to Mercy. She pulled Mercy's face down to her and kissed her cheek. "Certainly, Dr. Mercy Teller. You and I still have much to discuss. I look forward to your next visit or telephone call. I think I will take that nap now, I do feel a bit tired."

After they had exchanged contact details, Mercy left her grandmother and found Alexi waiting for her in the hotel lobby. He walked her back to the room where she and Jack had originally met with Dmitri and his brother. She found Dmitri and Jack talking quietly. The two of them stopped at her entrance and stood.

Dmitri said, "How is Sonia doing? Well, I hope."

Mercy said, "She is. She was growing tired and I had to leave her so she could rest." She changed her tone of voice to a softer quality and stepped closer to Dmitri. "I want to sincerely thank you for your care for Sonia. I realize you have your reasons for doing so and they may be very complex, but I thank you just the same. Janos Parasca, though he is my biological father, will never receive any love or respect from me, and doubly so for what he did to my mother Tresa, my grandmother Sonia and even my adoptive mother, Martha. But I can respect you for some of what you have done. I share the anger and rage that you must feel against Parasca and on Sonia and Tresa's behalf, I thank you for what you do. I am even grateful for the revenge you seek on Janos Parasca, for it is not something of which I am capable, but I find myself glad that <u>you</u> are."

Dmitri's face softened, his lips relaxed from their tight line, and his shoulders relaxed. His eyes gazed at Mercy questioningly, almost hopefully. He turned to Alexi, and said, "So, brother, is she not almost like family already? The way she talks and acts, the way she is calm in the face of opposition, but able to disagree and still be straightforward in her thoughts? She knows what we are and what we do, knows that our motives may not be entirely pure, but is able to accept what good we do for the sake of the ones who may benefit."

Dmitri turned back to her. "Mercy, I am grateful for the opportunity to assist your grandmother. Sonia's every need will be seen to by my staff for the rest of her life. She deserves to spend her remaining days in what comfort I can provide."

Dmitri paused and reached into a pocket and retrieved a phone that was vibrating. He glanced at it and arched an eyebrow. He said, "Please forgive me. I need to make a phone call." Dmitri stepped from the room and Alexi followed.

Mercy went to Jack and sat by him on a couch. She asked, "How did your time with Dmitri go?"

Jack said, "It was all right. Dmitri wants to hire me and I put him off. Why is it that all of the bad people want us to work for them? Parasca offers us a job, now Dmitri. Who's next, some terrorist group?"

Mercy said, "You did right by putting him off. I told him I respect him, not that I trust him. Seriously, Jack. I think we'll be able to do our own consulting if we ever get back to the U.S."

Jack said, "You still want to try that even though we'd likely be heading off in different directions on different jobs for different clients?"

Mercy said, "I've been thinking about that. What if we go as a team or not at all? We could work on proposals and present them together. We could offer ourselves at two for the price of one."

Jack chuckled, "How would that work? Do we double our rates so we could afford to do that?"

Mercy had a half-smile on her face and said, "Maybe. The point is this: we don't need to work for Parasca or Dmitri. Some jobs aren't worth it no matter what the pay. We can work for ourselves. We just need to keep on saying no when they offer the money."

Jack said, "Agreed."

Dmitri walked back into the room with Alexi close behind. He said, "My salvage ship has found and brought up the metal sarcophagus and the shield. It is on the way back to the port at Varna. Parasca has a ship that is following mine. They've been sending messages threatening legal and police action to stop the theft of what they say are 'vital PetroRomania assets.' I think we may need to go to Varna. Perhaps you would like to be there when my ship docks? If so, may I offer you a ride?"

Mercy said, "Dmitri, that sarcophagus must never fall into Parasca's possession. It contains something very … dangerous. If Parasca gets control of it and opens it, there could be horrible consequences."

Dmitri said, "We have no intention of letting that happen. Tell her, Alexi."

The younger brother spoke and said, "We have arranged for special transport of the freight and have spread substantial bribes around the port of Varna. No matter what Parasca's people do, the salvage crew from our ship will move the sarcophagus to a special heavy-duty transport truck, one of our own, and with a protective convoy, it will move the sarcophagus out of Varna, to the Bulgarian-Romanian border and then proceed to our facilities at Constanta. Because of the extreme weight of the sarcophagus, we will need to carefully proceed on specific roads that can handle the tonnage. It will be slow, but we'll have it in the end."

Dmitri said, "Parasca's people don't have a leg to stand on as far as salvage laws go. We did the work to get there first, we have possession of the items, and that counts for almost everything. Even if we were to lose a court battle for ultimate rights to the salvage, that would take years of legal wrangling. As long as I am alive, he will never get that sarcophagus or the shield."

Dmitri continued, "But Mercy, I invited you to ride with me. Wouldn't you feel better if you saw for yourself that the sarcophagus and shield were safely kept from Parasca? I know I won't sleep until they are well away from his grasping hands. Come and ride with me. We will go to the airport and hop on my jet and be in Varna in a couple of hours."

Mercy considered the proposal seriously and finally said, "I believe I will accept your offer. That thing must never be in Parasca's hands again, and I will sleep better if I know it is safe. Jack, let's go with them."

Jack said, "Fine with me. You must have spread a lot of euros around to make all of this happen so quickly."

Alexi said, "We did. It was necessary. We hope to be able eventually to make money on what we can learn from the metal or the sample of universal language on the sarcophagus. To do that, we need to make sure

Parasca doesn't have possession of the items."

Mercy looked appalled. She looked back and forth between Dmitri and Alexi and said to them, "You know about the metal and the universal language? How?"

Dmitri raised a hand as if to calm her. He said, "Mercy, you knew I had people on the *Fortuna*. I also have people within PetroRomania. They relay all manner of information to me that is helpful. For example, this." Dmitri waved at a briefcase-sized black box on the sofa next to him. "My people in PetroRomania learned of this and my man Vasya obtained it for me before you ever got to the *Fortuna*."

Mercy looked confused. "I don't know to what you are referring. What is in that case?"

Dmitri said, "Better to just show you. Alexi, would you do the honors?"

Alexi Slokov stepped to the case and lifted it. He moved to a table in the large sitting room and set the case on it and opened it. Inside, there was a transparent glass enclosure that held a large skeletal left hand, with its fingers spread wide. It seemed absurdly large and the span of the fingers from tip of thumb to tip of little finger looked to be almost forty centimeters. It had at least twice the reach of a normal human hand. On the third finger, there was a gold ring.

Mercy said, "Is that what I think it is?"

Jack said, "Wasn't there a missing hand on that giant skeleton we found at the bottom of the Black Sea?"

They both turned to Dmitri. He said, "This discovery was made right after that anachronistic steel dagger was found and was the first recovery of skeletal remains from the *Fortuna*. From the size of it and the fact that the giant skeleton that you dubbed 'Goliath' was missing a left hand, I think it will be safe to assume it belonged with that find, but testing would be necessary to be certain."

Mercy looked at the giant hand wistfully and said, "Yes, testing would be necessary, but I'm afraid all records of what we found on the *Fortuna* were lost when that ship sank."

Dmitri smiled and said, "On the contrary, dear Mercy. PetroRomania may have lost it all, but I did not. I have a complete backup of every file, every photograph and every test up to the moment the *Fortuna's* network connection was severed. Parasca may have lost it, but I didn't. For as long as I live, everything he has, everything he gains, I have to take it from him."

Jack said, "Weren't a courier and a chauffeur killed in the taking of this from Parasca? I mean, let's just be honest about this so we all know what the stakes are. You had two of Parasca's people murdered to obtain this, didn't you?"

Mercy looked soberly at the Slokov brothers. They both shrugged, almost in unison. It struck Mercy as a sad, if comic admission. She shook her head, but before she could say anything, Dmitri said, "That was my doing, not Alexi's. I hired the Russian that I called Vasya and gave him carte blanche to do what was necessary to obtain this artifact and to send a strong message. We were dealing with people who only understand force, and as we expected, they killed people of mine in retaliation. It is a messy business, but it is true, that I gave the okay for such actions."

Mercy said, "Dmitri, I can't condone this kind of thing and just so you understand me clearly, I can't work for you or your company. We may cooperate now on something such as making sure this sarcophagus stays out of Parasca's hands, but I can't be part of your organization. Your aims, goals and methods are just too different from my own."

Again Dmitri shrugged slightly and said, "I understand, but as a gesture of goodwill, please take this artifact. It does me no good, and putting it in your hands will be just as effective in keeping it away from Janos Parasca as if I held it in my own. You may be able to study it and learn something from it. Also, the ring on its finger was obviously made with some skill and may be of interest in your research. Take it."

Mercy looked at him steadily, her surprise at the offer turning to acceptance. She nodded, stepped to the case and closed it. She carried it horizontally so as to keep the artifact inside oriented parallel to the floor and stepped back to Jack.

Alexi said, "Shall we go to the airport and on to Varna?"

They filed from the room silently, all four lost in their separate thoughts.

* * *

On Dmitri's jet, they remained silent until after the takeoff for Varna, Bulgaria. Dmitri spoke at last and said, "There are several more reasons why we should be working together on this effort, even if you won't accept my offer of employment."

Jack said, "And what are they?"

Dmitri said, "First there is Varna. My salvage ship is bringing the sarcophagus into port there, it is true, but that is not the only thing happening in Varna. As I understand it, for many years there has been an archaeological dig there at an ancient graveyard. They have uncovered hundreds of gravesites there and many of them date back to four or five thousand B.C. Recently there have been some discoveries of even older gravesites there within the necropolis. Some of what has been found is quite disturbing."

Mercy said, "What is the point, Dmitri? What does this have to do with us?"

Dmitri held up a hand, as if hoping to quell interruptions. He said, "I found out about this other archaeological work in Varna because of my sources within Parasca's organization. It appears that there is a corrupt government antiquities officer responsible for the Varna necropolis site and those that study it. He has been in touch with Janos Parasca about funneling 'lost' items to him from the site. Some of them have the familiar bull symbol on them that you would recognize from the sarcophagus lid."

Jack said, "Dmitri, as I understand it, that bull symbol is common throughout many ancient cultures."

The older man answered, "True, true. But what is not common is what they found next, a large subterranean crypt complex."

Mercy's interest piqued considerably and she sat forward in her seat.

He continued, "According to this official, they found a massive stairway going down into the earth and at the bottom, a wide hallway that led into a large triangular chamber. One wall of the chamber seemed to be made from a strange, nearly translucent metal of some kind."

Mercy felt goose bumps form on her arms. She looked over at Jack uncertainly.

Dmitri said, "But that was not the worst of it. There was a plaque on the metal that had words on it that were readable by anyone in their own native language. It said, 'Architect of the Abyss.'"

Mercy felt sick. *Not again! This can't be happening again! How can there be another sample of the universal language that has been found, just now?*

Jack's face was deadly serious. He said, "It was in the universal language, the same kind of writing we found on the sarcophagus?"

Dmitri said, "Yes, it appears to be. I can't imagine it being anything else. This seems to be the same writing with different words than on the sarcophagus. According to the antiquities officer, no one knows what the phrase 'Architect of the Abyss' means. The two words architect and abyss don't seem to go together, even in a search of the internet. However, that isn't stopping the man from offering to help Parasca get away with all of the finds in the newly discovered crypt."

Mercy said, "Jack, if this is some other horror from Moloch's time, we can't let Parasca get to that either."

Jack said, "You're right, of course."

Dmitri said, "And there is the second reason that I think we should continue to work together for the time being. One of PetroRomania's top researchers has been keeping me informed of a project that is near and dear to Parasca's heart."

Jack muttered in amazement, "Is there anyone in Parasca's employ that doesn't work for you?"

Dmitri laughed, "Well, as you know, he is not one to inspire undying loyalty. But, let me continue, please?"

Jack motioned for him to proceed with his story.

Dmitri said, "PetroRomania's research group has isolated a single crystal from the tip of the original dagger that was found by the *Fortuna*. You may remember it is also composed of the miraculous steel of which the sword, shield and sarcophagus are also constructed. They used a new process to grow that crystal into a two meter long thread of the same metal. They have learned how to manufacture it and it has some wonderful properties that will make it immensely profitable. For example, it has incredible tensile and shear strength. It is also superconductive at high temperatures."

Jack leaned forward and said, "What? Are you joking? That would be a world-changer."

Dmitri said, "I am not joking. Parasca is a fool about scientific things and doesn't have the vision to understand what he has. I am no scientist, but I try to keep track of such things as well as any layperson may. He has neglected his research staff, insulted them and threatened them enough so that I was able to recruit his head of research, Dr. Ozera. As soon as I can extricate the good doctor from PetroRomania, I'll figure out how I can license the technology to other companies."

Mercy said, "You're sure you don't want to just sit on this invention in order to protect your businesses? Your companies transport oil and gas, so why shouldn't you just withhold these discoveries to protect your interests?"

Dmitri's face crinkled in disappointment. He said, "Mercy, I'm surprised at you. Why should I take such a narrow view? Just the fact of the metal's superconductivity could be worth more to me than all of the value of my other businesses combined. It would be very shortsighted of me to try to hold on to a nugget of gold when I can have the whole gold mine, wouldn't it?"

He continued, "Besides, the oil industry isn't going away anytime soon. There will always be uses for petroleum even if we find other ways to fuel transportation. It's too valuable as a lubricant and chemical feedstock to become worthless on the world market. Almost all plastic comes from hydrocarbons at the present. If we stop burning it in engines, we will still have many other uses for it. Don't fret about my companies or my bank accounts. I'll do just fine as the holder of a patent worth billions of euros."

Mercy said, "Dmitri, you don't know everything about that metal. It can also be used for very dark things that I can't completely describe for you. You have to be careful with it. Dangerous is the least of it. That metal can be used for extremely evil ends. Just because your scientists can produce the stuff doesn't mean you should do so."

Dmitri wagged a finger back and forth and said, "Mercy, everything can be used for good or evil. A knife can cut an apple or slit a throat, but it is not the fault of the tool that one time it is used for good and the other for evil. This metal is a discovery on the same level as the creation of the computer. I will leave others to work out the morality of whether such things are used more for good than evil. I believe in only a few things and one of them is this: if I have something that others want to buy and at a price for which I am willing to sell, then let business be done. Mine is a simple world."

Mercy shook her head in irritation. *It's like talking to a feral child. He looks human, but he has no understanding of right and wrong, good or evil. For him, everything is a transaction. I need to remember this. As long as he still hopes for future transactions with me and Jack, we'll be safe. When he sees no chance of 'letting business be done,' then he'll jettison us.*

CHAPTER 28 – RETURN

"Where all life dies, death lives, and nature breeds, perverse, all monstrous"
— John Milton, Paradise Lost

Janos Parasca turned away from the corpse of the woman. *Very nice. Surprisingly, Karras brought me a satisfactory catch this time. Mature but attractive and she had a lot of life in her. She did not give up easily.* He smirked at the body. *It seems almost a shame to have used her up so completely. Perhaps in the future I can learn how to keep people alive for a longer time, to drain them slowly, let them regenerate and then use them again and again. Hmmm. That is a thought to pursue.*

He looked at his hand where he held the sword. A crackling ripple of reddish energy ran along the blade. *Now that I know how to handle the energy and force it into the blade for storage, I can drain people like sponges and save their life forces for use whenever I have need.* His free hand had a light pink scar on it, from a practice cut that he had finally learned to heal. *I need to get better at that. Surely I'll be able to do it next time without leaving a visible scar.* With that free hand, he motioned to the corpse. It rose into the air.

I can feel the weight of it, but this life energy from the sword is like a multiplier to my natural strength. With it, I can lift ten or a hundred times more than my unaided muscles depending on how much power I let flow. I wish I could just incinerate the body to ash. If I could do that, I'd not need Karras to dispose of it. I need to learn how to do that. Parasca lowered the body back to the couch where she had lain before, walked to the door and opened it. He spoke softly to the man out in the hallway.

"I am finished with her. You can take her away now."

Karras stepped into the room and surveyed the situation. He looked more frightened than normal.

After all of the transients and homeless vagrants he has procured for me over the years, now he looks afraid. What is wrong with this fool? Is he finally losing his nerve, or

201

does he suspect something?

Parasca forced his voice to take on a concerned tone and asked, "Is something the matter?"

Karras said, "No, no. It is nothing, Chairman Parasca. I shall take care of this matter for you."

His voice now solicitous he said, "But why do I see a look of fear on your face? Why are you concerned about this ..." he motioned at the corpse, "when you've been unconcerned by such in the past?"

Karras said, "It is nothing, sir. I will take care of the situation." He moved to the side of the body, but before he could touch it, Parasca grabbed him by one shoulder and spun him around.

Karras' face instantly took on a look of pain and he involuntarily reached for his shoulder where Parasca gripped it. Janos Parasca felt the bones in Karras' shoulder flexing under his grasp and heard the man gasp. Parasca realized that he must be gripping too hard and relaxed his hold. Karras looked at him in open terror.

I am extremely strong again, perhaps even stronger than I was in my youth. He is terrified of me. Good. Parasca stepped back from Karras and spoke with concern again, "You are afraid of something about the woman. What is it?"

Karras' voice trembled slightly. A bead of sweat ran from his forehead and down one cheek. He said, "It is the cruise ship from which she came. You told me to look for a certain type of woman, a single passenger on a ship, that could be separated from the crowd and could be deceived into coming with me. I did as you requested and brought her here. Now, I have just found out minutes ago that her ship has been held from departing. For an entire day. This is not normal for cruise liners, so it must be that the authorities in Athens are placing the hold on departure. I assume it is because their passenger manifest shows someone missing and there is suspicion of foul play. I need to find out if that is why her ship remains in port. I don't want any authorities to begin asking questions and I don't want any suspicion to fall on us."

Parasca's facial expression shifted from concern to blankness and then he smiled wickedly. "You mean you don't want any suspicion to fall on <u>you</u>."

The man looked stricken. He said, "Well, <u>I</u> didn't kill her."

Parasca's face held the evil smile for a second and then it vanished and was replaced by a look of anger. He said, "But you kidnapped her. Who will believe you didn't kill her too? Or were you planning on turning me over to the authorities to save yourself?"

Karras shook his head in disbelief. "No, of course not. It never occurred to me."

Parasca's tone went flat, almost monotone and he said, "Any time you feel like talking to the police, remember how many kidnappings you've carried out. Remember how many times you were accessory to murder, and always remember that I keep records of each of these catches of ours." He motioned to a ceiling mounted video camera. "I know you've been watching the recordings of me and my guests, Karras. I know you enjoy watching them over and over. But you've seen some things in the last few sessions that is unnerving you, haven't you? Have you wondered about me? Have you wondered what has happened to me? Have you wondered about what I can do now that I wasn't capable of before?"

Karras swallowed nervously. He bent down and drew the body over one shoulder. He said, "I'll just take care of this so it won't be in your way." He straightened slowly and carried the body over his shoulder, its purpled face lolling near his belt, its throat covered in hand-shaped bruises.

Parasca moved between the man and the door. He said, "Be very careful, Damon Karras. Don't do anything foolish. Do you know all of which I am capable? I think not. Don't make me demonstrate." Parasca stepped to one side and motioned the security man to the door of the room. Just as the man stepped through the door, Parasca called out a final time.

"I know you haven't yet had time to review the recording of what just transpired in here with me and the woman. I advise you to watch it carefully, all the way up to the point where you enter the room. Once you have done that, you'll want to think over what you've seen. You'll wonder if you are going mad. You'll be tempted to run away, to flee. You'll fear for your life. Just remember that I already know that you'll have these thoughts. Remember what I'm telling you now and that you won't be able to get away from me. Think about this: the only way you'll survive the night is if you accept what you've seen and return to me. You need to come back to me here and ask for my permission to let you stay, to continue working for me. Who knows? I may grant your request. If you don't ..." Parasca tilted his chin to indicate the body that Karras carried. He repeated, "If you don't, remember that body and what you saw me do in the video. And if you try to run, I suggest you kill yourself before I catch you. Now get out."

Damon Karras moved into the hall as quickly as he could while carrying the body. He stepped to a gurney that he had positioned outside the room and hefted the corpse unceremoniously onto its surface. He pushed the gurney away without looking back at his employer.

Janos Parasca closed the door, turned back to his room and smiled. *I almost hope he does bolt and tries to flee. But no, it's harder to find someone like him that can take care of details than it is to find guests.* His phone vibrated and he reached for it, noted the caller and answered it.

Parasca switched effortlessly to the voice he thought of as 'caring employer' and said, "What is it Alex? Feeling better?"

"Yes, Mister Chairman. Thank you for your concern. I wanted to call you about a message that came through your email system. I don't think you've had a chance to look at it because it showed as unread. As you know, with the absence of Director Gachevska, part of my job is to filter your email for possible security concerns. I think you will want to read it."

Parasca felt a twinge of annoyance. *What is this man doing? Has he gone soft after one simple injury? Why would he call me about an email?* He said into the phone, "Oh? Why do I need to read it?"

Lacusta said, "The email appears to have been sent by someone in Bulgaria that claims to have one or more archaeological artifacts that might be of interest to you as additions to your collection. Of further interest, it seems to have been read and answered by Director Rakslav Gachevska."

Parasca said, "What? I thought Rakslav died in the wreck of the *Fortuna!*"

Lacusta said, "Yes, that is what we all thought. He has not reported back in for work, but I have determined that he or someone using his security credentials has logged into our network and checked his email. He has also sent email and looked at several files on our network."

Parasca said, "Where is he? Why hasn't he tried to contact me?"

The security officer said, "Unknown. We have done a trace on the path that the director or whoever is impersonating him used to gain access to the company email system. It went through the public internet and to the internet addresses used by a shipping company that operates in the Mediterranean Sea and Black Sea. Perhaps he was rescued by one of their ships in the area of the *Fortuna* when it sank. Would you like me to check on that possibility?"

Parasca said, "Yes, but you said I should read the email. Why? If it is just an artifact that I might be interested in for my collection, that is of small importance. Why should I drop everything and read that email?"

Lacusta said, "It is the content of the message that the writer of the original email sends and the reply that Director Gachevska makes."

Parasca said, "I don't have time to do that. Just read the pertinent parts to me over the phone."

Lacusta read the subject line of the email and Parasca burst in, interrupting the man.

"… may be written in universal language? What is this? How could this man know of what we saw on the *Fortuna?*"

Lacusta waited for Parasca to process his thoughts then after receiving the go ahead, continued reading the entire email containing Krastyo Balev's original message and the reply.

Parasca said, "That sounds like Rakslav and that is a typical cagey response from him to this Balev character. I remember that man. He is scum, but useful in acquiring collector's items for me from time to time. He is a government official on the take and channels items into the antiquities black market for people like me so he can enrich himself. His team probably stumbled on this grave site by complete accident. Interesting, but also upsetting. If this is anything like the last time we found one of these universal language inscriptions, it could be bad news."

Parasca continued, "So Rakslav is alive. He also sent a copy of his reply to my email address, so he expected me to see this and his reply. He is not trying to hide from me, but may be hiding from someone else. Who? The authorities? Dmitri's group? It might be Dmitri's people. Or Dmitri's brother. I saw Rakslav take out Dmitri's man on the *Fortuna* right before the ship sank. If Dmitri survived, Rakslav might be on the run from that man's people."

He spoke again directly to Lacusta. "It is good that you alerted me to this. I will travel to Varna now. My people have been having difficulty with another salvage ship that got to the *Fortuna* first and is now headed into Varna with items they got from the wreck site. I need to be at Varna anyway to make sure we regain control of what has been salvaged from the *Fortuna*. While I am there, I may need to visit this necropolis and see for myself what they've found. If I have to deal with it, so be it. I don't want another out-of-control situation developing like happened on the *Fortuna*."

He continued, "Alex, I need you to arrange for a security force there in Bulgaria. Contract with a local high-security firm and get twenty men out to the Varna docks for the first thing tomorrow. Make sure they are well armed. It may come to a standoff and if that happens, I want to have superior firepower. Do you understand?"

"Yes, Mr. Chairman."

"Good. Now, do you have any word of Dr. Teller or Jack Truett? Where did they go after the fiasco in the corporate apartment where you were injured?"

"We managed to find someone at the Bucharest train station that saw two people matching their description. We then found that two people of the same description paid cash for first class tickets to Timisoara."

"Timisoara? Yes, I suppose that could be Dr. Teller. She spent several years there when she was younger. Also, her mother and grandmother lived there. But why would they have gone to Timisoara?"

"Unknown, Mr. Chairman. We don't have any further indications of where they went in Timisoara or if they are still there. I have people continuing to attempt to trace them."

Parasca said, "Good. Anything else?" Lacusta replied that there was not and Parasca ended the call.

I have to get to Varna. My people on the salvage ship I sent out there saw a large metal container being raised. That other salvage ship must be Dmitri's, and they've got the sarcophagus. That thing must never be opened again. I can't face that monster again. If this new tomb complex has the same universal language writing, it may be related to

Moloch. That has to be stopped as well. Moloch by himself was monstrous. If there's another similar creature in the Varna Necropolis, it could be the end of everything, and certainly the end of me.

CHAPTER 29 – RETURN TO LIFE

"For the mind and spirit remains invincible, and vigor soon returns"
— John Milton, Paradise Lost

Professor Russo lay on the floor of the chamber coughing violently, choking in the greenish fog that rolled over him. Henry and Maria held their breaths and rushed to him, helping him rise above the mist so that he could catch a breath of cleaner air. The smell of the vapor was sickening and made Henry's stomach clench and his bowels quaver. *It's like meat that has rotted beyond all reason. If a person had to remain in this stink, madness would be the only option besides suicide.*

Maria gagged and almost vomited but was able to keep control of her stomach. Henry felt faint and had to steady himself, but between the two of them they managed to get the professor away from the crypt opening and out of the dissipating fumes. Russo finally got his breath back and the three of them tried to assess the situation.

Maria said, "From here it looks like there is a large figure, four to five meters in length on the floor of that new chamber. It looks vaguely human in shape. Could it be a large container for a body, like an Egyptian sarcophagus? It's too dark in there; I can't tell if there is another opening leading from that room."

Henry said, "As soon as I get my legs back under me, I'll take the light and go in there to see what we have. The reason we opened it was on the off chance that there was an opening on the other side of that metal door that would let us get back to the surface. If there isn't, we'll have to come up with another plan."

Professor Russo ceased coughing, regained his composure and said, "I think I'm feeling strong enough again. I'd like to go with you. This is an amazing discovery. I don't want to miss it."

Maria said, "Neither do I. We will all go in there together or not at all. No one stays behind."

The three of them rested a bit longer, took drinks of water, helped Russo to his feet and Henry lead the way with his phone's dim light. They stepped to the metal door, now lying flat on the floor before the opening. The entryway to the crypt looked to be between six and seven meters wide. Henry took a careful step over the threshold and the other two followed him.

Inside the vault chamber, Henry saw the large thing on the floor. *Could it be a sarcophagus? I don't know. It looks awfully irregular.* He also noticed again the noise he had forgotten over the last few minutes. There was a dripping sound as of a viscous liquid falling onto the metal floor of the room. He looked up to the ceiling of the revealed chamber and saw that there was a thick substance almost like mucous oozing into a droplet every two or three seconds and splattering to the chamber floor near the large form. In the dim light, it appeared to be the same color as the choking vapors that had receded a few minutes earlier and the stink from it was identical. *What is that stuff?*

Maria stepped closer to the four and a half meter long thing lying on the floor of the chamber and held up her phone. She looked at the face of it and sighed. "I'm going to turn up the brightness. We need to know what this is." She adjusted it and the sudden increase in light level nearly blinded them for a few moments. When she could see again, Maria gasped.

Henry's mind whirled. *It's not a sarcophagus, but it should have been placed in one.*

Maria spoke the thought they all shared in common. "It's a corpse!"

* * *

Henry broke the stunned silence that had held them for nearly thirty seconds after Maria's statement. He said, "Couldn't it be a statue though?"

Maria said, "I don't think so. Look at the anatomical detail. That kind of artistic form wasn't developed in sculpture until the time of the Greeks. If you compare it with the paintings and carvings in the rest of this complex, I don't think it is possible for it to be a sculpture. It's too realistic for the art of the time."

Professor Russo said, "Well, it's a massive corpse." He circled the still form and began describing it, almost as if dictating to a student taking notes. He was so lost in thought that he seemed to ignore the pain from his hastily splinted arm. "It's curled up, almost in a fetal position. It is naked, but the skin seems to be leathery, somewhat like smoked meat in appearance, though it looks moist. It is humanoid in aspect but double or triple sized in every dimension. The head is large, about a half-meter in width, but the skin of the creature is stretched tightly and one can see the lips and gums have receded to reveal a skull-like face. The back of the creature is arched, even beyond what would be expected from a fetal-position curvature. There is a large, curved shape to the shoulders and backbone. I am almost certain this creature would be a hunchback if it were standing."

He continued, "The hands are clasped together ... no! They are bound together. There is a chain that is wound closely about the wrists. It looks like the chains are very tight. Assuming this is real and not some kind of hoax, I would wager this gigantic being was a prisoner when it was placed in here. The chains are so tight they cut all the way to the wrist bones. It must have been in immense pain."

Henry said, "This is making me very unsteady. How can there be a giant corpse in here? There are no such things as giants. There have been many hoaxes of giant remains, but never a real example that held up under scrutiny. This thing however, is twice the size of a Kodiak bear."

He continued and asked, "Also, how was it preserved like this? Why didn't it rot away, or at least decay to a skeleton? This thing still has emaciated flesh on it. You can see the skin, and under it in many places sinews and tendons. It looks like a victim of starvation. Look at its sunken eyes. Why hasn't this rotted away to dust?"

Henry continued, "And why the chains? There would be no reason to chain a corpse, so I agree with you, professor. If this is real, it must have been buried while it was alive and still chained. Somehow they captured the creature, placed it in here and locked it in. We thought this tomb complex was a burial place of honor. I think in actuality, it is the resting place of a monster."

Maria interrupted. "What was that? It sounded like someone screaming."

* * *

Krastyo Balev floated in a flickering half-world of heat and sharp teeth. He felt things biting his arms and legs. He twitched and tried to shake away the unseen creatures that gnawed upon him, but however often he shook them off, in moments they returned to bite him again. He felt feverishly hot. He twisted and moaned in sweat-soaked garments. *Why am I so hot? Why are things biting me?*

A cracking, shredding sound filled his head like the breaking of a giant tree. The splintering sound went on and on. *What is happening to me?*

Suddenly, he awoke to teeth-grinding pain and tried to sit up. His body attempted to obey, but couldn't follow through. His awareness leapt back to him with the pain in his pinned legs. The darkness held him tightly. He felt rising panic at the possibility of dying in this place where no light might ever come again.

Balev screamed, "Help me. Somebody help me. I'm trapped. Help me!" He struggled weakly but couldn't move. He shouted as loudly as he could. The sound echoed. "Help! Help!"

* * *

Maria said, "Someone is definitely shouting. The sound came from the passageway that leads to the Grand Staircase."

Russo said, "It was Bulgarian. They are shouting for help."

Henry said, "At least one of us has to leave this and go see. I'll do it."

Maria said, "We'll go with you."

Russo said, "The two of you go. I'm going to sit down and rest a little. The pain from this," he indicated his broken arm, "is wearing on me."

Maria looked conflicted. She spoke with passion and said, "I don't like for us to be separated. Who knows what could happen?"

Russo said, "I know. You are very kind to this old fellow, but really, I'll be fine right here. I don't think this one is going to do anything to me." He indicated the giant body. Russo smiled a little against the pain and said, "He's even older than I am."

Henry said, "Maria, if you want me to stay with him, or if you want to stay, we can do that, but at least one of us needs to go so we can give aid to whoever is calling for help."

Maria was torn. She looked at the professor and back to the passageway. The cry for help came again, this time weaker than before. She nodded her head decisively. "We both go." She started to hand her light to the professor, but he demurred that he didn't need it while they were gone. She helped him sit down, back braced against one wall. She and Henry set off for the Grand Staircase.

At the base of it, they listened and heard nothing.

Henry shouted, "Is anyone there? Call out so we can find you!"

In an instant, a weak voice spoke in Bulgarian somewhere above them on the destroyed staircase. "Here! I'm here! I'm trapped. Help me!"

Henry started up the stairs, threading his way between boulders and debris. Maria was only a step behind and cursed under her breath. "I recognize that voice. It's that worm, Balev."

* * *

It took them some time, but they finally climbed up the ruins of the Grand Staircase, threaded their way through boulders, collapsed ceiling and dirt and came to within a meter of the first landing, the original site of the side passageway in which they had been trapped after the cave-in. Henry called out and they determined the direction of Balev's voice, but could not see him. The debris at the landing and particularly the side opposite from the collapsed tunnel was piled high and jumbled.

Henry spoke *sotto voce* to Maria and said, "I don't know how anything survived in that collapsed section. I can't see him at all."

Maria said, "Keep him talking. I'm smaller than you and can crawl up there to find him; I'll try to locate him while you occupy him. The way I feel about him though, he might be better off if we left him in there. If we get him out, I might have to strangle him myself."

As Henry spoke with Balev, Maria took the phone they used for light and climbed in and around the boulders. At some points she could not spare a free hand to hold it and instead clamped it between her teeth. She slipped and nearly fell a dozen times. *We can't afford any injuries at this point. I have to be extremely careful.* She closed in on Balev's voice and finally spotted him. *This is bad, very bad.*

Balev was at the bottom of a stacked pile of large rocks and boulders. She caught sight of his face about two meters below her vantage point. He was wedged in a small space between large rocks on either side of him. His lower torso was covered over in rock and soil. She saw no way to get to him and absolutely no way to extricate him. *It was a wonder he wasn't crushed into a paste. We'll need heavy machinery to get him out of there and that may not do the trick either. I can easily see him crushed accidentally even if rescue workers are able to get to this site. But I can't feel too sorry for him.*

Maria said, "Balev. Look up here. Do you see me? If so, nod your head."

Krastyo Balev nodded his head vigorously and cried out, "Get me out of this! If you don't get me out of here immediately, I'll have your permission to work at this site revoked!"

Maria stared at him in open-faced astonishment. *The nerve of this man! Making threats at a time like this.* Amid the dirt and grime of the current predicament, Maria's face took on an icy expression. She said, "Stop that this instant. You're in no position to make threats or demands. And from what I see, there is no way we can get you out of this situation without heavy earth-moving equipment. We're trapped in this complex just like you and are hoping for rescue as well. You'll have to be patient."

Balev's voice came from below. "This situation is your fault. If the three of you hadn't been down here, I wouldn't have had to come down here as well. Now I'm hurt and trapped. I could die. I'll see that you are banned from Bulgaria. You'll never enter the country again!"

Maria shook her head in disgust. *The man was horrible before. Now he's delusional as well.*

She said, "Our bigger problem is leaving here alive. We'll have to worry later about anything else. Can you raise one hand? I'm going to lower a bottle of water to you. Try to take it." She positioned herself as nearly above him as was possible and lay down on the top of the rubble pile. She extended one arm down and held the bottle of water out to him. Incongruously, as she looked down at him and stretched her hand to him, she saw something that looked completely out of place. Down at the bottom of the hollow in which he lay, about a third of a meter from his right shoulder, was a small plastic box with a selector switch and a large button on its face. *What is that? It looks like a remote control of some kind. What is it doing down there?*

She heard the man grunt with exertion and her attention jumped back to Balev. He managed to raise his good arm and reach for the bottle. It hung suspended from her fingers just a slight few centimeters away from his fingertips. Maria shifted, leaned downward further, stretched to her limit and saw Balev make contact with the bottle. He snatched it from her hand and in a moment, had the cap between his clenched teeth. He unscrewed it and in a few moments he was gulping water greedily.

Maria said, "Slowly! Drink it slowly! You don't want to vomit it all up do you? Then what good would it have done you?"

Krastyo Balev slowed down and sipped. Maria said, "I'll be right back." She climbed slowly back to Henry while Balev protested and cursed her for abandoning him. He shouted about the dark, about her and Henry and Russo and turned it into quite a long tirade. Maria smiled grimly to herself. *Keep cursing the ones that have to help you, Balev. It will make it so much easier for us to do what we don't want to do anyway.*

She made it back to Henry and spoke to him in a whisper. "He's stuck at the bottom of a large pile of rubble. I don't know how he survived at all, but he caught a lucky break, I guess. There is no way we can help him right now beyond the bottle of water I managed to get down to him. If he is to get out alive, it will take heavy equipment. He says he is hurt and I don't doubt him, but he tried to blame this all on us! I wanted to tell him that his guilty conscience was trying to shift the blame, but I kept my mouth closed. Well, closed as much as I could."

Henry said, "There's no exit through the crypt. For all the trouble we put into opening it, all we found was that giant corpse." He paused, devastation hanging heavy in his voice. "We're still trapped. I don't know what to do next."

Maria said, "We can't help Balev and Professor Russo won't be much help with his injuries. Help may be coming from outside, but that could take a lot of time. I don't know if we have much time. Whatever happens, it's up to us."

Henry lifted up something that he'd held at his side. He said, "I found this while you were talking to him. It was very dark and I only had indirect light from your phone, but this thing was very close to me and I found it by the wires trailing from it. We might be able to use this in some way if it is what I think."

She said, "What is it?"

Henry looked at it carefully in the increased light from the phone Maria held and said, "I think it's an explosive wired to a detonator. It has been labelled 'three.'" He said, pointing at the label. "Well, one of two wires is attached to it anyway. The other one came loose."

* * *

Something had changed. The troubled sleep continued its insectile clicking rhythm in his fever slumber, but something had changed. *What? Where am I?* His thoughts continued their gnawing slow pace, but something was different. An errant thought splashed across the surface of his mind like a rock skipping on water. *A smell. It's an odor. Something smells different.*

A dream image somehow now familiar ran through his mind. It was that skeletal figure with its hands cupped to the sides of its thin face, calling out to him. It was still distant, but somehow he knew it was closer than the last time. *Last time? When was the last time? There is no time, just as there is no water. I'm a husk. Oh, for a drink of water.* The dreamer tried again to swallow in his sleep, but his throat was tight and the hardened, corded muscles still would not move.

The skeletal figure spoke. *Have I had this dream before? Wait. Am I dreaming?* The thin figure seemed to be shouting something else now. "Lord Moloch lives yet … he is very close … you must awaken and give aid … awaken … help him." *Awaken. If only I could awaken.*

"…Lord Mulciber! Moloch is near!"

The dreamer's mind roiled and horrible thoughts swirled through him again. *I am Mulciber! I am sleeping and must awaken. I am still caught in a dream, but something is different. Something has changed. A smell. What is that smell?* A thought formed and shot to the fore. *It is water. It is the smell of water!* He surged toward the wall separating dreams from the conscious mind. *There is water. I must have it!* He broke through the wall and shattered the barrier. He felt his mind breach into consciousness like something from the deep.

He was awake. He could not open his dry eyes and they hurt bitterly, but he lay there listening and though he could not yet breathe, the minute air currents moved slight scents into his nostrils. He could not open his wooden mouth. His body was twisted in agony, every muscle in the grip of a fiery metallic cramp. He could not move his lips, or breathe. *But I am awake.*

What woke me? It was something that resembled a skeletal creature intruding upon my dream-state. It told me that Moloch was near. Truly? The last memory I have of

Moloch was seeing him being trapped just as I was. I was chained … ah! I think I can distantly feel the chains still around my wrists. They closed Moloch into a large chest, then flew away, carrying me to … here I suppose. Michael closed me into a metal vault and I heard crashing and rumbling and then I went mad. He shied away from thinking about that. He did not want to go in that direction again.

He heard a sound. It was speech of some kind, low and mumbling. *Someone is nearby. I cannot move, but I can use my mind. And I do smell water. Oh blessed water. Somehow, I have to get a drink. Just one drink would help.*

In his dark but conscious thoughts, he concentrated and felt for the nearby mind. *It is one of the humans. It is talking to itself. Ah. He is in the dark now, but has seen me and wonders about my twisted form.* Mulciber would have laughed bitterly if he'd been able to laugh at all. *My. Twisted. Form. The Creator's empowered agent Michael twisted me when he carried out the Creator's curse. He said it fit my twisted mind.*

I used to be an angelic being like all others that stood in the Presence. I could have any form I wanted, but whatever form I chose, was always beautiful. Everything I created was always beautiful. Beauty was my ideal. When the form, the function, the spirit, the mind, the thought, all lined up in simplicity, elegance and intelligence; that was when I was complete, when I was happy. It was when I created beauty.

Mulciber snapped his mind back. *I mustn't let my mind wander lest I drift back into unconsciousness. I have no energy to move, and my body has too long been unused, but I smell the water. I also smell fresh air. There is air in here. The human must have somehow opened my crypt.* Mulciber knew that Michael must have placed a complex lock on the crypt that would have required intelligence to decipher. That was the limit of Michael's creativity though: complexity. He and the other Archons had always tried to best Mulciber's preeminent creativity with their own use of sheer complexity. It was their answer to his inspiration, but it always failed. Mulciber's designs and his efforts were so far beyond anything the others did and his were always surprisingly, elegantly simple.

The Creator had praised Mulciber's projects, creations and designs, but had always found it necessary to warn him. The Creator had said, "You take pride in what you make, but you should also have the courage to exercise humility. Others do not have your gifts, it is true. But where did your gifts come from? Did you create them yourself, or did you cultivate them?"

That always infuriated me. It was a distinction without meaning. Of course I created my own gifts. They didn't exist until I developed them. But the Creator wanted me to think I was given my abilities. Even then the Creator was trying to humiliate me and lower me, but I didn't realize it until later.

The human in the crypt with him continued thinking about Mulciber. *He finds me awe-inspiring, yet repugnant. He quotes to himself a human poet: 'Majestic though in ruin.' Hmmm. That has some truth in it. I am surprised that a human thought of such a thing. Do they have some potential after all, or may even a beast accidentally stumble upon deeper reality sometimes?*

Mulciber's mind continued to clear with thoughts and memories snapping into place. He only had two of his physical senses, hearing and smell, but he felt the machinery of his thoughts gathering speed. *I have no energy for my body: it functions with only the barest whisper of life. But I may have enough mental energy to command action and compel obedience.*

Mulciber launched a gentle mental probe into the human's mind, gathered information, discovered the man had a small cache of water nearby and also realized the human did not notice Mulciber's mental intrusion. *Good. That will make this much easier. I will not waste effort on total compulsion then. I'll introduce thoughts and the creature will think it acts on its own. Only if it balks will I need to exert control.*

Mulciber reminded the human that it was thirsty. The man agreed mentally and felt for its small cache of water. There was a moment of reluctance on its part to 'take more than its share.' It appeared that the human had comrades that it expected to return soon and they would also expect to receive a share of the water. *That won't do. I need all of the remaining water. This body won't function at all without getting moisture into its tissues.*

Mulciber probed and saw that the creature thought of his form as 'the giant corpse'. He mentally nudged the human to remember it deserved a drink of water. As the creature procured a container of the liquid from its cache, he introduced a thought: 'I wonder what effect water might have on the giant corpse? I shall pour some on it to find out.' The creature tried to recoil from the thought as if it were profane in some way. Mulciber had to bear down on the thing's mind to overcome its repugnance. In a few moments, Mulciber felt the container of water pressed to his still form's mouth. Mulciber found the creature's reluctance to act growing stronger by the moment, so he seized complete control of the human. He forced it to keep the water container by his mouth. Mulciber sent commands to the creature and soon, he had it putting droplets onto the skin and gently massaging the moisture into Mulciber's parched flesh.

Once his lips were flexible enough, Mulciber forced the human to push the spout of the container between them and fill his mouth with the fluid. The water soaked into his flesh and Mulciber had the man empty more into his still form. He had the creature open additional containers to use again and again, and though it would not be enough to revive him fully, Mulciber knew it would be enough to alleviate some of the pain that consumed his body. He quickly compelled the human to use the last of its cache of water to rehydrate his form.

* * *

Maria said, "Explosives. It's just one more confirmation that we were trapped intentionally and the man who intended to murder us has been caught in his own trap. Now that we have this, we should use it on Balev. It's what he deserves."

Henry said, "I don't disagree that it might be satisfying, but I don't want to lower us to his level. I have something else in mind."

Maria asked, "What?"

He said, "What if we placed it up at the top of the Grand Staircase right at the stone door? If we could create an opening to the outside, even a small one, we might get out or at the least, call for some help."

Maria said, "Interesting. How would we set off the explosive?"

Henry said, "I want to study this detonator and see if I can figure it out. There doesn't seem to be a way to set a timer or activate it, but there must have been a way to do that. I'm certain the only reason this didn't explode the first time is that the other explosions must have loosened this connection before the blast. If we can figure out how to detonate this remotely and crack open the stone door above this crypt, we might be able to attract enough attention to get rescued."

Maria turned her head suddenly as if remembering something. She hissed, "Henry! What would a remote control for a detonator look like? Would it be a small box half the size of a pack of cigarettes with a large button and a selector switch?"

Henry looked her in the eyes and said, "It might be, but I don't know. Have you seen something like that?"

She said, "Yes." She pointed at the rubble pile where Balev was trapped. "In there, right near his shoulder is a small plastic box with a button and a selector, almost like a remote control. The positions on the selector each have a number on them from one through four."

Henry's eyes grew larger. "He did try to kill us all, didn't he? He must have had the side passageway wired with explosives and set them off with a remote control. The concussion ran wild and the wiring to this one failed. He got caught in the collapse." Henry looked at the device he held. "I think I should wait to reattach this wire until we get that remote away from him, shouldn't I?"

Maria said, "Yes. But I have an idea. I will try to get in there nearer to him. As much as I hate him, I need to see if there is any first aid he needs, and I need to do it right away. If I can get close enough for first aid, I will do what I can to help him, but I will also snatch the control and bring it with me when I come back out."

Henry said, "Is there enough room? I thought you could just barely reach his hand before, and that was with him stretching as far as he could as well."

Maria said, "I know. It is very tight in there and I don't know if it will be possible to crawl in further. We have to get that remote, though. It's the only way to set off the explosives from a safe distance."

Henry said, "And while you're doing that, I'll work my way further up and get to the top by the stone door if I can. Once I get there, I'll find a crack or opening into which to put the explosive." He stopped and pondered for a moment. "Just one more thing: we found number three and I'll bet one and two were used to collapse the tunnel originally when we were first trapped. Where is explosive number four?"

CHAPTER 30 – AMBUSH

"Art thou that traitor angel? Art thou he who first broke peace in Heaven...?"
— John Milton, Paradise Lost

Night was falling as Janos Parasca stepped off his private jet at the Varna, Bulgaria airport. His new PetroRomania assistant stepped forward and offered to carry Parasca's briefcase.

Parasca snapped, "What is the latest? Where are the salvage ships and have they started unloading the cargo yet at the dock? What about my security team? How are they positioned?"

The other man said, "Our salvage ship, the *Baltic Rage*, arrived second at the wreck site of the *Fortuna*. The *Vlad* wouldn't back off and so the *Rage* stayed close and observed the salvage operation. They tell me that no helicopters have come or gone from the other ship and they are now waiting outside the harbor for further instructions. The *Vlad* was contracted to Intercon Transport and has docked. It appears they are readying for the beginning of dockside freight operations. A large crane is moving into position, apparently to offload the salvaged items. An extra-heavy-duty truck has pulled up to the dock near the ship and may be the intended receiver for those items. Everything so far has been tightly coordinated by Intercon Transport."

Janos Parasca cursed. *Dmitri is being very efficient. He got his people to the Fortuna site before mine and now he is trying to get the goods off and away before I can do anything about it. Where does he think he is going to hide something like this? He can't succeed. Well, he hasn't seen my surprises yet.*

He said, "Tell the *Baltic Rage* their services are not needed any longer. Of course, they will receive no completion bonus since they didn't make the recovery of the items from the site of the *Fortuna*. What about my security team?"

The assistant said, "They have arrived at the dock warehouse we leased. It is near to the salvage ship *Vlad*. They are preparing to move at your signal. The last word I had five minutes ago was that they need only a few more minutes to get ready to begin execution of the action plan. They should be almost set by now."

Parasca said, "Good."

He and his assistant moved to Parasca's nearby car, a Bentley. The driver stepped out and opened the driver-side rear door for the assistant while Parasca's new bodyguard stepped out of the passenger side front seat to open the rear door for Janos. The car drove the few kilometers from the private airstrip to the dock warehouse where his security team was readying to deploy.

His assistant led Parasca inside and a few dozen steps into the warehouse's large ground floor area where his mercenary force was finishing their final check lists. Parasca saw the heavily armed men lined up and at attention. One officer seemed to be issuing last minute instructions to the men while another walked from man to man checking their equipment. Each man carried a military-grade rifle capable of full-auto or semi-auto fire and also carried holstered sidearms. All of the men were dressed in completely black uniforms, black shoes and pullover stocking masks that would allow them to move less conspicuously in the night outside.

The assistant went over to speak with the officer in charge of the security detail. Parasca and his bodyguard took an elevator up to the top floor and they exited through a metal door onto the roof of the warehouse building. The looked out at the dockyard and the *Vlad* below. Bright flood lights cut through the darkness and the dockside crane looked like a massive insect crouching over the *Vlad*. Only one crane at the Varna docks had the capacity to lift the sarcophagus and it was brand new. The crane's cables were being secured to the steel I-beam pallet on which the sarcophagus sat. Parasca looked slightly to the left at the heavy-duty transport truck and saw that a steel container with its lid open was already on the bed of the truck. *It won't be very long now. It looks like Dmitri's team is ready to have the crane lift and move the sarcophagus over to the truck. They'll set it down inside that container. Once the lid is put in place, that will be the last time anyone will see Moloch's sarcophagus if I have anything to do with it.*

Parasca looked to the edge of the rooftop and saw that two of his men were setting up tripods. He nodded in recognition at one of them and took out his phone. He sent a text message to his assistant in the lower warehouse level.

The message read, "Tell the commander to get his team into position."

Parasca couldn't have heard anything in the warehouse below, but he imagined the security force receiving his order and jogging to the exit closest to the *Vlad*. There they would split into squads of four to deploy to their various positions. *Dmitri won't know what hit him. I wish I could see his face when all of this starts.*

* * *

Rakslav Gachevska walked down the gangway of the *Vlad* to the dock. *I want to be there when the sarcophagus is placed on the truck. I have to be sure I get Lord Moloch to a secure place before the sarcophagus is opened. He needs to be able to get a lay of the land before anything else. I need to help him understand his situation, so I have to peel the sarcophagus away from Dmitri's people and also keep it out of Parasca's hands. I suspect Parasca has people here at least to observe and Dmitri would have sent a security team to guard this shipment. Where are they? Ah, that must be them.*

Eight armed men in dark green uniforms jogged up to the truck. Four went to the front of the heavy-duty transport that would receive the sarcophagus and the other four ran to the back of the truck. Each group arranged themselves into a semicircle facing outward so their fields of vision overlapped and still covered all points of the compass. They held combat rifles at ready across their chests.

Rakslav walked over to the first one he came to and said, "We'll be ready to bring the shipment down soon. Is this all of the security team?"

The guard said, "Who are you? Are you from the *Vlad*?"

Rakslav pointed at his ID badge. "Yes. I'm with the union and am here to make sure everything goes safely. I came over to make sure everything is in place before my men set it down into the truck's container. Is this the security team for Intercon Transport? Is this all of you?"

The guard said, "No, it isn't all of us, but what do you care? There are more in the vehicles that will be driving in front of and behind this truck. It's not your concern anyway."

Petr Ivanov came down the gang plank and walked to Rakslav and the security guards. He spoke to Rakslav. "This is none of your concern. These people are with me. You can run back to the union and give them your report."

Rakslav ignored him and walked over to the giant heavy transport truck. He was joined by two dock men with belt radios that came over and climbed up on the back of the truck. They spoke into their radios and waved up at the crane operator. The sarcophagus began to lift from the *Vlad*.

Rakslav stood at the rear of the truck and pondered. *This is going to make it harder. I don't know where all of Dmitri's security forces are and I've only got a few minutes left before the crane moves the sarcophagus into place.* Rakslav patted his underarm holster and the one on his back. His fighting knife was still in place on his leg sheath. *My weapons are ready, but am I? I have a feeling things are going to get very messy before the night is through.*

* * *

Mercy and Jack leapt from Dmitri's car as it slowed to a stop at the Port of Varna. Mercy shouted across the roof of the car at Dmitri, "Is that it? Is that your salvage ship?"

Dmitri said, "Yes, I think so, but I can't see the ship's name. There it is, the *Vlad*. That's the one."

Jack said, "That's got to be the sarcophagus that the crane is lifting."

Mercy said, "We've got to get people there. That thing must not be opened. Ever."

They watched as the huge box swung out over the truck and began its descent. Two men stood atop the truck and guided the crane operator with radios. The load slowed its descent when it came within a few meters of the container. The two men on the back of the truck spoke busily into their radios as they guided the crane operator in his approach. The sarcophagus lowered a bit more and one of the men used a guide rod to gently rotate the sarcophagus a few degrees for its final descent into the container. The load went down into the metal container and out of sight. A few minutes later, the crane hoisted its cables up but stopped the ascent. The two men on the truck positioned themselves to the side where the hinged lid of the container hung. They radioed back to the crane and the cable began swinging back over toward the two men.

Dmitri said, "Those men are going to get the lid closed with the help of the crane. I have armed guards around the truck and also in escort vehicles that will be driving in front and in back of the truck. We'll get it away from here safely and into one of my warehouses. We'll lock it up securely so no one can get to it ... wait!" Dmitri interrupted his own statement.

Loud cracking and popping noises carried through the air to them.

Jack said, "What's that?"

Dmitri said, "Get down! It's gunfire!"

* * *

Rakslav dropped to the ground near the gangway of the *Vlad* and lay flat. By the familiar cracking sounds of the shots being fired and by the lack of a characteristic echoing boom, he knew the rounds were all subsonic. He automatically filtered out and eliminated an entire category of rifles and ammunition from consideration. He saw one of Dmitri's guards fall down, clutching his face, blood between his fingers. Rakslav heard more shots and noted the chunking sound they made when puncturing metal. There was also the falling pitched whine of bullets ricocheting and that meant high-velocity missiles that were tumbling out of control. That also meant danger to people not even being aimed at.

The two workers that had been on the dock side of the crane operation leapt off of the truck and, apparently not taking any chances, ran a few steps and jumped off the dock and into the water below. *That's probably the safest place to be right now. It's where I'd be headed if I didn't need to do something right here.*

Dmitri's seven remaining guards had moved to the front passenger side of the truck for cover and were all crouching low. Rakslav drew his pistol from his shoulder holster and gauged the direction of fire from a few muzzle flashes. He began crawling toward the back of the truck while keeping a watchful eye on the direction of fire. He felt rather than heard a projectile whiz by his head. He heard a ping off of the side of the truck and felt the spray of sand and gravel where the bullet struck the ground near him. He cursed and crawled faster.

He made it to the end of the truck and crouched near one of its huge tires, putting it between him and the line of fire. He quickly checked his gun to make sure that the crawl to the truck hadn't gummed it up. He verified that it was clean and the action still worked. He patted his knife and other gun and hazarded a quick look out from behind the tire. He saw a squad of four advancing. A booming rifle shot echoed through the air. *Ah. That was a supersonic shot. They have at least one sniper laying down cover fire for that approaching squad.*

Dmitri's men at the front of the truck ducked out and returned fire, some at the approaching men and some in what they must have hoped was the direction of the sniper fire. One of the men in the approaching four-man squad fell. Dmitri's men ducked back behind the truck, but one was too slow and a booming sniper round took him through the head. He fell flat on his back, spread-eagled with arms flung wide. Rakslav noted approvingly that only a portion of the dead man's head was still attached to the body. *That was an amazing shot. Do not get in that sniper's sights.*

One of Dmitri's merc's radios crackled and Rakslav strained to hear. A voice shouted from the radio through the gunfire.

It was Dmitri. "Get that truck moving! They're trying to hijack it!"

One of the men climbed up onto the running board and opened the passenger side door. He climbed into the cab, but the snipers must have seen him. Several shots boomed with the accompanying sound barrier shattering rebound. Shot after shot shattered the windshield and the man that had been in the cab fell backward and tumbled onto the pavement like a ragdoll.

The five remaining men huddled down and began shouting at each other. Gunfire erupted from behind Rakslav back in the direction of the *Vlad*. Rakslav looked and saw eight more men piling out of two Hummers.

They aimed at Parasca's three-man squad as they ran toward the truck and their five comrades. *These must be Dmitri's chase vehicles.* One of Dmitri's men fell from another sniper round through the forehead. *Again a headshot! I wish I could hire that guy!*

Rakslav heard a yell and then an explosion from the direction of the front of the truck. He looked back just in time to see bodies falling to earth. *Must have been a grenade! They probably took out all five of the guys sheltering beside the truck.*

The three-man squad ran up, firing as they ran. The remaining seven men from the Hummers hit the dirt. Rakslav was caught between them and ducked under the bed of the truck and crouched behind the driver's side back set of wheels. The wheels were gigantic and tripled on each side of the trailer. It was obvious this was a super heavy-duty model. *It would have to be to transport the sarcophagus.* Rakslav restlessly checked the clip in his gun, making sure it was full. Satisfied, he crawled closer to the front of the truck.

He heard constant gunfire from the two sides and every few seconds booming rounds of sniper fire. *It's a butcher's yard out there.* There was a loud explosion followed immediately by a second one back by the Hummer group. *Two more grenades.* Fire went silent from that direction. He heard running footsteps coming from the front of the truck and two men jumped onto the running boards and then into the cab. *It must be a couple from the four-man squad at the front. I guess they lost another in the fire fight.* Rakslav considered jumping out from under the truck at the driver's side, but before he acted, the sniper guns sounded again. Bullets hit the dirt on both sides of the truck. *The sniper is putting down suppressive fire aimed at any stragglers sheltering by the truck. He can't see me but suspects I'm here. Smart.*

The truck engine rattled to life and Rakslav felt it shift into low gear. The truck above him started to roll forward and Rakslav realized he had to do something quick. His cover was leaving and in moments there would be nothing between him and the sniper but air still smoky from gunfire. He ducked and crawled to the end of the truck as it rolled past him centimeters above his head. As the rear of the truck approached, he pivoted and turned to face the front of the truck. The tailgate passed over him and he leapt to his feet, ran a few steps, grabbed and jumped onto the end of the flatbed. He crouched behind the container that held the sarcophagus and was out of the line of fire for the moment.

* * *

Parasca said, "What's happening down there? Why did our squad start firing before the sarcophagus was completely secured and the lid closed?"

Alex Lacusta said, "I suspect they saw Dmitri's people approaching the transport truck and decided they couldn't wait." He held the sniper rifle at ready and the scope to his eye. He watched the truck pull away with the relic loaded into the container and scanned the ground for any survivors among the scattered bodies. From his vantage spot on the roof near Parasca, he had a good view of the battlefield but saw no one alive. *Where did that big fellow go? I'm sure he's not among the dead, but he's not where I thought he'd be, under the truck. I know I saw someone hiding there.*

The truck continued right toward the building where he crouched on the edge of the rooftop in front of his tripod mounted rifle. *Still no sign.* The truck turned down the road in front of their warehouse and out toward the entrance to the docks. Two of the other security squads had secured the entrances to the docks and neutralized the Varna port's own security people. *The truck would have no more trouble...*

Lacusta did a double take. As the big vehicle turned the corner in front of him, he'd seen someone on the back of the truck by the end of the container holding the sarcophagus. He smiled to himself, moved the scope slightly to pull the face of the stowaway into view. *It's the big fellow alright. Now I'll just rack up another headshot...*

He pulled his finger around the trigger, tightening and preparing to squeeze. The man's face turned and looked in his direction. Lacusta looked at the man in his rifle scope and was stunned. He felt paralyzed. *I recognize him! It's Director Gachevska!* He took his finger off the trigger.

Parasca said, "There's someone on the back of the truck by the container. Shoot him!"

Lacusta pulled the scope away from his eye and looked up at Parasca. "Chairman, that's one of ours. You didn't tell me he'd be here. When did Rakslav Gachevska get to Varna? He didn't come with the rest of us."

Janos Parasca looked at Alex like he had grown a third eye in the middle of his forehead. "Rakslav? Rakslav is down there? What is he doing in Varna?" The two men looked at each other and then back at the truck as it turned a corner and was lost to their sight.

* * *

Dmitri's face was red with anger. He pulled out his phone and began shouting into it. "What just happened? How did so much of my security force just get mowed down?"

Mercy stepped back from Dmitri, looked at Jack and beckoned him over. "Did we just see what I think we saw? It looked to me that someone hijacked the sarcophagus right out from under Dmitri's people, killing a lot of them in the process. And I'm guessing the hijackers are probably working for Parasca."

Jack said, "That's what I saw too. This is bad, Mercy."

She clenched her fists and squeezed her eyes shut. Her face suffused in anger, she spoke from between tight, bloodless lips. "This is much worse than bad. Parasca will have the sarcophagus now. If he sets Moloch free, there'll be untold carnage. We've got to do something!"

A man ran at them, waving his arms. Dmitri said, "Good. It's Petr. He can take charge of the security team and get my truck back. Everyone else, get back in the car. We're going after them. Petr can rally the security people and get those Hummers rolling. We're not going to let Parasca get away with this. I won't let him take anything from me ever again!"

CHAPTER 31 – RELEASED

"For what peace will be given to us enslaved, but custody severe?"
— John Milton, Paradise Lost

The heavy truck rumbled through the gates of the Port of Varna, waved on by the last of Parasca's security force. Rakslav crouched at the back of the container holding the sarcophagus. He held onto one of the cables that secured the container to the truck bed. The lid of the open container rattled against the side where it hung. *Maybe I should climb inside. Perhaps I could open the sarcophagus and release Lord Moloch. I know there are three latches that have to be undone.*

Rakslav stood up carefully and held onto the corner of the three and a half meter wide container as best he could. He heard gunfire and the screeching of tires behind and turned to look. Two Hummers roared through the security gates. Each vehicle had men hanging out its windows and firing machine guns into Parasca's men at the security booth by the port entrance. Behind the Hummers followed an expensive luxury car.

Rakslav decided he'd best act now before the following vehicles caught sight of him. He leapt up and caught a hand on the lip of the container. His shoulders bunched, his huge biceps flexed and he pulled his chin up to the lip and continued the pull up to the middle of his chest and then to his waist. With an ease that would have astonished any bystander, he lifted one leg up and over the lip of the container and brought his two hundred and eighty pound bulk over into the inner part and lowered himself into a crouch on the top of the sarcophagus.

Most of the lid was as he remembered it from his time on the *Fortuna*. The difference was a large, bubble-wrap encased flat package duct-taped to the middle of the lid. *That must be the shield. The salvage team found it on the sea bed near the sarcophagus. They must have wrapped it and secured it in this way.*

Rakslav ignored the smaller package and touched the near-translucent metal of the sarcophagus' lid. He gazed at the rampant bull figure engraved into the surface of the impenetrable metal. He reached for the plaque and saw it was still there and still awe-inspiring. The letters resolved as he looked at it and in the Bulgarian of the gutter that he had first learned as a child, it said, 'Trapped until sorry.' but to English speakers he knew it would appear as 'Imprisoned until repentant.' He'd regained Lord Moloch's tomb at last. Lord Moloch would be free again soon, and Rakslav would be with his god once more.

* * *

Mercy stared at the window next to her. In the glass near her head was a shatter mark where it had been broken in a small circle about an inch across. The bullet that had been aimed at her head had been stopped by the multiple layers of bulletproof glass in the thick window. The shatter spot was surprisingly small, but Mercy couldn't help feeling a little shaky about it. *A bullet was inches from my head and aimed right at me. I would have been killed if not for this glass.*

Dmitri's brother, Alexi turned from the front seat and said, "You like that, Dr. Teller? I paid an amazing amount of money to get that glass from an arms dealer of our acquaintance. He found this experimental new material that the U.S. government had been testing. He said the outermost layer is called ALON. He called it an optical ceramic and that it is some kind of aluminum. I didn't care about that of course, but I did care when he promised me it could withstand even .50 caliber armor piercing rounds. I guess he wasn't lying."

Mercy touched the glass and spoke in a subdued voice, "I guess not."

Their car swept up behind the nearest Hummer. Dmitri shouted into his phone. "Pull up alongside the cab of that truck! Force them off the road or something!"

Mercy heard the small voice coming from Dmitri's phone. It said, "They are staying on the port road headed northwest. The truck may be too wide for the lanes on the highway without special escort."

Dmitri said, "Forget about that! We've got to catch up and get control of that truck. What is out to the northwest? Why would they be driving there? They can't hope to outrun us."

Alexi said, "The airport is there. They might try to fly it out of here."

Dmitri said, "What? That truck and the load are too big and heavy."

Alexi said, "Not for one of those giant freight planes."

Dmitri looked at his brother, fear and disbelief in his eyes. He started to say something but was cut off by Jack Truett.

Jack spoke loudly and suddenly. "We've got more company." He pointed a thumb to the rear window. A limousine raced up behind them. Mercy looked out the back window and her face flushed red with anger.

She said, "It's that monster, Janos Parasca. My father."

* * *

Parasca leaned forward in the front passenger seat gazing fixedly out the front window. He never sat in the front seat, but this time, he wouldn't allow anyone else to sit there. His driver was at the wheel, his assistant was in the back and crowded in next to him were Parasca's bodyguard and Alex Lacusta. He caught sight of his daughter, Mercy Teller in the car in front. She looked as furious as he had ever seen her. *What is she doing here? Has she taken up with Dmitri? How else to explain it? Well, dear daughter, on the Fortuna, you were full of surprises, but this time, I will have some surprises for you.*

The driver's eyes were fixed on the road and the cars in front of him. "Sir, the Hummers up ahead have gunmen with rifles. The windows on this car are bulletproof against small caliber handguns, but not high-powered rifles. You could be in danger if they start firing at us."

Parasca shot back brutally, "Never mind that. You just drive and keep your mouth shut. I hate it when people think I am interested in their idiot jabbering. Drive and keep quiet. Just stay as close as you can to that car right in front of you. If you understand me, nod, but do not talk."

The driver squeezed his lips together and the muscles in his jaw clenched. He nodded his head up and down once and stared straight ahead.

Imbecile. Where do all of these idiots come from? Is it too much to ask that people be silent and do their work and nothing else? Parasca turned to Alex Lacusta in the backseat and said, "Where did Rakslav Gachevska come from? Why didn't he notify us that he was alive and coming to Varna? More importantly, why didn't we know he was here?"

Lacusta said, "We deduced he was alive from the email that we found where he had replied to that Bulgarian official who was offering to sell you some archaeological artifacts. He didn't try to conceal that email trail. Director Gachevska is very capable of leaving no electronic footprints behind when he cares to, so I would conclude that he wanted us to know."

Parasca said, "You should have shot him when you had the chance. If he were working with us, I would have known. He would have contacted me and let me know he was alive. He would have come back to Bucharest and helped us. He might have been able to catch Mercy Teller when she came to that corporate apartment. He might have had a better idea to incapacitate her than mixing sedative drugs into her pills." He frowned at Lacusta. "Luckily, <u>my</u> idea of using that stun pistol worked, even if your part of that scenario almost got you killed." Parasca's frown turned into a glare. "Rakslav must be working for Dmitri now. He didn't conceal that email correspondence because he wanted to keep us guessing. And his gambit worked, didn't it?"

Lacusta said, "Yes sir. I did not suspect the director of betrayal. Your explanation makes sense to me."

Parasca was slightly mollified and spoke to his assistant. "Get some more security people mobilized and the ones waiting at the airport ready. Tell those at the Varna Port to pull out and follow. We need more people with us in case something else happens."

He turned back to the action in front. The huge truck carrying the sarcophagus rumbled ahead of them on the freeway. His two men driving the truck had orders to take it to the Varna International Airport where he had a heavy 747 freighter aircraft waiting. It was capable of carrying a third more than the weight of the truck and the sarcophagus combined. The rear ramp would be down and the truck would be able to drive right up into the airplane.

The plane would take off for Istanbul, at least that was its filed flight plan, but Dmitri would never know where it ended up, even if he had connections at the Varna Airport. The plane was going to be diverted in flight to another destination that Parasca would choose once it was airborne. The pilot had instructions and a large bonus riding on his ability to fake a minor emergency like a faulty fuel gauge that would send the plane to Parasca's off-the-cuff intermediate landing site. *Not even the pilot knows where he will go yet. He also doesn't know where he'll be bound once he lands and takes off again. That way, no amount of spying does Dmitri any good. The pilot was contracted for this one job and is not an employee of mine, so Dmitri could not have known of him in advance. And, if in spite of all these precautions, Dmitri finds out where the plane finally lands, then I will have evidence of something that I've suspected for a long time, that the PetroRomania network has been completely compromised.* Parasca was sure though, that once the plane was in the air, it would be the end of the affair as far as Dmitri was concerned. Most importantly, the sarcophagus would be out of his rival's reach.

* * *

Rakslav Gachevska tried to hold on as he lay on top of the sarcophagus. It rumbled and shook in the truck's container, sometimes sliding into the inside wall of the steel box. Rakslav saw two sizable dents that had been put into the steel walls of the container and he was having a very difficult time trying to stay in one place. *I've got to get those latches open, but it's almost impossible with the motion and sliding going on. The work crew didn't have a chance to secure the sarcophagus inside before the hijacking started and now this truck is being driven much faster than it ever should be. It will be a miracle if something disastrous doesn't happen.*

He heard honking and a crunching sound on the passenger side of the truck. *Someone just lost an argument with a very large piece of rolling steel. Anyone close better pay attention to that. This driver is not stopping for anything.* A siren began to wail and Rakslav whistled under his breath. *Now we have the police getting involved. What's next, the Bulgarian Army? What a mess this whole thing is turning into. What were Janos Parasca and Dmitri Slokov thinking? They've gotten to the point that they don't even care if the whole world sees them have a shoot-out in the middle of a major city. Well, I don't care about either of them. I've got to free Moloch.*

He didn't dare crawl down into the space between the sarcophagus and the interior wall of the steel container. With all of the sliding and shifting of the load going on, if he were caught down in there when the sarcophagus slid in the wrong direction, there wouldn't be enough left of him to wipe off with a paper towel. He grabbed onto the hinge side of the sarcophagus and felt a slice in his right hand like a paper cut. He cursed himself for forgetting that the edges of the thing were sharp. He wiped his cut hand on his stolen uniform and moved more carefully. He turned and looked at the opposite side and found the three latches. *I need to wait for a calm moment and swing around. I've got to time this perfectly.*

The sirens came closer and Rakslav heard the police speaking through a bullhorn like PA system. They were commanding everyone between the truck and the police car to clear out of the way. Though Rakslav could not see the reaction, he imagined what it would be. A moment later he had his suspicions confirmed and heard the sounds of multiple guns opening fire. There was the screech of tires and another crashing sound. *Now we get deeper into this dark water. There will be dozens of police on us in minutes. They will descend on us like wolves. I must hurry.*

After the sounds of the crash faded away, Rakslav took a chance, flipping around and throwing himself across at the closest latch. He grabbed onto the large mechanism and rode out the next few bumps and slides. The latch was twice as wide as a normal man's hand splayed wide. He had been on the *Fortuna* the first time the latches had been opened and had seen it done. The crew on that ship had used long pry bars to lift the latches. He didn't have any tools and would have to do the work with his bare hands.

Rakslav braced himself as well as he could and pulled at the latch strongly. He felt no give in the mechanism. He held tightly to the latch with both hands and repositioned his legs under him. He flexed his arm muscles and then his legs. His arms creaked and he pushed up with his legs. *For a count of ten … one, two, three…* He held the pulling tension on his arms and the latch and his mind blanked of everything but the force he exerted. Veins in his face bulged with the pressure. *Eight, nine, ten. Nothing.* He relaxed his exertion but kept enough hold to retain his balance against the shifting load on the truck. He pulled himself toward the latch and brought his face up to it and studied it. It was hard to make out the working of the nearly translucent metal mechanism, but he decided he had been putting too much upward force on it and not enough outward force to pull the latch away from the side of the sarcophagus. *If only I could chance putting myself down there between the edge and the inner wall of the container, then I'd get a better angle.*

He felt the truck turn a corner and the load shifted ominously, completely smashing closed the space that he'd considered putting himself into only moments earlier. The truck's bed rocked and Rakslav felt it lift up on one side then slam back down. The sarcophagus slid back to the other side and left the opening again. *I would have been a greasy smear on that wall. What is this maniac driver doing? Some of the opposite side wheels left the road for a moment. You can't drive like that with a heavy, unstable load.*

He decided it was now or never. *I have to open these latches now before anything else happens, before the truck stops and definitely before Parasca or Dmitri get control of it. I may never get a chance if I don't do this immediately.*

Rakslav put his feet against the edge of the sarcophagus and his back against the inside wall. He crouched down, legs bent almost double at the knees, stretched his hands down between his legs and took the latch in his hands. He used all the strength of his two hundred and eighty pounds and the force of his legs and lifted. He felt no movement but gave it a count of ten. *Everything I've got. Deep breath and release some. This will be a long, hard pull. Don't want to black out. One, two...pull harder...three, four... harder...* He felt the latch swivel, smoothly but extremely tightly. *This thing was made to take a lot of force to open. I can feel the inner resistance of the spring. It not only doesn't want to open, it wants to reclose. I didn't think of this. It's not just a question of getting it open, but keeping it open. I've just got to keep going until it reaches the catch point.* He pulled and the latch continued its swivel. Before it reached perpendicular, he felt a click. He released his grip and the latch stayed open. The sarcophagus shuddered underneath him. *Now, for the next one.*

* * *

Mercy saw the leading Hummer take advantage of a clear space on the driver's side of the huge truck and surge forward. It accelerated into the opening and the Hummer's passenger-side gunmen leaned out his window and started firing into the other truck's driver-side door. Most of the shots went wild but some struck the door and one shattered the driver's window. The big truck's brake lights blazed on and it suddenly slowed with convulsive jerks, the trailer slewing dangerously to one side, narrowly avoiding a jackknife.

The trailing Hummer slammed into the rear of the slowing truck carrying the sarcophagus. The airbags deployed in the front seat. The Hummer's driver-side rear door flew open at the impact and a guard in that vehicle was thrown out and sailed fifty feet into oncoming traffic. Mercy saw a taxi going the opposite direction hit the airborne man in the middle of its windshield. Mercy thought she saw the guard crash through the windshield glass. His body went all the way into the car, not even leaving his feet hanging out of the windshield. Mercy momentarily wondered if the dead man had crashed through the safety glass separating the taxi driver from the passenger compartment and into the back seat, ultimately landing beside a horrified taxi passenger.

The Hummer beside the freight truck swerved to avoid the bigger truck and tipped up on two wheels. The driver of the larger truck must have drawn a pistol because Mercy saw muzzle flashes from the driver's seat and saw the windows on the Hummer shatter and spall at the points of impact. The big truck stopped its slewing and put on the gas again, accelerating away from the wrecked Hummer behind and gaining a little distance from the other Hummer that had been firing on it from beside.

Dmitri shouted, "Don't let it get away. It's trying to get to the airport! Get closer!"

Dmitri's driver swerved around the wrecked Hummer and chased after the truck carrying the sarcophagus. Mercy looked at the crash site as they sped by. The occupants of the Hummer weren't moving and smoke billowed out of the engine compartment. Another body hung, tumbled half out of the open door from which the airborne passenger had come. Traffic was stopped on the opposite side of the road and the taxi driver was out of his car, arms waving in the air. Mercy looked over at Jack, speechless for a moment but then found a few words.

She said, "We've got to stop all of this chaos somehow."

Jack said, "I know, but how?"

* * *

Rakslav braced himself and pulled with all of his considerable strength, this time making sure to use his muscle in the most advantageous way. The latched lifted slowly and stiffly against his applied force and clicked into place a few moments later. He wiped sweat and blood from his face and hands. A large gash through the left sleeve of his shirt showed shredded flesh. That entire arm dripped blood but he still had his strength even if he'd momentarily had the wind knocked out of him.

Got to hurry. The next time this truck slams its brakes on and I go flying against the inside container wall, I could just as easily bounce out and onto the road. As it was, I smashed into the upper edge and took this ripping cut to my arm. I can't help Lord Moloch if I get killed. Now, for the last latch.

Rakslav Gachevska wiped his bloody hand against his pants and crawled toward the third latch.

* * *

Dmitri shouted into his phone, "I don't care! Get your police forces out ahead of the transport truck and put up a roadblock before it gets to the airport! Between your payments and all of the palms that had to be greased for this operation I paid a half-million Euros to make everything happen here in Varna. Get your police to help us rather than chase us! We're trying to get the truck back that was hijacked. Stop the truck for us and this will all be over quickly. No, I'm not paying you any more money. I gave you enough. Just remember your reputation for fighting corruption. You don't want word of bribe-taking to surface about yourself now, do you?"

Dmitri hung up on the caller. As he pressed the button to end the call on his phone, Mercy heard a tiny panicked voice shouting unintelligibly from the other end.

Dmitri spoke with disgust. "Chief of Police! What a fool. He should take care before I have to have something done about him." Dmitri shifted, looked at Mercy and his expression changed. He actually smiled at her, his lips parted in a doting, indulgent and somehow terrifying grin.

He spoke with a note of reassurance. "Don't worry, my dear. I have a feeling that today is my day. Maybe I'll put an end to Parasca for good. After all he's done to me, to you, to your mother and grandmother, by the end of day he'll be paying for it all. I can't wait. I hope I get to see his face before the end."

Mercy looked at him in disbelief. *Dmitri is completely insane with hate at Parasca. He is like Captain Ahab going after Moby Dick. He can't think of anything else. What are we going to do? How are we going to get out of this situation?* She looked at Jack.

He leaned close to her and whispered. "We're caught in a madhouse."

Apparently seeing an opening, the Hummer in front of them roared up alongside the truck with the sarcophagus. Petr Ivanov leaned out the passenger side and fired at the bigger truck's driver. The transport truck swerved to keep the Hummer as far away as possible and abruptly made a right turn off of the main road and into a narrower side road. The passenger side wheels lifted up off the pavement by two feet. Mercy thought the truck would tip over, but somehow it made the corner. The Hummer's tires screeched as it went wide, was forced to stop suddenly and back up to make the corner. Dmitri's car made the corner and raced up behind the big truck, now the closest vehicle.

Mercy saw out of a corner of her eye a sign in English and Bulgarian. She read the legend, but at first the meaning didn't register. Then, in a moment of recognition, she twisted around to see the receding sign on the two-lane road they were now on. She had seen an arrow on it pointing in their direction. The English version of the wording on the sign had said, "Varna Ancient Cemetery (Necropolis).' *That's the other place we were going to investigate here before all of this exploded in our faces; before Parasca resurfaced.* Mercy looked out the back window and saw Janos Parasca in the car behind. Their eyes locked and their two expressions showed mirrored reflections of fury.

* * *

Parasca shouted, "What is that idiot doing? Why did he turn down here? This isn't the way to the airport!"

Lacusta said, "The truck driver was taking fire from the lead Hummer. He turned to evade."

Parasca slammed his fist down on the dash of the car. He glared at Lacusta and said, "Shut up! No one is to talk unless I say so!" He turned to his assistant. "Haven't you raised that driver yet?"

The man spoke carefully and minimally. "No sir. Not yet. I've received word from the other group that stayed behind at the dock. They are on the way now and are about five minutes behind us."

"That won't be in time." Parasca said. He looked up and saw Mercy looking back at him from the car in front. She had a very angry look on her face and he glared back. *We have to get back on the highway to the airport.*

* * *

Rakslav rolled across the top of the sarcophagus as the truck bed tilted. He smashed into the inside wall of the container and groaned in pain. The wheels of the truck slammed back down onto the road. *That was one of my ribs breaking. I know that feeling. I can't take much more of this.* He forced himself to crawl back to the third and final latch and braced himself. *We're on a straightaway. Do it now.* He wiped blood from his hands and away from his eyes. He couldn't remember when or how he'd gotten a cut that was bleeding into his eyes. *Too many falls, too many cuts; I've got to finish this.* He braced himself and pulled. *I can't let exhaustion and this battering stop me. I've got to get this done.* He strained and pushed with his legs.

The truck suddenly lurched from one side to the other. Rakslav felt the tendons in his arms and shoulders pop. The muscles in his shoulders corded. The container shook and seemed to rotate to the side. Every blood vessel on his face felt like it would burst from the strain of his effort. The latch began to open. Rakslav gave one massive, final pull and felt the latch click into position.

* * *

Mercy was certain the road they were on was too narrow, but the remaining Hummer raced past Dmitri's car and up beside the huge truck with only inches to spare between the two vehicles. Petr leaned out of his window one final time and emptied an entire clip into the driver side of the transport truck. The large truck swerved again, but this time, it didn't straighten up immediately. It weaved in the narrow road, drove up onto the curb and back into the road and smashed into the Hummer.

The Hummer was sandwiched between the giant lurching truck and the building on its left. With what seemed to Mercy like amazing fragility, the smaller vehicle seemed to fold in from side to side like an accordion. She saw men inside the truck uselessly trying to shield themselves with their arms from the truck carrying the sarcophagus. Mercy felt a scream trying to build within her. *No! Don't let me be watching when someone is crushed to death!* The Hummer imploded in an orgy of crunching metal and smoke. The side of the building gave way and the vehicle was lost from sight in a collapse of masonry.

The big truck lurched away in the other direction. From her vantage point, Mercy saw the shattered driver's side window. There seemed to be no one at the wheel, but she saw a bloody arm hanging limply from the window. The vehicle careened off the opposite side of the road and into a vacant field with some darkened buildings and trees in the distance. The trailer rotated away from the truck and jackknifed into the cab.

* * *

Rakslav knew the truck was skidding and sliding precariously. He felt the back end of the trailer slew into a jackknife maneuver and knew his own death was almost certainly upon him. Unable to prevent it, he tumbled wildly across the width of the container, struck the opposite wall, bounced off the top edge of the open container and felt himself go airborne.

* * *

Mercy felt the familiar sensation of time dilating into an agonizingly slow cadence. The ticking of her internal clock decelerated into a low rumbling and she seemed to know what was happening in the entire scene of carnage at once. Her peripheral sight failed but all else turned into ultra-bright clarity in her remaining tunnel vision.

The jackknifing trailer swiveled toward its truck cab, its giant wheels no longer turning, but locked and skidding across the dirt and grass of the open field. Clods flew in the air in slow arcing waves. The two halves of the truck smashed into each other and the entire crippled vehicle pivoted and turned as it continued pin wheeling. The trailer's side struck a berm of earth in the field and the massive load overbalanced and pulled the rest of the truck with it. The vehicle rolled and parts, pieces and even bodies seemed to fly off in all directions as if from an explosion. The massive weight of the rear load carried the truck, the container and the sarcophagus into a rolling, thunderous snowball of wreckage that sprayed across the length of the field. The truck cab seemed to head off in one direction and disintegrate into a smoking ball of wreckage. The trailer continued rolling, flipping and tumbling in another direction.

She felt the energizing pulse of energy and knew that someone had just died in the wreck. Ever since this macabre dance had begun back at the dock yards, she'd been feeling the familiar surges of energy, this one seemed muted, as if something else had been nearer and had taken most of the energy for itself. Time jerked from slow back to normal speed and Mercy felt disorientation and vertigo. She gasped in a lungful of air and realized she had been holding her breath for an unknown length of time. The extent of the field of wreckage was almost incomprehensible. Everyone within the car was still. Finally, Mercy broke the silence.

She shouted in the confined space inside Dmitri's limousine, "Out! Open the doors. We've got to get out there to the sarcophagus and secure it."

They threw open their car doors and immediately heard the sounds of gunfire erupt from behind them.

* * *

Janos Parasca felt his panic mounting. The truck with his hijackers tumbled and rolled into a smoking ruin in the field and he screamed at the driver to stop the car. Mercy and the others were jumping from their car. Parasca leapt from his vehicle and shouted to his bodyguard and Lacusta, "We've got to hold on until the rest of my security forces arrive. Open fire. Kill all of them if you can."

The bodyguard crouched down, pulled a pistol from a chest holster inside his jacket and started shooting at Dmitri's car and its occupants. Alex Lacusta knelt behind the edge of the car, opened a case and started assembling his Sako sniper rifle.

CHAPTER 32 – LOYALTIES

"Then were they known to men by various names,
and various idols through the heathen world"
— John Milton, Paradise Lost

Henry was perched precariously at the top of a pile of rubble just underneath the stone door. From his vantage point, he could see cracks and chips in the door above and using a hammer that he had found with the few tools they had scrounged, he freed a large, deep shard of cracked stone near the edge of the door and set it beside him on the pile of rock. *This should be wide enough to accept the explosives.* He lay on his back and placed the bomb in the crack and used the stone shard he had just freed to wedge the explosive in place with the wiring trailing down to the detonator. The device was marked with a piece of adhesive tape upon which was written: 'three.' One wire from the explosive was still not attached to the wireless detonator.

He turned and looked down the rubble-strewn stair. He flashed his cell phone three times in rapid succession in a prearranged signal, paused, repeated and waited.

* * *

Maria saw Henry's light flashing from above and gave the acknowledgment signal with her own phone. She moved to the pile where Balev was trapped and climbed back in place above him.

She said, "I'm back. I've brought some first aid supplies and am going to try to work myself in closer so I can treat you."

He said, "You were away too long! You can't do this to me. I'm going to report you to the government and have you thrown out of your doctoral program."

She sighed and rolled her eyes at the hateful irrationality of the man. She interrupted his complaints and said, "Do you want first aid or not? I can just go away if you like."

He switched tactics and demanded that she in no way was allowed to leave and must help him immediately. She shook her head in disgust and gritted her teeth in readiness for what she knew was ahead. She shifted and probed, crawled and twisted down into the jagged hole of rubble. There were several false starts and dead ends, but finally, hanging headfirst, she reached down and found she was further in than before. *But can I make it back out? I'll have to chance it.* She inched downward, feet trailing out of the hold above. She was within arm's reach of Balev.

His eyes peered up at her hatefully, not an ounce of gratitude showing. "There you are. Took your time, didn't you?"

She ignored him, not daring to glance at the plastic remote control near him lest he suspect the main reason for her visit. He scolded and reproached her, Henry and Professor Russo, but she tried to tune him out. She took the first aid kit out of a side pack that she wore and laid it out on the man's chest. Not used to being inverted like this, the blood pounded in her head but she tried to ignore that as well. She examined his face, arms and chest and did what she could, cleaning wounds and cuts with prepackaged moist towels, applying ointment and bandaging where practical. She couldn't make out any details of the condition of his buried legs. *That will have to wait for a rescue team, if they ever find us.*

She found his broken arm to be in bad shape, the cast shattered and blood slowly oozing from the wrapping. She managed to find pain pills in the first aid kit and gave him a strong dose with her remaining water. While he closed his eyes and drank the pills down, she reached out, palmed the remote control and slipped it into the first aid container.

She folded up the kit, stowed it at her side and backed out slowly. He protested loudly and obscenely when he realized she was leaving him behind. He accused her of everything that seemed to occur to his twisted mind, but she tried to pay no attention. She had to retrace her route and became frightened a couple of times, but with great effort, she succeeded in backing out of the pile of twisted wreckage where Krastyo Balev was trapped. For the entire twenty minutes of painstakingly slow exertion that it took to extricate her from the pile of rock, he cursed and threatened her. He told her what he would do to her sexually when he was released and how he would humiliate her.

Something snapped in Maria. *How dare he say that about me?* She pulled herself forcefully out of the last part of the hole, gasping from the effort and turned back to him. She shined the light down the hole at him and saw his evil, pain-wracked face. She pulled the remote control out of the first aid kit and held it in her other hand so he could see it.

Her face took on a look of scorn and she said, "You evil pig. Even though I help you, only words of hate come out. You even promise to violate me in every way. Yet, it is you that caused your own predicament. Henry and I know that you tried to have us killed. We found the explosives you had placed in the tunnel to bring it down on our heads. We even found this!" She showed him the remote.

"It was right down there beside you all the time, but I grabbed it and brought it out, just now. I knew from the first you'd tried to kill us, but this is now the proof. So don't worry, I will not lose my position, it is not I who am in trouble, it is <u>you</u>. Your own government will be very interested in finding out that you traffic in black market artifacts and then try to murder people in the process, won't they?"

"Bitch!" Balev shouted.

Maria left him cursing behind her and moved away from the hole, leaving him in the darkness. She lifted her phone up and gave Henry the three flashes of light that signified completion of her task.

* * *

Professor Russo's mind felt clouded and helpless. It seemed almost as if his thoughts were wrapped in a thick layer of impenetrable gauze, muffled and opaque. He seemed to be doing things that were completely out of character for him, but he could not stop. He had no control over his body, no control over what he did. He had been forced to take bottle after bottle of water to the giant corpse and place it between the dead lips, pouring it onto the face and eyes. He had been made to rub the limbs as if to chafe them and restore life. He had been compelled to massage the face and hands of the giant creature. He had been forced to study the chains on the wrists but had not been able to determine a way to remove them. He had tried to recoil in disgust from touching the corpse, but had been unable to act. His limbs would not obey and seemed to be controlled by something else. He thought he heard commands, but knew there was no sound. It was as if thoughts were coming into his mind from some unknown place, foreign, but irresistible.

Russo felt deeply frightened, but in a distant way as if he could see someone else's terror, not his own. *What is happening to me? Have I lost my mind? Am I hallucinating?*

Suddenly, in a surge, he felt the strength of the compelling force on his mind increase by an order of magnitude. If he had thought it irresistible before, now he found it impossible to separate his view from the overriding foreign thoughts that invaded him and controlled him. Now, he thought he heard a stream of conscious words: it seemed to be speaking to itself.

Within the chambers of Russo's own mind, it spoke inside of him: *People are dying nearby. I feel the rush of life energy, the death drafts swirling into me. Now that the crypt door is open I can feel life energy again filling me. Sweet power, it won't take too much of this until I can move.*

Russo felt pushed and shoved into a smaller and smaller region of his mental landscape and his thoughts, feelings and senses were being cut away from him bit by bit. In a tiny corner of Russo's mind his own voice seemed to scream in tones more shrill and desperate. *Someone help me! I'm trapped, and something monstrous is controlling me!*

* * *

Henry felt more than heard a deep rumble that seemed to roll like thunder for several seconds. It shook the pile on which he crouched and loosened some dirt that sifted into the still, underground air. He held his breath for a moment and then seeing no collapse, climbed quickly but carefully down the pile of rubble. He had reconnected the wire after receiving Maria's blinked message and needed to get as far away and down from the explosive as possible. *The best position will be beyond the bottom of the stairs and back in the large crypt room. In fact, the safest place will probably be in the metal vault with the corpse, if the remote control will work that far away.*

He continued climbing, but with a small portion of his mind, he wondered what to do about Krastyo Balev. *The man is an attempted murderer, there is no doubt. He's also likely a grave robber who peddles antiquities on the black market. He's a scoundrel who has attempted or succeeded in molesting every young woman with which he comes in contact. But does he deserve to die? Maria would say yes, without a doubt, and I can't fault her for feeling that way. But, what do I do about the explosives overhead? We have to set them off to have a chance of opening the door, but won't that endanger Balev, and if it does, do I want that on my conscience?*

Henry made it down to the staircase landing level and found Maria. She silently held up the remote. Henry heard Balev's voice cursing and saying the most incredibly vile things about Maria. Henry blushed in the dim light.

He said, "That's truly disgusting. What has gotten into him? Why is he going on like that?"

Maria showed a satisfied smile in the dim light and said, "He knows we have the remote and he knows we know about the explosives he set in order to kill us."

Henry asked, "How did he find that out?"

Maria said, "I decided I'd had enough of his foul mouth and all of his bile, so I told him we knew. I feel better now. He seemed to get even more upset after that." She smiled. "What a pity. Cursing like that must be thirsty work. Too bad he can't get himself a drink."

Henry raised his eyebrows, listened to Balev for a moment, looked at

Maria again and shrugged. "Well, I had almost worked myself up to some sympathy for the man, but hearing him now, I think I'm over that. Let's go. If we are going to set the explosives off, we need to get as far away as we can. I suggest the crypt room. Balev can take his chances like the rest of us. Besides, he's probably more protected than we are. Let's head on down further: we need to check on how Professor Russo is doing, anyway."

They moved down the rubble-strewn remains of the Grand Staircase and reached the bottom.

Maria said, "I don't see any reason to wait any longer. We should set it off and see if we get the door up there opened."

Henry said, "First let's check on the professor and warn him." Maria nodded and they moved into the crypt chamber through the large arched opening at the base of the stairs that lead into the next room.

They looked toward the crypt chamber where its door lay open on the floor. They saw dimly into the crypt where the large body still lay. Maria stopped suddenly beside Henry and grabbed his shoulder tightly. Her grip was surprisingly strong.

"What is he doing?" She hissed.

Henry squinted into the darkness. The giant body lay contorted on the floor, but Russo seemed to be standing on top of it, looking down on the corpse from above. *What is the professor doing? Why would he be standing on top of those remains like that?*

Henry's skin crawled as he watched the professor lean over the giant dead face and start massaging it. Russo knelt down on the thing's chest and seemed to be fondling its face.

Maria gasped a breath in and shouted, "Professor! What are you doing? Stop!"

Henry's eyes were caught by something shiny reflecting light back at him. He looked to the ground of the crypt chamber and saw over a dozen water bottles scattered around the giant corpse, all with lids missing.

He said, "Maria, look at all of the empty bottles. What has he done?" The two of them ran to the crypt opening to confront the older man. They saw Russo indeed kneeling on the corpse, apparently trying to massage the face of the dead thing. Its ancient skin seemed to glisten wetly in the feeble light.

Maria's shouted, "Professor, why have you thrown away all of our water? Why did you pour it on the corpse? What were you thinking?"

Russo turned to them and said nothing. His eyes were blank and did not meet their gazes. He looked like a man that was sleepwalking. Maria stepped over to him and reached for the arm that was not splinted.

She said, "Come down off of there! Are you sick? What's the matter with you? You shouldn't be touching that thing. You could damage it. And, you've wasted our water. What if we can't get out of here and need it?"

Russo ignored her and shook off her grip. He turned back to his task of massaging the now moist skin. She backed up a step and turned to Henry, her eyes wide with confusion and some small amount of fear. Her brows arched in concern and her lips parted slightly, she mouthed silently to Henry, "He's gone insane!"

* * *

Rakslav lay on his side, trying to make sense of what he was seeing. The moonlight illuminated his surroundings, but from what light he had, everything seemed to be smoke and confusion, rubble and dirt. His eyesight gradually came back into focus and he saw the ground directly in front of his face. A large, dark shape was coming toward him. Whatever it was drew closer and loomed over him. Something took hold of his limp body and a deep, rumbling voice spoke in a language that seemed to skip past hearing and go directly into thought. His body didn't seem to want to work. He couldn't feel his fingers. Rakslav's feeble thoughts trickled out. *I opened the sarcophagus ... I had to help Lord Moloch get out ...*

The giant being holding him said. "Your thoughts tell me enough. I am still weak due to my re-imprisonment, but it did not last long enough to render me completely helpless this time. As soon as I had air to breathe again, I recovered quickly. From your thoughts I can see that you have worked faithfully to free me. I always reward that kind of loyalty. Those that are not so loyal would be well advised to flee before they fall into my hands. What of the other one that served me on the ship, the one your thoughts call Janos? Where is he?"

Recognition flooded into Rakslav. Lord Moloch had returned, and a vast sense of relief engulfed him. His mind raced over the recent events since the sinking of the *Fortuna*.

The large figure said, "You think he is nearby, possibly? Hmmm. That one resisted me back on the ship and he's not the kind to remain loyal unless one hovers over him. I knew he was faithless then, but when I catch him, he will understand the full import of what he has done. I punish nothing more severely than faithlessness."

Moloch asked Rakslav, "Where is the woman that fought me? What happened to her?" He paused as if listening to Rakslav's thoughts. "You don't know ... but I sense some use of the power nearby ... could that be her? I taught her some uses of it. I tried to capture her, contain her defiance and break her so she could be useful to me, but not anymore. This time, I will destroy her. Wait ... I sense an artifact. There is the sarcophagus that imprisoned me, yes, but there is something else ..."

Rakslav mumbled, "Great Lord, it may be the shield. It was recovered with you from the sea bottom. The last I knew, it was attached to the sarcophagus. I would fetch it for you, but I cannot move."

It continued speaking to Rakslav, "You are injured. Ah, I sense your neck is broken and you will die shortly. I'm afraid then your usefulness to me is nonexistent anymore." He paused again as if debating something internally. "Though, it's such a pity to lose my only useful servant here. And after all, you did release me from that box. But I haven't enough energy to spare for healing you properly. Not yet, anyway. Still, I suppose I could … Ah, I have it. If the shield is here as you say and we recover it, there is more than enough power stored within it. In the meantime, I must preserve you and your knowledge of this world until I can retake the shield."

Moloch concentrated on Rakslav's broken form and the injured man fell into a deep sleep. "That should keep you barely alive until I can do this properly." The giant's head snapped back up as if smelling something on the night wind. "Wait. There is that small use of power again …"

Moloch stopped, turned and faced away from Rakslav, widened his eyes, drew a breath in over his teeth in a hiss of astonishment and said, "… Mulciber?"

* * *

Maria said, "Henry, I'm terrified! The professor is acting like he is possessed. What should we do?"

Henry stood looking at Russo and wondering. *This is crazy. I have to snap the professor out of this.* He said to Maria, "I'm going to try to wake him up from this state he's in." Henry stepped back to the professor.

The older man was muttering to himself. "I need more energy. Water isn't going to be enough. I need more humans to die." The hair at the nape of Henry's neck rose.

He stepped closer and said, "Here now, professor. Please wake up. I think you're sleepwalking or something. You're having some kind of nightmare." Henry reached out a hand and grasped Russo by the shoulder. Russo stopped his efforts at rubbing on the giant corpse's face. He pivoted his head on his neck until Russo's face pointed directly at Henry. Russo's eyes did not immediately track and a second later, swiveled in their sockets to look at the younger man.

A chill of terror ran through Henry. *Why did his eyes have to catch up with his head's movement? That's not natural.*

Russo jumped at Henry with arms outstretched, even the one that was splinted. Maria yelped in surprise and Henry tried to backpedal and stumbled, falling back on his hands. Russo lunged at Henry and threw himself at the younger man's throat. Russo's hands grabbed Henry's neck and started squeezing. Russo's face showed no emotion, not rage, hunger or fear. The older man's face held no clue as to what currents swept through the man's mind.

How can he be so strong? One arm is broken and he is acting as if nothing has happened to it. He is paying no attention to it even though he must be in agony. How is that possible? Russo knelt on Henry's chest with his knees and squeezed vice-like hands around his throat. Henry couldn't breathe. He felt his heart pounding in his chest which uselessly tried to force blood into his head past the constriction at his throat. Sparks and flashes of light danced across Henry's sight. He heard a roaring sound in his ears like a train passing close by.

There was a thudding sound and Henry saw Russo's head flinch to the side. An impact came again and this time Henry saw the source of the sound: a meter long wooden board slammed into the side of Russo's head. The man grunted and fell off of Henry, his hands momentarily coming loose from around Henry's neck. Henry gasped a breath in and saw Maria swing the board back to her shoulder, preparing to swing again.

Russo rose and Maria swung at him again but the man held out his splinted arm and took the impact of the wooden plank. Maria winced as she saw too late that she hit him square on the break in his arm. Blood oozed quickly into the torn cloth holding the splint in place and dripped to the floor. Russo seemed to feel no pain and lunged at Maria. She danced back and pulled the board to her shoulder, preparing to use it again when an opening presented itself. Henry got to his feet, ran up behind Russo and shoved him from behind, pushing him sprawling.

He shouted, "Maria, let's get out of here and up the Grand Staircase. He won't be able to follow us easily."

Maria shot past the fallen man and darted out of the crypt. Henry followed behind but saw that Russo was climbing again to his feet. Henry ran but thought he heard the older man behind him, mumbling, "Kill them both. Need their energy."

They ran away from the crypt and into the hallway leading up to the Grand Staircase. They went almost at a run, dodging the now familiar stones and strewn rubble. Henry looked back and his blood went cold. Russo lumbered out of the crypt room and toward the foot of the stairs. He started climbing after them. A line of dark, bloody splotches trailed away from Russo's broken arm in the direction from which he'd come.

Henry said, "He's after us. Keep climbing."

Maria's face took on a look of determination as she clambered around a large block of stone. She looked behind them and her eyes sought out a target near her feet. She seemed to find what she sought and kicked a twenty kilo rock down the stairs toward Russo. It bounced high and wide over Russo's head. Russo paid no attention and continued climbing, going more slowly than Henry and Maria.

Russo seemed to be talking to himself in a low monotone, "Keep going up the steps, grab the female first and then the male. Throw them down the stairs to their deaths one at a time. I need their lives."

Henry and Maria climbed up to the landing level and she took another heavy stone, lifted and threw it underhanded down the stairs. It bounced nearer to Russo and kicked up some smaller stones that struck him glancing blows as they hurtled down the stairway. Russo shrugged off the impact and kept on climbing. He gained speed and moved faster, climbing over the stairs, rocks and rubble. Maria threw another rock that hit him squarely, but did not stop him. Russo paused and then regained his momentum and charged on. Henry braced himself to try to push the older, bigger man away, but Maria grabbed him by the arm and pulled him up on the largest pile on the landing.

Henry followed and said, "Isn't this where …"

Maria interrupted him and said, "… where Krastyo Balev is, yes. It's also the highest point on the landing without climbing the last flight to the door. We'll try to push him away from here. We'll be at the top and he'll be coming from below so maybe it will give us the advantage we need to keep him at bay."

They clambered up, turned and stood back up and found that Russo was only a meter below them. With his face completely passive, Russo reached for Maria's right leg and grabbed it, pulling her off balance. Henry grabbed at her and almost fell but managed to hold on. She kicked with her other foot and Russo staggered back, releasing her leg. She stood, reached into her side pouch first aid kit and pulled out something plastic and rectangular.

She muttered under her breath, "We may need this soon."

Russo charged up the small slope and tackled Henry by both legs. Henry crashed onto the mound. Dirt and rocks cascaded down the inside of the mound and rained down on Krastyo Balev.

The trapped man screamed at them in helpless anger. "What's going on up there? You're burying me!"

Maria took a rock in her free hand and smashed it into Russo's shoulder. The bigger man released one of his hands grasping Henry, swatted the rock from her hand and seized her by the wrist. He drew her arm to him as if reeling her in. She fought, but his strength was incredible. He pulled her close enough that she saw his dead eyes staring unseeingly in her direction.

Henry kicked with full force, planting the sole of his boot into the side of Russo's head. Russo was staggered and slid a meter away and down before catching himself. Henry scrambled to his feet and reached for Maria to help her up. She took Henry's outstretched hand and started to rise.

Russo spoke into the air, not looking directly at them, "I must kill them as painfully as possible to maximize the energy loss at the planar barrier, but do it quickly. I need their deaths…"

Maria screamed at Russo, "Get out of him, you devil! What are you, that monster from the crypt down there? Get out of his mind! Let go of him!"

Russo charged up the short slope, leapt on them and hurled them both down onto the pile. Maria lost her grip on the remote and she heard it clatter on the rocks. She heard Balev shout in rage below. She fought to rise, kicking at the form that used to be Russo. His hands held onto her like clamps and he pulled her toward his face. Henry pummeled Russo with both hands, kicked at him and twisted. Henry shouted at Russo in what sounded like furious anger, not helpless fear. Maria felt proud of the fight Henry showed. She felt horror and loathing at Russo, but not a paralyzing fear. She felt proud of both of them.

Russo's mouth was bloodied where Henry had been punching him. The larger man spoke one final phrase through those dark-red cracked lips, "Kill them now."

From below them, beneath the twisted pile of rock and debris, Krastyo Balev's voice called out. "I have it! I have the remote! I will have the last laugh after all!"

The cavern above them exploded in a hailstorm of stone.

* * *

In the dark of the hole where he lay, trapped and encased, Krastyo Balev grinned from ear-to-ear and pushed the button on the remote. The cave rumbled and Balev felt waves of self-satisfaction roll through him in rhythm with the shuddering of the complex. *Those two smug fools haven't beaten me yet. I'll get out of here and the only thing left of them will be their crushed corpses. What they know will die with them.*

He imagined the looks on their faces as the rocks above tumbled down, bouncing and rolling as they careened toward the young man and woman. He thought of what the terror on Maria's face would look like as she saw Henry trying to flee from the avalanche. He savored the thought of her watching as a boulder smashed Henry's head, dashing it into a bloody pulp in front of her very eyes. The smile spread over his face and he pictured Maria screaming in terror as a wave of mixed rocks and soil rolled over her, filling her mouth with choking, suffocating dirt. *How delicious!*

Balev was jerked from his momentary daydream by a jolting shake and a grinding wrench of the stones around him. A single glint of dim light from above shone into his confining cell of rock and he saw a sight that paralyzed him. The large, flat stone above his head tilted and scraped the other rocks nearby. It wrenched, pivoted and slid. Dust sloughed toward him and the table-sized rock rushed down straight toward his forehead. He felt the same helpless fear he had wished on Henry and Maria moments before and gasped in one last breath. His final moment of consciousness was nothing but an overwhelming and nameless feeling of terror. Then the stone smashed into his skull, crushing it like a piece of eggshell.

* * *

Professor Paolo Russo felt the compulsion smothering him. In the distant, tiny corner of his mind that still seemed to be the home of his remaining thoughts, he cowered in agonizing pain. He still saw what his body did, but could not stop the senseless actions. He was being forced to fight Maria and Henry, to attack them, to try to kill them. It was beyond belief.

He had watched the pursuit and struggle, he heard words coming from his own mouth that could only have come from that thing that seemed to control him, for he knew now that it <u>was</u> a demon that had taken him over and manipulated his every step.

The monster they had found in the crypt, that misshapen, desiccated ogre must have taken over his conscious functions and still held him in thrall in spite of all of the injuries he'd suffered. His broken arm, his broken ribs and split mouth, his now missing teeth had not shaken the thing's hold over him. Somehow, it had diverted all pain reception to the tiny corner of his being where Paolo Russo still lived. He felt the pain of the breaks, fractures and bruises, but could do nothing about them. The pain did not trouble the being that was his undisputed master; instead the pain was all channeled to Russo. Somehow this was a crowning indignity: robbed of all control, forced to commit violence against his will, yet still compelled to suffer the pain received from someone else's violence.

Russo saw the climax of the struggle with Henry and Maria and felt the concussion of the overhead explosion. He felt the monster that controlled him order his gaze upward, saw the plummeting dark shapes of tons of rock descending to commit a final and merciful coup de grace to him and sighed with poignant relief. A fleeting thought went through him. *Not even a monster like that can keep me suffering after I'm crushed. I'm sorry Henry. I'm sorry Maria. I wish I could have resisted this thing. God speed to you both.* Russo felt something slam into him from above and all went mercifully dark.

* * *

Mulciber felt the sudden rumble and then two crashing pulses of life energy suddenly flooded into him as they were released at the moment of death. His eyes opened with agonizing, painful slowness. He felt as weak as a babe, but words came from his throat as painfully and coarsely as if produced by a rasp.

"Nearly free." He said and he almost relaxed with the knowledge of how

far he had come and how long he had lasted. *Now, to get loose of these chains.*
Then he sensed Moloch's mind nearby.

* * *

Mercy crouched behind Dmitri's bullet-riddled car with Jack, Alexi, Dmitri and their driver. The pistol fire from Parasca's car had kept them pinned down initially, but the gunfire had ceased a minute or two ago. None of them had ventured to look out, lest they find with deadly certainty that the stoppage had been a ruse.

Dmitri hissed, "The stupid police should be here in moments. Then we'll get out of this."

Mercy felt panic building in her. She was almost certain she had heard some thoughts that felt all too familiar. It was as if she had caught a snippet of one side of a conversation and she feared Moloch was the side to which she had listened.

She heard the rumbling of one or more large vehicles. She looked back down the street they had come and saw what appeared to be two large unmarked trucks. Behind them and further back she thought she saw flashing lights. The leading truck pulled forward and behind it a second truck turned and parked sideways across the road, completely blocking it to further traffic. The rear gate on both trucks opened and four men in black gear piled out from each truck. They looked heavily armed and prepared for anything. A siren chirped from the street beyond the truck that was parked across the road. A loudspeaker blared in Bulgarian.

"Attention! This area is restricted and under police control. Drop all weapons and lay down where you are or you will be fired upon. This is your only warning."

In response, Parasca's men opened fire.

* * *

Mercy felt the ground rumble. A second shockwave travelled through the earth and beneath her feet. The force seemed to have come from behind her where the heavy truck with the sarcophagus had tumbled to a stop a minute before. Mercy said to Jack, "I need to even the battlefield here. I'm going to take care of some of those men and will be right back. Keep safe."

Jack said, "Mercy, wait! Why not let the police do their best first?"

She said, "There's no time for that. Moloch's on the loose. I'm sure of it. According to Dmitri, the shield was also recovered with the sarcophagus, so I need to find it before Moloch does. While all of that is happening, there are bullets flying every direction at once. I need to get this situation under control before all of us get killed."

Before Jack could say anything else, Mercy went into her concentration state and saw the glowing blue line trailing away from her hand that signified her connection to the Creator's source of power. She dashed from behind the car where they had been crouching and she saw that the world had slowed to a crawl. In her heightened state, she ran at Parasca's car first. A nicely dressed tough was aiming a pistol toward Dmitri's car. To her, the man seemed mired in amber, nearly unmoving. Mercy ran at him, wrenched the gun from his hand, grabbed him by the arm, planted her feet and threw him. He sailed through the air past the rest of Parasca's group, over the heads of the black-garbed security team defending Parasca from the police and into the side of one of the trucks in which they had arrived.

She turned and saw another of Parasca's group turning toward her from only a few feet away. She recognized him: he was the man that had shocked her with a stun gun back in Bucharest at her apartment and that she had stabbed while paralyzed by using her newly acquired telekinetic ability. He was swiveling and bringing around toward her a large rifle with a telescopic sight. As slow as everything moved around her, he still had the rifle almost pointed in her direction. She saw his finger tightening on the trigger and she realized he was going to shoot at her from point blank range. She grabbed the muzzle of the gun and twisted it and herself, holding the barrel pointed slightly away from her. The gun rocked with a slow explosion, she saw a jet of flame come out of the barrel and a projectile flew from it in a slow, smooth line.

She experienced several things at once: a burning sensation in her hand where the metal of the gun barrel had scorched her; a pressure wave of slowed sound thudded through her from the supersonic projectile; from the corner of her eye she saw the bullet penetrate and destroy the head of the man dressed in a chauffer's uniform who crouched right beside Parasca; and lastly, she felt the pulse of death energy surge into her from the dying man.

She tore the sniper rifle from Lacusta's hands and slammed the butt of the rifle into his temple. The man crumpled slowly. There was a third man who seemed to be in the act of cowering lower. Mercy ignored him because he looked to be unarmed. For Janos Parasca, she slammed the butt of the rifle into one of his knees and then dropped it. He toppled over in pain and she dashed off to see about Parasca's commandos in black.

* * *

Parasca groaned in pain, a red haze covering his field of vision. *My knee must be shattered! It was Mercy, I'm sure of it. I could hardly see her, she moved so quickly, but it had to have been her.* He lay on the ground hugging his leg and surveying his group. The bodyguard was gone; it looked like he'd been thrown by some massively strong force. The driver was dead with his face blown apart. Lacusta was unconscious at least. There was a bloody wound on his temple and he wasn't moving. The only one unharmed seemed to be his assistant who was cowering against the side of the car. Parasca cursed his luck. The only way to remedy this situation now was a drastic one. He needed his ace in the hole.

He shouted to the assistant, "Help me to my feet! I need something out of the car."

* * *

Carrying the unconscious Rakslav, Moloch trotted away from the explosions and into the field where the sarcophagus lay open on its side. *If those sounds are from the same kinds of weapons I experienced on that ship, I had best stay away. I can't afford the energy expenditure required to heal wounds from those cursed missiles.* He reached the overturned sarcophagus and studied it. His servant Rakslav had said the shield was affixed to the lid. Moloch could not feel any power emanation from it, so it must be shielded from him by the sarcophagus itself. The crystal steel metal was a nearly perfect storage mechanism for life energy, but because of that, it absorbed it nearly perfectly as well. It was why he'd been successfully trapped for these millennia: the metal absorbed and blocked the passage of energy, so no matter what he had tried to do in order to escape, he'd been unable to free himself.

He went around to the end of the box that had been his jail cell and looked at the underside of the open lid. It was dark with only moonlight above, but Moloch thought he saw something there. He reached under and found the object stuck to the lid with some kind of sticky substance that had cloth on one side and adhesive on the other. He pulled the package loose and held the object to his chest. *Now I can feel the power in it.* It had a wrapper of some flexible material that seemed full of large bubbles. He tore the wrapping off and held the shield in his hand. A slow smile spread over his face and he sighed. *Ah. Now I remember what it was like to have power and to spare, though it hasn't as much in it as the day Mulciber and I made it. First, I must heal this creature so I can use its knowledge. Then, I have to locate Mulciber.*

CHAPTER 33 – UNEARTHED

"Deeds of eternal fame were done, but infinite;
for wide was spread that war and various"
— John Milton, *Paradise Lost*

Mercy ran in the dark at speeds even she had trouble believing. *I'm fast, but this new power-enhanced rate is faster than anything I've done before. I first started seeing these bursts of extreme speed on the Fortuna, but now it's consistent and I move even more rapidly. I might be able to outrun a car at full-speed.* She sprinted to the cab of the nearest large unmarked truck and stopped. None of the combatants were close to the truck she hid beside: all seemed to have moved to the other truck fifty feet away that was blocking the road.

There were eight men dressed in black uniforms and black masks, obviously outfitted for night work. The men were positioned at several spots near the end of the truck furthest away from Mercy. Each one deliberately seemed to be choosing targets and firing patiently. *I'm betting they are fighting a delaying action at the moment, keeping the police pinned down. They'll hold this spot until more police forces are brought up or Parasca's people are ready to leave. Then, they'll hop into this truck beside me and take off, leaving the other truck for the police.*

Mercy studied the spacing of Parasca's men and decided to take out two men that were hanging back from the other six. *Time to thin the herd.* She reached out with her mind and sought the guns they held in their hands. After a minute's mental struggle, she decided against trying to pull the guns away telekinetically since she didn't know if she would be able use her ability on more than one object at a time. *I've got to disable them, but I don't want to kill unless there's no other way. I don't want to turn into a cold-blooded killer like Parasca. I'll do myself in before I turn into someone like him!*

She heard a rhythmic chopping sound from beyond the unmarked truck

Parasca's men were using as a blockade. *Sounds like a helicopter.* A blaring loudspeaker shouted in Bulgarian above the chopper's blades. "This is your last warning. Drop your weapons now or you will be shot." The helicopter rose above the truck and all heads followed its ascent.

With their attention riveted overhead, Mercy decided there would not be a better time to act. She ran at incredible speed from her place of cover, came up behind the furthest man to the rear and closest to her and with one hand covered his mouth and with the other, wrenched his weapon arm behind the man's back. He arched his back with the pain of having his arm forced beyond its flexibility limit. Mercy tore the weapon out of his hand, slammed the butt of it against his head and the man went limp. She dropped the gun. In Mercy's hyper-fast state, it began to settle toward the ground as if it weighed no more than a feather. She released his body which also seemed to float in slow motion to the earth.

Mercy moved nearly instantaneously up behind the second man. He did not realize his comrade had been taken down and was caught completely unawares, still staring up at the helicopter as he sighted along his gun toward it. He began squeezing the trigger on his rifle to shoot at the chopper. Mercy reached with her left hand over his left shoulder and across the man's face and pulled him down backwards as she delivered a punch to the back of his head. The man's legs went out from under him, his arms shot up toward the night sky and his rifle flipped end over end. Mercy snatched it out of the air and dashed back past the first man, grabbing his rifle along the way. She crouched beside the first truck to hide.

A spotlight shot out from the helicopter overhead and lit up one of Parasca's remaining six men. He seemed pinned like an insect in a collection. A loud echoing crack rang out and the man flopped seemingly boneless to the ground. *The chopper has a sniper marksman too.* Parasca's other men dove for cover and let loose a fusillade of shots at the helicopter. The flying craft rose higher, apparently to get up and out of range of the harassing fire.

Mercy saw that the remaining five men hadn't yet noticed the two fallen men. She hefted one of the rifles and tossed the gun upward. She concentrated and took it under control mentally. The gun hung suspended in the air about five feet above the ground. *I haven't yet figured out how to paralyze people like we saw Moloch do, but let's see from how far away I can direct this.*

The gun moved through the air like a missile and smacked into one man's back. He staggered forward but managed to catch his balance. *Stupid. My aim was off. So the gun can only move as accurately as I direct it from a distance. If I can only see things murkily in a searchlight, it can only move accordingly. That's not a huge surprise.* The man next to her target saw him lurch forward and turned to try to catch him. He saw the rifle hanging in midair and started to do a double take, but the rifle rotated and slammed into his face. He went down in a spray of blood from his shattered nose.

Mercy heard another powerful rifle shot echoing, but this time, the sound came from behind her, not from the chopper aiming at the ground. The spotlight on the helicopter abruptly went out. *So, Parasca's sniper is in action again. That man looked like the same one that stunned me. He must be pretty tough to bounce back so quickly. Now he took out the searchlight. There are too many dangerous things flying around this place. And now I can't see anything with the light out. Maybe I should take care of that man of Parasca's for good. He has been a constant source of pain to me.*

The helicopter reacted quickly and rose and moved back toward the police lines.

She brought the floating rifle back to her and turned to look for Parasca's car. She found it and saw that the sniper had to be hiding around the front corner of that limo and taking his shots from that vantage point. At her current location, the bulk of that car was between her and the sniper so she had no line of sight to the shooter. She dashed around at full speed, swinging wide and came back to Dmitri's car. *I think I'll check on Jack. Maybe from here I'll be able to see Parasca's sniper and figure out a way to take him out.*

At that moment, she felt a sharp prick of pain as if someone had stabbed her with a pin on the back of her head. She spun around looking for the source of the sensation. At least a hundred yards away, she saw a brightly glowing light hanging in midair, out in the middle of a field. It would have been the right height for a streetlamp except there seemed to be no buildings or streets out there. She also saw an immense figure moving out there that appeared much larger than even the biggest man. Her heart seemed to constrict within her as she realized that pin-prick sensation she'd felt must have been from its use of death energy. *Oh, no. It is that creature again!*

* * *

Moloch moved in the direction that he had sensed Mulciber, while still carrying the unconscious form of Rakslav Gachevska. *Was that really Mulciber's mind I heard? I only caught a fleeting sense of him for a moment. Now it's silent again and I sense nothing.* He came across rectangular pits in the earth that were spaced in a regular grid pattern. They were comparatively small, about a third his size, and they made it difficult to move rapidly in the moonlight. He stepped as quickly as he could through the place and came to a larger, deeper pit. He could not see details well in the dim light of the moon, so he used a small bit of the power stored in the shield to place an immobile globe of light hanging in the air just above his head.

He examined his location and noticed that the area seemed also to be rectangular in shape though much larger than the other pits. This one had a stone floor. There was a dark zone at one corner of the rectangular area and Moloch moved to it. He set Rakslav down nearby and studied him.

Shall I do this now, or wait? I think now. He will be helpful to me if he regains full use of his body. Otherwise, he is merely a burden. I will do it now and do it as quickly as possible. Moloch drew again on the shield. He blasted the flow of energy into the man's form with not the slightest concern for easing the shock of the rapid healing. Rakslav's body twisted and writhed in agony. His head jerked side to side and bounced repeatedly on the stone on which he lay. At last Rakslav curled to his side, vomited and lay panting.

Moloch frowned in distaste and said, "Move away from this stone door, slave. You served me well in the past, now do so again. It is the only reason I restored you to health. I can take your life from you just as quickly if you do not serve me well, so be sure that you do." Moloch made a gesture of dismissal. Rakslav moved quickly to his knees and stumbled off of the stone door and to the edge of the pit.

Moloch said, "I do not want to make a mistake this time as I did a few days ago on that large ship where I was initially revived. You know this world as it is now and have shown some resourcefulness in getting me free again. Tell me what I need to know right now before anything else."

Rakslav rose shakily but spoke clearly, "Lord Moloch, there are enemies nearby. They have weapons that can hurt you and kill humans." The steady sound of gunfire and booming rifle shots punctuated his words. Indistinct voices called out over loudspeakers. The drone of a helicopter overlay all of the other chaotic sounds. "I can hear that they have an airship that may carry heavier weapons and can observe movement from great distances. They have ways to speak from afar with their captains that will allow them to summon even heavier weapons and armed soldiers. We will be overrun quickly if this happens. I suggest we make a strategic retreat and make plans from a safe location."

Moloch looked down at Rakslav with one of his eyebrows arched. *This human speaks as one who knows and grasps strategy and tactics. His mind shows no deception. I made the right choice to restore his health.*

Moloch spoke, "Where is this safe place and how can we get there in a way that our enemies do not observe our retreat?"

Rakslav said, "There are large vehicles over there that we can use, brought by some of those that are fighting. I will procure one for us. In the confusion of the battle now taking place over there, I hope we can escape undetected. I have some ideas for a safe location from which to plan. With a vehicle, we will be able to get away from here and be on our way. The problem will be the airship. If it observes us escaping, we will be pursued."

Moloch said, "If that happens, I will deal with it. First, though, I need to free a comrade."

Moloch examined the stone door again and spotted the corner where there was a large, shattered place that revealed an opening to something below. It was large enough for a human to enter, but not for Moloch himself. He moved his face down to the opening and listened. He thought he heard the sounds of one or more distant voices. He sent his thoughts through the opening, down into the greater darkness below, questing for minds that could be queried and searching for his lost ally.

I have him. That's Mulciber.

Moloch held the shield in one hand and grasped the jagged edge of the broken door in the other. He opened himself to the vast lake of energy still stored within the shield and felt it pour into him like water over a cataract. *This is what it feels like to live again.* Reddish bolts of energy crackled from him, trailing upward and away in fractal shapes of ozone-stitched glow. His muscles bunched and he lifted at the broken edge of the door. He tore the entire mechanism of the thing from the earth like a broken tooth from its socket and threw it away. It flew through the air, landing with a jolting crash thirty meters away.

Moloch stepped down into the inky darkness and shouted Mulciber's name in triumph.

* * *

Maria woke up to painful coughing in darkness and to the smell of thick dust. Pain stabbed her in the leg and she struggled to remember where she was. *Why is it so dark? What happened to me?* The pain from her right leg was intense. *Madonna mia, oh, that hurts! What happened to my leg?* The darkness was pervasive and she could not see what was causing the excruciating pain. She was not even sure she wanted to see her leg because of what the pain might indicate. *What if it is horribly maimed? Please don't let me lose my leg!*

She coughed a minute longer and finally forced herself to stifle the next few spasms. She moved her right hand to her face and brushed away a thick layer of dirt and pebbles. After a few more coughs, she calmed herself and concentrated on her leg. She tried moving it and found it wasn't stuck, but just the effort of shifting it sent bolts of pain lancing through her. She gasped and stopped trying to move the injured limb. She tested the other and determined that it was very sore and probably deeply bruised but could be moved carefully. Her head cleared a trifle and she remembered what had happened. She called out.

"Henry! Professor Russo! Krastyo Balev! Is anyone there?" She heard only silence in response.

Her senses came back further and her head cleared a little. *I'm caught in another cave-in. This time, I seem to be the one that is trapped.* Her left arm was stuck, so she felt around her with her right and found large rock piles nearby and a massive block above her head, just centimeters away. Her body was covered in thick dust and dirt and smaller rocks. Her face seemed to be undamaged. The air felt close and there was no breeze. *Am I in a small air pocket? I may not have much breathing time.* She felt around with her free hand and found something smooth and rectangular. *What is this? It seems too regular. It's my phone!* Excitement surged through her.

She pulled it closer to her face. *Please let it be working! Please don't be broken!* She pushed the home button and the face lit up. *It works!* She thought in relief, but then her heart seemed to thud with a feeling of dread. *It only has 8% charge!* She felt deep fear that the phone would soon be dead. She glanced at the upper left corner of the screen and gasped in astonishment. *I have one bar of reception! I have a cell signal! The explosion must have at least partially opened the stone door overhead.*

She shook her head at her predicament. *I can't believe I forgot to turn off the phone function. We were trying to save every bit of power on our phones and I forgot to disable reception. Now I'm glad I didn't.*

She put it back to sleep, let the darkness settle around her and considered. Who should she call? Henry and Professor Russo were in here with her but she was pretty sure their phones were set to not be receiving calls. Besides, even if he was still alive, the professor was acting like he was possessed by a demon. Henry would already be searching for her if he could, so it made no sense to call him. *My roommate, Angelica: I could call her. She might be able to get help to us. I've got to take the chance.*

She pressed the home button again, flipped over to her contact list and pulled up Angelica's number. She pressed the call button. The phone's charge was down to 7% and she bit her lip. She heard Angelica's phone ringing the first, second and third time. On the fourth ring, a woman's voice answered the call and spoke with uncertainty.

"Hello? Maria, is that you? Where are you?"

"Angelica, listen. I only have moments before my phone runs out of power. Henry and I are trapped underground in a collapsed section of the Grand Staircase. The professor and Krastyo Balev are in here as well. Get help for us. I'm caught under a rockslide and think I may have a broken leg. My air is getting bad. Send help. Angelica, can you hear me?"

"Maria, I overheard about Henry's father and thought you'd left with him to go to London. Balev's security men told us the entire Necropolis' new section was closed off at Krastyo Balev's orders. The guards chased us all away from the dig site. We couldn't find Professor Russo. We …"

Angelica's voice cut off and the dim light from the phone went out abruptly. Maria's fear was confirmed: it was dead. She felt the cold grip of the pervasive dark. *I'm alone in here and my air is going bad quickly. I've got to stay cool and calm. If I get excited and hyperventilate, I'll use up all of my air very quickly.* She exhaled slowly and deliberately. Her thoughts spun. *What can I do now? I simply refuse to go down like this!*

Maria heard a loud, reverberating crash from somewhere above, followed a few moments later by a distant voice calling out in what sounded like thunder. She couldn't understand what it said at first, but her mind seemed to do a second pass at the sounds and it resolved into a single shouted, rumbling word: "Mulciber!"

* * *

Janos Parasca twisted and looked past Dmitri's group to the reddish bolts of lightning trailing into the night sky. Dread seized him and he knew that he was in deep trouble. Something in him spoke with a certainty filled with terror. *The monster is loose. If it catches me, it will know that I had planned to prevent its release. I am undone. I have to get away from here.*

He looked in panic at his remaining companions. Alex Lacusta had unexpectedly revived after only a minute of unconsciousness and had shot out the searchlight on the helicopter hovering above them. Lacusta was the only one he could count on. His assistant had helped him to his feet and retrieved the package from the trunk of the limousine, but otherwise was of no use in a situation like this except possibly to serve as a human shield.

Parasca unwrapped the package and took out the crystal steel sword. His leg had been hurt by Mercy when she attacked a few minutes earlier and he had to repair the damage before anything else. His earlier practice at healing would hopefully be enough to use the sword and then he should be able to effect some changes in this battle and more importantly, get far away.

He held the sword in one hand and painfully lowered himself down so that the body of his car was between him and Dmitri's group. He commanded Lacusta to keep Dmitri's people at bay and placed his assistant between him and the direction where the Bulgarian police forces were positioned. He concentrated on the sword and pulled on its stored power. Deeply focused, he somehow envisioned the injury and realized the knee joint itself had not been damaged, but the thigh bone just above the knee joint had been broken. Parasca gritted his teeth and positioned the bone back together as best he could. He let the power from the sword flow through and into his wounded limb, accelerating the healing that would have normally taken place at a much slower rate. The body knew how to heal itself, but normally proceeded at a slow pace because of the energy required. With the additional power made available from the sword however, natural healing could be sped up by an order of magnitude or more. Unfortunately for Parasca, the pain that always accompanied an injury was magnified as well by being compressed into the same limited healing period. His face became a rictus mask as the healing energy reknit the broken bones in his leg.

All during the excruciating process, his thoughts centered on one thing.

Mercy has to pay for this!

* * *

Dmitri Slokov shouted at Jack and Alexi. "Where is Mercy? Why isn't she back yet? Is she hurt?" Jack's thoughts roiled in concern for Mercy but paused for a moment at Dmitri's questions. *He actually sounds concerned. This man keeps surprising me.*

Jack said, "I'm worried about her too, but my better judgment tells me we shouldn't worry too much about her. She's incredibly powerful and strong, Dmitri. I think we're in more danger than she is. But with Parasca's sniper over there, we can't budge. He'll kill anyone that makes a single move into the open."

Alexi said, "What is taking the police so long? They should have had these criminals under control by now, shouldn't they?"

Dmitri said, "It's Parasca's sniper that has them acting so cautiously. Police departments do anything they possibly can to keep their men alive. They won't send them into a dangerous situation without exercising extreme care."

Alexi said, "I wonder … I've got it. Maybe I can help them spot the sniper. We know where he is, but the helicopter may not, especially with their searchlight shot out. If they know where he is, then they can take him out. Dmitri, send me the contact information for the local police that you've been using so I can relay the data to them on Parasca's sniper."

Alexi popped up for a half second, looked and ducked back down. He pondered and moved to a different location behind the car, looked out again and ducked back. This time, there was an echoing boom from the nearby rifle. Alexi checked a compass app on his phone and nodded his head in confirmation.

"He is twenty-five meters away to the southwest of us, hiding behind the passenger wheel well. That's enough information for them to go on. We've got him, Dmitri."

Alexi called the police contact that his brother had provided and gave them the details that he had deduced. He described their location and his calculated position for the sniper that had destroyed the helicopter's searchlight. A minute later, they heard the helicopter approaching again. This time, the aircraft tilted its nose down and pointed its immobile front lights down in the direction of Parasca's group.

Immediately, multiple shots came from the helicopter, obviously from multiple gunmen. Intermittently mixed in with the other shots, Dmitri heard the booming report from what he guessed was the chopper's marksman at work. Shots rained down on Parasca's group huddled by their limousine.

Though crouched down, Alexi raised his fist high and pumped it in triumph above the side of the vehicle. He shouted, "Dmitri, they're dead men now! The Bulgarian police are nailing them to the ground!"

At that moment, two things happened: first, a tumbling, ragdoll-like body seemed to fly through the air upward from Parasca's besieged group. It slammed into the helicopter with a sickening impact and cracked the front window. The helicopter veered away and back to the safety of the larger police group; second, a booming supersonic report echoed from Parasca's camp. Alexi jerked as a shock wave ran through him. He froze, a look of stunned surprise on his face. He looked at his brother Dmitri but immediately seemed to lose control of his body and fell face down into the dirt. Dmitri stared in disbelief at a new hole in the metal of the car behind Alexi and a matching crater in Alexi's back. The shot had apparently punched through the engine compartment, through the side of the car and into his brother. Dmitri stared in shock and denial and whispered, "Alexi?"

* * *

Mercy felt more surges of energy from those dying nearby. She experienced a heady, almost alcoholically intoxicating feeling. *I feel so wonderful and alive!* She heard the shots from the helicopter and imagined that Parasca's men were facing tough odds with that armored, insectile craft hovering above them all. She also felt the undeniable surges of massive power expenditure from the direction of the huge creature she'd spotted. She saw bolts of reddish energy lancing into the air and could no longer doubt or deny the grim meaning of it all. She heard echoes of powerful thoughts rebounding through the air and she knew Moloch was free and on the move. He was wielding the power of the death energy of thousands of souls, likely drawn from the shield. *I may be outmatched again, but I beat him before. I've got to see this to the end.*

She prepared herself to race to the giant where she could engage it, but her thoughts were interrupted when she heard the rattle of pebbles behind her. She ducked instinctively and sensed a whistling, high velocity object slicing into the side of the truck near where her head had been moments before. It cut into the steel of the truck's side and left a gash a meter long that penetrated entirely through the wall of the truck's cargo compartment. Mercy rolled and came up moving at full speed.

When she rose from her roll, she saw Janos Parasca standing with the crystal steel sword in one hand and a grim expression on his face that was changing into one of surprise. To her heightened senses, he appeared to be moving much faster than the others she had fought tonight, but still a trifle slower than herself. Apparently, he had moved silently up to her after the fusillade from the helicopter and swung the sword at her in a move calculated to decapitate her before she even knew she was in danger. The pea gravel he had kicked up had given her enough warning to narrowly escape the blade's swath. Her hearing and her speed had saved her. *But, they might not again. And so much for familial affection. I guess I shouldn't count on attending any Father-Daughter dances with this maniac.*

* * *

Henry wondered where he was and why he had a splitting headache. Consciousness was slowly gaining the upper hand in his mind and he seemed to swim through a dark cave toward a dimly lit but more familiar area. *Why do my eyes sting? And my head! It feels like it's going to burst.*

A sharp pain stabbed him in the left temple and he awoke with a moan. *Something is jabbing me in the side of my head.*

"Stop it!" Henry tried to shout. *Who is stabbing me? Oh, what is going on?*

His voice sounded dull and muffled, with no echo or resonance like would be normal. Henry willed his eyes to open but there was nothing to see. Henry was in darkness so total that it seemed like a physical substance rather than an absence of light. It was like being submerged in liquid, breathable ink that was completely opaque. Henry had a wild, stray thought: *What if this stuff can soak into a person? What if darkness like this can infect people and twist them into creatures that hate light, that hate anything healthy and life giving? What if that is part of what happened to that creature in the crypt?*

The pain in his temple jolted his wandering mind back into focus. He felt his eyes stinging, even though he could see nothing in the enfolding darkness. His head throbbed. He felt his pulse beating in his temples and neck. He tried to bring his left hand to his head to check the place from which the pain came, but his arm seemed to be tangled up and simultaneously weighed down by something.

Henry struggled for a moment to free his left hand to no avail. He paused and took a deep breath. *Let's see if I can move the fingers on my left hand.* He could. *So the hand is undamaged. It has that pins and needles feeling like it's falling to sleep. Ow. That is not pleasant. I wish I could see my surroundings. What about my other arm?* He moved his fingers on the right hand. *Feels like it's in my pocket, holding something … what is it? Oh, my phone. Maybe I can pull it out and get some light.*

Henry worked his right hand slowly out of the trouser pocket while holding onto the precious phone. It was a strangely difficult process, as if gravity were not working correctly. *What is wrong with me? This should be the simplest thing in the world, and I am having trouble with it.* At last the arm was out and he held the phone. He felt for the home button and pressed it.

The light was sharp and brittle bright to him, seeming to stab him simultaneously in the eyes and in the temples. He flinched from the pain and his hand wavered. He noticed with dread that the charge was almost gone. *It's down to 3%. I have a few moments left and that is all.* He glanced around and felt terribly disoriented. *What am I seeing? I can't understand any of this.* Then individual features in his line of sight started to make a small amount of sense.

His hand was holding the phone and drifting slowly on its own from the pocket to his chin and past his face. It stretched upward and stopped. *Why am I holding the phone above my head?* In the light of the object, he saw a gash on his right hand and watched a drop of blood form in the cut and run from the base of his thumb up to the tip of the thumb. It swelled into a large raindrop-like globe of red. The drop of blood leapt upward off of the tip of his thumb and Henry finally realized what was wrong. *The blood isn't leaping upward, I'm hanging upside down!*

In a wrenching shift, his viewpoint rotated sickeningly and he saw he was suspended facedown with his arm dangling below his head and blood dripping off his hand. A feeling of vertigo crawled through his gut and threatened to turn him nauseous, but the very lack of anything in his stomach worked in his favor. He got his bearings again and tried to concentrate. He reviewed his situation mentally.

I'm upside down and hanging from my legs. Feels like I'm supported at my knees. I'm in a hole of some kind that is very cramped and dusty. There is something dark below partially covered in dirt, about a third of a meter away from the phone in my hand. There's a horrible stink coming from whatever it is that is down there. The pounding in my head is from hanging upside down for however long I've been unconscious. My temple also hurts, but that must be something separate from just hanging upside down. My left arm seems to be tangled up or caught and has fallen asleep.

Henry tilted his head all the way back to look straight down. He followed a droplet of his blood as it fell from his thumb and landed in a spreading, muddy blotch at the bottom. He studied the thing below and tried to identify the stink. *It smells like feces and worse.* He looked from one side of the hole where he dangled and thought he could make out a dark, wet area there that had the shape of two long humps. The other end of the hole had another large wet place where a slab of stone was standing vertically. The wet area ended abruptly at the stone slab.

A rectangular edge with a kind of common regularity that seemed out of place for this space of crushed and smashed rocky chaos caught his eye. He looked and recognized the corner of the plastic remote that had belonged to Krastyo Balev. Nearby was one exposed fingertip, its nail just protruding from the layer of dirt and pebbles that covered everything down here. A dawning shock ran through him, but at first he only felt relief. *That finger belongs to a man. It's not Maria's, I'm certain.* He felt sick again as his thoughts continued. *It might be Russo. He was attacking us when that last cave-in occurred, but based on the fact that I'm dangling down in a hole and that is his remote, that finger must belong to…Balev.*

The man lay below him, mostly covered in dirt and debris. The man's head appeared to be crushed and buried beneath the vertical rock slab. The soaked earth at the spot must be sodden with the man's blood. The other end of the pile must be where his legs were buried under tons of rock, and again, there was a large stain, probably more blood. The stench from below was just what he had imagined: in death, the man's bowels must have voided. *Ugh. That would have been a singularly awful, but very sudden way to die. Can't say he didn't deserve it though, He set that last charge off himself with the remote and he had no one to thank for the result but himself. Now how can I get myself free from this?*

The light from Henry's phone blinked off. He was back in total darkness and he cursed under his breath. *All out of power: now what?* Henry pondered his next move. *I absolutely must get that remote. If Maria and I get out of here, we might need it for proof of what happened. I'll just have to fumble around by touch to find it.*

Henry struggled and stretched and eventually got close enough to reach to touch the area below where he had last seen Balev's hand. He groped around in the dark and finally touched the remote beside the dead hand. He took the device and prepared to shift his efforts to escape when he had another thought. *What if Balev had a phone on him? I need to check his body and see if he has anything Maria and I could use.*

Henry, still dangling inverted over the dead antiquities officer, gritted his teeth against the stink and by touch alone, searched the parts of the upper body he could reach. Henry found what must have been the man's belt and clipped to it was something hard and rectangular. *Perhaps it's a pager or a phone of some kind.*

Henry's pulse thrummed in his head painfully. He fought against the urge to try to see and willed his uselessly straining eyes to close. He felt carefully at the object he had removed from Krastyo's belt, trying to visualize the thing by touch. *It's about the size of a large phone. It's inside of a leather case that has a clip for the belt. I wish I could get my other hand free, but I'll just have to be deliberate about this. First, I'll carefully remove the phone from the case.* Henry eased the device slowly from its case with his one hand. He had it almost completely out when its screen flashed to life, startling him and almost causing him to fumble and drop it. It was indeed a phone, with a small button-style keyboard below the screen. The screen had text in Bulgarian, but it looked to be presenting a password request. After a few quick attempts at getting through, past or around the screen, Henry was forced to use the thing only as an intermittent light source. It lasted thirty seconds at a time before the login screen timed out but he reactivated it by pressing the space bar each time.

Consoled by the find, he held the phone in his teeth and recommenced searching Balev's body a final time. At the dead man's right shoulder, he found a strap that had been buried under the rock and dirt. He felt downward along the strap and located what was apparently a shoulder bag that was attached to it. He pulled the thing loose causing a minor dust cloud. The phone went out and he squeezed the thing with his lips until he felt the click on the space bar. The phone's light came back on. He gingerly opened the bag with his one free hand and dug through it.

Inside, Henry found two objects in the bag that were partially wired together. He pulled them out and whistled. *It looks like another batch of explosives partially connected to another wireless detonator.* The light from Balev's phone timed out again, but not before Henry saw a label attached to the detonator. It had the numeral 'four' written on it.

He gasped at the discovery, but before he could do anything else, he heard a distant rumbling. Through the debris above him, he thought he heard a sound like a muffled shout from a mighty voice. There followed a lumbering, descending pounding as of gigantic footsteps marching closer to Henry. He felt a growing fear well up inside of him. *What is happening now? What is coming down the Grand Staircase?*

CHAPTER 34 – DUEL

"Well hast thou fought the better fight"
— John Milton, Paradise Lost

Parasca said, "Did you see the way I chased off that helicopter? I used the power in the sword to lift my guard's body and smash it into the chopper's front windscreen. I almost took them out on the spot."

He held the sword in front of himself like a barrier, his arms straight out at her, the pommel gripped in two hands almost like a golf club with its head up in the air. Mercy winced and saw immediately that he was not comfortable with it as a weapon. *I'm no expert, but at least I had a few fencing lessons and once saw a demonstration of proper long-sword technique. For fencing, his grip is two-handed and wrong, way too tight. He is holding the thing stiffly and perpendicular to his arms in a bad posture. For long-sword fighting it should be back above his head and shoulder and ready for a swing. He's using neither technique. He's seen too many movies and thinks he's going to bluff his way through this.*

Parasca stood with what he apparently thought was a warding stance and said, "You are such a disappointment, daughter. I tried to make this easy for you so it would be over quickly, but you wouldn't cooperate. You are unarmed. I, on the other hand, have this magnificent weapon and I have learned how to use its powers in amazing ways. What do you have? Nothing."

Mercy stood in a half-crouch as if prepared for a knife fight, knees apart, elbows away from her sides, hands forward and palms down with her fingertips all about an inch apart. *I need to be ready for a lunge so I can try to disarm him.*

She said, "I have enough. And you should be silent. You have nothing to say that I am interested in knowing." Her words radiated coldness.

Janos Parasca said, "Really? You seem to have taken up with Dmitri

Slokov. Do you really know him? Do you know what kind of scum he is? Do you know what he does for pleasure? Would you like me to tell you what your new business partner is involved in? Perhaps you don't know about all of his various sordid enterprises, his drug dealing and human trafficking, for example?"

He waited for her as if wanting her to take the bait, but she said nothing. Instead, she gave a lunge feint that forced him to dance back a step. She smiled slightly at his instincts. He noticed her expression and frowned. *He is a little slower than me, and I haven't yet shown him how fast I can move when I want to. From that swing and the way it cut through the metal wall of the truck, he's very strong and much more capable than I would have guessed from his age. I suppose he has the demon's genetics just as I do, and with it some of the strength and speed. I would guess he's stronger than me, but not as fast. Does he have the endurance I have, I wonder? From his reactions so far, the only kind of fighting he seems to know is street brawling.*

Mercy said, "As if I could trust you to tell the truth. I don't trust him <u>or</u> you, so nothing you say is going to sway me. Just be silent."

Parasca's eyes widened in outrage, and he charged her, drawing his arms back, then delivering a two-handed swing aimed at her midsection. She darted back and away from his strike.

He said, "You dare a lot speaking to me like that."

Mercy held her balanced stance. *All right, I think I've got his timing down.* She smirked and said, "Not used to anyone speaking their minds? It's a weakness to only surround yourself with those that agree. Maybe you should allow your people to be more honest and direct with you. Then perhaps you wouldn't be left in the dark so much and always end up caught unawares by Dmitri's people. They're all over your organization, you know. PetroRomania is riddled with moles. Your information leaks like a sieve. Dmitri knows practically everything that goes on in your company. How do you think he found out about all that was happening on the *Fortuna*? How else would he have been able to beat your salvage operation to the *Fortuna* site?"

His face clouded in anger. He seemed to bite back a response and instead said, "Well, maybe you have some information that I would be interested in knowing, then."

Her face took on a derisive expression and she said, "Really? Why should I tell you anything? Stop wasting time and attack me, you feeble old man."

As if in answer, he charged her again, but was moving much more quickly. He drew the sword into an overhead motion like a tilted, spinning helicopter blade. She ducked under and charged him, trying a disarming motion. She grabbed his hands and twisted, trying to wrench the sword pommel from his grip. He held onto the blade and swung a shoulder into her to try and bowl her over. She let herself roll with his motion but was up on her feet before he could bring the sword around for a follow-on cut. She was ready again for him and he now held the sword in a more practiced way. *He was bluffing and only pretending to know nothing about sword fighting. The man is crafty.*

He asked, "Why did you travel to Timisoara, Mercy? I know you went there. Was it to see your grandmother? She must be getting very old these days. Dmitri's people there aren't really trained as guards you know. They won't be able to protect her. She's liable to end up in a horrible accident when I decide her time is up." He paused to let his words sink in.

Mercy watched him calmly and coldly. *I'm not going to let him get my goat. I'll just check with Dmitri after this is over to see if his security needs to be beefed up to protect Sonia.*

Parasca continued trying to taunt her. "Your mother really was a slut, you know. She wasn't good at it, but she did have quite the appetite."

Mercy said only, "What a pathetic, evil thing you are. The only shame that I feel is because I am related to you."

He said, "They say that 'blood will tell.' You've got some of the same blood as me Mercy, and if you think I'm pathetic and evil, you indict yourself as well. You can't get rid of your heritage, daughter. Just remember, you have more than my genetics. You've got your mother's genes as well."

She said, "I know all about hers and I'm proud of that. You were the corrupting force on her. You were the one that abandoned her in that prison and left her to die. If there is any justice, you'll end in Hell."

He laughed. *That sounded a little fake to me. He's just trying to keep up a brave front, now.*

Parasca said, "You seem to believe in all of this supernatural nonsense now, so just know that if I end badly, you'll likely be joining me in whatever place there is reserved for those of us with 'demon' heritage."

She looked at him, an appalled expression on her face. *This man's self-deception is monumental.* She swept one arm as if indicating the world around them and said, "After all of this, after Moloch rises from thousands of years of imprisonment, after seeing the universal language, after being miraculously healed by that monster, after seeing levitation, telekinesis and having your very thoughts read, you still think there is some kind of materialistic explanation for all of this? I know what kind of scum you are, but I never thought you would be mentally defective. You're living in a dream world if you can't accept the evidence all of us have seen and experienced. The supernatural is real. No other conclusion is possible."

He shook his head slowly and Mercy thought unconvincingly. "Perhaps all of this will be explained by science eventually. 'Supernatural' may be what primitive people call natural things that they don't understand. You, my daughter, still have a primitive mindset."

She felt a tingling sensation and realized he was drawing on the power in the sword. She quickly stepped back two paces and saw something coming at her from the corner of her eye. She threw herself to the ground but took a glancing blow to the top of her head. She felt the wind of something large rush past and turned in the direction of the object. *It was too large for a bullet. What was that …?* She felt a chill. A boulder three feet in diameter stopped in midair and started moving back toward her. *Is that what he's been doing …?* She glanced in Parasca's direction and saw he wasn't standing where she'd last seen him. Panic grabbed her in the chest. *Where is he?*

She felt a massive blow to her jaw and went rolling. Blood sprayed from her mouth but she stopped her roll and came up in a kneeling position. Parasca stood where she'd been a moment earlier, his arm still swinging from the backhand blow he'd delivered to her. She spit a mouthful of blood out and wiped more blood from her eyes. *I must be bleeding from the scalp. I'll have to take care of that later.* She considered Parasca. *So now he can use telekinesis too. I thought he was just bragging about chasing off the helicopter. What else can he do, and why did he hit me with his hand rather than the sword? He just wasted a chance to kill me.* She felt a ticklish sensation again, this time like something was moving behind her eyes. *What is that?*

Parasca stalked toward her, the floating boulder drawing up beside him and keeping pace with him like a granite bodyguard. He said, "I can read your thoughts too, Mercy. I didn't kill you because I wanted to see your expression when you realized I had mastered these new abilities. I wanted to see you understand your hopeless situation. Now I've seen it, and as delicious as it is, I say, 'Goodbye daughter.'"

So that was the sensation I felt, like some worm inside my head. He was rifling through my thoughts. I need to learn how to shield against that. But I've no time to lose, now. Have to strike before he does anything else. She drew on the thread of blue energy that connected her to that distant throne room, letting its entire capacity flow into her in a solid stream. The thread seemed stretched to its limit and she felt incandescent with its flow of power. *Hope that's enough.* She inhaled and held a deep breath and felt the blue thread expand from its spider web thickness into a larger cord-like sinew of light. More power than before rushed into her.

She didn't wait for him to close the distance, but shot straight at him like an arrow from a bow. She saw his gaze lose its focus on her and she knew she was moving faster than he could track. She saw the sword lift up as if readying to strike. She raised her left arm to ward off his sword arm and simultaneously lowered her right shoulder as she rushed him. She slammed into him with her charge and took him off his feet. His sword arm came down involuntarily and she grabbed it sight unseen when it came in contact with her raised left. This time, she took a different approach and didn't try to seize the sword directly. Instead, she twisted his hand with her own and felt Parasca's wrist shatter as she wrenched. The sword tumbled away from his grip. The small boulder fell suddenly to the earth and Mercy slammed Parasca down, back first into the ground, plowing a short furrow with his body.

She didn't wait for him to take any counter action: she smashed her fist down into the middle of his face and crushed the man's nose. She saw his eyes roll up in his head, saw him lose consciousness and then stood up over him. She checked him for any signs of deception. *He's really out. I wish I had some way to secure him, but he'd probably get out of whatever I did. I won't kill him even though he deserves it. I don't want to become any more like him than I already am. I guess I'll leave him for the Bulgarian authorities.*

She walked a few short steps and took the sword in hand. She was ready for its effects and fought off the surge of wild energy. *The Counselor warned me against using death energy. This thing is full of the stuff and I've got to be very careful with it. Sure would be nice to release all of this, though. The people who gave their lives to fill this with energy deserve nothing less.*

Mercy moved away from Janos Parasca's unconscious form and glanced out toward the open field. *There's that feeling again: more of the death energy being released. Moloch must be there.* Mercy took a deep breath and felt the elation and near rapture of the increased flow of the energy coming through the now thicker cord of blue. *This must be the stuff of life itself. I feel like I could do anything!* She took one step and then another toward Moloch.

* * *

Dmitri Slokov screamed in rage and grief, "Alexi! No, it can't be! Alexi!"

Jack Truett put his hand on Dmitri's shoulder but didn't say anything. *What can you say to someone who loses their closest friend and relative at the same moment?*

Dmitri's eyes darted crazily around. The portly man seemed to have snapped. "Alexi, I'll get you to a doctor. We can still save you. Jack! Do you know CPR? We can revive him!"

Jack looked at Alexi and didn't see any hope of this working, but he checked Alexi's pulse and started the cycle of chest compression and breathing assistance. *Dmitri, he's dead. Alexi is dead. But I'll keep trying.*

Between breaths, Jack said, "Maybe the police out there have some emergency medics with them. You should call them."

Dmitri's darting eyes snapped back to stare at Jack and he seemed to focus for a moment. "Yes. You're right. Hold on, Alexi!" Dmitri called the police again. After a minute of obviously futile talk, Dmitri slammed the phone on the ground.

Dmitri said, "They won't move medical support in until after the scene is pacified." He lifted his chin and as if in answer, shots rang out again. One of the booming supersonic rounds sounded followed by fire that might have come from the police. *Parasca's sniper must still be active.*

Jack looked up from the fruitless CPR and said, "That sniper is the problem. He has to be taken out, but the helicopter doesn't want to risk another direct hit."

Dmitri's face took on a grim expression of hatred. "That sniper is the one that shot Alexi." In a mercurial change, his face melted into grief and he motioned Jack away from Alexi.

He said, "He's dead. I know it." Dmitri clenched his fist in front of him. "Somehow I knew he was gone the moment he was hit." Dmitri hung his head over Alexi's chest. He was silent for a handful of seconds, then straightened. He lifted his handgun, checked its load then took Alexi's pistol and checked it as well. He gave his own gun to Jack and took Alexi's. "That sniper is a dead man and I will kill him with Alexi's own gun." He started to rise, but Jack put a hand on the man's arm.

Jack said, "Wait, Dmitri. Don't just run out there and get killed. We need a plan. That rifle takes at least a second or two between shots. If we charge, we need to wait until right after it fires."

Dmitri was in no mood to wait. "There's no time." He rose to move, but before he had come up from his crouch, the booming sound of the rifle rang out again. The projectile punched through the car where Alexi had fallen and missed Jack and Dmitri both, but hit Alexi's inert body again with a final, insulting blow. Dmitri screamed with berserk rage and darted around the end of the car. He dashed faster than Jack would have thought possible toward the sniper's lair behind Parasca's car, firing Alexi's gun as he ran. Jack moved out and around the other end for a moment and fired his handgun several times at where he thought Parasca's sniper hid, trying to lay down some additional covering fire. *Dmitri's headed right down the throat of that rifle. God help him.* Jack said a little prayer and prepared to charge as well.

* * *

Moloch's gigantic form clambered over the rubble on the way down the broad staircase. The globe of light that he had created earlier preceded him down the flight. He passed a human body, partially crushed under a large block of stone. It looked to be a man in late middle age and dressed strangely as seemed to be the custom in this age. He wondered momentarily at this place and its construction but dismissed the stray thoughts as immaterial to his present mission. He sent his questing thoughts out ahead.

Mulciber! Are you here?

Thoughts fired back at him instantly. *Yes, I am here, but I am very weak and my hands are wrapped in crystal steel chains. The last thing I remember from before was*

Michael and his host trapping me and confining me in a cell. I was in there for longer than I know. I have been back and forth from the shores of madness a dozen times. But I seem to have been saved by some blundering humans that appear to have puzzled out Michael's lock on my crypt. I took mental possession of one of the humans and learned a few things from him, but I am still very weak. The creature died as I was commanding it to kill other humans for their life energy. At its death, I took its life energy and that of another that I felt dying, but I am still too weak to do much else. I might be able to move slowly with help.

You'll do more than that. I have the shield that we made ages ago at one of the blood forges. It still contains much of the power we instilled in it at its making. I am bringing it to you.

Moloch felt relief flood through Mulciber's thoughts. Moloch reached the bottom of the staircase and went through the passage toward the large chamber. Mulciber's thoughts grew stronger as he approached.

What is going on in this world now? It has been so long since we were free. Where are Michael and his host? Does he know we have been let loose from imprisonment? Is the Creator taking a hand in matters here on Earth?

Michael is nowhere to be seen. I don't know if he knows of us or not, but from the small bit of this world I have seen, the humans have completely overrun it. The Creator seems to be letting matters run their course, whatever that means presently. Perhaps Michael and the other Archons have orders to back off and leave the Earth alone. If that is the case, we might have free rein at least for a time.

But if we are to succeed in the long term against Michael, we must gain more energy and more weapons like this shield to use against enemies whether human or angelic. We need to make more of the crystal steel. And, we'll need more of the angelic blood who can fight with us using the power contained in these crystal steel weapons. We can never hope to defeat the Creator himself, but if we make the costs high enough, He might decide to sequester us in a way that would leave us free once again in our own realm here on Earth.

Moloch found the mouth of the crypt and crouching down, looked inside. He hissed at the sight of Mulciber's emaciated form and the other's contorted face turned and looked at him. The dry, red eyes blinked slowly and painfully.

Mulciber's voice came out in a dry rasp. "Loose these chains, get me out of here, get me well and then we can make some plans."

Moloch examined the links that cut into Mulciber's wrists. At first he despaired of ever loosening them, since he knew that the metal was impervious to manipulation by any life energy he could wield. *How did Michael do this? Once the metal is made, it absorbs all life energy and so is impossible to alter except by … ah. That's it.* Moloch had found two links of the chain that appeared to be melted.

He said, "I have ill news. The chain seems to have been secured on you by fusing two links together."

Mulciber sighed. "It is what I feared. As I designed it, the metal resists all manipulation by spirit energy because it absorbs it. The only way to shape it after forging is with fire. It will have to be melted using tremendous amounts of energy to which neither you nor I would have had access without the shield artifact. I have not the strength and cannot see well enough yet to do this. Draw from the shield and burn through the chain."

Moloch grimaced. He rolled Mulciber's giant form to one side and pulled the stiff arms as far away from Mulciber's torso as possible, exposing the chained wrists. He held the shield and focused his thoughts. He drew the stored energy from the shield and pulled a focused thread of it into his right index finger.

He said, "Brace yourself."

Mulciber rasped, "You know that is not possible. Burn it anyway."

A fiery streak blazed from Moloch's finger and bathed the fused chain in licking flames. The color of the fire ran up rapidly from red to orange and yellow. The fire tightened into a beam that turned greenish for a moment and then blue. Finally, it shrank into a thread that blinked into a brilliant searing purple beam of fire. Mulciber groaned. The atrophied skin of his wrists peeled and blackened, exposing bone. The fingers of his hands curled involuntarily into contorted and uselessly charred knots.

The violet flame from Moloch's finger deepened and went almost black. At the same instant, the fused chain link slumped into glistening liquid droplets that splattered onto the floor of the crypt. Moloch stopped the fire and pulled back. Mulciber lay trembling.

After a few minutes, he stopped shaking in agony and gave a slight nod. Moloch flooded him with healing force and then finally held out the shield and laid it on Mulciber's chest. After a time, a red glow shone from the shield and bands of light began to swirl from it and into the prone form. Mulciber began to manipulate the energies in it into flowing lines of force that penetrated his weakened body, lacing through it and reinforcing it in an armor-like shell of energy.

As the other worked, Moloch touched the crypt wall in which Mulciber lay. *There is so much crystal steel here, fashioned by Michael with the Creator's power. What if we could put this in the hands of our own legions? We could store nearly limitless death energy and use it to fight and take back what we had before. We must get to the point where we can reestablish ourselves, prepare for the fight and make any battle for Earth too costly for the humans or Michael's forces. We've rested for thousands of years now. It's time to retake this world.*

* * *

Mercy found the opening in the earth that lead downward into the cavernous complex. She sensed large flows of death energy deep below. *I have to face Moloch again and this time, Hayden isn't here to sacrifice himself for me. I won't have an unexpected gift of energy from a dying friend. I don't have that stone dagger of Parasca's that drained energy from Moloch last time. This time, Moloch knows about me and won't be surprised. I could have hoped he'd be groggy and disoriented from his re-entrapment, but judging from the amount of energy being used below, that seems to be a fool's wish. Whatever is happening down there, it is being done in earnest and with purpose.*

She looked down the rubble-choked stairway and decided against climbing. She spotted a flat section of stone three feet wide a short distance down the passage and pulsed some of her energy toward it. It lifted and came to her smoothly. It stopped before her, flat side up and seemed to wait. She stepped onto it. She and the levitating rock glided diagonally down the hole, floating effortlessly above the wreckage a few feet below. *I'm going to have to do this alone again and hope that whatever happens, it will be enough. Please, let it be enough.*

Mercy made a small globe of light at the tip of one finger. It clung to her as if it were a glowing ladybug resting on her fingernail. *Amazing. I just thought of a light and somehow it happened. What are the limits of these capabilities?* Mercy floated down the Grand Staircase on her platform of rock. She came to a plateau-like area on the slope of debris and slowed her descent. *What is that? I thought I saw something glowing in that pile of rubble.*

Mercy spoke in a soft voice, "Hello? Is anyone here? Can you hear me?"

Two voices spoke suddenly and at the same time, overlapping so that Mercy could make no sense of what they said. She had only been able to tell that one voice had been male and the other female. There was a one second pause followed by the female voice speaking.

The woman said, *"Madonna mia!* Thank goodness you are here. Help us, please!"

Instantly a man's voice spoke, but in a muffled tone as if covered over with a thick blanket. "Maria, is that you? Did I just hear you Maria? Where are you? It's me, Henry! I'm down here near Balev's body. He's been crushed to death!"

* * *

Mulciber stood up, a woven armor of reddish light supporting his twisted and emaciated frame. He said, "This will have to do for now. My body is too weak for the moment without aid. I'll have to replenish it with more energy, food and water before it will function well enough."

Moloch said, "But what is this you've created around yourself? I've never seen it before. And why expend this amount of power? I can easily carry you from this place."

Mulciber said, "Think of it as armor over my body that I animate with my thoughts, not my limbs. My physical form still lives, but is not strong enough or recovered enough yet to be fully functional. The form Michael cursed me with on this plane never was very robust, but now after untold ages imprisoned, it is weaker still. And, I refuse to leave this prison while being carried like some sickly thing. My body may not be vital, but my mind is as active as ever."

He took a step and then another, the red, translucent covering sparkling with laser-like glints. It did indeed resemble a full suit of armor, though molded tightly to his form. It took on the emaciated contours and added two centimeters of thickness to every surface. It rippled and moved as he raised both arms and winced in pain.

Mulciber said, "It moves me well enough and obeys my commands, but it stretches my atrophied muscles in ways in which they cannot yet easily move. Alas, this cursed form." He looked over his limbs, winced again in the unaccustomed pain of movement, but then smiled slightly. "Yet, it is so good to breathe and move again."

Mulciber faced Moloch and said, "What happens above? I feel death energy coming in surges from nearby. Is there a battle?"

Moloch said, "There is, though it is between the humans themselves. There are some factions of them fighting above. They are not as primitive as they were when we ruled here in past ages. They have much more powerful weapons at their disposal than we knew then. They have devices that can throw metal pellets from long distances with devastating force. I have felt the bite of those things in this flesh and while they cannot kill us, with enough hits, they can render us helpless from injury, forcing us to use large amount of power to heal ourselves."

Mulciber said, "Interesting. I will want to acquire some of these devices to learn their function. Who would have thought the humans capable of such inventions? They seemed like little more than intelligent but belligerent animals to me in our time. Do you have a plan?"

Moloch said, "One of the humans, a very resourceful and persistent one that serves me willingly, is acquiring a transport of some kind that we can use to get away from this current battle, regroup in a safer location and plan our next moves."

Mulciber seemed impressed. "Very good, brother. We need to understand this new situation in which we find ourselves. I need some time to recover and study the human hierarchy and the structure of their society. You will want to understand their martial capabilities. We'll need to grasp it in its entirety if we are to take it over. I am ready. Let us leave this place."

Moloch stepped into the larger crypt antechamber and moved toward the exit leading to the ruins of the Grand Staircase with Mulciber's glowing red energy armor stepping behind. One of Mulciber's feet crushed shards of white plaster into powder that had moments before been pieces of a large painting of a bull. The two giant figures left the antechamber and went through the archway leading to the stairs.

Instantly, Mulciber's head jerked upward and to the left, looking up the ramp of the stairway at a swirl of reddish energy that swept overhead. He said, "What is that?"

* * *

Dmitri's gun blazed as he dashed across the meters separating him from Alexi's killer. *I don't care if I die, as long as he's dead too.* The ground was uneven and Dmitri almost stumbled twice. Once he thought he'd turned his ankle, but he bulled through and found he could keep charging. His heart pounded and his vision seemed to go red. He distantly heard the booming sound of the rifle again and thought he felt something pass very close to his head. *You can't kill me yet. You owe me for Alexi first.*

He completed the dash across the ground separating him from Parasca's car. He rounded the corner by the front bumper and found a man dressed all in black in mid-reload motion. The man looked up, met eyes with Dmitri and tried to leap to one side. Dmitri fired point blank at the man and hit him again and again. Dmitri kept firing until he heard the constant click, click, click of the empty chamber and then finally stopped. The sniper was slumped over and bleeding from multiple wounds. Dmitri saw a name spelled out on the man's chest: 'Lacusta.'

Dmitri saw Jack run up and assess the situation. Jack put his gun arm down by his side. Dmitri's face grew red with undissipated fury and he kicked the dead man, picked up the man's sniper rifle and heaved it as far away as he could. Dmitri screamed and shook his fist at the sky, then turned back and stumbled toward his car and Alexi's body. Dmitri wept and collapsed by his brother.

Jack shook his head and headed off to find Mercy.

* * *

Mercy directed her floating platform of rock down to the landing and stepped off. She used the energy flowing in her to lift the stones and rocks that were pinning the other woman. The scene was lit by a small light glowing from Mercy's fingertip. Maria seemed to watch carefully as Mercy worked.

Maria finally spoke while pointing at one of the levitating boulders, "Who are you? How are you doing this?"

Mercy lowered the stone and moved to where she heard Henry's voice. "We don't have time for me to explain right now. You can be sure that I am here to help you. You also need to know there is something very dangerous down there. We need to get you and your friend to safety." She pointed further down the slope to where a dim light shone through the opening leading to the crypt antechamber room.

Mercy called down into the hole to Henry, "Are you injured?"

He said, "I have an arm that is trapped and I can't feel the fingers in that hand. I think it may be just tangled up in a way that is preventing blood flow. Other than that, I'm hanging upside down and all the blood in my body feels like it has settled into my head. I would really appreciate help getting out of this. Oh, and there's Balev's dead body down here. It stinks horrendously."

Maria smiled slightly at Henry's statement and dragged herself painfully to Mercy's side near the opening from which Henry's voice came. Maria didn't know exactly what was wrong with her leg, but she believed her knee to be crushed at the very least. *At least it's not amputated.* Mercy began levitating more rocks and boulders from where Henry lay. She set them aside as quickly as they came loose.

Mercy said, "We'll get you out. I need you to keep talking to me so I know you're still okay as I move this debris away from you. Tell me about yourself and what you've found down here in this complex."

Henry spoke and told Mercy about their dig and the events that had lead up to their current predicament. Maria joined in the narration.

Maria said, "I know this will sound incredible, but we saw things down here that defy explanation. Besides the universal language samples, when we got into the crypt, the remains there didn't seem to be decayed like we would have expected. Our own Professor Russo became deranged and attacked us like a man possessed." She looked sadly over at the still form she'd found a few minutes earlier. "He was crushed when that last explosion blew a hole in the stone above. Please don't think we're crazy when we say that there may be supernatural things going on here."

Mercy reassured her that she did not doubt them. She said, "In the last few days, my entire world view and ideas about religion and the supernatural have been turned upside down. It would be hard to tell me anything now that would be too difficult to believe."

Maria said, "That thing in the crypt, I think it is a monster of some kind. It was trying to kill us by possessing the professor and making him attack us. I heard it speaking insane things through the professor's mouth. But that thing is not all. I also saw a giant creature step past me in the dark before you came down here. It walked down the stairs and either did not notice me or did not care about me. It went past me and called to the monster down in the crypt and seemed to be going to its aid. What is all of this? Do you know what is happening?"

Mercy felt a chill as if an artic wind blew through her. "You say there was a monster down in the crypt, and another giant creature that went past you calling out something? What did the thing that passed you call out?"

Maria said, "It shouted, 'Mulciber!' It called out the same word that we found on the plaque on the outside wall of the inner crypt."

Mercy blanched and said, "Are you sure it said, 'Mulciber?' The same word you found on the plaque?"

Maria said, "Yes. The phrase is burned into my memory: 'Evil Mulciber, killer of innocents, scheming ally of the foul monster Moloch. Judgment awaits you.' It's written in a language that anyone can read as if it was their mother tongue. Frankly, that terrifies me too."

Mercy's stomach roiled and she felt nauseous. She said, "It should terrify all of us. I think the monster that went past you was Moloch. He must have been going down the passage to bring Mulciber out. The two of them are like, well, think of them as arch-demons. We've got to get you and your friend out of here, now!"

Maria said, "Henry and I thought it was referring to some mythological creatures or the deities of the people that built this complex."

Mercy continued, "They're not legends or myths. They're real. Very real. And, they will kill people by the thousands without a second thought." Mercy paused and shouted down to Henry to make sure he was still alright. "Henry, talk to me some more. Tell me about yourself and your family."

He said, "I'm Henry Travers. I'm an archaeological postdoc student here at the Varna Necropolis..."

Mercy looked stunned. She interrupted him. "Henry Travers? Are you related to Hayden Travers?"

Henry's voice paused down below. Mercy looked at Maria who returned the glance with wide, sad eyes. Maria nodded as if in confirmation to Mercy.

Henry said, "Yes, he's my father. I had heard that his ship had gone down in the Black Sea. I was trying to leave and go to London to my mother when this cave system began collapsing and trapped us. Do you know my father? Do you know what happened to him?"

Mercy's face fell and she seemed to be washed over by a wave of grief. She bit her lower lip, took a deep breath and said, "I am so sorry, Henry. I am so, so, sorry..."

Maria's breath caught and spoke in a whisper, "No."

Henry's voice seemed to catch in his throat as he said, "Tell ... me what happened."

Mercy said, "Your father saved my life. He literally sacrificed his life to save mine. He died on the *Fortuna*, I saw it happen. I am so sorry. He was a dear friend to me. He was probably the best man I've ever known. I miss him so much. I still can't believe he's dead."

Maria's face filled with sadness and concern. Her eyes welled up.

Mercy lowered her head for a moment and then her expression grew grim. She looked at the sword that she still carried in her hand, looked back at the hole where Henry was still trapped and said, "I am going to get you out of here alive if it is the last thing I ever do." She pointed the sword at the rubble pile and her other hand as well. She said, "Up! All of you!"

A sudden surge of power from the sword blasted through Mercy. She showered the raw energy over the mound of rock and stone. Each individual piece of the hundreds of boulders suddenly moved from its resting state into a cloud of levitating, slowly swirling grayness twenty feet over their heads. More rocks and boulders swept upward from the stairway landing and into the orbiting ring that moved above and around Mercy.

Mercy felt a racing torrent of the death energy from the sword sweep through her, raising goose bumps on her arms and setting the hair on her head standing on end. The power came with strange sensations, almost like a taste. *It's nearly sweet … it feels wonderful … intoxicating … seductive and something else … addictive?* It pulsed and flowed inside her like a geyser wanting to be released. *I feel like I can do whatever I want, that I need to do whatever I want.*

She heard a shout down at the base of the staircase and saw two gigantic figures down there, one of them glowing within a fiery red aura. Suddenly, she knew what she had to do.

CHAPTER 35 – ARCHITECT OF THE ABYSS

"Men called him Mulciber; and how he fell from Heaven …
sheer over the crystal battlements: from morn to noon he fell …
dropt from the zenith like a falling star"
— John Milton, Paradise Lost

Mulciber shouted in a rasp, "Watch out! That thing up there is …" His words were interrupted by a barrage of stone, rocks and boulders flying towards them as if shot from hundreds of cannons. A few leading projectiles reached them first and Moloch was smashed backward by a large one to his chest. Mulciber's glowing red armor took hit after hit from large and small projectiles alike. Mulciber reached for the power he'd drawn from the shield and began raising a barrier, but each hit forced him proportionally backward, and then the main body of the cloud of debris arrived and Mulciber and Moloch fell to the storm of rock, each of them hit by dozens if not hundreds of the missiles.

Moloch took bruises, broken bones, lacerations, deep wounds, shattered ribs and broken hands and fingers where he'd tried to protect and shield his eyes. He was smashed back into the antechamber and rolled into the wall where he lay unmoving for a moment.

Mulciber's partial shield and energy armor took the brunt of the fusillade, but he too was smashed, blasted and bruised into senselessness by the onslaught. He collapsed to the floor right under the archway leading to the antechamber room. In a few seconds, he was covered over in a mound of rock that built up on top of him.

* * *

Mercy yelled in triumph, "There! Stay down there!" She felt exhilarated and more alive than she'd ever experienced before. She wanted to try a hundred things at once, to throw off all restrictions and blaze like the sun. *You know, there is no one that can tell me not to....* She noticed a buzz in her head and felt a nagging thought that seemed to be trying to get her attention. She heard a suppressed voice, not one of the old voices, but what seemed to be her own voice asking uncomfortable questions. *Am I tipsy? Am I drunk?*

She ignored the errant thoughts, looked down the slope, became annoyed at the relative darkness down there and flourished her hand, "Let there be light!" A nagging thought came back to her again. *What are you saying? Get ahold of yourself, woman! You're not some goddess, so stop acting like one!*

But wild power raced from the sword, through her body and turned into blazing, blinding light like noon on a summer day. It filled the cavern complex from one end to the other. It was too bright for her at first and she had to shield herself while her eyes adjusted. Gradually, Mercy made out the pile of rock at the bottom of the ruined Grand Staircase and felt giddy with her success. *I did it! Moloch and Mulciber, both defeated at once! They are out of the fight! Now who can I go up against?* She looked around as if hoping for more opponents. She felt dazed and transcendent at the same time. She hummed a tuneless song to herself and felt very pleased.

* * *

Maria's voice rang out as she crawled the rest of the way over the landing to where Mercy had removed all of the rest of the stone. "Henry! Are you alright?"

Henry nodded and said, "Yes, I'm alright except for this hand: it still has no feeling in it. Hopefully it will wake up now without all that weight on it. First, look what I found." He held out the bag.

Maria said, "That can wait until later, can't it? Where did you get the shoulder bag? You didn't have it before."

He said, "It was Balev's. It's got another explosive in it that can be set off remotely."

Maria said, "What? A fourth one? Well, there were four positions to the selector switch on the remote. Too bad I lost it down the hole with Balev. Unless…" She looked at him questioningly.

He said, "Yes, I recovered it. The remote is in the shoulder bag also."

Maria said, "Get it out. We may need it." She looked back at Mercy and saw that the woman was swaying slowly from side to side and seemed to be humming. Mercy's eyes were focused into some indeterminate distance and she seemed to be oblivious to Maria and Henry. Maria shook her head in Mercy's direction and said, "I think something is wrong with her."

* * *

Mercy's mind seemed to race in many directions at once. Her small, insistent voice seemed to be shrieking for notice, but it could not get her attention. *Got to focus! What's happening down there? Where are Moloch and Mulciber? Make sure they're down for the count or at least secure them somehow, but do something! What's wrong with me?*

She noticed at some level that she was singing a childhood melody and seemed to be swaying in time to it. She felt somehow that was extremely funny and started chuckling. *I'm the one that defeated both Moloch and Mulciber. I can spare myself a little bit of celebration, surely?*

She looked over the cavern, its every corner illuminated with her light. *My light. Let there be light!* She chuckled again. She heard a low rumbling sound from below. She looked down the slope and saw the large, new pile of rocks shift and slough to one side. A large, shimmering red shape stood up in the midst of the rock. It looked up in her direction and even with the distance separating them, somehow she felt it was smiling at her.

* * *

Mulciber shook off the stones, stood and flexed his misshapen form. *It's not enough that I have to use precious energy to heal my stiff and unresponsive body after that avalanche. It's not even enough that I also have to continuously use prodigious amounts of power to fuel this spirit armor. But when I fear we have been overmatched as we are crushed under the onslaught of these boulders, I think, 'What else can be done to us? How can the entire cosmos conspire against us like this?' I had thought that one of Michael's host or even Michael himself was attacking us and we would have been undone in our weak state. But chance has spared us. Instead, we are opposed by some human snippet drunk on death energy. I will make quick work of this one.*

Mulciber sent a mental probe at Mercy, using the same means and force he'd employed to take control of Russo's mind. *She has a rudimentary mental shield, only enough to be effective against the unbodied. I could penetrate it and take control of her, but she has the sword artifact. She's intoxicated by the death energy she draws from it, but she also has a direct power conduit from the Creator. Not a very large one, but the only one I've ever seen attached to a human. Ah, and it is growing slowly larger, expanding and gaining capacity. This one must be a favorite of one of the Archons or the Creator itself. I don't know what will happen if I seize her. I don't want to damage the sword either. We need it. Between the shield that Moloch has and the sword, we should be able to do what needs to be done. So instead of killing her and chancing some errant surge of power that wipes out the remaining stored death energy in the sword, let me see what happens when that protection from the Unbodied is compromised. Perhaps she'll destroy herself.*

Mulciber's probe turned into a lance of mental force. It cut through the membrane of Mercy's protective barrier like a knife slicing through a wineskin. *But that isn't enough. That split will last until she brings her shield back up. I need to make sure she can't reestablish the shield for a while.* Mulciber used his mental probe and set it into Mercy's mind. *There. I'll be able to listen in on her thoughts for a while. And, that type of probe is extraordinarily painful, so she won't be able to concentrate enough to redo the shield. That should last for a few hours at least.*

* * *

Mercy felt the tingling sensation again, similar to when Parasca had tried to insinuate himself into her head, only this time, it felt more subtle and much stronger, as if something were sniffing at her thoughts rather than trying to read them. She tensed and lifted another mass of projectiles from the boulders and rock scattered below the landing, preparing to hurl them down the staircase.

Suddenly, her head felt like it had been split open like a ripe melon. She felt a burning, stabbing pain as if something white hot had been jabbed into her skull. Inside her mind, a cacophonous sound like an ocean in full storm poured into her, lifting her mind on a tide of voices, thousands, millions of them screaming for attention. *Not this!*

The Torturer's voice called to her above the further voices in its familiar and dread tones, "You thought to hear me no more, but I have all of the patience of eternity. The worst pain of all is the pain of loss. Though you'd lost almost everything, you still had your sanity. You will not have it for long, I fear. You know too well this time all that you've gained and now the full import of what you've lost. Before, you thought your voices to be signs of insanity. Now, you know us to be malevolent beings. Oh, yes. There, I can taste your horror while I attach myself to your unshielded mind, sipping on the wine of your life force. Ah…" It seemed to moan in ecstasy. Mercy wanted to vomit, but was pummeled by other familiar voices.

The voice she knew as the Professor said, "Of course, you know about us in an academic sense, now. You realize that we are external to you but can reach your mind when improperly shielded, as you are now. Did you know that we attach parasitic spirit tendrils into your psyche, and draw on your life energy much like a blood leech? It is all very fascinating, of course…"

The Cannibal screamed in her head, "Enough! Eat! Devour its mind!" The voice fell into incoherent grunting.

Baby Benny shrieked, wept and cried piteously. The thing sounded like it was the one being eaten alive, but Mercy knew that it too was settling in on her mind like some maggot boring in and wallowing in her decaying thoughts and eating the substance of her life.

The Jailor said, "Now you are truly trapped. You are confined within your own mind and besieged by us from without. I am so grateful to Lord

Mulciber for the opportunity to taste of you once again. For years we drank of you daily, sipping your energy while you thought us to be but the ramblings of your sick mind. Now, you know that we are your jailors, your torturers and those who dine upon you."

Mercy felt attacked from all sides. *I have to block them out again. I've got to remember how I did it, but I feel so disoriented and foggy headed. And the pain!*

The Jailor said, "Poor child. You will not block us so easily this time. We are boring into you even now. It will be impossible to dig us out."

* * *

Maria sat next to Henry, pain creasing her dust covered face, her broken, bloody knee staining the leg of her work coveralls. She shook her head at their sorry condition and looked over at Henry. He was caked in dirt and one arm hung uselessly.

"How did we get mixed up in something like this?" She asked and glanced at Mercy who stood transfixed in apparent agony. "She's almost like some kind of good sorceress, but she doesn't look so good now. She levitated that barrage of rocks and threw them down on those two monsters, but since then, she looks like someone caught in a vise."

Henry's voice was growing unsteady, "She knew my father. She said Dad sacrificed himself to save her." He stopped and regained control of himself. "If she knows Dad, and was his friend, then we can trust her."

Maria said, "I think you're right, we can trust her. But what is happening? I feel like I've fallen down the rabbit hole into an evil Wonderland. Oh no. Look down there. I think we're about to have company."

Down at the base of the stairs, two giant forms came back into view and began walking upward. One of them glowed red. This time, Mercy Teller didn't seem to be in any condition to intervene.

Far above them, a familiar voice called out. "Maria! Are you down there? It's Angelica! I'm here with some of the other students. There's some kind of shootout going on nearby and we had to go the long way around to get here. Are you down there?"

Maria and Henry locked eyes and she shouted, "Angelica, go back. There's something very dangerous coming up your way. You need to go back! Get away from the opening! It's not safe!"

Henry motioned to the side passage that they had gone into earlier with Russo and Balev. He said, "I think we can get to some cover over there. Since Balev's third explosive failed to go off, the opening to the side tunnel is still there at the edge of the landing. It's probably not very deep before the caved-in section of the passage starts, but maybe we can hide in there and those creatures will pass us by."

* * *

Mercy struggled to slam a shield into place over the voices and pain, but it was almost impossible to think. *It's just like I did with the last shield! Why won't it work?* The rush of energy through her seemed more than adequate for the task, but she couldn't seem to concentrate. She cursed her luck and the power. The voices of the Unbodied hammered her mind. They were commanding her, threatening her and somehow it was worse this time than ever before. *This time, I know they are real. It's not a psychosis. It's not some imbalance of brain chemicals. These are real creatures and they are trying to attach themselves to me like monstrous ticks.*

What is the matter with the power from the sword? It was working fine before. It seemed to work alright when I was using the energy in it to bombard Mulciber and Moloch with those rocks. It seemed to work for offensive uses when I was reacting instinctively. But now…oh wait.

She looked at the hand that held the sword. Red light glowed from within it and pulsed into her arm almost exactly like the weapon had a heartbeat. She looked closer and felt sick. Red tendrils of power appeared to have issued from the crystal steel sword and crept to her hand, <u>penetrating</u> it. They looked like thin tentacles with barbs on the ends that had dug into the skin of her hand. She recoiled and tried to fling the sword away but found her hand clenched involuntarily around the hilt. She could not let go of it.

No, this can't be happening! She looked around wildly and saw that Henry and Maria were crawling to a small side tunnel. *Good, maybe they can escape this disaster.* She looked below and saw Moloch and Mulciber walking slowly up the stairs toward her. She felt chilled with fear.

The Counselor warned me against using the death energy stored in the sword and shield. It was too much for me and too intoxicating. I couldn't keep control of it. Now it has hooks in me. A moment ago, I felt transcendently powerful and thought I'd defeated Moloch and Mulciber. Now, I'm battered by the voices, the sword has taken hold of me and Mulciber and Moloch are back and almost on top of me. What can I do? Do I have any choices left to me?

She stood and tried to fight off the urge to tremble. *I could go down fighting, but that won't stop these two from being loosed on the world. It is <u>my</u> task to stop them. Somehow I must.* She looked at the sword. She heard the screaming voices in her head. She saw the thread of blue light that connected her to the Creator trailing away from her other hand, the one opposite the sword. It was pulsing with the rhythm of her heartbeat. *It seems brighter and thicker. I wonder.*

She moved her hand with the blue cord over to the opposite one that was spasmodically clutching the sword. *I have to let go of this thing. It's full of death and suffering. Only something that is damned can ever use this. Let go of it!*

* * *

Mulciber walked up the stairway, stepping carefully between blocks, stones and other rubble toward the stunned human female that had been the source of the rain of stones. *She is strong and that thread of power from the Creator is gaining in capacity. The Unbodied are tormenting her with her shield temporarily out, but she is fighting. I want this one, but she'll need to be broken first.*

A small, supplicating voice whispered to him. "Lord Mulciber, I abase myself."

Mulciber frowned as if he'd smelled something rotten. *How dare one of them speak to me!* "I have no patience for you, vermin. Get away or I shall take what energy you have. It would bring you unendurable suffering, but provide only the merest nourishment to me for my effort. Away with you before I decide to do it anyway."

The voice said, "Lord, I only spoke to you because Lord Moloch earlier sent me as a messenger to you while you were still confined. I know that you heard me in your dreaming state. He had told me to say to you in part, 'Tell Mulciber and tell my followers that I live yet...'"

Mulciber's anger slowed and he said, "I remember that. While I dreamt uneasily, a voice came to me with that message. Since you speak truly, I will not punish you for stepping beyond your station this once. And now, this conversation is truly ended. You presume too much in speaking directly to me."

The voice persisted, "Lord, I would ask a boon of you in payment for my service."

Though many things had happened to him in the last few hours, Mulciber felt completely astonished for the first time since he had awakened. *This Unbodied speaks to me like this?* Mulciber said, "Truly? You ask for payment? You astound me. Why shouldn't I just destroy you in an instant?"

The voice quavered, "I am one of the loyal ones. There are some of us in the lower ranks that still seek to serve you and the other Archons, you and Lord Moloch, that is."

Mulciber almost laughed. *The boldness of this one!* He asked sarcastically, "What boon do you request?"

The voice sounded like it grew hungry in tone. "That you grant me the woman's mind and life energy. Those of us, the Unbodied, must always draw power from the minds of the humans, but this one is especially energetic and powerful. I desire to grow fat on her energies. I want her exclusively for myself, apart from the other Unbodied. I want to keep her mentally bound and confined, my prisoner and prize."

Mulciber chuckled, "Ah, it's a question of appetites then? I understand you finally." Mulciber pondered for a moment. "Well, as payment for your service, you may have her for a time, solely yours. You will not destroy her completely though, for after some period, I will require her from you. I want her broken mentally, so that she can be useful for me at some future point. I do not want her driven insane. Cause her all of the suffering you desire, extract as much energy as you can from her, but leave her mind largely intact. I want to understand why she is a favorite of the Creator's. I want her knowledge of this latter time and, who knows, I may be able to use her for my own ends."

The greedy voice said, "I understand and am grateful." It giggled slightly.

Mulciber noted the creature's laughter and asked, "What is your name?"

It said, "The others call me the Jailor."

Mulciber peered again into Mercy's mind and saw her fruitless struggle to push out the Unbodied and reclose her shield. *She does things by instinct, and mostly very well, but she has not had ages of practice. And, she does not know the finer points of shields. She has not yet understood the probe I set in her. Let's change the game on her again.*

Mulciber eased back on the probe, leaving nothing but a tiny thread, made sure that the Jailor was on the inside and shot a mental blast against all of the other Unbodied. The spirit creatures fled from the shock wave and away from Mercy. With the pressure and pain suddenly relieved, Mercy gasped and Mulciber felt her slamming her mental shield back in place. Mulciber quickly wove an outer shield over Mercy's inner shield and smiled. *What will she do with this situation, now?*

* * *

Rakslav ducked and ran back toward the scene of the firefight. The helicopter circled over the site and that gave him a sense of direction to travel. It sounded like the gunfire had dropped to intermittent levels, and therefore he assumed that the local authorities were gaining the upper hand. *The police will be crawling all over the area soon. I don't know what has happened to Dmitri or Parasca, and I don't care. I hope they shoot each other's brains out.*

A loudspeaker from the helicopter was demanding the immediate surrender of all parties and that any that wished to live had to immediately lay down their weapons and lie face down on the ground. *It may not be easy to steal a truck from under their noses.*

He sprinted over the field for a short distance to a tree. He stopped beside its trunk and saw he was twenty meters from the nearest of the white cargo trucks. There were bodies that lay interspersed over the ground. *I doubt that any of these are voluntarily surrendering. They all look dead. There's no way*

I'll be able to find keys to the truck unless they've been left in it, and I don't have time to search the bodies. I'll have to hope it has on old style ignition setup that I can hotwire.

He ran the last twenty meters to the truck and grabbed the door handle. It came open and he piled in. He felt in the ignition and found no keys. He searched the cab and the overhead visor without any luck. He reached under the dash and felt in the dark for the ignition wires and found them. He pulled them loose and touched together the two that would have been connected through the ignition switch. The truck's engine rumbled to life.

Now to move this thing quietly back to that dig site, without being noticed. No lights. Move slow. Look somewhere else, Mister Helicopter.

He put the truck in low gear and eased out the clutch. The truck began rolling slowly toward the dig site.

* * *

Angelica Costa pulled herself away from the lip of the pit, Henry and Maria's shouts still ringing in her ears. She did not understand how it could be so brightly lit since none of the electric lamps seemed to be the source of the light, but she did understand that something was terribly wrong.

Two gigantic figures had started climbing up the rubble-strewn stairway below. They looked three times the size of any human and that would have been enough to put fear into Angelica, but one of them also wore some kind of translucent red armor that shone as if it contained its own light source. The other carried a shield that was also glowing with reddish light. Both of them looked massive in size and strength, and were completely, incredibly beyond all explanation. They looked like they were five meters tall. *Giants? How can there be giants?*

She waved off the students who also crouched near the lip of the complex entrance. "You heard them! Get back. Henry and Maria are getting to cover down there. We need to do the same. Something awful is coming out. But first, I need to do one more thing."

She pulled up the camera she carried, leaned over the edge one final time and zoomed in on the scene below. She took a continuous stream of shots until she counted to fifty and then stopped, backed away from the hole again and led the students to the nearby tree line in the ancient cemetery.

CHAPTER 36 – DESPERATION

"So bent he seems on desperate revenge
that shall redound upon his own rebellious head"
— John Milton, Paradise Lost

Mulciber and Moloch stepped onto the platform of the landing, only twenty feet from Mercy. Her body still seemed transfixed and her face wore a determined but anguished look as her eyes tracked the two demons. Her hand still gripped the sword that pulsed with red, fiery light. Her other hand covered the first and seemed to be trying to steady the sword hand.

Moloch spoke, a tone of recognition mixed with fury. "This is the one that threw the rock slide down on us?" he asked. Mulciber nodded.

Moloch said, "Because of her, I had to use precious energy to heal wounds and broken bones just now. This is also the one that put me back into confinement on that ship. Her life is mine. I will finish her." He stepped forward to seize Mercy.

Mulciber said, "Wait, brother. I have rendered her helpless at the moment by breaking her shield and unleashing the Unbodied on her. Let us then consider our next move well, lest we venture into error."

Moloch looked at Mulciber questioningly and with a bit of annoyance. "Why? What is it to you what I do with her? She is nothing but a human female. Why should you stop me or even slow me down? She made me look weak when we fought on the ship and that is enough. I will not let her live."

Mulciber shrugged off Moloch's annoyance and said, "She has a power thread that is a conduit to the Creator. That can only mean she is a favorite and has been chosen for some task. If we kill her, we lose that power source. Think what it would mean to have all of the power we wanted, needed or desired again if we could but tap into her conduit."

Moloch gestured emphatically, "I already thought of that and tried to get access to her power back on the ship. I managed to siphon off some of the power before she closed me back in that sarcophagus. Granted, it is a direct tie to the Creator, but it is too small to do us any real good. We would be forever starving for power compared to Michael and his hosts."

Mulciber stepped in front of Moloch and said, "Didn't you notice that her thread is expanding and thickening? It is growing in capacity by the minute. I already sense more power flow in the last few seconds through it. If it continues to grow, it could be a very real supply for us."

Moloch's irritation seemed to increase. "Get out of my way. I'm going to kill her and crush her into paste right here on these stairs. I'll drink up whatever power is in her and whatever is left in her conduit. That is all I will say on the matter."

Mulciber said, "No. We need her broken and obedient but still alive. If we are to reestablish ourselves on this world, we will need followers that can use the power, and she carries her own source of power with her. If we can turn her into a follower we won't have to supply her with death energy. Until we find more of the other Fallen, we need her."

Moloch spoke angrily and said, "I won't have it. After what she did to me, I won't allow it!"

Mulciber didn't back down from the confrontation. He looked at Moloch and said forcefully, "I've already rendered her helpless. She is caught in her own battle now and can't fight back against either of us. We need her power source and if we can break her, we gain the use of her ability. I won't let you kill her until we see if she is salvageable."

Moloch roared at Mulciber, the corded muscles in his neck straining in rage. "Get out of my way! She tried to crush us under a rock slide just moments ago, you fool! We have to kill her before she grows stronger. She defeated me in combat just a few days ago. She can wield the power: humans can't do that. Do you know what that means about her? She's not just a favorite; she's got to be one of our blood. She had to have come down through some of those human women we took ages ago."

Mulciber shouted back at him. "Few of those infants ever survived, but if she's a descendant and she dares to oppose us, that means the Creator is using some of our own against us. And that is all the more reason to turn her. We could even use her as a breeding mare to create more of the humans that have access to the power. We have to keep her alive. Enough of this. You can't have her!"

Moloch roared and leapt on Mulciber, slamming the shield into him. Great shimmering sparks of red flew from where the shield touched Mulciber's glowing red armor. Mulciber staggered back from Moloch's bull rush until he steadied himself against a wall adjacent to the landing.

Mulciber shouted at Moloch, "Stop! You're wasting power!"

Moloch said, "Then get out of my way!" Moloch grabbed Mulciber's left arm and threw him to the side and toward the stairs leading downward. Mulciber looked like he was about to tumble down the long flight when he suddenly righted and floated above the plunging stairway.

Mulciber's voice grated, "So now we both throw away rivers of power. What fools we are!"

* * *

Mercy heard internal momentary silence and relaxed mentally. Only the merest whisper of sound remained and Mercy considered it to be just an echo. *I did it. The shield is back and the Unbodied are gone again. Oh, thank you! Thank you! Sweet silence!*

She looked and noticed the two demons again. They had made it up to the landing and seemed to be fighting against each other. Mercy felt relief. *Maybe they'll each destroy the other. At the very least, they should be able to do a lot of damage to each other. Perhaps I should move away from them…*

She backed toward the side passage where she saw Henry and Maria hunkered down just a few feet from the opening. She took a few steps and then remembered the sword in her hand. She stopped and again placed her hand over the top of the sword hand concentrated. *I need to let go of this thing.* She felt the flow of power begin through the thread that lead back to the throne room where she first met the Counselor. She let it move into her body and suffuse into her flesh. She let it fill her as water fills a container. It soaked into her entire body, except for the hand holding the sword. Something there prevented its passage and blocked its action. She kept the energy flowing into her, because there seemed to be a leak: something was drawing on the power she pulled through the thickened tread. *Maybe it's the shield I'm maintaining that's draining the energy.*

She concentrated on her sword arm and visualized it relaxing in the warmth of sunlight. She imagined the blue glow soak into thirsty tissues. She looked and saw a reddish energy hook slowly withdraw from her hand and retract into the sword pommel. One after the other, as she maintained the flow of the life-giving energy, she saw the hooks retract and release her flesh. Finally, the last one came free and Mercy felt the sword lying in her palm, free to do with it as she willed.

She felt victorious. *Now to throw this away…*

The Jailor's voice spoke from within her. "Not so fast. I think I will want the energy in that for myself."

Panic washed over Mercy at the sound of the voice within her. *But I drove out the Unbodied! How could one of them have stayed behind while all of the others were forced out?*

The voice said, "You thought you pushed them all out? You thought you drove out the rest of my fellows? You didn't. It was Mulciber and he is now my patron. I did him a favor and now he has given you to me. Solely. Your mind is your prison cell, I am your jailor and now <u>I am locked in here with you</u>!" It laughed at her.

Mercy frantically brought down her shield to push the creature out. She felt the energy release and she knew the shield was down. She also noticed she still had a steady energy leak and realized it was not due to maintaining the shield. *It has to be this worm in my head that I always called the Jailor.*

She fought against the creature's insistence and dropped the sword to the ground. She felt its power drain from her and felt exposed and naked. *I let go of my crutch. Now let's see if I can stand without it.*

* * *

Jack walked quietly through the trees toward the pit that had a searchlight-bright beacon of light shining from it. *I'm pretty sure Mercy came this direction. If I can get close enough to look in, I hope I can spot her. There shouldn't be a problem with light pouring out of it like that.*

He moved closer to the excavation while staying under the trees. He heard some whispering voices and looked in that direction. He saw a group of about a half-dozen people, all looking to be in their twenties. He listened.

One of the group, a pretty young woman, pointed at the back display on a camera and said, "…and look at this picture. It's that tall blond woman again. She's holding a silvery, almost translucent sword!"

Jack smiled. *At least I know where Mercy is. There isn't anyone else that could fit that description.*

* * *

Mercy shuddered at the demon trapped in her head with her. Her shield was down, she was certain, but now she sensed an outer shield of some kind and not of her own making. It seemed unbelievably smooth like the inside of a glass globe. *The Jailor is certain he's been 'given' me as his plaything by Mulciber. That's who must have put up this shield. I doubt I can easily break something put up by one of the Fallen. What can I do?*

The Jailor said, "Nothing. You can do nothing. Isn't it delicious? You are trapped in your own head, unable to force me out. Your thoughts can no longer reach outside. You may not even be able to use the power any longer outside that shield. In the meantime, you and I will be closer than lovers. As close as maggots are to rotten meat!"

Against her will, Mercy felt her hand begin to move toward the sword she had dropped.

The demonic force within her laughed. "Pick up the sword, Mercy. Let me feel the power in it channeled directly through you to me. I'm through with hiding or laying low. No more drinking a tiny sip of you and sharing your energy with millions of others. I can do whatever I want with you. Mulciber has handed you over to me. He said, '... cause her all of the suffering you desire, extract as much energy as you can from her, but leave her mind largely intact.' But when he returns and finds you drained and all but dead, your mind a quivering shell of madness, I will just say, 'she was weaker than I thought' and it will be too late. But you should be grateful to me. He means to enslave you, break you and use you against the Creator. He means to use you as breeding stock, to form a corps of hybrids that can use the power. I will be much more merciful to you than that. I will be much quicker."

Mercy nearly gagged at the images the demon brought into her mind, and she tried desperately to pay no attention to the thing as it kept talking. *Can I close it off or sequester it away from the rest of my mind? Could I wall off a section of my mind with that creature within? Would that leave it still able to damage me from the inside? No, I can't leave it to rummage around in my mind.*

"Prison cells are small places and this one is so small only one human mind can exist inside it," the Jailor said. "But there will be more room for me when your sanity is in tatters."

Her hand continued downward toward the sword. With two inches to go before her finger touched it, she struggled mightily against the coercion and managed to slow the movement by a hair. *How is it controlling me like this? It bypasses my consciousness and takes over my body? How?*

The Jailor said, "The physical body, so rooted in its animal needs and appetites is the easiest to manipulate. Why are you surprised? It is the hardest thing for a human to control, so why wouldn't it be immensely simple for a demon to control, especially from within your own mind? Your body is your true jail cell and I control it now."

She tried to visualize the Jailor. *I reject your attempt to confine me. I won't give up my sanity or my physical body to you!* Her hand was a half-inch from the sword and stopped moving. *I've driven you things out before. How did I do it?* She remembered it had to do with the imagery she had brought to mind. *That's the way it seems to work for me. What do you look like? Where are you?* She imagined a massive covered stadium, similar to the one she'd pictured when she'd first learned how to drive out the Unbodied. At the center of the domed area, she imagined herself standing alone, tall and fierce. She held the image and a diseased and pock-marked satellite appeared like a tiny moon orbiting her. Its surface was covered with boils, sores and open wounds that oozed thick pus. It swirled around her, globules of its disease bubbling out like lava and raining down on her.

There you are. If you were a moon, that's what you would look like.

The Jailor said, "You see a version of reality but it is just a metaphorical representation. It would be just as true to imagine me as a maggot eating away at your dying body. The underlying truth is this: I am infesting you and eventually, I will poison you and kill you."

I found out in the throne room that for me, reality can sometimes only be understood as images. It's the best my mind can do sometimes. I can grasp a model when I cannot grasp the entirety of the reality. It's a crude representation, but it will do.

She held the image of the Jailor's tiny diseased satellite in her mind and looked for the thread connecting her to the Creator. A bright blue band like the arc of a rainbow swept from her hand and off into the distance. It went through her image of the domed stadium and she imagined it cut through Mulciber's outer shield as if it were no obstacle at all.

She allowed the blue energy from it to spread through her like the warm glow of a summer's dawn. She pulsed with the renewed life of it. The blue band of energy thickened and broadened, carrying more and more life into her. She looked at the orbiting creature that represented the Jailor and knew what she needed to do, but consciously avoided mental pictures or giving a name to what she intended.

With her mind, she reached and pushed at the Jailor, altering his orbiting course, nudging him bit by bit. The effort was enormous, but felt strangely similar to the telekinesis she had already learned. *I'm only shifting its position a little at a time.*

The Jailor said, "A fruitless expenditure of precious energy. Do you wish me to be impressed? I am not. This merely proves that you need to be broken and humbled. You need to serve a more focused and stronger mind. Stop this needless waste at once!" She paid it no attention and continued pushing the thing further and further from its original orbit. She felt more power move through the thickening band of blue light. It grew more brilliant and began to grow lighter in color.

The Jailor said, "What a mindless beast you are! What is it you think to accomplish? You are using enough energy to lift mountains, and for nothing!"

She bore down as if putting every last ounce of her strength into the effort. The Jailor's satellite shifted drastically, encircled in a glow of crackling energy. Bolts of blue lightning rained down on the Jailor. He started screaming.

"Stop it! What are you doing?" It shrieked.

The Jailor circled around her one last time in a wildly irregular orbit. It swung wide on one side of her and flew in close on the other. On the opposite side of its eccentric revolution, the Jailor flew straight into the blue arc of power that seemed to rise from Mercy like a pillar holding up the vault of heaven. With a shriek of agony from the Jailor, he was sliced in two and then each piece fell into a swirling vortex that sucked the tumbling halves into the arcing blue band. The Jailor disappeared. The blue thread pulsed once and expanded incrementally.

Mercy gasped at what she had just seen. She listened, but the Jailor's voice seemed to have been permanently silenced.

* * *

Moloch lunged at Mulciber and shouted. "That woman must die! She humiliated me. No human has ever done that."

Mulciber backed away, hovering in the air out of the bigger one's reach away from the landing. "It is what I've been telling you! Since she's a hybrid, she can touch and use the power that normal humans can't perceive. But it has to be more than that since she has that conduit to the Creator's power. It means she's been in contact with one of the Three. I can't imagine any but one of them sanctioning such a connection. And with that type of close involvement on the part of the Three, we can't afford to bring their direct scrutiny down on us by killing her."

Moloch stopped trying to reach Mulciber and stood at the edge of the stairway and shouted, "We can't just let her go."

Mulciber floated closer and said calmly, "No need to worry. I placed an outer shield around her mind and trapped an Unbodied in with her. That should break her down mentally. I also put a probe into her mind. She won't be able to dislodge it or even sense it, but I will be able to tap into her from anywhere." Mulciber motioned in the direction where he remembered Mercy had been standing. She was not there, but the crystal weapon she had held was. He looked puzzled.

He said, "Here is the sword." He retrieved it. "But where is she?"

* * *

Mercy recovered from the destruction of the Jailor and eyed the globe-shaped shield that Mulciber had built around her mind. *How can I break through this thing?* She tried to reach out to Jack's mind like she had the previous day. There was nothing. *I can't hear him at all. In fact, I can't hear anything including the huge roaring voices I should be able to pick up from Moloch and Mulciber. I can't hear Parasca's mind either, but of course, he might be still knocked out.*

Mercy looked more carefully at the translucent shield. *It reminds me of crystal steel's structure with the carbon nanotubes filled with iron, except this is completely transparent like the iron component was left out. That would make it similar in structure to a diamond, but of course, this is immaterial. It's not made of carbon tubes or crystals, it's made of ... what? Just energy? Hmmm.*

Mercy visualized a closer view of Mulciber's shield, moving to within a hairsbreadth of it. She couldn't make out the finer structure of it: it looked like a type of smooth glass. *I wish I could use the power to zoom in, but I don't know how yet.* She looked over at the portion of the shield where the blue cord passed through, seemingly unobstructed. *How does it do that?*

She moved her viewpoint to the blue thread and followed it to the shield. She saw it go right to the barrier and without any seeming disconnect, it continued on the other side. *It passes through, so why can't I?*

Mercy tried to aim a smaller thread of the power right at the shield and it passed through without a pause. Her thoughts though, could not travel through. She tried, but each time she attempted to reach through the barrier to touch Jack's mind, she was met with blank silence. Her thoughts bounced back.

If only I were completely made of the life energy. She pondered, stymied. Another thought occurred to her. *What if I am made of the life energy? What if that's all any of us really are?*

She brought her awareness back to her body, retreated from the visualization she had built and rested her thoughts for a moment. She heard again the sounds of struggle between Mulciber and Moloch. There was a violent fight going on with Moloch insisting she must be killed and Mulciber wanting to 'break' her instead. Mulciber also said he didn't want to attract the attention of the Creator by killing Mercy and severing the connection between her and the blue thread of power.

Mercy felt she only had moments to act, but she knew she had to undo Mulciber's shield. *He cut through my shield that kept the Unbodied out. I need to slice through his now. I need to stop trying to control the power, but instead just let it work.*

She let go of trying to master it and relaxed. She imagined herself being carried on a current of blue, rolling water. She felt herself drawn into the massive flow that had been funneling into her and now she felt herself carried into it. The thread seemed that it would be too small to hold her entirely within it, but it broadened to fit her consciousness. She somehow knew she was approaching Mulciber's shield wall and she wondered if she would be crushed against its diamond-like surface.

She reached the interface and for a moment saw herself on the inside and outside of it at once, and then the shield was behind her. She hadn't broken Mulciber's shield, but she had escaped it by riding out through the blue thread.

She heard a thought from somewhere else, perhaps from someone else. It said, "Anyone that is carried by the power can break through any barrier."

Mercy snapped back into the full possession of her body. She distantly heard Jack's thoughts and knew for certain that she had escaped Mulciber's mind trap. She saw Moloch and Mulciber, still struggling, then turned and saw Henry and Maria. She jumped to the passageway entrance where they were trying to shelter themselves from the fight.

She said, "Come on. I need to get the two of you out of here quickly."

Maria said, "Take Henry out first. I can't walk. My knee has been shattered."

Henry said, "No, she should go. She's hurt worse than I am."

Mercy said, "You're both going. Come out of there. I'll carry you both if I have to."

Henry said, "But what about those two? Won't they just catch us and kill us? We wouldn't last long against things like that."

Mercy said, "I'll move us quickly so they don't catch us. They're bigger than me, but I think I'm faster."

Henry said, "I found an explosive left by the saboteur that caused this whole debacle. Why don't we start up the slope, then I can set off the explosive. It would at least slow them down and it might give us enough time to get away. What do you think?"

Mercy said, "It's worth a try."

Mercy lifted Maria easily and draped her over her shoulder. With Henry, she helped him come out of the passageway and seeing he could walk, she looked to the rubble-strewn slope and decided it would be faster if she used the levitating stone again. *I'm without the sword now. Can I pull enough energy through to do this?* She concentrated and the stone rose and came to her. *It seems even easier than before.* She asked Henry to step onto it and then helped Maria up to the small floating platform. Maria leaned on Henry.

Mercy sent the stone rising rapidly to the top of the slope and saw Henry step off with Maria. She brought the stone back down and turned. Mulciber and Moloch stood facing her, both breathing heavily, but no longer fighting. Mulciber held the sword she had dropped. Moloch held the shield.

Mulciber said, "You broke out of my shield and destroyed one of the Unbodied. It was a minor spirit, but still, it was an immortal and you annihilated it. Even the Creator itself doesn't often resort to irrevocable disintegration. You can be a vicious little creature, can't you?"

Moloch said, "I told you she had to be destroyed. She is gaining more ability each day. If you'd not forced us both to profligately throw our strength away in a fruitless battle, we could have finished her by now."

Mulciber spoke angrily, "I had this creature under control until you forced my attention away from it. This is your fault."

Mercy glanced up at the opening above. She saw what looked like two faces, both male. One was Henry's. Was the other person Jack? *I have to get them all away from here.*

She called out, "Henry! Throw it and set it off! I'll take care of the rest!"

She saw a small package drop. Mercy sent out a wave of force, pulling at all of the broken boulders, stone and rubble, pulling them toward her. The thousands of pieces started moving and then more slid and more quickly.

Henry's object landed in the shifting, accelerating mass and exploded with a shattering boom. Mercy opened herself to the entire volume of the energy in the conduit and guided it into a ferocious pulling force. At the same moment, she leapt into the air. A wall of rock, like a mountain in motion, slid down toward Mercy, Mulciber and Moloch.

* * *

Rakslav drove the truck as silently as possible, letting the idling engine pull the vehicle. In the dark, he had many obstacles to avoid and was unable to steer clear of all of them. He felt the familiar speed bump-like mound that indicated he had rolled over another body. *I hate that feeling.* A car came into view and he swerved to avoid it. It was, or had been, an expensive limousine. There were multiple bodies near it and he avoided those when he turned to miss the car itself. Some meters away, there was another body and it was right in his path. He braced himself for the squishy feeling of running over another highly compressible mound, when something made him slam on the brakes. The truck shuddered to a stop.

Rakslav hardly knew why he had done that, but he felt a hunch calling to him. He set the brake and flung open the door and stepped to the ground. He walked around to the front of the truck and looked at the body that lay only centimeters from the front tires.

"Well, well. Janos Parasca. What have you gotten yourself into now?"

Rakslav bent over to examine the body and was startled to find a strong pulse. Rakslav straightened up, pondered and went back to the truck cab. He searched the tool compartment behind the front seat and came back to Parasca with some rope and a few bungee cords. *This won't take long.*

* * *

Mercy rose up and out of the pit while clinging to the edge of a levitating rock. She coughed from the cloud of dust, let go of the rock and fell to the earth. She tumbled to a stop and Jack ran to her and helped her get behind some nearby trees.

Mercy panted, "We've all got to get away from here. That rock slide won't hold those monsters for very long. We need to be gone by the time they come back out. First, though …" She turned to the hole in the earth one last time and waved her hands as if cancelling something. The light pouring out of the hole blinked out.

Jack herded the students away from the site. Several of them assisted Maria and Henry. All of them moved back toward the city as quickly and as quietly as possible.

* * *

Rakslav drove quietly and continued his trip across the mostly open field. As he approached the brightly lit opening in the earth, he saw a cloud of what appeared to be dirt billow from it and then the light went out. Concerned, he backed the truck into place by the large opening where Moloch had left him earlier. He'd had to carefully avoid all of the open dig sites while driving with no lights. *I don't want to do this again anytime soon.*

He opened the truck cab door and stepped out. He worked the door at the back and slid it up, revealing the large open cargo area. Rakslav looked at the tied up body that was the sole occupant of the back of the truck. He looked down into the dark hole leading to the complex below and wondered when Lord Moloch would return. *He will be glad to see who I've found for him.* Rakslav Gachevska smiled, noticed a sound then turned his head to the side. *What's that?*

A knot formed in his stomach as he heard, then saw the helicopter flying toward him. Its nose tipped downward and its remaining headlight illuminated the underground entrance, the truck and Rakslav himself.

A loudspeaker blared into life from the helicopter. "Drop your weapons. Stand where you are and raise your arms over your head. If you do not comply, you will be shot."

Rakslav paused and raised his arms slowly, his fingers splayed open to show he was unarmed. The chopper hovered above him, suspended in the air like a praying mantis examining its supper. He stood immobile, but looked up at the machine, squinting against the glare from its lights. He thought he could make out large cracks in its windshield and there seemed to be multiple bullet holes scoring its body.

The machine hovered lower. Its loudspeaker boomed again. "Lie down on the ground."

Rakslav didn't move. *They plan on holding me here until the police on the ground arrive. We've got to be long gone by then.*

The loudspeaker sounded out, "Lie down! This is your last warning."

Rakslav began to crouch down, but the loudspeaker blared again, "Halt! Whoever you are coming out of the dig site, halt or you will be shot!" There was a sudden shouted curse and the voice of the pilot could be overheard, "Look at the size of those things!"

Rakslav looked over at the opening to the dig below and saw two gigantic figures step out and onto the ground. Moloch held the crystal shield and another figure surrounded by a glowing red aura held the sword. A high powered rifle boomed from the chopper and sparks flew from the shoulder of the second figure. It staggered back a step but caught itself and looked up at the hovering machine.

The huge being spoke a single word that shook Rakslav. It sounded like the embodiment of all flame and torment: "Fire!" A fountaining stream of seemingly liquid flames blazed into the air and pinned the helicopter like an insect on a needle. The pillar of fire shot through the bottom of the craft, filled the passenger compartment with an inferno and blew out of the top of the machine. Flames swirled around the spinning blades and the engine intake sucked the fire in and through. Faint voices screamed for mercy from inside the cab as the engine exploded. The vehicle crashed to the ground and a secondary ball of fire exploded upward from the wreck.

Rakslav ran to Moloch and said, "Great Lord, we must leave quickly before more of these arrive."

Moloch nodded, looked at the flames of the downed helicopter and followed Rakslav to the back of the truck. Moloch turned to the other figure and spoke as if they were resuming a conversation that had started before the helicopter had been encountered.

Angry sarcasm seemed to drip from his tone, "Mulciber, do you still think she is tamable?"

Mulciber said, "No. She's progressed too far. She could never be contained now. There was a chance to break her, but that would have been days or weeks ago, before she started using so much power and before her conduit had expanded so greatly. Still, even at that, her mortal body can only handle so much of the power before burning up. She is near that capacity now. We have both of these," he indicated the sword and shield. "And though they are both nearly depleted now, when full again they each will far surpass her capacity. She still has no conception of what we can do with them when we are back to our full strength."

Moloch said, "And she will have no one protecting her." He glared at Mulciber and motioned at the sword and shield. "Our next move must be to gain much greater sources of energy to feed these. To do that, we need to be some place where there is constant death on a large scale."

Rakslav stepped forward and said, "I believe I can help you find what you seek. There is always a terrifying amount of death where we are headed. The Middle East is near."

He motioned to the open back door of the truck and indicated they should enter. Moloch nodded and started to climb in.

Rakslav said, "Also, I found someone you might be interested in becoming reacquainted with." He pointed at the body lying on the floor of the cargo area.

Moloch looked down and smiled.

* * *

Janos Parasca was a small child again. He heard the rumbling of diesel engines above and saw an avalanche of bloody carcasses, bones, blood and intestines being pushed over the edge and down into the pit where he and the other war orphans waited. They fought for the edible scraps, but not with each other, for the very concept of edible changed when you had to fight against rats for the privilege to eat. The feral children scrabbled over the pile like cockroaches on garbage, snatching and gnawing at bones with trailing bits of raw, red gristle.

He heard the engine roar more loudly, looked up and saw the giant bulldozer's blade push another towering mound of the slaughterhouse's offal off the edge, but this time, it was right above him. He tried to get away, to climb over other boys, to claw his way out from under the mountain of blood and gore that hung suspended in space above him, but it landed on him like a fallen star. He was crushed and suffocated in the wet darkness, his mouth full of blood, his lungs full of blood, death suffusing and drowning him forever. In his darkened eyes, he saw the faces of every one of his victims, past and future. From the first child he had killed for its food while still a child himself, to the woman he had strangled at his island only a day ago, he somehow felt that the blood he drank was theirs, all theirs. *How can there be so much blood in the entire world?*

The rumbling roar of the engine somehow grew louder. The ground under him trembled and he was shaken to his core. A jolt hit him and seemed to squeeze him in the chest. His consciousness swam back to the surface and he realized he was awakening. *Oh gods, thank you! Thank you that I wasn't back at the slaughterhouse pit. It was only a dream!*

He awoke and opened his eyes. He couldn't focus at first, but still felt the rumbling roar of a diesel engine. It was dark, but not completely. Something large nearby glowed hazily like hot coal. His eyes cleared a little and he saw what looked like a hideous gargoyle statue that was wrapped in a glowing red layer of armor. Parasca's skin crawled when the thing's head swiveled and looked at him. Its lips moved and it spoke.

The monster said, "It is awake, and its mind shows traces of having recently used the death energy. It seems to be another hybrid like the woman. How fortunate this is, but how strange that we should find another of our descendants so quickly."

Parasca felt enormous pressure in his chest as if a giant were squeezing him. He felt something large exhaling its hot breath close to him. He turned in that direction and saw a huge, familiar face studying him. Moloch looked at him with open glee.

Moloch said, "My traitorous priest. You served me duplicitously and I can read the truth from your own mind. You had the chance to rescue me from the sea bottom but decided not to. You wanted me kept imprisoned so you could be free of me. Now you're mine." Moloch held the sword with one hand and Parasca saw a reddish glow building, its remaining energy being brought to bear.

Moloch's grip on Parasca's rib cage grew tighter. Parasca felt bones splintering and shattering, then quickly felt the jolt and agony of sudden healing. The monster did not hesitate, but broke Parasca's arms, legs and feet in sequence. After each, he healed the man again and proceeded to break more. Moloch crushed and healed, shattered and smashed and healed him minimally again and again. Parasca did not know what was worse, the pain of the injuries or the pain of the rough healing so he could withstand more injury. *Not this! No nightmare could be worse than this!* He continued screaming and screaming endlessly, his throat bloody with pain and terror. He felt his mind slipping into madness.

* * *

Dr. Caba Ozera removed the USB thumb drive from his laptop and put it in his pocket. He disconnected his computer from the PetroRomania network and made sure his wireless connection was turned off. He ran a program to hard format the drive in the laptop and then removed the drive just to be sure. He put the drive in his briefcase and left the dead laptop on his desk. He took a small box out of a desk drawer and examined it briefly. He noted the slim, nearly translucent metal of the dagger in the case. He nodded to himself and placed the item in his briefcase. He turned off the lights and left the PetroRomania research lab.

Once in his car, he opened up the app on his phone that allowed encrypted message traffic and sent a text to one of Dmitri's tech people. It read, "Everything is wrapped up. All data that was needed has been copied to a thumb drive, my laptop has been formatted and the hard drive removed. I have the item. We are ready for reset."

Ozera pulled his car into Bucharest traffic and turned on the radio to a classical station that was playing one of Mozart's operas, *The Philosopher's Stone*. Ten minutes later, his phone vibrated and he read the message: "Reset has completed."

Ozera smiled. He finished driving, parked his car and walked into the Bucharest International Airport. He had a flight to catch.

* * *

Dmitri Slokov slumped in the police cruiser, shaking his head slowly in numb disbelief. *Alexi is dead, and that monster Parasca is responsible.* The Bulgarian police came and asked him more questions. He pled ignorance to everything, claiming that his car had been shot up by thugs that seemed to be firing at each other and now his brother was dead. Dmitri didn't have to fake any of the tears.

His phone vibrated and a message came through. "Reset has completed.

Ozera has boarded his flight and has the item. Files are secure."

Dmitri keyed in a message, "What about Parasca's personal staff?"

The return message read, "Fled or killed by our team. Parasca's security man at his island retreat surrendered and has some data for us. It sounds interesting. There's lots of photographs and video. It looks incriminating. Greek authorities might be very interested."

Tears dripped from his chin and onto the phone. He had to wipe it off before he could key in his answer. Dmitri wrote, "Good. I want it all. We'll use all of it. I'll have his company yet." He shook with grief and rage. He clenched his trembling fist and shut his eyes tightly. *No more tears until Parasca pays. And pays. And pays.*

* * *

The truck drove out of Varna and headed west toward the highway that would connect with one going to Istanbul. Rakslav sat in the cab, concentrating on his driving and on keeping the truck unobtrusive. He heard what could only be Parasca's screams through the wall of the truck. The throat-rending shrieks went on and on, kilometer after kilometer. Three hours later, the screaming had not yet stopped.

CHAPTER 37 – EPILOGUE: PRIESTESS

"Let us seek Death; or, he not found,
supply with our own hands his office on ourselves"
— John Milton, Paradise Lost

5580 BC

The oil in the lamp was running low and the flame began to flicker. The shadows around the sick woman wavered and the haggard face was almost visible in the midst of the regalia of her office. An errant breeze blew through the windows and the downy, colored feathers of the headdress rustled gently on her brow. The folds of her soft robes moved feebly with her hesitant breaths. The woman shifted slightly and a soft jingle sounded from the gold of her earrings and bracelets. The necklace draped around her held several items: the heavy gold medallion bearing the bull symbol, the medal with the hammer and fire symbol and lastly the cylindrical jewel that had been found at the door of the crypt when they had first uncovered it. The sick woman's withered hands lay beneath the necklace and the nearly skeletal fingers rose and fell with the slow, uneven rhythm of her breathing.

The tall young woman stood in the doorway to the chamber and looked at the old priestess before her. *How did it all happen this quickly? It was just five years ago that she took me as her acolyte and only two since she elevated me to priestess. One year ago, she showed me the construction at the crypt. Two moons ago, the swellings developed on her neck. Now she is dying.*

Melka motioned to one of the attendants hovering nearby and pointed at the flickering oil lamp. The woman moved quickly but silently and took it away to refill it. The light was dimmer in the chamber now that it was lit by one less lamp. She stepped closer, moving carefully so as not to disturb Chalara's rest.

She sat on the stool next to the bed and studied her mother's ruined face and wispy hair. The disease had ravaged her in a matter of weeks, reducing her fabled loveliness to this rubble of flesh. *You were always a radiant beauty, high priestess and the wife of a god. You looked the part for so long with your golden hair and the face of a queen. You guided your people through the years after the deluge and led them to rebuild and rise again. They think you cruel, but I know that is wrong. Cruelty is what strength feels like to those that are ruled. You taught me that.*

The attendant returned with the refilled lamp but stood back, waiting for a sign to approach. Melka nodded. The woman replaced the lamp on the table and then moved back into the shadows again.

Melka turned to gaze again at Chalara. *What do you do when your mother is dying? What should I be feeling? Others hold feelings of love and affection for their mothers.* She reached out her hand and lightly cupped it to one cheek of the sleeping woman. *But that is not for us, is it Chalara?*

Chalara's eyelids fluttered at Melka's touch. They opened slightly, then wider. She spoke in a coarse, dry rasp. "Daughter. A drink." Without looking away from her mother, Melka motioned to the attendant, the acolyte that had refilled the lamp. Melka sensed the young woman move to her side. Melka held out her hand and spoke in her low contralto, "Water."

In a few moments, a bowl was in her hand and Melka held it to the sick woman's lips. Chalara drank a few small swallows and sighed.

She whispered, "Is it ready?"

Melka replied, "The crypt is ready, Mother. The workmen are finishing today."

"Did they cover the blasphemy as I instructed?"

"Yes. The taunt by Lord Mulciber's captors has been covered over as you wished, with a painting of a bull."

"Good." The sick woman lay back, catching her breath. The exchange had cost her much energy. She lay there for a minute breathing laboriously. Melka did not speak as Chalara gathered her strength. When the sick woman spoke again it was with eyes shut in exhaustion.

"Are you ready to carry out our plan to close and seal the crypt for their return?"

"Yes, Mother."

Chalara opened her yellowish, sickened eyes and looked into Melka's. "Will you do all of it? Will you finish it?"

Melka said simply, "Yes."

Chalara relaxed. A smile of relief came to her and Melka saw a momentary glimpse, like a memory of her mother's healthy face, unclouded by sickness. Chalara spoke again.

"Must you go now?"

"Soon, but there is still time."

Chalara considered and closed her eyes as she whispered. "I've not been a gentle mother to you. I did not raise you to be a soft child. I raised you to be your father's daughter. From a babe, you grew up here in Varnach, never knowing your father, never knowing his power, never seeing his face. You never saw him destroy armies. You never knew his fierceness or his anger. You never knew the fear he inspired." She stopped and opened her eyes again to look at Melka. Chalara's voice rose in volume "But though you never saw him, I see him in you. From that first day when I brought you to Varnach and you drank the life of the dying, I saw him in you. You have your father's strength and his will. You have your father's thirst. You are the Lord Moloch's daughter. Go and finish the crypt. You had the dream and so did I. The crypt must be finished so they can return."

Chalara slumped back, her racing pulse obvious in the veins at her temple. Melka bent over Chalara's form and unfastened the necklace from her mother's throat. She took the cylindrical jewel off of the golden chain and held it. She took her mother's hand and gently squeezed it and said, "I am Moloch's daughter. I am also yours. I will return. Rest."

She released the sick woman's hand and stepped to the small altar by the wall. On top of it lay a dagger, its stony blade stained dark. Melka took the knife and felt visions sweep through her of countless deaths, of rivers of blood, of gaping wounds, of life power loosed.

She turned to the acolyte attendant one final time. "Prepare for the ceremony. Bring the High Priestess as we planned." With the stone knife in one hand and the cylindrical jewel in the other, she smiled and walked from the chamber.

A few minutes later, Melka paused next to a newly dug grave that would soon be put to use. At the opening leading to the crypt below, she told the guards to stay behind at the top of the stairs.

She said simply, "Some may come this way. Let no one leave until I return."

Melka descended the broad staircase. She wore the cylinder secured to a thong around her neck. In her right hand she still carried the stone knife. The stairs went down into the earth in a wide descent with a comparably high ceiling. After all, this stair was intended for use by Lord Mulciber when he came out of his crypt.

Years ago, her dream had said that on some distant day, the crypt would be opened and Mulciber would return to this land. How long that might be from now, she did not know, but when her mother had dreamt the same dream on the same night, Chalara had known to have her people start work immediately. That night, all of this had been set in motion.

She continued walking down to the middle landing where the foreman met her. He and all of his men had been working into the night to complete the crypt. Torches were spaced regularly in the halls. At the landing, she stopped in front of him. At two meters, she towered over him and all of the other workmen. He looked up into her eyes.

"Priestess," he spoke tentatively, "The queen … I hope she will approve of our work here."

Melka looked down at him and spoke without expression. "That will depend on what I report back to her, won't it?"

He gulped, nodded and led her into the smaller southern corridor. She had to bend her head a little to negotiate the passageway, but they walked through it and around a corner until they came to the balcony overlooking the crypt antechamber.

Below, final cleanup was completing with only polishing still underway. Dust and debris had been swept away and most of the men stood in rows waiting for her to review them and their work. She surveyed the crypt chamber, the giant metal door, with half of it thickly plastered over and elaborately painted like a bull. She knew the message the plaster and paint concealed. Amongst a pattern of crosshatched lines and written in the Angelic tongue in the wondrous metal, it had said, "Evil Mulciber, killer of innocents …" Melka knew the rest of the inscription. Chalara had been right. That message had to be concealed since it could not be removed.

Melka looked from one end of the crypt to the other from her vantage point on the balcony and nodded. It looked right. All was complete but one thing. She motioned to the workmen below.

"The painting of the bull on the plaster, I need it covered up for a few moments." They looked confused, but she offered no explanation of her request, but only stood there looking at them, expecting them to comply. In a minute, some of the men rigged up a rough cover for the painting. After that was finished, she spoke to the assembly.

"You have done exceedingly well. Your families will think of you when they remember this place. As I and my mother have foreseen, there will come a day when the great god Mulciber comes out of this crypt. On that day he will no doubt survey this place, admiring your workmanship and thank all of you for what you have done. For you shall all be here to welcome him."

One of the older workers below shouted, "I hope I live so long, my lady!"

The other men were horrified at the man's outburst. One did not speak to the queen or her daughter without permission. They shushed him and told him to be silent. Melka merely looked down and smiled. She beckoned to their foreman who, seeing her permission to approach, stepped up beside her.

Melka smiled at him, turned back to the men below and continuing her smile said, "You will be here to welcome him, but you will not live so long." She grabbed the foreman by the back of his neck and lifted him up and out over the balcony. The men below gasped. The foreman shouted in surprise and attempted to grab onto the arm that held him. He shouted at her in fear and confusion, "What? My lady!"

Her arm held his two hundred pounds effortlessly over the ledge and she turned him in midair to face her. His eyes were caught in hers and his mouth opened in a soundless shout. She held out her other hand with the stone knife and held it before his gaze. The men below raised a unison shout of dismay. She calmly lowered the knife to his waist and plunged it in one side and ripped the blade across to the other side. The shouts from below changed to cries of terror as the man's entrails gushed from the wound and onto the horror-stricken crowd below. Savoring the blast of his death energy, she dropped the dead man onto them, and leapt over the side and into the workmen beneath the balcony.

She grabbed man after man and slit their throats or plunged the knife into hearts, guts or heads. Each death gave her a massive surge of life energy. Some of the men tried to rally and bring their tools to bear, but she fairly crackled with energy and strength. She swatted aside all attempts at defense and took not a single wound though she was soon drenched in blood. She waded through them, cutting them all down, breaking necks and spines, tearing arms from sockets. She felt a reddish glow suffusing her and surrounding her. *I can do anything!* The last man standing was the older man that had called to her from the crowd. He looked at her in terror and simply kneeled and put his head down. She severed his spine with one stroke of the blade. Her flesh prickled as she absorbed his death draft. Red sparks trailed and spread from her fingertips. Her entire form was encircled in a globe of energy.

She walked to the covered painting and pulled down the spattered cloth. *It wouldn't have done to have this painting all ruined with splashed blood.*

She stepped among the corpses and through the entry at the back of the antechamber leading to the broad steps. As she expected, there were shouts and cries at the top of the stairs. The guards held back the workmen that had escaped her attack in the antechamber. She stalked up the stair. One of the workmen above screamed.

"She's coming! Let us through!"

The spears of the guards blocked the workmen's escape and Melka blocked the staircase to the antechamber. There was no place to run.

Melka, bursting with death energy, charged the remaining distance to the half-dozen laborers and laid into them like a ravening lioness. She stabbed, bit, ripped and smashed the men into bloody pulp. Screams, wails, grunts and moans echoed through the passageway. Blast after blast of force from their departing lives caught her and charged her with new, rending fire. Each surge carried her mind deeper into a feral, wild territory of ecstasy and pain.

When the last cry went silent, Melka looked up from the crushed throat she had been tearing with her teeth. She heard gasps from the guards at the door. They huddled back from her at the entry to the stairway, their eyes wide in awe and fear.

She rose from the corpse she had been shredding. Blood ran from her mouth. Her tunic was red from neck to hem and gobbets of flesh and hair clung to it in clumps. She stepped forward and towered above the guards. She reached out for one of the spears and took the point in her hand. The terrified man released the spear to her instantly.

She took the spear, one hand at each end of the weapon, moved the shaft behind her head and against the back of her neck and stretched. She curled her head back against the wood of the spear shaft as if scratching an itch, while simultaneously pulling the stout wooden pole toward her. The shaft flexed, curved like a bow and then smoothly snapped behind her neck. Her bloody lips parted in a smile at the breaking of the spear. She leapt at the guards.

A few minutes later, she kicked their dead bodies into the descending stairway, tossed the useless spears after them and moved to the stone slab that lay next to the stairway opening. She walked to it casually, and suffused in a seven meter wide nimbus of blazing life force visible only to her, she lifted the slab with one hand. Its massive weight meant nothing to her in her state of elevated consciousness and murderous power. The hinged stone flipped over as easily as a windblown leaf, effortlessly swinging over and down into place. She took the cylindrical jewel from the thong at her throat and placed it in the hole in the stone that had been carved by one of the masons specifically to receive the jewel. She felt the click of the lock, pulled the jewel out and stood in the center of the stone slab. *Now for Mother.*

The sounds of chanting came from the temple and Melka saw the procession starting on the path leading her way. She waited until the line of priestesses carrying Chalara's litter came closer and they all could see her blood-drenched form. They circled around her and set at her feet the small platform on which Chalara lay. When she was convinced they were all there and had been awe struck by the gory sight of her, she closed her eyes and held up her arms, the stone dagger in her right hand. The power flowing through her seemed to concentrate in her skin and she smiled slightly. *This feels almost like when I use the power to keep those unbodied voices away, only infinitely more unbridled.*

A visible glow seemed to emanate from Melka's face. It grew brighter until one of the acolytes involuntarily raised her hand to shield her eyes. The glow increased until all of the women were either shielding their eyes or clenching them tightly shut. Waves of heat shimmered from Melka and she felt the blood soaked tunic sizzling against her skin. The garment burst into flame and sloughed away. The blood and offal on her skin turned to ash and flaked off. The glow lessened and she stood naked on the stone slab, towering over the prone form of her mother.

Chalara's voice whispered. "Daughter. Finish it."

Melka kneeled beside her, placed the cylindrical jewel back on Chalara's necklace, cupped her hand by her mother's cheek again and raised the knife.

She shouted, "The High Priestess offers herself as a willing sacrifice!" and plunged the dagger into Chalara's chest.

A searing bolt of energy lanced from Chalara's still form, through the stone knife and into Melka. The tall woman twisted and shrieked in agony and then stood, blazing like a torch. She raised one hand and released a lightning bolt up into the heavens above.

"I am the daughter of Moloch. I am now High Priestess."

She motioned to the cowering women and they lifted Chalara's form and laid it in the waiting open grave. Melka strode up beside her mother's resting place and held her hand out over the corpse. A soft glow of bluish light seemed to cover Chalara's form. For a moment, the disease and the years seemed to melt away and Chalara appeared youthful and beautiful once more. Then, her flesh turned to ash and fell away, leaving her bones, her ornaments and her jewelry.

Naked, Melka turned to the other priestesses. One of them brought her a robe and she took it, draping it around her. She walked down the path toward the temple. *Now things will change. These human cattle will long for the easy days of my mother's rule.*

The stories of Mercy Teller and Melka will continue in Uncreated Night, planned for the summer of 2015

If you would be interested in receiving updates on future books, please write to:
johngrashambooks@gmail.com
Also, check out the author's blog at:
www.johngrasham.com

ABOUT THE AUTHOR

John Grasham was born in Texas, grew up in the Los Angeles, CA area, but returned to Texas to finish high school and college. He has a B.A. in Music from Abilene Christian University in Vocal Performance. He spent years working in Dallas, Anchorage Alaska, Houston, did time as a road-warrior consultant criss-crossing North America and now lives again in the Dallas area. John is a throat cancer-survivor and his voice is almost all the way back to what it was.

He's been writing fiction and creating stories to tell his kids and grand-kids since they were old enough to sit in his lap. His supernatural thrillers, "Forever Fallen" and "Darkness Visible" are found under contemporary fantasy and horror.

Made in the USA
Charleston, SC
27 August 2014